The

GOLDEN
GURU

The

GOLDEN
GURU

The Strange Journey of
Bhagwan Shree Rajneesh

JAMES S. GORDON

THE STEPHEN GREENE PRESS
Lexington, Massachusetts

For Sharon Curtin

First published in 1987 by The Stephen Greene Press, Inc.
Published simultaneously in Canada by Penguin Books Canada Limited
Distributed by Viking Penguin Inc., 40 West 23rd Street, New York, NY 10010.

All photographs credited to Rajneesh Foundation Europe are reprinted
by permission; all rights are reserved by the copyright holder.

Library of Congress Cataloging-in-Publication Data
Gordon, James Samuel.
The golden guru.
Includes index.
1. Rajneesh, Bhagwan Shree, 1931–
2. Gurus — Biography.   I. Title.
BP605.R344G67 1987   299′.93 [B]   86-33509
ISBN 0–8289–0630–0

Designed by Deborah Schneider
Printed in the United States of America
by Haddon Craftsmen
Set in Clearface by AccuComp Typographers
Produced by Unicorn Production Services, Inc.

CONTENTS

Part II Rajneeshpuram

Part III Breakup

ACKNOWLEDGMENTS

This book is about Bhagwan Shree Rajneesh and his present and former disciples. It couldn't have been written if he and they hadn't been generous with their thoughts and feelings, their lives, and on occasion, their living space. At times Rajneesh and some of his disciples were reticent or refused to speak with me; sometimes he and they equivocated or lied. In the end, however, reticence and openness, truth and fiction were all useful to me, all elements in the complex compound of religious search and communal experience, of Master and disciple, creation and destruction, that I was trying to describe and understand.

In addition to those whom I quote or describe in *The Golden Guru*, a number of other people have helped my understanding and guided my journey with and among Rajneesh and his disciples. These include particularly Ma Veet Mano, Ma Prem Gitesho, Ma Prem Sunito, Swami Prem Bodhen, Ma Prem Prasado, and Ma Bodhi Samma. Non-disciples who have been touched or troubled by Rajneesh who have also been generous with their time and observations include Josh Baran, Kerin Hope, Ted Mann, Win McCormack, Cary Schay, and Hillel Zeitlin.

During the years that I have been exploring meditation practices and traveling to ashrams and communities in India and Oregon and elsewhere, almost all of my friends and family, my colleagues and patients have had to cope with my preoccupations and enthusiasms. Some have been particularly interested, sympathetic, and helpful. These include William Alfred, Rudy Bauer, Marshall Berman, George Blecher, Gregg Calvert, Amrit Desai, Max Heirich, Steve Hersh, Gary and Ann Kaplan, Jackie Mendelsohn, Ann Patterson, Jim Statman, Marianne Tamulevich, Laura Tennen, Phyllis Theroux, and Suzanne White. I am sorry that two men whom I admired and cared for—Gregory Bateson and Dick Price—will not be able to read what they helped stimulate me to write.

This book began years ago as a chapter in an as-yet-unfinished survey of new religions in America for which the Ford Foundation gave me a grant. Tom Quinn, my editor at McGraw-Hill, continues to support and encourage that book. He has been patient with me while I have taken the very long detour necessary to write this one. Bill Whitworth, of the *Atlantic*, commissioned the article on Rajneesh and his disciples that eventually grew into *The Golden Guru*. Tom Begner, of the Stephen

Greene Press, saw the book in the article perhaps even before I did, and has shepherded its progress ever since. Rickie Harvey, also of the Stephen Greene Press, has made sure I did what I said I was going to, and Peggy Anderson, my copy editor, helped me to do it. Ann Geracimos, Robin Carter, and Loraine Hutchins endured my deadlines and handwriting and typed earlier versions of the manuscript with remarkable good cheer. Maria Sessa typed the final version and, when my confidence about the manuscript flagged, reassured me that all was or soon would be well.

Sharon Curtin has read everything I have written. My book and I are better for her sharp challenges and loving suggestions.

The quotations from Bhagwan Shree Rajneesh are drawn from about 50 of the more than 350 volumes of his discourses to and dialogues with his disciples. Where I have not cited the particular volume for a quote, it has simply been to avoid cluttering the text with titles.

Most of Rajneesh's books in English, video and audio tapes of some of his discourses, and audio tapes of his meditations are available from Chidvilas Publishing, Boulder, Colorado. Two volumes of *The Book of the Secrets*, the Rajneesh text that I first read, are now published in the United States by Harper and Row, as are *The Mustard Seed*, Vasant Joshi's authorized biography, *The Awakened One*, and several other collections of Rajneesh's discourses.

Rajneesh's thoughts on a wide variety of subjects are alphabetically arranged according to topics and collected in three volumes of *The Book*. His meditations are assembled in *The Orange Book*. An in-depth presentation of his disciples' view of Rajneesh's life and work through 1984, with photographs, is contained in two lavishly produced volumes, *The Sound of Running Water* and *This Very Place the Lotus Paradise*. All are available from Chidvilas. A detailed investigation of Rajneesh and his disciples appeared in a twenty-part series in the *Oregonian* in June 1985. Hugh Milne's book *Bhagwan: The God that Failed* is published by St. Martin's Press. Frances Fitzgerald has written a long reportorial account of Rajneeshpuram, which is included in *Cities on a Hill* (Simon and Schuster).

The

GOLDEN
GURU

PROLOGUE

I heave myself out of bed, dress warmly. I go out into the early morning, across the yard, over the fence, and into the barn. I let the chickens out and go up the stairs to the loft. Better to begin before I think too much. I stretch, take a few slow, deep breaths, and turn on the tape recorder. I stand in the middle of the floor, away from the corncrib and bales of hay, and close my eyes against distractions. The music begins—electronic, repetitive, insistent—and so do I, inhaling and exhaling deeply, in through the nose, out through the nose, pushing it out faster and deeper, like an engine gathering a head of steam.

My hands are in fists close to my chest as I pump my arms; I feel resistance, in my arms and shoulders and neck. I pump harder, trying to break through. My stomach begins to knot. I breathe faster and deeper, feeling the pains in my solar plexus. I retch and nothing comes up, breathe again and retch again. "Let it happen. Don't indulge it," I remind myself, and I focus again on the breathing—harder, faster.

My mouth tastes of metal and there are pains in my arms and chest and legs. I breathe faster, deeper, breaking the crude, comforting rhythm I have established. I fling my head around on my neck. I begin to wonder how much of the first stage's ten minutes is left: five minutes, no, probably seven. I breathe till I feel my chest is going to burst and just when I think I can't possibly do any more, I hear a voice in my head—Shyam's, Rajneesh's, my own?

"Only one hundred percent effort will do."

I feel despair dogging my effort. Have I ever done anything one hundred percent? I try harder, pump my arms up and down like a crazed chicken, breathe in and out so fast and deep my nostrils close. In my mind's eye I see Rajneesh sitting in a long white gown on a chair. He is smiling at my resistance, at all the pain that, it suddenly seems, I am making for myself.

Something moves. It is as if my body is enlarging and contracting to match the dimensions of my breath. The breathing has a momentum, a will of its own now. I am being breathed. I am exhilarated, awake, smiling, an amazed and delighted witness of what, miraculously, no longer seems like effort. Now I feel—this seems absurd to me—that something wants to jump out of my body. Maybe I am going to leave my body, watch it from the rafters of my barn, like one who has had a near death experience watching, as if from the ceiling of his hospital room, while doctors clamor over his body. Fear comes. What will happen? Will I lose my body and die? I feel myself resisting. My effort is no longer total and the pain is back and breathing is a burden, and I am worrying that I will always be afraid. I pick up the pace again and laugh at myself, at the games my mind plays.

The music changes. This is the second, cathartic, stage. The beat is more insistent than before. When I have done this meditation with a group of people, the screams and shouts fill a room that is hot with effort. I have heard sounds of bodies falling to the ground, and fists and feet pounding on pillows. Today, alone in the cold morning air, I hear my own angry voice rising high in the barn. I shout and flail and stamp, and scream like a damned soul or a child in a tantrum. "Mommy! Daddy!" I shout over and over, as if I were an infant too long left alone. Now obscenities are pouring from me, curses against nurses, playmates, teachers. Tears and great wrenching sobs. I sweat and cry and become a child of one and two and five and seven again.

After a while my limbs feel like lead and my voice stops in my throat. My effort feels forced, mechanical. And then I am into it again. "Get it out. Get it out," I say to myself, punching the air, as images of bullies and critics and lovers, Shyam and Rajneesh, pass before me.

In ten minutes the music changes again. This third stage is the most painful part, jumping and shouting the Sufi mantra "hoo." I jump as high as I can, throwing my arms up above my head. I land hard on my heels, bringing my arms down, shouting, bringing the sound, as the instructions say, "deep into the sex center," just above the pubic bone. I land and shout and jump and land and shout. Very soon I feel I can't jump again. It's too much. I try it another way. Now instead of jumping I thrust my pelvis forward when I shout "Hoo!" This feels good. For a while I am hooing up a storm.

Soon the pain in my arms begins to build. I want to sob. I try to shout it away. The "Hoo, hoo, hoo" changes to "Oooh," a wail. I lower my arms just for a moment and feel a worse pain in them, this time compounded by a sense of defeat and cowardice. I raise them into the air and jump again. In a few moments my hands seem suspended, as if some presence is reaching down to hold them high. I'm happy now.

"Stop," says the voice on the tape. I freeze, my hands not as far up as they can reach but still painfully high. Sweat, cold before it leaves my face, pours off me onto the wooden floor. All the injuries I have ever had speak to me: the torn ligaments in my knees, my strained lower back, the arm I broke years before. New pains emerge. Cramps rise like steam in my calves and upper back and shoulders. A terrible ache is building in my raised arms. I cannot imagine fifteen minutes immobile in this position.

"Become the witness," I tell myself. "Slow down. Breathe evenly. Move within the pain." Curious now, savoring its subtleties, I follow the pain from knee to back to arm. It disappears for a while and when I tense, returns. God,

my arms hurt. I have not, I notice, been totally still. In the agony of challeng-
ing gravity, my arms have moved down slightly. "Does this qualify as move-
ment?" I ask myself, a casuist in a barn. I strain to be still.

Finally the music begins again. At first I am awkward, as if rising from bed
after a long illness. I stumble wearily from one foot to the other. My body falls
into some remembered dance. The tempo increases. Now the music seems to
carry my body as if it were a suit of clothes, and the music, moving within,
were flesh and blood.

Like a Red Indian I dance stutter steps that widen into circles. I feel strong.
Now I am the Hindu deity Shiva, now Nataraj, the dancing god, now Krishna
piping softly to the gopis, the cow girls who adore him. Now a cow girl myself,
feeling soft and delicate. As the music grows more lush, my body widens,
expands, like a flower opening. I am turning. My arms extended now, the right
one palm up, the left one palm down, I whirl like the dervishes I never ima-
gined I could be. Faster and faster, then slower, feeling the center of gravity just
below my navel. My eyes open, revealing the bright morning sun on the beams
and bales of hay. The boards of the walls and the pillars of the barn flash
past. My mind is quiet. I'm smiling.

When the music ends, I fall, hardly dizzy, laughing, to the floor.

I'd first done Dynamic Meditation in De-
cember 1973 in a workshop led by Shyam Singha, an Indian acupuncturist and osteopath. It was during a phone call from an old friend in England that I first heard
of Shyam. My friend, Richard, a laconic and skeptical man, had been unashamedly
enthusiastic. He told me about this "mad Indian" Shyam Singha, who had put him
on a fast and stuck needles in him and changed his life. The most remarkable thing
was the call itself: it was the first time I had ever spoken to Richard on the telephone.
Until his treatment by Shyam, he had been so hard of hearing it was impossible.

When Richard asked me to set up a workshop for Shyam in Washington, D.C.,
I readily agreed. For six years I had been trying to use the techniques of psychotherapy
and of the therapeutic community to help people go through and learn from psychotic
experience. In 1971, as a chief resident in New York, I had set up an experimental
ward in a mental hospital; now, as a research psychiatrist at the National Institute
of Mental Health, I was working with counselors in mental health programs for teenagers—hot lines, runaway houses, communal group homes.

I realized that there was a biological component to the young people's mental
illness but believed that the tranquilizing drugs that suppressed their symptoms frustrated the possibility for self-discovery. I had come to understand that for many people,
severe psychological problems could, if treated appropriately, be an experience of
self-discovery as well as an illness. During my years at NIMH, I had begun to wonder
if there weren't ways to work with troubled people that would promote the same
kind of supportive and transformational experience on a biological level as psychotherapy and a therapeutic community did emotionally.

What I had read about the theory and practice of acupuncture —its holistic view of mind and body, its concern for restoring balance rather than treating symptoms, its concept of the "healing crisis"—led me to believe that it might be such an approach. What I heard from Richard about Shyam made me think he could help me to learn it.

Shyam, when I met him, proved to be a strange, powerful, mercurial man, generous and expansive one minute, gruff and cryptic the next. He wore custom-made Savile Row suits and shirts, but his black hair rushed in curls down to his shoulders and his yellow eyes were wild. Shyam stayed at the farm where I lived outside Washington, a tropical guest in a winter landscape. We shoveled snow from the driveway in the morning and had bacon and eggs for brunch. At night he cooked for us, fish stews into which he emptied the whole spice cabinet; rice pilaf studded with fennel and cumin, cardamom and coriander seeds, peppercorns, raisins, and onions; salads of mixed fruits, vegetables, and nuts, pungent oils and chilies, sugar and salt, wine and brandy. While he cooked, Shyam explained the laws of yin and yang and how they governed both the way he was making our meal and the medicine he practiced. He told me stories of the wandering monks he met in China and the barefoot saddhus —holy men—his Kashmiri father had brought home to dinner. Leading meditations in the workshop I had organized at the Washington, D.C., Runaway House, Shyam reminded me more of the shamans I had read about and the curanderos whom my patients in the South Bronx had consulted than of any physicians I knew.

Around Shyam's neck and over his Christian Dior tie he wore a locket with a picture of a smiling balding man. "Who is that?" I asked him. "My sweetie," he said, laughing. Later, he told me that the man's name was Bhagwan Shree Rajneesh and that Rajneesh had devised the Dynamic Meditation we had done. "He's my gurushmuru," Shyam joked. In India, he explained, people sometimes wore a picture of their guru. I was surprised that someone so self-assured, so accomplished, and so irreverent would be another man's disciple and wear his picture like a lover's.

I was originally interested in the techniques Shyam used in his medical practice, but I soon found myself equally drawn to the meditations he had learned from Rajneesh and the connections Shyam drew between meditation and medicine. As words, they both had the same linguistic root, he explained. Medicine was directed toward healing body and mind, meditation to healing the spirit. Several months after Shyam returned to England, I began to practice Dynamic Meditation on my own. At first I did it without music, marking a blank tape to signal the time intervals of the different stages. Later Shyam sent me a tape of the musical accompaniment that one of Rajneesh's other disciples had composed.

Until I began Dynamic, meditation had been just a word to me. I had been intrigued by it as I had been years before by psychoanalysis. Meditation seemed like a tool to explore and help free me from unconscious, self-deprecating thoughts and behaviors, a practical way to become more relaxed, more at home with my place in the natural and social world in which I lived. In fact, there had been moments during my own psychoanalysis that I thought of as more meditative than analytic. On some occasions I had watched my free associations—some horrifying, some joyous, some bland—sail effortlessly through my mind. On others I had felt a sweet, peaceful connection to the couch I lay on, the room I was in, the analyst who sat behind me, and all the experience that had and would shape me—that was at that very moment shaping me.

But meditative techniques had always seemed inaccessible and unpleasant. When I tried Zen meditation, watching my breath move in and out of my nostrils, I felt terribly uncomfortable. My thoughts raced around inside my head, my legs twitched, and my back ached. Every few minutes, hoping for a quick reprieve, I sneaked a look at the kitchen timer I was using. At the end of twenty or thirty minutes I was often more agitated than before I started and even more discouraged about my ability to meditate—whatever that might mean.

I knew people who did Transcendental Meditation, but it had never attracted me. They sat quietly for twenty minutes twice a day and said a Sanskrit mantra, or sound, to themselves. They claimed that repeating the sound was both relaxing and enlivening, but I had my doubts. Some of these people seemed depressed and dulled, almost as if their meditation was a soporific. Others were obsessed and obsessive. What they might have gained from the twenty minutes of calm twice daily they seemed to lose in the tenseness of their preparation, in the sanctimoniousness that limned their intention. At the time I first heard about TM—as they called it—I couldn't imagine sitting still for twenty minutes twice a day. I resented the idea of paying $200 to a TM teacher who would select my mantra for me. And, in any case, I didn't want to turn out like those people.

Dynamic seemed different. I discovered that an hour of its activity would bring me to a surprising inner stillness. I found that during the sessions I was expressing emotions that hadn't surfaced in several years of psychoanalysis and resolving conflicts that intellectual understanding had not affected. It was also an incredible physical workout. After I did Dynamic I felt purged and relaxed, alert, and generally more intuitive and less judgmental.

The longer I practiced Dynamic the more I appreciated it. First of all, it was democratic. I could—anyone could—do it. No priests or gurus were needed, no initiation fees or secret mantras. All I had to do was use the capacity for effort that years of school and sports and work had taught me. Then, after the activity, the calm and stillness, the quiet pleasures of a relaxed body and an uncluttered mind might come of their own accord. The way I felt afterward reminded me of what it was like to stand in a hot shower after a day of playing football, basketball, or tennis.

But there was more to it. Each stage had its own purpose, and they all seemed to fit elegantly together. Breathing fast and deeply invigorated my body and disrupted my habitual and sometimes obsessive patterns of thought: the breath churned my unconscious. In the second, cathartic, stage, images and feelings that had been long and deeply buried emerged, played their dramas out in my mind and body, and disappeared again. The third stage was a mystery to me. Sometimes the jumping and the sound of "hoo" produced a subtle physical feeling—a vibration, a movement, as of something alive deep in my pelvis. This, I imagined, was the energy that Indians called kundalini. They said it lay coiled like a serpent at the base of the spine, ready to rise to the crown of the head, clearing away emotional and mental blocks and producing as it rose sadness and desperation, sexual feelings, anger, love, creativity, and psychic abilities. I had read in modern books on yoga that this energy had a controlling connection to the neurological and endocrine systems but was separate from them—and not yet capable of being registered by scientific instruments.

Before, kundalini had seemed like a fable to me, fascinating and appealing, but as improbable in its way as God talking to Moses through a burning bush or Jesus raising the dead. But now I was sometimes aware, toward the end of the third stage of Dynamic Meditation, of something moving as elusively as neon up my spine, flashing like lightning in my limbs. Standing still in the fourth stage I felt as if my body were being reclaimed by these electric scouts. When, in the fifth and final stage, I danced, I now sensed myself moved by a force more powerful, more inventive, than any I could consciously summon.

As I did Dynamic day after day I began, like someone training for a marathon, to discover I could go beyond physical limits that I had always believed impregnable. I found satisfaction in the effort I put out to reach these limits and freedom and power as I pushed beyond them. And sometimes at each stage—breathing, jumping, shouting, standing still, dancing—almost as a by-product, I found myself being simultaneously a quiet, nonjudgmental witness.

Soon after taking up Dynamic Meditation I began to read Rajneesh's books. I wanted to see if his words were as illuminating as his techniques. Besides, by this time Shyam had become my acupuncture and meditation teacher, and Rajneesh was, in some way I didn't understand, *his* teacher. I was curious about him.

The books I found had been badly printed in India on already browning paper, but the contents were a happy surprise. They were collections of talks on religious texts he had given in Bombay in the late sixties and early seventies. They turned out to be colloquial, sophisticated, and funny. In his commentaries on the *Upanishads* he aptly used Marx and Maslow, Plato and Heidegger, Freud and Beckett, to make points that were intelligent and, so far as I knew, original. He brought directness and a wry, dispassionate clarity to the subjects he touched on: politics, religion, birth and death, madness and meditation. He had a knack for making previously impenetrable religious texts accessible, for demystifying esoteric techniques. In his hands, Buddha and Jesus and Krishna and Shiva were thoroughly modern spiritual psychologists, reminding us of what we already knew but had somehow forgotten.

All religions, Rajneesh said, "although separate" were one. The differences among them were basically accidents of time and place and culture. All of them, in Rajneesh's reading, had the same basic message: Go inside; the kingdom of heaven is within; celebrate the divinity of your own ordinary lives.

"When John the Baptist said [in Matthew 3], 'Repent ye for the kingdom of heaven is at hand,' he never meant that this world was going to end. He simply meant that YOU were going to end and before you die make contact with the other world. In Aramaic," Rajneesh went on, "repent meant to return to your source, come back to your original being."

The way to discover this original being was through self-knowledge. "You have to peel your being the way one peels an onion. Go on peeling. . . . You will find layers within layers and finally when all the layers are discarded or eliminated you will find in your hands pure nothingness . . . emptiness. . . . Shunyata [the Sanskrit word for emptiness] is your essential core."

"I teach you a totally different kind of religiousness," he said in a lecture on Zen. "It is that of meditation. You do not have to worship. You do not have to pray. It is not a question of discovering God. . . . The first and only inquiry is to know who am I in this body, mind mechanism? What is this miracle of consciousness?"

Though Rajneesh borrowed from and was influenced by many religious traditions, there was—particularly in his early work—a distinct and distinctly interesting flavor of Tantra. Before I read Rajneesh, I knew only that Tantra was a very ancient, culturally marginal religious practice; that there were both Hindu and Buddhist Tantras; and that some aspect of Tantra, the so-called left-hand path, had something to do with using sexuality as a path to spirituality. But the books I had looked at—aside from their extraordinary pictures of the erotic statues at Khajuraho—had seemed dry, obscure, and incomprehensible.

The Book of the Secrets was different. In it were Rajneesh's commentaries on the *Vigyana Bhairava Tantra*, an ancient self-help manual in the form of a dialogue between Lord Shiva and his consort Parvati. The *Vigyana Bhairava* presented 112 techniques for transforming consciousness (*vigyana* means "consciousness," *bhairava*, "the state beyond consciousness"; *tantra*, from a Sanskrit word related to weaving, may be translated "method"). Some of these used breathing or visual attention or sensory awareness—"When on a bed or a seat, let yourself become weightless, beyond mind"—for coming to a state of blissful, thought-less spontaneity. Others made use of touch and sexuality.

Tantra, Rajneesh explained, was not a religion. It was a scientific, psychological method but not one that utilized retrospective analysis or interpersonal understanding or behavior change or effort, as most modern psychotherapies did. Tantra's method was awareness. One simply did what one ordinarily did—ate, drank, breathed, worked, played, made love—but became more aware of one's actions and thoughts and feelings. Soon what had been denied or repressed or ignored, encysted in the body and enshrined in neurosis, would be observed, reawakened, and admitted to the circle of thought and feeling. Only then could one behave in the fully human, loose, and natural way that Tantra described. Only then would it be possible for energy—Wilhelm Reich had called it "orgone energy," Tantra called it Shakti—to flow freely in the body. Once this happened it seemed one might experience the ecstasy of moment-to-moment awareness that Tantra celebrated.

Rajneesh applied the Tantric approach to sexuality in several ways. First, he said, sex was to be explored and enjoyed as a part of life. So long as the desire was there, it should be satisfied. Religions that tried to suppress or sublimate sexuality or that encouraged celibacy were destructive or perverted. They would produce frustrated, hypocritical, and sadistic people who would condemn in others what they denied in themselves.

Second, sexuality could itself become a meditation. It was not mutual masturbation or an athletic activity, but a dance. Meditative Tantric sex was, Rajneesh explained, an experience of relaxation, a gentle mingling of the male and female energies, which animated all of life. The physical act of intercourse was both the emblem of and the avenue to internal harmony, to the realization of the "coincidence of opposites" within oneself and the universe. It was a way for a man to unite with the female in him, for a woman to include and assimilate the male in her. If used properly, meditatively—not simply as a relief or release—sex itself could become "the door to the divine" and "a meeting of you through the other." Sex had to be accepted, used, and fully experienced. Only then, when it no longer held sway, when it dropped of its own accord, could it be "left behind."

Sometimes as I read, I closed Rajneesh's books angrily. There were inaccuracies in the quotations, quotations not attributed to their sources, interpretations that seemed tortured to fit his meaning, repetitiveness, bad jokes, contradictions that appeared to be unexamined rather than paradoxical. In those moments I compared his books unfavorably with the brilliant early writings of the Tibetan lama Chogyam Trungpa, Alan Watts's careful popularizations of Zen, or Idries Shah's discourses on Sufism. But a few months later I would notice another volume in the bookstore and pick it up to see what he had to say about the tales of the Hasidim or the verses of Lao-tzu.

Rajneesh might not always be accurate, but there was an unmistakable authority in his voice. He spoke of the founders of the world's religions and their scriptures as easily, as intimately, as confidently, as E. M. Forster did of novelists and their novels. "I am not a scholar," Rajneesh explained in a talk on the verses of an eleventh-century Tibetan Master, "I live [Tilopa's words] again. I give them a new idea, a new shape, a new being. I really make him again contemporary."

In the mid-1970s Bhagwan Shree Rajneesh and his disciples and their practices were all but unknown in America. Other unconventional religious teachers and the groups that formed around them were, however, very much in the news and on peoples' minds. As many as 3 million to 4 million young people had turned their backs on conventional Christianity and Judaism—and on their expected role as students at prestigious universities—to preach and proselytize, to pray and meditate, as Scientologists and Children of God, as members of Reverend Sun Myung Moon's Unification Church and Swami Prabhupada's International Society for Krishna Consciousness and some two thousand other groups.

Their parents were hurt, bewildered, furious, and vocal. Why had their children given up their religion, comfort, freedom, intelligence, to follow "cult" leaders who seemed to offer only mind-numbing prayer and poverty? Had they been brainwashed and infantilized by these men and their authoritarian organizations? What, such parents asked the National Institute of Mental Health, were their children getting out of these groups? What were the leaders of these groups getting out of their children? And how could they get their children out?

In 1974 as part of my job at NIMH, I began to look into the cult phenomenon. I first tried to put the current proliferation of cults into a historical perspective. Most of the world's religions had started as cults, forming in times of crisis around charismatic teachers who had had a striking, and strikingly resonant, spiritual experience. Christianity and Buddhism, for example, had begun in times of social, religious, and psychological disorder, in rebellions against the rigidity and formalism of Judaism and Hinduism. Both Jesus and Buddha served as examples for and magnets to contemporaries whose needs and aspirations had been unfulfilled by the traditions in which they were raised.

Beginning with the Puritans, who came in revolt against the orthodoxy of the Church of England, America, with its open land and freedom from traditions, had been a particularly attractive sanctuary and breeding ground for new and schismatic religious groups. The Great Awakening of the eighteenth century provided new, more democratic, and accessible vehicles for religious feeling. In the early nineteenth century utopian communal experiments—the Transcendentalists' Brook Farm, John Humphrey Noyes's Perfectionist community at Oneida, New York—and millenarian movements such as the Mormons and the Millerites flourished. Later, hundreds of thousands of Americans were attracted to the religious philosophy and healing practices of Christian Science and the New Thought Movement, Theosophy, and Anthroposophy.

Moving out of the library and into the field, I began to speak with members of America's newest religious groups and visit their centers—from 1974 to 1986 I conducted in-depth interviews with between eight hundred and nine hundred people in more than forty groups. I did their meditations, shared their sacraments, participated in their meetings and workshops. I lived in their communities for days or weeks at a time and met with many of their leaders. I spoke with people who had left groups on their own and with a number who had been kidnapped and "deprogrammed"; with parents who were active in the nascent anticult movement and those who felt fine about their children's involvement with the Hare Krishnas or the Moonies.

It became clear to me that what was being labeled a monolithic and destructive cultism was in fact a religious revival, at least as widespread as any of its predecessors, that the cults themselves varied enormously in origins, size, practices, membership requirements, and doctrines.

Transcendental Meditation, for example, had initiated several million Americans into a simple practice familiar to countless Hindus. The vast majority of TMers continued to go about their lives as students and workers, pausing to meditate on their mantra for just twenty minutes, twice a day. The Unification Church, by contrast, had a complicated theology and required a total commitment of time, energy, and money. The church often encouraged members to reject the lives they had led and the people who were important to them.

Some organizations, such as TM and est (a consciousness-changing group that denied it was a religion but owed much to Scientology and Zen), were vast bureaucracies appealing to the urban middle class. They seemed to draw people who wanted to decrease their anxiety or improve their functioning or brighten up their self-image but were wary of more profound, potentially life-shaking, change. The Farm in Tennessee and the Love Family in Seattle, Washington, were, on the other hand, tight communes built on the LSD-informed spirituality and apostolic communalism of the hippie life-style of the 1960s.

Some of the people I talked to had been going through times of personal upheaval when they committed themselves to these groups. Many who joined the Unification Church, for example, had just matriculated or were about to graduate from college and felt lonely, unsure, in need of guidance. Some had recently broken up with husbands or wives or boyfriends or girlfriends. Others, including a number of Hare Krishnas with whom I spoke, had been strung out on drugs. A few had been clinically depressed or on the verge of psychosis.

Many others who joined new religions, particularly those who did so when they were older, did not seem to have experienced any devastating personal crisis. They felt they were seekers and spoke to me of a desire to find a more meaningful way of living with themselves and others, a more direct experience of a God that some of them had tasted in psychedelic drugs. They wanted to learn from a teacher who had himself transcended the ordinary conflicts of identity and intimacy, who had traveled the path to greater understanding and peace. And they wanted to be part of a community of like-minded seekers who might somehow make a difference in a troubled, and indeed endangered, world. There needed to be—they all said it differently: a change in consciousness; more godliness; more love; a way to unite Eastern meditativeness and Western activity; a new world religion—a way of being and an organization to make each person whole, to unite all of us. And it needed to happen soon, before we blew ourselves up.

As I began to develop a clearer picture of the groups I was studying, some of them, particularly the more dogmatic and authoritarian, troubled me deeply. The ultrareactionary politics and deceptive recruiting of the Moonies and the sometimes deceitful soliciting of the Krishnas were ugly. So too was the paranoid aggressiveness of many of the Scientology staff. If they lacked the power to confine their adherents physically—the sine qua non of brainwashing or true coercive persuasion—these and a number of other groups exhibited many of the characteristics that critical observers had noted: aggressive recruiting; near total control of the milieu; the use of guilt and shame to manipulate members for a "higher purpose"; suppression of doubt; and separation of the blessed "us" within the group from the benighted "them" outside.

Other leaders and their groups were far less rigid and clearly had valuable traditions to transmit and lessons to teach. These groups balanced devotion to the guru or teacher with the self-discipline of meditative practice and tended to attract older, more sophisticated adherents. The Tibetan Buddhist psychology that Chogyam Trungpa presented at Naropa Institute in Boulder, Colorado, and the Sufi techniques that Pir Vilayat Khan taught were remarkably sophisticated tools for self-knowledge. The sitting and walking meditations of Zen and the South Asian Vipassana tradition were spare and elegant. Swami Muktananda seemed somehow to be able to give shaktipat, to transmit to his followers by touch and glance some kind of enlivening energy. The Divine Light Mission, the Krishnas, and some of the hip communes provided members with a sweet and loving, if sometimes limited, saccharine, and authoritarian way of life.

However, none of the teachers or their practices interested me as much as Rajneesh. I took every opportunity to visit the small Rajneesh meditation centers that were opening in Miami and San Francisco, and did much more reading and many more interviews with Rajneesh's disciples than my work at NIMH required.

There was something very appealing about Rajneesh's personality as revealed in his tapes and books. He seemed original, idiosyncratic, surprising. If he was serious or hypnotically seductive one minute, he would almost certainly be abrasive, profane, or iconoclastic the next. He might interrupt a long and eloquent discourse on Buddha's *Heart Sutra* with a joke from *Playboy* or an arch aside about Indian prime minister Morarji Desai—"I have nothing against him personally, but he is a representative of a corrupt, decadent order."

Rajneesh seemed larger, more inclusive, and in many ways more down to earth and more relevant than other actors on the spiritual stage. The techniques he taught, like Dynamic Meditation, were easily accessible to the uninitiated as well as to disciples. He commented on many religious traditions—Zen, Sufism, Vipassana, Yoga, Taoism, Christianity, and Judaism—in ways that made each tradition come alive, but he had so far resisted creating a religious dogma of his own. Instead of presenting meditation or religion as an alternative to psychotherapy he was developing an approach that integrated them. I heard that at his ashram (religious community) in Poona, India, Rajneesh used psychotherapy groups as a way to bring what was repressed and unconscious to the surface, and meditation as a tool to develop a different attitude toward the thoughts and feelings that had been exposed. Most religions emphasized the opposition between the unconscious and higher consciousness. Rajneesh said the exploration of the former was a necessary step toward the latter.

Self-exploration, silence, and meditation were important to Rajneesh, but so too was celebration. He believed the body was to be nourished and enjoyed as well as explored. Asceticism was, Rajneesh maintained, only a disguised form of masochism. It led not to spiritual purity but to self-righteousness and repressive puritanism. The world, Rajneesh said, was to be embraced, not abandoned. He believed that wealth, which more traditional gurus shunned, was actually the precondition for spirituality. Only wealthy people living in a wealthy community had the freedom and leisure to transform themselves. Those who extolled poverty did so only to keep their followers in line, to forestall earthly rebellion with promises of spiritual riches.

Rajneesh's stated aim was to unite the materialism of the West and the spiritualism of the East. "I teach a sensuous religion," he told his disciples. "I want Gautama the Buddha and Zorba the Greek to come closer and closer. . . . My disciple," he said, "has to be Zorba the Buddha. Man is body and soul together. Both have to be satisfied."

As I listened to Rajneesh's tapes and read his books I thought of Proteus, the elusive mythical shape-changer; of Lao-tzu, the Chinese sage; and of the Ba'al Shem Tov, whose ecstatic celebration of the divinity in daily life illumined the eighteenth-century Hasidic movement. Most of all, however, Rajneesh reminded me of George Gurdjieff, the twentieth-century Armenian spiritual teacher who, I later found out, was one of his favorites.

Gurdjieff, who spent time in esoteric schools in Asia Minor, India, and Tibet, had in many ways anticipated Rajneesh. He had forged from his experiences a method by which he could make Eastern wisdom relevant to Western seekers. And, like Rajneesh, he had created communities in which his followers could begin to integrate the physical, emotional, and mental aspects of their functioning. He had used ancient Christian chants, dance, meditations learned from Tibetan yogis and dervishes, physical disciplines, sexual excess and abstinence, exaggerations and lies, even alcohol and violence—anything that worked—to wake his followers from their habitual ways of seeing and reacting to the world around them. Gurdjieff's first students were Russians, but later talented sophisticated western Europeans and Americans came to live with him.

By the late seventies, I had begun to meet some of the orange-clad westerners who were returning as disciples from Rajneesh's ashram in Poona. They were a disparate collection of attractive, restless people: therapists who were "into" Gestalt and primal scream, investment bankers who financed movies, schoolteachers who worked as models, and businessmen who had become dope dealers and then masseurs. These new disciples, or sannyasins as they called themselves, did not appear to be as well-integrated and awake as I would have expected Rajneesh's students to be. They seemed as a group self-consciously hip, and smug about the man they breathlessly called "Bhagwan." Still, the unlikely, contrasting stories they told about Rajneesh and his ashram intrigued me as much as the strange tales I had read about Gurdjieff.

In one evening at a raucous party at San Francisco's Paras Rajneesh Meditation Center, I heard the ashram described as "sweet and blissful" and a "continuous orgy"; a gateway to the collective unconscious and an escape from all troubling thoughts. It was a hell of psychological and physical confrontation for some and a heaven of effortless cooperation for others. Rajneesh himself was variously a saint and a demon, a lecher and a celibate, an intellectual giant and a holy fool. The more contradictions I heard, the more curious I became. I knew that sooner or later I would go to Poona to see him.

PART I

POONA

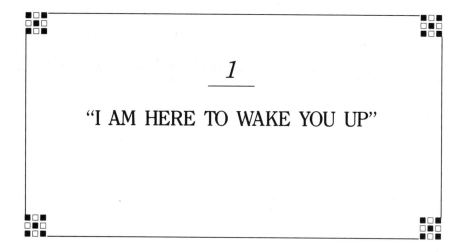

1

"I AM HERE TO WAKE YOU UP"

In May 1979, a month before the monsoon season began, I arrived at the Shree Rajneesh Ashram in Poona, a former British hill station in the state of Maharashtra, about one hundred miles southeast of Bombay. As part of my work at the National Institute of Mental Health, I had spent the previous six weeks in India visiting medical researchers and learning about India's traditional systems of healing. This was to be the first step in setting up collaborative research projects between the United States and India.

I had moved from ashram to laboratory, from hospitals where Western-trained physicians were using ancient Ayurvedic herbs and oils to treat schizophrenia and arthritis, to forest huts where community psychiatrists were learning from local healers. I spent time with psychophysiologists studying the effects of pranayama (yogic breath control) on brain chemistry and others who were trying to find the physical correlates for the chakras, or energy centers, that the ancient scriptures had described. And I had meditated with the yogis, clad in white dhotis, whom they were studying. Though the efforts of the Indian investigators were disorganized and severely underfunded, I found widespread interest in making a marriage between Western scientific methodology and indigenous healing systems.

Originally I had hoped to include the Shree Rajneesh Ashram in my studies. After all, it seemed to me that Rajneesh and his disciples were embarked on a significant experiment. Though I did not yet know the details, it was clear that their effort to combine Eastern meditative and Western psychotherapeutic techniques was on a scale far larger than any similar undertaking in the East or West. The idea had interested NIMH, but a State Department telex from Delhi had quashed it. The Shree Rajneesh Ashram was not a "suitable place" for me as a "representative of the U.S. government," certainly not a site for a joint research project.

The consul in Bombay reported that there had been two suicides at the ashram, that many people had experienced serious injuries, including broken arms and legs, in therapy groups. There were rumors of drugs and prostitution. The Indian government was said to be investigating. It was only four months since 911 members of the Reverend Jim Jones's People's Temple had killed themselves or been killed at their remote settlement in Guyana. The embassy was taking no chances. Poona, NIMH was warned, might become "another Jonestown."

The suicides and murders at Jonestown had troubled me in the months before I went to India. Preoccupied, I had read every newspaper and magazine account I could find. I reviewed for the *New York Times* the quickie books that appeared on Jones and Jonestown. On NIMH's behalf I went to San Francisco to talk with people who had left Jones's fold before the temple went to Guyana and with those who had survived in South America. I watched and listened to tapes of Jim Jones and pored over temple documents.

Jones had been an overvalued yet cowed child; an insecure, violent adolescent; and an insincere, manipulative adult. As a minister he was a caricature of the Christian missionary and the apostolic communitarian. He had used his charismatic presence, his fine voice, and his good works to seduce the gullible and needy, old people on Social Security, poor blacks, and idealistic and naive middle-class whites. Under attack, threatened with exposure in San Francisco, he fled. In the Guyana jungle, isolated from the restraints of the larger society, drugged with amphetamines, and drunk with his own power, Jones reigned supreme, and his sadism and self-destructiveness emerged unchecked.

Jones's history and the fate of the People's Temple were cautionary tales necessary for anyone evaluating a charismatic leader and his group. But in spite of the reports of suicides and of violence in some of the ashram groups, I did not believe that Rajneesh and his disciples were courting a similar destiny. The context and the characters seemed quite different. Insecurity and sadism and hypocrisy and control were themes that wound their way through Jim Jones's life and echoed in his words. Rajneesh seemed nothing if not direct and secure. The disciples I had met were, if obnoxious, still educated and mobile, skeptical, independent, and free from economic ties to their leader. In his published work, Rajneesh seemed to encourage independence, not submersion in the group, to push his disciples to know, not forget, themselves. His therapy groups were open and freely chosen, his ashram easily visible in the middle of a city. In general, the equation of Rajneesh and Jones, the Shree Rajneesh Ashram and Jonestown, seemed instructive but inaccurate.

The Indians whom I met in my travels seemed unconcerned about the comparison with Jonestown or the possibility of a massacre. They had seen too many gurus ("We are a religion-mad nation," one senior scientist had told me) to be alarmed by one more. Rajneesh's name was, however, familiar to almost everyone with whom I spoke, physicians and psychologists, herbalists and hotelkeepers, pundits and rug merchants. His books — already about two hundred had been published in Hindi and another seventy-five in English — were in every stall in Benares and Bangalore, in Delhi, Chandigarh, and Coimbatore. Everywhere I went, the name Rajneesh evoked the Indian equivalent of the response that the name of the mayor or the Yankees' owner might in a New York City cab driver. Lips puckered and heads shook as my informants declared him either a rotten spot on an ancient and honorable culture or a breath of fresh air in the miasma of Indian life, a bum or a hero.

Nearly everyone I spoke with agreed that I should go to Poona, to see and experience Rajneesh. "He is a phenomenon," one physiologist who had visited the ashram told me. Nor, he assured me, did it matter that I had no reservations for my four-week stay. "These things," he said, "take care of themselves." It was, he added, better that I go as a private citizen than a government employee. "In the end it is better for you to be on your own. The government connection would only inhibit. Perhaps instead of hearing God's voice, you would be listening to President Carter's."

----------------■□----------------
□■

Most of the ashrams I had seen in India were spartan and primitive, crowded, arid, and dusty. Their pilgrims seemed forever bent in prayer or work. Men and women kept their distance from one another. The Shree Rajneesh Ashram was a complex of new and brand-new buildings on six acres in an elegant neighborhood.

Standing at the gate, my bags in hand, I could see plate glass windows shining in the hot Indian afternoon. Long-haired men and women, mostly Western, all in orange clothing—long, loose gowns and cotton pants and shirts—were sitting on a low wall or walking slowly along spotless shaded walks that crisscrossed gardens where thousands of carefully tended plants glistened with water. Many of them had their arms around each other.

The Moonies I had visited were like bees around a jam pot. They flattered and fluttered and wanted to know everything about me, a new visitor, as soon as possible. Est graduates, with their name tags and smiles and questions, were like battleships moving relentlessly toward me, "into my space." Members of other new religions, although less demonstrative, all went out of their way to make me feel at home. At the Shree Rajneesh Ashram no effort was made to seduce or recruit me. "You have come," the people at Reception seemed to say, "because you wanted to. We are here. Bhagwan"—the Blessed One, as they called Rajneesh—"is here. Enjoy your stay. Make of it what you will."

Darshan, a laughing Indian woman at Reception, tells me there is no place in the ashram for newcomers to stay. Four thousand or five thousand people are currently in Poona "to be with Bhagwan." Only six hundred disciples—sannyasins, she calls them—a fraction of those who work full time in the ashram, actually live on the grounds and eat in the ashram canteen. As many as two hundred people, I later find out, have bought their tiny apartments for $6,000 or more.

The rest, even those who tend the gardens, prepare the food, or edit Rajneesh's books, stay elsewhere. According to their income and inclination, they live in Western- or Indian-style hotels, in rented apartments, in tents they have pitched, or in huts they have built by the river. Some of the newcomers are staying where I eventually choose to, in the two-hundred-bed "dormitory" across the street, where whole Indian families bunk down side by side with young Westerners locked in sweaty embrace.

There are, I learn, several major parts of the ashram program. Each day two meditations are done, Dynamic at 6:00 A.M. and Kundalini—a four-stage shaking, dancing, awareness, relaxation meditation—in the evening. Most of the newcomers' time is usually spent in therapy groups: there are some sixty different therapies, from art therapy and encounter to hypnotherapy and primal scream, designed by Rajneesh to peel the onion of their conditioning. Dozens of kinds of individual therapy are also available—Gestalt, primal scream, deep tissue massage, shiatzu, foot reflexology, rebirthing, Rolfing, tarot, chakra balancing, and many more—the whole panoply of the human potential movement and esoteric practice. "Many of the best therapists in the West," Darshan tells me proudly, "have come to Bhagwan." From the eleventh to the twenty-first of each month the groups are suspended. Then there is a meditation camp. Each day, five different hour-long meditations can be done.

Once I find a place to stay, I am told, I should come back to "speak with Arup." I should tell her what experiences I have had with meditation and therapy, and she will recommend groups for me. The next morning at eight I should be sure to come to "Bhagwan's daily discourse."

While cleaners mop the sweat that early-morning meditators have left on the marble floors of the huge open tent called Buddha Hall, I line up outside with two thousand others. This month, as he does every other month, Rajneesh is speaking in Hindi, a language that neither I nor the other Westerners understand. When I ask about the discourses, one elegant old man assures me that Rajneesh is "the most remarkable orator in Hindi, like Churchill in English." The old man and about half of those waiting with me are Indian. Some have come in the four buses parked just outside the gate.

I have been told that when Rajneesh speaks in English his audience is twice as large and his commentaries set the tone for life in the ashram. "When he was talking on Jesus," one man tells me, "everyone seemed to be passionate, intensely active. Love filled the air. When he spoke on Lao-tzu we drifted peacefully around the ashram." On alternate days he answers his listeners' questions, sometimes contradicting the gloss he has made on a text and then, two days later, contradicting his contradiction. He may counsel one sannyasin to doubt more, another to trust completely, and a third to forget about doubt and trust altogether.

We pay our five rupees (sixty cents) and file between two women who lean toward us to sniff our hair and bodies. Those who wear scent are forbidden entrance or, if their only offending part is their hair, turned back to put on a scarf. "Bhagwan is asthmatic," I am told, "and allergic to many things." LEAVE YOUR SHOES AND MIND OUTSIDE, a sign admonishes.

Those of us who are not sannyasins sit in the rear of Buddha Hall, to the left. Men and women in orange gowns tidy the rows, patrol the aisles, and maintain order and total silence. Our segregation and their martial bearing make me uneasy. Those who cough—apparently Rajneesh is quite sensitive to germs and noise as well as scents—are asked to leave.

Soon Rajneesh arrives, in a yellow Mercedes. He is wearing a white gown. He walks toward the dais, his hands touching in front of his chest in the posture of namaste, or greeting. A tiny Indian woman who I soon find out is his "secretary," Ma Yoga Laxmi, is at his side, carrying a folder that contains his few lecture notes—a quotation from the scriptures he is commenting on, the jokes he plans to tell.

As he lifts the skirt of his gown, Rajneesh seems to glide up the stairs toward his armchair. He sits, crosses his legs. Laxmi hands him the folder. I hear the faint, distant blare of horns and the low roar of scooters in the city streets. Closer by is the sound of many birds. Silence seems to rise like steam from our bodies toward the roof of the temple. In a few moments Rajneesh begins.

He is indeed a remarkable speaker. He caresses us with his voice, bathes us in sibilants. His pauses are dark and full of promise. He shifts tone like a halfback turning a sharp corner. Even in Hindi it is clear to me that the careful exposition of some difficult doctrine has ended, that a new voice, sly and confidential, is rising to tell a dirty joke.

Rajneesh uses his face and hands like a great melodramatic actor, a figure from Yiddish theater. He calls us with his liquid eyes, or widens them in pleasure or mock surprise like Zero Mostel. He tilts his head to underscore understanding, carves rounded figures in the air with his long, delicate fingers, gathering us to him. He invites and seduces us but never badgers or harangues. It is as if he is speaking first for his own pleasure and only very secondarily for an audience of which one somehow feels privileged to be a member.

As I watch him day after day, Rajneesh seems insubstantial, elusive, almost not there. Some personality remains: the irreverence, the gentleness, the anger that suddenly erupts and just as suddenly subsides, the vanity of his gowns, and the whimsy of the hats he wears daily. But all these characteristics seem as separate from him as his gown, and as easily put on and off.

I recall a story about Bodhidharma, who two millennia ago took Buddhism from India to China. It is said that he became enlightened after sitting for nine years facing a blank wall. It is also said that while he sat, his legs withered away. Commentators say that this is only metaphorical, that it was only his concern for lower or worldly things which disappeared. Watching Rajneesh move in and out of his car, listening to him speak in Hindi, responding to his greetings and his farewells, laughing at jokes I can feel but not understand, I have the persistent sense that he too is all but withered away.

Chandra Mohan Jain (the name Rajneesh, from the root *raja*, or king, was added later by his family) was born on December 11, 1931, in the village of Kuchwada in the province of Madhya Pradesh in central India. He was the eldest of eleven children. His father, Babulal, was a Jain, a member of an ancient Indian religious minority whose great leader, Mahavira, was a contemporary of Buddha and, like him, a religious reformer. Babulal was a cloth merchant, as was his father before him.

Rajneesh's birth and early years are shrouded in the kind of mystery and contradiction, the great expectations and great danger, that fill the early histories of other heroes, messianic figures, and shamans—Moses and Jesus, Krishna and Gurdjieff. Even his own accounts as recorded in *Glimpses of a Golden Childhood* and synthesized in disciple Vasant Joshi's worshipful biography, *The Awakened One*, differ. Both books seem as much the stuff of self-consciously created legend as of historical fact.

Joshi, for example, emphasized Rajneesh's self-sufficiency, the solitary nature of his lifelong quest—"After my grandfather's death," Rajneesh declared, "aloneness became my nature"—the unwavering trajectory of a mission that began seven hundred years before, in a previous incarnation. Rajneesh presented himself as a pampered child, the cynosure of the doting grandmother who cared for him in his earliest years ("My Nani was my first disciple"), the adored protégé of mad wandering Babas—holy men—who immediately recognized his "potential."

According to Rajneesh's account—and the one his godfather, Ambalal Patel (Bapuji), gave to me—several astrologers refused to cast his natal chart, predicting either that he would die young or face death every seven years. One reportedly said that if he lived apart from his family he might cheat death. Then "his life would be fairly long and he would have the great personality and light of a leader, a path indicator for the world, like Buddha or Mahavira."

Rajneesh spent much of his early childhood with his maternal grandparents and his godfather. His grandparents, said Rajneesh, "were feeling very lonely, so they wanted to bring me up." His grandfather, who had named him Raja, and his grandmother treated him "like a prince." He was a very bright but sickly child. Several times he almost died, of smallpox and asthma. When he was five his younger sister died. He seems to have been quite disturbed by her death. He reportedly refused food, dressed as a Jain monk, and carried a begging bowl.

From the time Raja could speak and walk about the village, he was said by villagers with whom I talked to have exhibited the mixture of solitude and provocativeness, of indifference to others' opinions and leadership, that would characterize his adult life. Stories of his self-reliance and his brash challenges to the learned, powerful, and pompous—school authorities and priests—abounded. According to his autobiographical accounts he was the one who asked embarrassing questions of the swamis and pundits who enjoyed his grandfather's hospitality, the boy who brought the snake into the elementary school classroom. Some who lived in his village saw him as selfish and spoiled, others as gifted, talented, and justifiably self-absorbed.

When he was seven, Rajneesh watched his grandfather die "slowly and painfully" of a stroke that robbed him first of mobility, then of speech, hearing, and sight. After his grandfather's death, Rajneesh seems to have made the kind of decision not uncommon among children who experience a terrible early loss: by distancing himself from others, he would protect himself from experiencing such wrenching pain again.

"His death," Rajneesh remarked in a discourse years later, "to me became the death to all attachments." From then on, "whenever my relationship with anyone began to become intimate, that death stared at me." He realized, sadly at first and then with a certain "happiness," that he would be alone. "For me the possibility of anyone else becoming my center was destroyed in the very first steps of my life." Rajneesh became preoccupied with death and the desire to risk and face it. He spent time with dying people, watching, like some precocious psychologist or anthropologist, their decline and the reactions of their relatives. He followed funeral processions to the local cremation grounds and often spent time sitting there.

He also began to experiment on himself. Death had taken him by surprise, given him great pain; now he would try to understand and master his own fear of it. He began spontaneously to detach himself from external sensations, to lie down and imagine that his body was as heavy, inert, and lifeless as lead or marble. At fourteen, an age at which the astrologers had predicted he might die, Rajneesh elected to face death: he spent a week in a deserted temple, "waiting for death." A snake came and moved over his supine body and went away. "Fear," he reported, "had disappeared. If you accept death there is no fear . . . a distance is created; life with its worries moves away . . . you become aware of . . . something deathless."

Rajneesh also began to treat his entire village, starting with his family, as an experimental laboratory. Like many adolescents, he was rebellious. Unlike others, he seems to have been the master, not the victim, of his rebellion. He seemed to know exactly how far he could safely push his parents and what would be most distressing, infuriating, or embarrassing to them. In pictures he looks smug, intense, angry, mischievous, knowing, but not happy.

He played elaborate, sometimes sadistic, tricks on villagers who annoyed him — on several occasions he staged dramas of ghosts and spirits to frighten the gullible and superstitious, including a hapless tutor who had done him no harm. He was a leader among the village boys, devising challenges and ordeals for them. Ajit Saraswati, a childhood companion who became a physician and one of Rajneesh's first disciples, told me about young Raja's nighttime expeditions. On moonless nights he led Saraswati and the other village boys up narrow trails onto the ledges high above the river Shakkar. Then he guided them along the cliffs and onto a high railway bridge that spanned the river. Rajneesh would always jump first, goading, shaming, teasing the others with his example.

During these years Rajneesh also loved to dive into the whirlpools that formed when the river was swollen by the monsoon. He would let the force of the whirl take him, faster and faster, in tighter and tighter circles, till finally, at the narrow point at the bottom of the whirl, he was thrown free. Surrendering to the pull of the water, he later explained, was like surrendering the ego, the will, allowing it to die.

When he wasn't playing pranks or experimenting on himself or his family and friends, Rajneesh was reading. He loved books, loved ordering them by mail and unwrapping the parcels when they came. He loved reading and rereading them; loved to possess them and to carry them around with him. Like young people everywhere — and perhaps most particularly like young people in small towns — he read because books took him out of his own narrow world and because they gave him comfort while he remained in it. They were his friends and they helped him understand himself and his family. They gave him a taste of his own possibilities as a man and a writer, and for a larger, richer, more complex world. The Russian novels seem to have been his favorites: Gorky's *Mother*, Turgenev's *Fathers and Sons* ("I used to force my poor father to read it to understand the gap between himself and me"), and Tolstoy's *Resurrection*, which he believed "contained the whole spirit of Jesus."

Rajneesh's late teens were a time of turmoil and contradiction. He fell in love and his girlfriend, Shashi, died. He advocated socialism and became disillusioned with it, denounced Gandhi and deeply mourned his death. He mocked religion even as he looked for answers in the Jain, Christian, and Buddhist scriptures. He read esoteric books; practiced magic, yogic breath control, and self-hypnosis; and hypnotized his friends and family. He spent time with the eccentric babas who had taken him under their wing and met the people—musicians, politicians, sages, and saddhus (holy men)—to whom they brought him.

At nineteen Rajneesh the small-town rebel and prankster went to college in the relatively large city of Jabalpur. At first he resembled the Western Bohemians who were his contemporaries, a rebellious, poetic, mystical, lazy young man who debated with skill and energy, charmed some professors with his wit and intelligence ("He had an understanding far beyond his contemporaries," one recalled), offended others, and often neglected his studies. He was, he said, asked to leave one college because a professor objected to his continual classroom challenges. In his second college he elected to stay home rather than conform to the strictures of the classroom.

Soon he seemed more basket case than beatnik. He continued to challenge the received ideas of his friends and teachers, but his precocious self-assurance disintegrated. He felt alone and insecure. He suffered from disabling headaches. "For one year," he recalled, "it was almost impossible to know what was happening. . . . Just to keep myself alive was a very difficult thing, because all appetite disappeared. I could not talk to anybody. In every other sentence I would forget what I was saying."

He said he ran up to sixteen miles a day "just to feel myself" and spent days at a time lying on the floor of his room counting from one to one hundred and back again. He sat in high trees to meditate. Once, he reported, his body fell to the ground but his "consciousness" stayed in the air, connected by a glittering silver cord to his navel. He felt the "connection . . . between this physical body and the spiritual being . . . disintegrate." During this year his hair and beard were wild, his eyes preternaturally bright.

Rajneesh had the sense he was going through an extremely important change. His concerned parents believed he was going crazy. They took their son to one physician after another. In the West, indeed in modern India, there would have been little doubt about Rajneesh's condition. To most observers the situation would have looked less like an ordinary adolescent identity crisis and more like an incipient psychotic episode. Doctors would probably have hospitalized him; tranquilizers might have been prescribed.

As it happened, Rajneesh was seen by a Vaidiya, a traditional Ayurvedic physician, who construed his symptoms differently. The Vaidiya believed that the symptoms were those of divine intoxication, that the apparent breakdown was actually a kind of breakthrough. Rajneesh, the Vaidiya said, was "reaching home."

Rajneesh said that on March 21, 1953, at the age of twenty-one, he did "reach home." He became enlightened. Seven days before, he "stopped working on myself." For years, "lifetimes," he had been "struggling," "seeking." Now he no longer felt the need. Like Buddha, who had passionately practiced every ascetic and esoteric discipline for six years before simply sitting, Rajneesh was now ready to stop searching. Then "effort was necessary." Now it was beside the point.

In that recognition, that giving up, "a new energy," "a new freedom" came. During those seven days "it was as if I was exploding, as if I was mad with blissfulness." On the night of March 21 he awoke to feel "throbbing life all around me . . . a great storm of light, joy, ecstasy." He rushed out of the house he shared with his cousin and into a garden he used to visit daily.

"There was no gravitation," he said years later. "I was feeling weightless. . . . For the first time the drop had fallen into the ocean . . . I was the ocean. . . . The moment I entered the garden everything became luminous . . . alive . . . beautiful." He sat under a Maulshree tree. There was no time, and "the whole universe . . . luminous, throbbing, became a benediction."

Enlightenment is very difficult to characterize, impossible to certify, and — especially for the consumption of credulous and eager seekers — easy to counterfeit. "The way that can be described," said Lao-tzu, "is not the way."

The English word *enlightenment* is obviously associated with light. The concept is Buddhist, but both the concept and the imagery of light are far broader than the Buddhist tradition. The Hindus speak of an equivalent state of "god realization"; in Zen it is kensho; some Neoplatonic and Christian sects have used the word *gnosis*, or knowledge. The Sanskrit word *guru* means "one who brings light out of darkness"; Christian saints are depicted with halos of light.

The enlightened person, the person in whom light dwells, sees clearly, no longer, as the Christian apostle Paul put it, "through a glass darkly." Enlightenment is also closely associated with waking. Buddha literally means "the awakened one." Gurdjieff often spoke of "waking people up." Waking up, one sees what is already there.

Enlightenment in these traditions is thus as ordinary as it is rare. The turmoil that usually precedes it is considered preparatory catharsis and includes preliminary, though wildly unfocused, glimpses of the state toward which one is moving. Enlightenment itself, however, is seen to be more like recovering one's true self than acquiring anything new or special, extraordinary powers. "Enlightenment," a Zen Master has said, "is simply this: When I walk, I walk. When I eat, I eat. When I sleep, I sleep." An enlightened person is not, Rajneesh said, "somebody who has reached the topmost rung of the ladder. Enlightenment is getting down from the ladder; getting down forever and never asking for any ladder again, becoming natural."

Outwardly, Rajneesh seemed much the same. He went to classes in the same desultory fashion, argued and debated as provocatively as before. He received his B.A. in philosophy in 1955 and his M.A. in 1957. But, he said, he did things with a new ease. He was no longer concerned with ("attached to") the outcome of his actions. The process of detachment, begun when his grandfather died, and accelerated with his challenge to death at fourteen, was, he said, complete. Now he was allowing his life simply to be, rather than striving to shape it. He was no longer searching for or testing himself. The feeling of "eternity," of "each moment, a miracle," continued.

After he received his master's degree, Rajneesh taught philosophy, first at Raipur Sanskrit College, then at the University of Jabalpur. He was by this time a widely known and controversial figure in the city. Many people in and out of the university community acknowledged the exceptional intelligence that had enabled him to overcome the deficiencies of his early education in a small town. He had even then, according to one of his university colleagues, a "golden tongue" in Hindi and a firm command of English, to which he came later in life than most of his fellows. He was a subtle logician, a cunning debater, and a popular lecturer. It was said that he had studied Gurdjieff and the Russian mystical philosopher Peter Ouspensky deeply, that he was a powerful hypnotist and knew many esoteric methods of healing.

Many people, including one of his former professors, began to come to him for help with physical and emotional problems.

There were rumors of a less savory side as well. Some I heard while traveling in India in 1979, others came to me later. It was said that after he put some women in trance, Rajneesh stole their gold bangles, and that he "impregnated" the daughter of the man who built him his first meditation hall and then convinced his cousin to claim paternity. Surendra Kelwala, now a psychiatrist living in the United States, was an adolescent in Jabalpur during these years and knew Rajneesh. "He was," Kelwala said to me several years after I returned from Poona, "the brightest man I have ever known . . . with the best memory, but he had a habit of lying a little bit."

Kelwala remembered that Rajneesh accumulated disciples and then "dropped" them as he moved from the middle class of Jabalpur to its wealthier citizens, then from Jabalpur to Bombay, the capital of India's commerce and home of its film stars.

In 1960 Rajneesh began to travel around India, lecturing to students, religious groups, social and political organizations, and public gatherings. He moved quickly from one city to another, attacking India's most cherished institutions and beliefs, spreading a gospel of doubt and disquiet. In 1965 several of Bombay's Jain business-men formed the Jeevan Jagruti Kendra (Life Awakening Center) to support Rajneesh and propagate his teachings.

During this time these men—and other Jains—seem to have believed that Rajneesh had the potential for becoming a Tirthamkara, a great teacher in the Jain tradition of Mahavira. Most were disappointed. By the late sixties Rajneesh had come to view the Jainism of his childhood as a prototype for the narrowness and stupidity of all organized religion. He relabeled Jain asceticism as masochism, celebrated the sexuali-ty that Jains condemned, and mocked the elaborate dietary prohibitions and strict nonviolence (the Jains strain their water and wear masks so as not to injure insects that might otherwise be imbibed or inhaled) that characterize Jainism and set its adherents apart from other Indians.

Rajneesh soon broadened his attack to include all orthodoxies. All of India's ancient religions, he maintained, were now dead; their priests were hypocritical, petty tyrants, lulling their followers with empty ritual, oppressing them with fears of damnation and promises of blessings in this life or the next. He told his audiences that socialism, to which virtually all of India's major political parties gave lip service, was a dead loss, socializing only poverty. India's whole attitude toward sex—from arranged mar-riages to the suppression of sexuality in adolescence to the clandestine affairs of adulterous men—was, he said, life-denying and perverted.

During 1968–69, Gandhi's centenary year, Rajneesh focused his attention on the sainted Mahatma. He declared that Gandhi, whom in many ways he respected, had always been a Hindu chauvinist, not really ecumenical. He was a "masochist" who loved to manipulate others by starving himself, a pervert who refused to make love to his wife and, as an old man, brought naked young girls to his bed. Gandhi's *Experi-ments with Truth* were actually, Rajneesh confided, deadpan, "experiments with food and sex."

"With or without reason," Rajneesh said a few years later, "I was creating controver-sies, creating criticisms." Looking back, one can see these attacks as the adult version of the child Raja's uncompromising insistence on speaking "truth to power"; the fulfillment of his identity as an adolescent rebel in his family, school, and town; and the beginning of a strategy for attracting as much attention as possible.

During the 1960s Rajneesh was called Acharya (Teacher). As word of his rhetorical skill spread, he drew increasingly large crowds. Men would overhear a few words while hurrying home, Surendra Kelwala told me, and would stop for hours. Occasionally in cities like Bombay as many as fifty thousand assembled to listen to him.

Rajneesh aroused a variety of emotions. Many Indians were infuriated by his sweeping attacks on traditional, widely accepted religious practices and political and social values. Others were scandalized by his well-known love of women and fast cars. Physicians, psychologists, and scientists who were interested in Rajneesh's views told me they had been disturbed by the way he presented them. They found his public confrontations with Hindu priests and Jain monks and Muslim mullahs ugly and dangerous. "India," a distinguished physician whom I met in Bangalore told me, "has always been known for its religious tolerance," but "this man has gone too far." The uneasy truce among religious leaders and the subcontinent's pluralism depended on mutual tolerance if not respect. Attacking another man's religion and his guru—not to say savaging Gandhi—was in poor taste.

Besides, many well-bred scientists confided in me, Rajneesh was so arrogant. Virtually every other religious teacher in India certified himself by his connection to his guru and to a lineage that might stretch back beyond written history, perhaps to an incarnation of the god Shiva or Vishnu. Rajneesh said that he had no guru and usually, according to those who heard him in the sixties, didn't acknowledge his debts even to obvious sources like Gurdjieff and Ouspensky. He often seemed to claim that he was the sole origin of and authority for his teachings. Even in his account of his past incarnation, he did not include any mention of being anyone's disciple.

Still, there were many Indians who nodded in recognition when Rajneesh spoke. Religious tradition might provide reassurance to most, but to some it was simply a burden, a barrier, as oppressive, restrictive, and irrelevant as the caste system that helped sustain it. Rajneesh's fiery presence and the freshness, indeed the outrageousness, of his message attracted the curious and adventurous, the déclassé and the disaffected. These were Indians whose heterodox opinions or social concerns or questioning minds were already putting them in conflict with their religion or their family. They saw in Rajneesh a modern man, critical, sexually liberated, psychologically minded, antiestablishment. They felt ready to examine the blind spots and limitations that he was probing. Cosmopolitans like Shyam, marginal types like a gambler uncle of Laxmi, speculators, bureaucrats, performers, unemployed graduate students, wealthy urbanites—all came to listen.

Once Rajneesh had his audience's attention he could proceed. If a listener granted the possibility that one religious or cultural commonplace might be inaccurate or hypocritical, then he or she might be open to other heretical ideas. Even if what Rajneesh was saying wasn't altogether accurate—and the more erudite could easily pick out distortions, exaggerations, and inaccuracies—they could recognize the germ of truth in his words, the taste of, to borrow a then current Western word that Rajneesh himself often used, authenticity.

In the West in the mid-sixties, educated young people were experimenting with the expanded consciousness that marijuana and psychedelics offered, and with new forms of community—more loving and cooperative, less fearful and competitive than the ones in which they had grown up. They were listening to Mario Savio, Stokely Carmichael, Abbie Hoffman, and Danny the Red, and reading books by Herbert Marcuse, R. D. Laing, and Norman O. Brown. They were participating in movements against racial discrimination, the war in Vietnam, and the university bureaucracy, and they were attempting to make these movements responsive to personal—including sexual—needs as well as social hopes and political realities.

At the same time in India, a number of young and not-so-young people were attending Acharya Rajneesh's lectures and contemplating the possibility of a related but particularly Indian revolution: a total change in consciousness, a new religionless religion.

V. N. Shah was a young, hardworking civil servant with a wife and family when he first heard Rajneesh, in 1964, at a series of lectures sponsored by a Jain youth group. Shah was in many ways a conventional man: "My concept at the time," he told me twenty years later, "was a traditional Indian one. I believed that first I was a good boy in my family, then a good citizen in society and a good parent; finally, perhaps, I would become religious." On the other hand Shah, who had a master's degree in commerce, was "very much a person who questioned, a man who tried to understand and experiment."

After hearing Rajneesh speak, Shah's "world turned topsy-turvy. . . . Rajneesh said unless you are religious you can't be good and if you try to be good you can't be religious. You will land yourself in hypocrisy. He made a mockery of [every kind of priest] and of all the rituals I had practiced for thirty-five years." At every opportunity Shah returned, "to hear this man speak.

"I was a man who experiments, not the type that falls in love," he reassured me, shaking his head from side to side, a motion that in India implies emphasis rather than negation. "I wasn't interested in magic," he went on. "I had seen many persons like Sai Baba [a contemporary South Indian guru], who could make things appear and disappear. I had decided that I would be with a teacher only if he fulfilled certain conditions.

"First," Shah, a bit of a pedagogue, ticked them off on his fingers, "everything he achieves has to be achievable by me. Second, I would be with him only if he had something different from all the available religions or"—touching his third finger—"if someone had a modern approach to the eternal truth in religion and could implement it in day-to-day life. Finally, in whatever he was offering there must be no cunningness, no desire to get something from me.

"I applied all these to Bhagwan," he sat back now, stroked his long white beard, crossed his slim legs, "and found no problem. He was speaking only from his experience and asking me to accept what he said only if my experience confirms it. He was ready to unconditionally share whatever he had." Shah took his family and friends with him so that they too could see and hear this man and test his teachings. He later helped organize some of Rajneesh's lecture tours.

At this time Rajneesh reminded Shah and others of Jiddu Krishnamurti, another itinerant speaker who infuriated the Indian establishment. In the 1920s Krishnamurti had renounced the role of "world teacher" for which Annie Besant and her Theosophist colleagues had prepared him. For the next sixty years he would inveigh against religious orthodoxy and its institutions, slavish devotion to tradition and to gurus, and, indeed, the blind acceptance of any received ideas, including his own.

J.K., as he was known, counseled his guru-seeking audiences to understand and think for themselves. "Forget about answers," he advised them. They should develop a "choiceless awareness," which would enable them to see through the hypocrisy, self-deception, and violence in which they ordinarily lived. But Krishnamurti was refined, eloquent, and arch, a surgeon wielding a scalpel on his audience's psychic aberrations. Rajneesh was, by contrast, fiery and confrontative, a rhetorical warrior assaulting the barricades of belief.

In 1964, in the hills of Rajasthan, in northwest India, Rajneesh began the ten-day meditation camps that would ensure his notoriety. "I am here," he announced in his first evening lecture, "to wake you up." The earliest camps were fairly sedate: talks twice a day to the several hundred people who came from all over India to attend them, quiet meditations (on the breath and the navel), and self-hypnotic exercises. Rajneesh taught the techniques carefully and responded to questions—about trying to conquer thought and whether one must renounce the world to become spiritual—with great patience. Most of his answers were identical to those he would give twenty years later: "Forget everything," he advised his listeners, quoting Ramana Maharshi, the Indian sage who died in 1950. "Live only in the present." Morality is not "constraint" but an "articulation of joy." "It is not the world one must renounce, but ignorance."

Though his point of view remained reasonably consistent, the tenor of his camps soon shifted. Rajneesh's aim was essentially the one followed by centuries of Indian meditation Masters: the dissolution of the boundaries that separated the individual from the cosmos of which he was an inextricable part; the experience of shunyata, the silent inner emptiness that lived, feared and unexplored, at each person's center; the development of a detached, vigilant consciousness that witnessed thoughts and feelings and actions. But the methods that he began to use were different from his predecessors'.

Meditation, he found, would not happen until people undid the "knots of negativity" in their bodies, minds, and emotions. Perhaps in a more relaxed, pastoral world the quiet within was more available. But in a developing society whose members were clinging to no longer relevant values while grasping for meaningless success, meditation was another matter. Agitation and catharsis were necessary to loosen the physical constrictions that chronic stress had created, the fixed patterns of thought and feeling that family and society had imposed. Only then would it be possible for people to relax; and only in this relaxation could one begin to experience the inner emptiness and unmediated connectedness with the natural world that were, after all, the essence of meditation.

By the late 1960s Rajneesh had begun to combine traditional techniques with expressive devices he had borrowed from Western psychology and particularly from the human potential movement. Bioenergetic exercises derived from the work of Wilhelm Reich and his pupils—screaming, crying, rolling eyes, and shaking—were performed in a sequence with Indian mantras, Tibetan humming, Sufi dances. Buddhists had compared their meditation to walking: years of practice would wear away the ego like an old shoe. Rajneesh was learning to use an electric sander.

Over the years Rajneesh devised dozens of meditations for different temperaments and occasions—active techniques for the morning, quieter ones for evening; meditations with mirrors and pillows, and with infants' pacifiers; indoor and outdoor meditations, meditations in automobiles and airplanes. He refined them, sometimes divided them into stages, and gave them names: Kundalini, the four-stage shaking, dancing, awareness, relaxation meditation that was done in the late afternoon; Nadabrahma, a Tibetan humming technique, could be done singly and in pairs, in the early morning or late at night; and Gourishankar, a candle-gazing technique so called because, according to Rajneesh, it "got you as high as Gourishankar [Mount Everest]." The best-known and most dramatic was the Chaotic, later called Dynamic Meditation.

Dynamic was in many ways a microcosm of Rajneesh's methods and his outlook. It was a synthesis of Eastern and Western techniques, a shock to habitual patterns of thought and behavior. It also was, at least on the surface, totally antithetical to the conventional Indian practices of prayer and meditation. No holy place or elaborate ritual was necessary, no worshipful attitude. There were no priests and no austerities. One could simply put on a tape and do it.

The Indians who came to the camps in the late sixties and early seventies shook and shouted, laughed and cried as they did Dynamic. Some shed their clothes and danced as if possessed. At one camp on Mount Abu, Shyam said, he laughed for ninety-six hours. Others who came sat in blissful silence for hours or days at a time.

Rajneesh presided, a small but now solid man, dressed only in a skirtlike lunghi, bright-eyed, bearded, bald except for a fringe of long black hair. "Give one hundred percent!" he would shout during the breathing and dancing, raising his hands. "Give total effort!"

In 1966, under pressure from his college administration, Rajneesh resigned his academic post. After two more years of traveling, and with the financial support of the Jeevan Jagruti Kendra, he settled with a few disciples in a large apartment in Bombay. He had, he believed, "extended [his] invitation" to all of India. Now those who were interested could come to him. He received visitors, answered questions, and gave daily discourses.

In Bombay Rajneesh began his commentaries on the world's sacred scriptures. Over the years he would explore with apparently indefatigable pleasure many dozens of them. He spoke about the *Upanishads* and *Vedanta*. There were ten volumes on the *Bhagavad-Gita*, many books on Buddha's sutras and on Bodhidharma and the Zen Masters who followed him. There were lectures on the songs of the Baul mystics and the poems of the Sufis Kabir and Rumi; two volumes on the fragments of Pythagoras and two more on Heraclitus; books on Lao-tzu, Chuang-tzu, and Lieh-tzu, the Taoist Masters, and on *The Secret of the Golden Flower*, the Taoist esoteric yoga. There were lectures on the Hasidim and lectures on the Gospels, both canonical and Gnostic, and on Tibetan and Indian Tantra.

Each text had its own validity. And, equally important, each could be used as a magnet. Rajneesh delighted in drawing people back to the tradition they had long ago left behind or were just about to give up. He would, he announced, show the lapsed Catholics and Protestants, the disillusioned priests and nuns who were beginning to come to hear him, "a real Jesus," a man who walked and talked and ate and laughed and spent his time with women. He would also help them to understand the real meaning of the miracles they had come to mistrust. Jesus didn't raise Lazarus from the dead, Rajneesh assured his listeners. It was a metaphor, not a miracle. Jesus was a Master and all Masters were calling their disciples out of the living death of sleep and ignorance.

"The real Jesus," he went on, "never died on the cross. That which dies is not really part of you." Christ was not the name of a person but "the name of the ultimate state of consciousness. It is exactly what we call in the East, Buddhahood. Jesus was only one of the Christs. Abraham was one, Moses was one, Lao-tzu was one, Krishna was one. Identifying with Jesus as a figure on the cross is simply a way for people to project their sadness." Jesus became "an excuse to become miserable," and the worship of his suffering was a form of pathology perpetuated by hysterical saints and repressed priests.

Besides, the idea was not to become a Christian. In fact it was idiotic to be a Christian and fall in love with Christ. "Once you have accepted yourself as becoming a Christian you have barred yourself from becoming a Christ. You have become a follower, and a follower is only an imitator. Drop being a Christian," he told them, "and start being a seeker of truth."

Rajneesh understood that each tradition would also attract those to whom its doctrines and tone were temperamentally congenial: the intellectual to Buddha's cool, dry paradoxes; the romantic to the poems of Kabir and Rumi; sexual adventurers to Tantra; the worldly man, the singer and dancer, to the tales of the Hasidim. "Have a little more freedom . . . look around," he coached his listeners. "Whichever flower attracts you, follow that. . . . You may be a Hindu by birth, but if you feel the Koran rings bells in your heart, then the Koran is your scripture."

Rajneesh, of course, was also casting his commentaries like nets, to bring disciples to him. "You can know Jesus," he told his listeners, "only through a man who has attained Christ Consciousness. Through me," he said with, I imagine, a smile at his parody of Christ's words, "there is a possibility to know Jesus."

In 1969, much to the surprise of those who had heard him inveigh against gurus and disciples, leaders and followers, Rajneesh initiated his first disciples, among them Laxmi Thakarsi Kuruwa. Laxmi had first seen Rajneesh in 1962, when he spoke to an all-India Congress party conference in Bombay. Then secretary of the Bombay Congress Women's Auxiliary, she was a funny, passionate, well-connected Jain woman who did social work and had a taste for chocolates and fast cars. She had a bright political future. She was at the time "a happy person" but still, she told me years later, somehow "not satisfied."

All that changed the first time she saw Rajneesh. "Laxmi" — she almost always used the third person when speaking of herself — "was born in a Jain family. So she expected a man with cloth in front of his mouth. When he entered and as he came near, one felt, 'One knows him.' As he started talking, the ears, the mind could not function. One look into his eyes and that was it. He called me with his eyes.

"The talk ended and Laxmi remained sitting like that, while the whole hall emptied.

The president of the women's auxiliary came in and said, 'What is happening?' Laxmi said, 'Oh, the lecture is over? I am in love with that man.' The president said, 'You are hypnotized.' And Laxmi's mother said, 'Oh, if he is a swami, a saddhu, then I am happy that my daughter is in love.' "

Several years later Laxmi went with her gambler uncle to one of Rajneesh's meditation camps. She did Dynamic and like Shyam found herself unaccountably, uncontrollably laughing. At six the next morning, "Bhagwan put his hand on Laxmi's arm and said, 'Laxmi come back.' And Laxmi came back. 'I did not feel to stop you,' Bhagwan said, 'but your uncle is a heart patient and some quiet was needed.'

"Then Laxmi felt that the clothes Laxmi was wearing, stretch pants, a brassiere, couldn't be worn. Her uncle said, 'Are you going to go naked?' Laxmi said, 'No, nakedness cannot be done but a clean dhoti can be worn.' " She felt no need of food or drink and had a sense that "everything was overflowing," that she was complete and content. Laxmi was converted, not to a religion but to a man.

Not long after, Laxmi became Rajneesh's personal secretary, a title that actually meant something like chief executive officer. She arranged for food and lodging for Rajneesh, scheduled his lectures and meetings, and asked for donations. Laxmi began spontaneously to wear orange, the traditional color of sannyasins, India's wandering renunciates. Then she decided that she was Rajneesh's disciple: "Laxmi said to Bhagwan, 'You must initiate me,' and Bhagwan did."

In 1970 Rajneesh began to initiate others into the order he and Laxmi were creating. They decided that all the disciples would also wear orange, as well as a mala, a necklace of 108 beads (which Rajneesh said represented 108 kinds of meditation) and a locket with a picture of Rajneesh. Orange was to represent "the color of the sun rising . . . live and vibrating." The picture, Rajneesh said, was not a form of idolatry but a reminder. "The picture is not mine. . . . I exist as an emptiness that cannot be pictured."

Rajneesh gave many of his followers Sanskrit names, which represented some aspect of their character or undeveloped potential to which they might aspire. Some he called by the names of sages and saints—Kabir, Krishna, Christ, Caitanya—with whom he felt they had an affinity. Sometimes he gave sannyasins back their own names.

The new name was prefixed, usually by either Anand or Prem. The former means "bliss" and was given to those whom he saw as solitary, meditative types. By contrast, the Prems—Prem means "love" — were more devotional. Other sannyasins were given names like Yoga (Union), Deva (Divine), or Dhyan (Meditation). All the male sannyasins were called Swami, for Lord or Master, and all the women were Ma, or Mother. Thus, Ma Yoga Laxmi. When, according to Rajneesh, the men came to their "ultimate flowering" they would become "masters of their own being." When the women "flowered" they would become a "motherly force."

To distinguish his disciples from the orange-clad sannyasins who wandered the roads and haunted the temples and bathing ghats of India, he called them "neo-sannyasins." He said that the old sannyasins with their begging bowls and staffs, their matted locks and dour looks, were rigid and life-denying. By contrast, his sannyasins were to be "joyous creatures, rebels and dancers moving to their own music."

The new wanderers would, he declared, be free, responsive to the immediate situation, creative, capable of being either loving or alone, and able to trust in themselves completely. They were to surrender to him, their "Master," but only "the ego, the false idea that you are somebody, somebody special." He was, he said to them, "not to be worshipped." He was rather to be "like a catalytic agent," "a sun encouraging the flower [to open], but in a very delicate way."

Rajneesh's understanding of the ego and his insistence on shedding it were in many ways at odds with what I had learned of modern psychology. Freud had postulated a tripartite division of mental functioning. In the center was the ego, mediating between the instinctual demands of the id and the harsh familial and cultural imperatives and prohibitions that were internalized in the superego. One of the goals of psychoanalysis was the reclamation for the ego of the territory previously governed by the id and the superego.

For psychoanalysis, the ego represented the highest aspect of development. It was the realm of conflict-free activity, of cognition and problem-solving, as well as of mediation and synthesis. It provided the individual with a sense of identity, a feeling of continuity with the past, and more or less secure expectations for the future. The ego was a realm of sanity. Its borders were proof against invasion by destructive instincts and intrusive self-judgments. The ego protected the individual from the dissolution that came from a symbiotic merging with another. If its boundaries were breached by overwhelming or oft-repeated traumas, they might become porous and ineffective. One's own thoughts might then be projected, heard as voices or commands from another, or indeed from God. One might feel that he was disappearing or was going to be engulfed by another. This confusion of inner and outer world was one of the hallmarks of psychosis.

In the introductory part of *Civilization and Its Discontents*, Freud noted that this inclination to abolish the boundaries of the ego and merge with what was outside was connected with religious experience. He said he could understand the appeal of the "oceanic feeling," the unbroken connectedness to the world. But he felt obliged to remind his readers that it was regressive, the vestige of a less rather than a more highly developed consciousness, a return to an infantile state in which the ego had not yet differentiated itself from the external world.

Rajneesh agreed that the ego represented an integrating force and that religious experience was related to the undifferentiated security of infantile—and prenatal—life. But for him, as for the mystics he had read, the formation of ego was a necessary stage rather than a goal, as much a barrier as an achievement. The developing ego enabled the growing child to differentiate himself from his impulses and his caretakers and the world around him. It allowed him to function with others as an adolescent, to become an adult in the world. But it also created a separation—an illusion of separateness—between him and the natural world, of which he was in fact an inextricable part.

According to Rajneesh and other mystics, people would at a certain point in their development begin to feel the pain and isolation of this separation. Their achievements might seem not only insufficient but unsatisfying, not only limited but limiting. They might feel a yearning to drop the characterological defenses with which they had armored themselves, to burst the structure that, left standing too long, had metamorphosed from a safe place to a prison. Now they wanted to recover the freshness and immediacy of childhood, the "visionary gleam" that Wordsworth described, to reestablish the connection with nature and their own naturalness. Many of those who entered psychotherapy or turned to religion were people who had reached this point.

In Rajneesh's view, conventional psychotherapy without the aid of meditation simply strengthened the ego, allowed it to become more flexible, more adaptive, more "cunning." The disease was not, he said many times, of the ego or the mind (he sometimes used the terms imprecisely, interchangeably). Ego and mind were themselves the disease.

Conventional religion, particularly in its fundamentalist forms, recognized the need for a deeper transformation, said Rajneesh, but wound up substituting an even more impenetrable suit of armor for the first. The ego of the born-again Christian or the Hindu fundamentalist was inflated and case-hardened with divine justification.

True religious experience, by contrast, would peel the ego away, revealing "layers within layers" of poses and defenses, beliefs, ideologies, attachments, hopes, fears—all the accretions of character and social roles that define and determine our lives. As the structure and support of psychological defenses and habitual patterns of behavior were stripped away, the individual might experience great pain—as if, Rajneesh said, one were "peeling . . . skin." With the removal of each layer one might become more vulnerable, more confused. At a certain point one might feel as if he were psychotic. The body itself might seem—as it sometimes does to psychotics or people taking psychedelic drugs—to be disappearing.

This state of total dissolution, of surrender of all that one held dear, would seem like death itself. But, paradoxically, it was the source and ground for regeneration. The annihilation of the old was a necessary precondition for the birth of the new. This shunyata (emptiness), Rajneesh said, was "your essential core." It was the womb in which the new man and new woman could be nourished and from which their reborn souls could emerge.

Rajneesh told his listeners that during this prolonged crisis of death and rebirth, they would begin to see the world with new eyes. They would know that the stability and security on which they had depended had been forced and was ultimately illusory. They would realize for themselves that only change and impermanence—what Buddha twenty-five hundred years ago called annicca—were real and natural. All attempts to halt the continual change that is the nature of life, to solidify it in character structure or to freeze it in interpersonal relations or career goals or religious dogma, would only reinforce and reestablish the ego—which needed to be dissolved—and bring more suffering.

There are some persons who embark on and complete the voyage of ego dissolution and transformation on their own. Rajneesh cited his experience of enlightenment as an example. Most often, a guide seems to be necessary. The guide has experienced the process and is now prepared to aid others in undergoing it. In the East he (usually, though not necessarily, it is a man) is called a Master. The relationship between him and his disciples provides the motive force for transformation, and reassurance and protection during the process.

The concept of a Master is repugnant to most Westerners. The very word, especially when capitalized, implies a dominion over others that is threatening, and ugly, to people who see democracy and self-determination as preeminent values. Christians will agree that Jesus was a Master—he is spoken of in this way in the Gospels—but he was unique, "the only begotten son of God." Anyone who now claims a similar authority is angrily accused of heresy, pitied as insane, or scorned as a con man.

In the East the Master is a familiar and attractive figure. In the Tibetan Buddhist tradition Masters like the Dalai Lama are said to be reincarnated periodically to perpetuate an ancient lineage. In Vaishnavite Hinduism the Master appears in response to the urgent need of a particular time or place: "When goodness grows weak," Krishna, the divine charioteer of the *Bhagavad-Gita*, tells the warrior Arjuna, "when evil increases, I make myself a body."

The Master is first master of himself. Only then and only with their consent, indeed their devotion, may he become the Master of others. He has accomplished that to which the seeker aspires: he has realized the divinity in himself. In becoming a disciple, one agrees to allow the Master to guide him toward the same goal, to help him strip away the ignorance and habits that prevent him from realizing it. In bowing down to the physical form of the Master, the disciple is acknowledging his achievement. At the same time, however, he is also acknowledging his own potential for realizing the divinity in himself, a divinity that is, after all, not different from the divinity in all of existence.

The Master is useful to the disciple in many ways. Because he has the same human form, one can identify with him. His realizations, even if remote and awe-inspiring, seem at least potentially attainable. And because he too is human, a relationship seems possible. He is the "Thou" to whom many "I's" can surrender. Loving him in different ways—as friend, parent, lover, teacher, or child—one experiences many forms of one's own capacity to love, many aspects of what is lovable in existence. Even a religion like Christianity, which claims only one long-dead Master, recognizes the value of this kind of relationship for promoting feelings of devotion as well as sectarian loyalty. Visual renderings of and prayers to Jesus as infant, rabbi, stern judge, and loving friend abound.

Often the Master is compared to a second mother. His eyes seem to the would-be disciple, as Rajneesh's did to Laxmi, to be as soft, accepting, and inviting as those of a mother gazing at her infant. He cares for his disciples' spiritual development as their mothers had insured their physical welfare. The disciple often describes his relationship with the Master in terms that have the primitive, childlike, and sensuous quality of a child's perception of a maternal figure. Buddha was said to have had a certain fragrance. Krishna dancing with his flute and his gopis—his cow-tending female devotees—was pleasing to the ear and eye. Jesus' followers commemorate him by eating and drinking his body and blood.

The Master has another physical quality, a powerful vibration or aura, a surplus of the enlivening electromagnetic energy that the Chinese call Chi, the Indians, Shakti. According to some traditional stories, Chinese Masters seem to accumulate this energy slowly through exercises like Tai Chi and Chi Kung. Indians tend to acquire it more suddenly in the course of experiences that resemble Rajneesh's "enlightenment." This energy, which the Master seems to radiate like an electromagnetic field, can be transmitted to others by a touch, a glance, or even the Master's silent presence or thoughts. Depending on the state of both Master and recipient, it may be experienced as comforting, cathartic, or disturbing. This transmission may have helped catalyze the uncontrollable laughter reported by both Shyam and Laxmi. Presumably, it was this energy which Jesus' disciples recognized in him, which enabled him to effect such remarkable healings.

In his work with his disciples the Master is eclectic and practical, sometimes ruthless and contradictory. He is not concerned with conforming to conventional ideas of piety, holiness, or saintliness, or conventional standards of ethics or behavior. "Truth," Buddha noted, "is what works," in this case, what furthers the disciples' development.

The Master's behavior is often startling, puzzling, and contradictory. There are stories of Indian Masters who lived in excrement. Ramakrishna, the nineteenth-century Hindu saint, dressed in women's clothes and fell into trancelike samadhi states in public places. Gurdjieff organized drunken feasts and orgies as well as meditations and sacred dances. Some Masters have trafficked in dramatic displays of power, miracles, or magic, depending on one's point of view. They have been reported to read minds and fly, to predict the future, heal the hopelessly ill, appear in two places at one time, and raise the dead. Virtually every day Sai Baba, who is reputed to have 5 million followers, "materializes" objects—ash, candy, Swiss watches—as he walks among his devotees.

Frequently the Master will be in conflict with his society and its norms. Society depends on structures, limits, and laws that have been established over centuries; the Master listens to his inner promptings and responds to the immediate situation. He will inevitably violate the boundaries of class and caste, even when he doesn't transgress the ordinary laws of Newtonian physics. The agnostic Buddha outraged Hindus whose baroque rituals, proliferating gods, and rigid caste structure had encumbered their religious impulse. Jesus infuriated spiritual and temporal authority, the rabbis and Romans. Lao-tzu, the paradoxical poet, boggled the minds of orderly Confucians. And the Ba'al Shem Tov, the Hasidic Master, danced in the court of dismayed rabbis.

The Master also serves as both a mirror and a screen for his disciples. His still presence reflects their fears and doubts, pleasures and fantasies, even as his untroubled surface invites the projection of remembered or anticipated affections and torment. In the disciples' eyes, the Master may become as all-powerful, all-knowing, all-loving, as the recollected or fantasized father or mother of infancy. He may at times be transformed through their guilt and shame into a threatening, judgmental figure.

It is clear that in some ways the Master resembles the Western psychoanalyst, and in this regard the appeal to Westerners of a Master such as Rajneesh—who explicitly discussed his disciples' psychological problems with them and combined modern psychotherapeutic techniques and meditative practice—would prove to be especially great. Like the psychoanalyst, the Master is an object of transference; he is committed to his disciples' development and responsive to the nuances of their behavior; yet he is detached from the outcome and from the disciple's progress.

There are differences as well. The Master has moved beyond the doubts and fears with which the analyst may still be struggling, the social and professional conventions within which the analyst—or any other therapist—must work. He is the detached witness of his thoughts and actions and emotions. Though he may live in the world, he is (as the Sufis say) no longer of it. He has finished his accounts with existence. All his energies and ingenuity are devoted to bringing his disciples to the state in which he lives.

Though the Master is more detached than the analyst, he is often far more involved with his disciples, who may remain with him not for a year or two or five but for a decade or even a lifetime. They may live with the Master and seek and take instruction from him in the most intimate details of daily life—cooking and business practices, child rearing and sexuality—as well as meditation and self-observation. They may, as many of Rajneesh's sannyasins would, devote their lives to projects of the Master's devising, living out and propagating his teachings.

Each step in this process increases the disciples' dependence and transference and makes them more bonded with, more vulnerable to, the Master. Correspondingly, each increment of his disciples' devotion and commitment makes it more difficult for the Master to remain aloof from the outcome of their actions.

To remain a Master rather than become a dictator, a catalyst rather than a controlling force, one must value the disciple's development and freedom more highly than the advancement of one's own person or the cause to which both Master and disciple have committed themselves. If the Master is seduced by his power over his disciples or by their devotion to him or their efforts on his behalf, he will become a dictator and a deceiver. Disciples, intoxicated with transferential fantasies and borrowed self-importance, will become dupes.

In the end, the goal of the Master is to help his disciples find the same kind of freedom as he has and, with it, liberation from him. Buddha liked to compare the Master to a boat. Once the disciple has crossed the river, the boat becomes superfluous.

2

"BE LIGHT . . . WEAR ORANGE . . . COME TO POONA"

In 1971 Rajneesh began to call himself Bhagwan, an honorific that literally means "the Blessed One" but is used in India to describe an incarnation of God. The name alienated many of the sophisticated Indians who had struggled to surrender to Rajneesh as a Master. To some it seemed as slavish and blind to accept Rajneesh as an incarnation of God as it had been to worship in the traditions he had helped them to reject.

Rajneesh enjoyed their consternation. "When I call myself God," he told them, "I mean to provoke you, to challenge you . . . so that you start recognizing that you are also divine."

Others, including V. N. Shah, put aside their objections to discipleship and to the name Bhagwan: "I didn't like it really or understand it," Shah recalled in conversation with me, "but I knew by then that he knew something I didn't. If I had to become a disciple to realize what he had realized, then so be it. If he called himself Bhagwan, that was perfectly all right, too. Perhaps it would assist me." Shah was initiated as Swami Anand Bodhisattva, nicknamed Asanga.

Westerners were coming to Bombay now as well as Indians. Hippies heard about the "sex guru" who didn't condemn drugs. Serious, self-conscious seekers made their way down from the ashrams and caves of the Himalayas to see the man whom so many traditional gurus and saddhus were attacking. Jet-setters dropped in just to check him out.

Catherine Venizelos, a Greek heiress, became Ma Prem Mukta. Soon after, a wealthy, energetic young Italian woman who had been meditating in Japan and Taiwan ended her around-the-world tour at Rajneesh's feet. Disillusioned by the failure of the European student movement, fascinated by meditation, and drawn, she later told me, by a powerful attraction to Rajneesh's "charisma," she became Ma Anand

Deeksha. A Canadian public relations man who, as he told me years afterward in Poona, had "seen and done everything and made more money than I could possibly use," stopped by on his way to the hippie-thick beaches of Goa and became Swami Krishna Prem. A lovely South African schoolteacher with waist-length blond hair came up from Goa to visit Rajneesh. She had been modeling and, most recently, acting in a movie. As a girl she had looked around South Africa and had wanted "all the bad people to disappear." Now she was looking for good and peaceful people. She and her boyfriend met Rajneesh in Bombay. The boyfriend left; she didn't. She went to a meditation camp on Mount Abu and soon became Ma Prem Veena (the Instrument the Gods Play On).

Some of the Westerners, including Krishna Prem, stayed in India. Rajneesh sent others, like Veena and, briefly, Deeksha, back to spread the word about him. Many of the next generation of sannyasins first heard about Rajneesh from Veena and from Shyam, who helped her start the first Western Rajneesh Meditation Center, in London. Christine Woolf, who would become Rajneesh's principal lover and caretaker Ma Yoga Vivek, came to India from England. So did Michael Barnett—soon to be named Somendra—a psychologist who had written a book, *People, Not Psychiatry*, and had started a therapeutic community in London.

Like Barnett, many of the people who went to the first meditations and heard the noisy lecture tapes that Veena and Shyam brought back from Bombay were already involved in the human potential movement. Therapies such as Gestalt and encounter groups had helped them to express rather than repress needs and feelings; the theory and practice of Wilhelm Reich and his followers had taught them to recognize sexuality and its suppression as forces in shaping their physical bodies and their relationships with others. Still, they felt trapped, unfulfilled.

Tantra as Rajneesh explained it seemed to be the means to help them to experience their feelings and sexuality so fully, so intensely that they would, in exhausting themselves, automatically prepare the ground for the relaxed self-acceptance, the self-actualization, and the ecstatic experience they craved.

Doing Dynamic, listening to the tapes, meeting Veena and Shyam, they felt rather than understood that this supremely confident man Rajneesh, with his soothing, seductive voice and his great knowledge of both Eastern meditation and Western psychology, had the power to take them where they wanted to go.

Hugh Milne, an earnest, energetic young Scots osteopath, was attracted by Rajneesh's open-mindedness and experimentalism, particularly about sex, as well as by Veena's good looks and her clingy, "exotic" orange robes. He believed he was a seeker, but he felt confused. Fifteen years later, in a disillusioned memoir, *Bhagwan: The God That Failed*, he described his state of mind in 1971, his need to "get out of this rut, this money-spinning trap" of professional success and material accumulation, his belief that sex could be the vehicle for him. Rajneesh seemed to know the way, to be the example he needed. "Bhagwan," he rhapsodized years later, "was a mixture of poet, artist, lover, sexual alchemist, sensual libertine, master magician, court jester, and without doubt one of the wisest men who had ever lived."

Another early, and more measured, listener was Paul Lowe, a forty-year-old man who had managed businesses before he and his wife, Patricia, founded the Esalen-like growth center Quaesitor (seeker) in London. Lowe had participated in encounter and Gestalt groups at the Esalen Institute in California with Will Schutz and Fritz Perls and had led groups in England. His center was thriving and he was well known and sought after. But he, like Milne, was still frustrated. "I had reached the ceiling," he told me years later in California, "the limits of my ability, of my understanding. I had a certain awareness, but I realized that I couldn't bring people beyond my own awareness. I knew that there was more, and when I heard this man I knew that he knew and I didn't." A few days later Lowe was on the plane to Bombay.

When Lowe and Milne and Christine Woolf and the other Westerners who followed came close to Rajneesh in his apartment, their minds seemed to stop. The questions they had brought with them melted away.

In those first meetings they were as eager as children, as clumsy and inarticulate with love as teenagers. "I felt," said Lowe, a large, graying man, "in the presence of someone, something inexpressibly vast. In Bombay he lived with us, but in another realm, everywhere and nowhere. . . . It wasn't what he was saying. He was just so different. I just wanted to be in his presence."

"I had the distinct feeling," recalled Milne, "that I had finally met my real father and teacher."

Sometimes Rajneesh made conversation. He asked his visitors where they had been and why they had come. Sometimes he sat with them in a silence he broke only to murmur, "Good, good," or "Mmh," or to chuckle softly. The pilgrims who had come across the world to meet him had a sense of being immediately understood and welcomed; sitting with him, looking into his eyes, they felt themselves silently, subtly penetrated and probed. He seemed to know almost at once all the places where their thoughts and emotions lay hidden. And in his knowing, there was acceptance, reassurance. He touched some of them physically as well, gently palpating the chakras, the energy centers described in yogic texts.

Even in the very first meeting, Rajneesh might suggest that a new arrival read a particular book, or do a meditation, or stay for a while in Bombay, or change his or her way of relating to a lover or relative, or indeed become his disciple. "Are you ready for sannyas?" he would ask, as if taking on a new name and wearing his picture and dressing in orange were perfectly ordinary and expectable. And within a few minutes or a few days many of his visitors would agree. Lowe became Swami Ananda Teertha; Milne was initiated as Swami Shivamurti (soon shortened to Shiva); and a wealthy, wandering American student was Ma Prem Chetna.

After their darshans (literally, "viewings") with him, Rajneesh's visitors often found themselves changed. They wondered if he had "done anything" to their chakras. It felt as if his touch or his presence or something about him was dissolving emotional blocks or evoking psychic powers that had lain dormant. Some felt dreamy and vulnerable, extremely sensitive to sights and smells, uncannily aware of their own and others' thoughts and feelings. Many of them felt Rajneesh's presence emanating from the locket he had given them, enveloping them, protecting them, insuring them against the damage they feared if they took the risks to which he was urging them. "Just hold the locket," he told them as he put the malas over their heads. "Think of me and I will be there."

Each morning, while the Indians on Bombay's Chowpatty Beach laughed at their antics and the sun rose over the water, Deeksha, Teertha, Shiva, Vivek, Mukta, and the other Westerners did Dynamic. During the day they transcribed Rajneesh's lectures and helped Laxmi organize Rajneesh's household. They wandered around the city and marveled at the miracle of being with this man who seemed now like a friend, now like a father, now like someone out of scripture—a Moses or Jesus or Buddha. Sometimes, catalyzed by Rajneesh's presence in ways they could not explain, they found themselves crying for days at a time. They relived unnamable sorrows from earlier in their lives, or perhaps, as some thought, other lifetimes. Often they laughed and played together like children who had just discovered long-lost sisters and brothers. In the evenings they sat with Rajneesh during the discourses he gave to disciples and to an increasing stream of visitors.

Some of Rajneesh's new sannyasins felt drunk with the energy that seemed to flow from their Master to them, the attraction they felt toward him. Their previous existence, ten thousand miles away in a cold climate, seemed unreal, lifeless. They loosened their hold on their careers and ambitions, their families and friends. They drifted in the hot mists of Bombay.

Rajneesh suggested that some disciples leave an old lover or take on a particular new one. He told several women to leave their young children in the West with husbands or grandparents: the children were, their new Master said, obstacles to their spiritual growth. Some did as he said. They cursed the choice and agonized over their loss, but in the end they did not want to leave this man whom they had come to love—to lose, as they saw it, their chance for enlightenment. When Rajneesh assured them that he would, by some esoteric means he did not define, care for their children's spiritual well-being, they were comforted.

Others wanted nothing more than to share their new joy with their families and friends. Two weeks after Paul Lowe arrived, he called his wife, Patricia. "Come immediately," he said over the terrible connection between Bombay and London. "Sell everything."

"I thought," Patricia Lowe told me years later, back in England, "that he was a bit daft. I had these two babies and had this big center in London." But she packed her bags and her babies and came.

To many of the women who came, Rajneesh became father, lover, and guru. To Patricia, who soon became Poonam, and to many others, he was simply a wise, avuncular figure. In the individual meetings that filled his days in Bombay, he counseled them about problems they might ordinarily, in other situations, have taken to a family physician, a minister, or a psychotherapist.

"I talked about my children," Poonam recalled. "India was difficult. Soma, my three-year-old, was volatile, angry, demanding. I wanted to hit her. I went to Bhagwan. He said, 'If you hit her now, you will continue a chain of violence that has been in existence for thousands of years and will continue for another thousand years. Sometime in this long chain there is an opportunity for someone to wake up and stop it.' He made me feel that it wasn't this one child but all children who were involved.

"He told me when I was angry at Soma I should go into another room and hit a cushion and spank it thoroughly and then go back and talk to her, free from the immediate situation, without the anger I felt at my mother who had hit me. He was so sensible about marriage, and children, sex, love, the whole human condition.

He was very beautiful with the children too. He wouldn't tell them what to do but would tell them to think about a problem for twenty-four hours and then come back and sit with him again."

Sometimes in his evening talks Rajneesh spoke of more esoteric matters. He dropped hints about a previous life that he had shared with his present disciples seven hundred years before. In that life, he said, he had "contrived" to be assassinated by a Judas-like follower. It happened when he was one hundred and six years old, on the eighteenth day of a twenty-one-day fast that would have led to his "final enlightenment." He had known then, with a prescience that gurus have often claimed, that he would need one more lifetime to finish his work, after which he could step off the wheel of Karma—cause and effect—and dissolve into the universe. In that lifetime, his foreknowledge had shown him, each of the three days his fast lacked would be stretched to seven years, and at the age of twenty-one he would be enlightened. Then, he told his stunned but flattered listeners, he would reassemble those who had been with him—now also reborn—to help him serve an endangered planet.

In early 1974, Rajneesh dispersed the Westerners who had gathered around him in Bombay. He sent some to do Kirtana—to sing and chant and dance in the streets of Indian cities. Others he dispatched to live and work on farms. One group went to live on property that the family of Rajneesh's godfather, Bapuji, either owned or managed—no one was quite sure which—near Baroda, some 250 miles north of Bombay. Later, thirty or forty others went to a farm in Kailash that Rajneesh's family owned. This was a particularly inhospitable location 400 miles from Bombay in central India's sweltering plains.

According to both Shiva and Teertha, Rajneesh had instructed the leader of the Kailash community to make an inherently difficult situation all but impossible. The farm was infertile, stiflingly hot, and populated with rats and scorpions. Sannyasins were told to keep a meditative silence and were required to work longer and longer hours with progressively less time off. When the farmers' endurance was exhausted by labor, heat, and dysentery, the rules were changed to accommodate them and then, as they regained their strength, changed again. Rajneesh had assured his disciples that he planned to establish a commune at Kailash, but this was almost certainly untrue. The place had virtually nothing to recommend it.

Hearing Teertha's account and, later, reading Shiva's book, I thought of young Raja leading his teenage friends high above the river Shakkar and of the famous device that Gurdjieff had used on the British literary critic A. R. Orage—publisher of Eliot, Pound, and Katherine Mansfield—who was one of his most distinguished students. Gurdjieff told Orage to dig a ditch to drain water from the kitchen garden at his institute in Fontainebleau. Orage worked doggedly for three or four days. Gurdjieff praised him lavishly, then told him to make the edges "quite equal." A day or two more of labor was required and more praise was tendered. And then, immediately afterward, Gurdjieff told Orage to fill in the ditch: "We don't need it anymore."

Like Gurdjieff, Rajneesh seemed to be promoting awareness through total effort and total concentration. And like Gurdjieff, he was teaching flexibility and nonattachment as well. External work, in a ditch or on a farm, was primarily a tool for internal change. One had to act as if it was of paramount importance and accept the fact that it might all be destroyed, reversed, or negated without warning or explanation.

Half the sannyasins, including Shiva, returned to Bombay; but Teertha and others stayed several months longer, until the experiment collapsed. It was, Teertha maintained, a successful if unpleasant enterprise, a good device for demonstrating to sannyasins the extent of their commitment to their Master.

While the farmers labored at Baroda and Kailash, Rajneesh dispatched a small group of sannyasins to open the Shree Rajneesh Ashram in Poona, a cosmopolitan and prosperous city some one hundred miles southeast of Bombay. More and more people—hundreds, not dozens—were coming to "be with Bhagwan." More space was needed. Money from wealthy Western sannyasins was available. With it Laxmi bought and renovated a six-acre estate in Koregaon Park, a posh Poona district. When the sannyasins had cleaned and furnished his new home, Rajneesh gave up his Bombay apartment and moved there.

At the new ashram, Laxmi was in charge, and Krishna Prem handled public relations. Mukta supervised Rajneesh's meetings with visitors and tended his gardens. Chetna helped her. Deeksha worked in Rajneesh's rapidly expanding library and later ran the ashram kitchen. Vivek, who Rajneesh said was the reincarnation of his boyhood girlfriend, Shashi, continued to be his lover, caretaker, and constant companion. Veena was back from London to help edit Rajneesh's books, and Poonam was dispatched to run the meditation center there. After he returned from Kailash, Teertha read questions at the morning discourses and typed Rajneesh's lecture notes; later he would lead the encounter group at the ashram. Shiva was Rajneesh's photographer and would become his bodyguard.

By the time I arrive in Poona in 1979—five years after the first sannyasins—the small community of disciples has become a huge multinational camp of seekers. There are orange-clothed sannyasins around me everywhere—in morning discourses and at meals in the ashram-run Vrindavan Cafeteria (named for Krishna's birthplace) and in the beds on the dormitory porch. They sweep every inch of ashram walks and scrub the bathrooms and tend the plants and labor in the workshops for weaving, printing, carpentry, and clothes design that marble the densely packed ashram. Sannyasins fill the hotels, pensions, and apartments of Poona. There are sannyasins living in tents and huts in fields near the river, and sannyasins eating and drinking in the bars and restaurants of the Blue Diamond, the nearby five-star hotel.

Orange-clad men and women weave on bicycles and motor scooters through the impossible Indian traffic—ancient cars and trucks, with horns more active than engines. They jockey on the Mahatma Gandhi Road with cows and water buffalos and rickshaws drawn by scooters, bicycles, or men. Young and lithe they walk in loose, translucent gowns, without underwear (Rajneesh has said at some time that underwear interferes with the passage of energy). They stop at stalls where Indian men and women with shrewd old faces and teeth red with betel nuts sell Kashmiri shawls and sandalwood elephants, papayas, pakoras and chilies, brass bangles, cotton pants and plastic raincoats. The sannyasin women, with their round hips and swinging breasts, their nipples and pubic hair pushing against the fronts of their dresses, drive the postpubescent, puritannical, sex-starved Indian males mad. Young men on foot and scooters stare and jeer and occasionally pinch or grab them from behind as if breasts and buttocks were so many fruits in the market.

Laxmi is still in charge of everything at the ashram—or, rather, she is the instrument through which Rajneesh directs day-to-day life and long-term planning. She decides where new housing will be built and who can live in it; what job each of the many new ashramites may have; how discourses and darshans and the medical clinic and the book publishing business will be run. But she is above all a surrendered disciple. She acts only for her Master and on his instructions. "Always remember," Rajneesh tells his sannyasins one morning, "Laxmi never does anything on her own. She is a perfect vehicle, that is why she is chosen for the work. . . . Laxmi has no idea of what is right and what is wrong. Whatsoever is said, she does." Laxmi now has two assistants, Ma Prem Arup and Ma Anand Sheela, who work with her in Krishna House, the administration building.

Arup, the daughter of a prominent Dutch banker, sits on Laxmi's right at the large glass table that serves the three women as a common desk. As Maria Gemma Kortenhorst, she founded the first Esalen-like growth center in Holland. She is a large, solid woman, straightforward, capable, reassuring. Officially Laxmi's assistant, she is particularly concerned with the human side of ashram life—assignments to therapy groups, the emotional crises that attend being in them or, indeed, living in Poona. One morning I watch her patiently counsel a half dozen newcomers who are unsure about which groups they should take. When a young woman in the dormitory becomes anxious and agitated, I ask Arup to keep an eye on her, and she arranges to meet with her weekly.

Sheela, a thirty-year-old Indian woman who is the daughter of Rajneesh's godfather, Bapuji, sits on Laxmi's left. She is Laxmi's secretary and almost, it seems, her shadow. Though she sits in plain view in front of a plate glass window, it is possible not to notice Sheela. She seems evasive, furtive, as she bends down to whisper to one or two women who kneel at her feet. Sheela deals with matters related to ashram administration and business, the nuts and bolts of its operation. I understand that she has spent time in New Jersey, majoring in art at Montclair State College, and that she is married to an American sannyasin once called Mark Silverman, now named Chinmaya. Sheela and Chinmaya, who has Hodgkin's disease (a kind of leukemia), started the first U.S. Rajneesh Meditation Center, in New Jersey in 1972.

Arup and Sheela are as instrumental and as receptive to Laxmi as she is to Rajneesh. If they were animals, Laxmi would be a bright, fluttering bird; Arup, a docile, faithful horse; and Sheela, a small, nervous dog.

During the month I spend in Poona, Rajneesh is not personally accessible to me. When I ask Laxmi for a private interview or even a few words in public with him at his evening darshan, I am turned aside. "Bhagwan," she says with solemn and irritating finality, "now speaks only to sannyasins," and for the most part only to those who are arriving or departing or to those whom he is initiating.

Sitting in Laxmi's office in Krishna House, an island of air-conditioned efficiency in the sweltering sea of a southern Indian summer, I plead my professional and personal interests. There is my position with the National Institute of Mental Health;

my friendship with Shyam; the years I have been doing Dynamic and reading Rajneesh's books; the book on new religions that I have now decided to write. It's to no avail. I'm angry and exasperated. Why doesn't he give interviews? Is he scared to talk one on one, to answer ordinary questions? And then, why won't he see *me*? I have impressive credentials and will understand him better than most. I start to laugh then, at myself. Surely my curiosity is frustrated, but my pride is hurt as well. A few days later I ask a second time.

Laxmi sends a note inviting me to meet with her again. "Ah, Jim," she says, wagging her finger, "you have not brought Laxmi chocolates," as if this somehow might have changed her mind. She offers me tea. "Laxmi will," she goes on, shaking her head from side to side, "of course ask him," raising her voice, vocally capitalizing the *H* in "him." Again the answer is no.

A week later, remembering the apocryphal story that in the East the Master must accede on the third, heartfelt, request, I ask again. A written reply, cryptic, distancing, condescending, but not unfriendly, comes back from Rajneesh: "I will be happy to work with you," he writes, "but you must come to know *me* through my sannyasins."

I have, of course, already begun this process. Some thirty thousand people, I have learned, many of whom will take sannyas, are coming each year to see and hear Bhagwan Shree Rajneesh. At any one time five thousand to six thousand are in Poona. In the early years the ashram relied on large donations—two dozen people, by Deeksha's estimate, contributed $50,000 to $75,000 each—and room sales to stay solvent. By 1979 these visitors from the West are paying for services. Each day two thousand to four thousand people are taking meals at Vrindavan; individual and group therapies for almost as many bring in large sums of money. Admission to discourse and sales at the ashram bookstore and boutique generate still more income. The total is well over $100,000 a month, perhaps as much as $200,000.

The ashram is packed with Americans, British, Italians, French, Dutch, Danes, Swedes, and especially Germans. Though English is the official language, the ashram rings with their accents. There are Japanese—most of whom speak little or no English—and New Zealanders, Australians, and Canadians. There are Hindu and Muslim Indians, disciples who are Jain like Rajneesh and Laxmi, Parsees and Christians. There are—as in almost all the new religious groups I have visited—a disproportionately large number of American Jews, including a few rabbis. There are many Catholics too, former priests and nuns and seminarians. There are doctors and dentists, academics, lawyers, businesspeople, minor movie stars, artists, craftspeople, and every imaginable kind of therapist.

They are, in spite of their similar orange dress and their malas and their shared veneration for their Master, very much individuals and individualists. Some are funny and disputatious; others are smart, sympathetic, and easygoing. There are emotional people and intellectual people, shy and passionate ones, sannyasins who adore Rajneesh as a lover and others who appreciate him as a trickster. They agree about only one thing: of all the religious teachers, Rajneesh is uniquely relevant to them. He accepts them as they are, with all their vanities and vices, and does not insist that they become holier or better. He is not solemn and dogmatic like other teachers, but as playful, as flexible, as loving, as intelligent, as they would like to be.

Some of the sannyasins are disdainful or vexed by my desire to understand and write about them and their Master. Why try to explain something that has to be experienced? "Take sannyas and you'll find out!" one man snaps. Most are eager to share their stories with me. They see it as an act that affirms our spiritual kinship. They are furthering my sadhana—my spiritual path, which for now involves research and writing—by telling me of their own. Others are simply happy to talk about themselves, to puzzle over what is happening to them, to participate in the ashram's favorite pastime, gossip.

Not long after arriving, I look up a young American woman whose parents have asked me to see if she is well. I have noticed her before I am introduced to her—a lovely, tall, slim woman with light brown curls and bright blue eyes who moves gracefully in and out of Laxmi's office.

We sit together on the couch in the waiting area. She speaks in the measured and slightly ironic accents of the American upper class, but simply, earnestly, a bit cautiously, as if I were an eager but obdurate and possibly dangerous pupil. Childhood words like "naughty" sprinkle her speech. She wants me to understand. Through me, perhaps her parents will.

As a child in New England, Krishna Gopa tells me, she felt overwhelmed by her parents' intellectual and aesthetic aspirations. She was bright and had artistic talent but believed that unless she became a Matisse—or at least a Mary Cassatt—she would be a failure. She found herself becoming increasingly "naughty," then angry and rebellious. She denied her talent, her intelligence, her femininity, and then her very physical being. Eventually, at twenty, she became seriously depressed, lost forty pounds, and was hospitalized as anorexic.

I have heard some of this from her parents and have been expecting to meet a fearful, rigid, defensive, inhibited girl, protecting herself with organizational cant. Instead I find myself talking to a beautiful, courteous, witty young woman who cheerfully works long hours in the office and flirts easily with the men who walk in and out of Krishna House—a walking advertisement for "Bhagwan's therapeutic paradise in Poona."

Staying in the dorm with me is Therese, who has just arrived in Poona. She is still groggy from the Thorazine she was given in a Canadian mental hospital. A few days before, Gilles, a young engineer who is with her, helped her escape. Eyes averted, speaking haltingly in the English that is her second language, she tells me her story: a childhood of abuse; schooling truncated by necessity; a short, brutal marriage followed by confusion and despair; some tentative visits to the spiritual communities that are springing up in Montreal; psychotherapy; antidepressants and antipsychotic drugs; hospitalization.

Several weeks later, as I am about to leave Poona, she seems if not cheerful at least hopeful. Her eyes are clear and her tongue is no longer thick. "Therapy in the West," she says as if it were a long time ago, "it was no help. It was only 'You are wrong. You are crazy. You need drugs.' Here one is a person, one is able to be."

Unlike Krishna Gopa and Therese, the vast majority of the people I meet in Poona seem to have been in good psychological shape before they came. Some are quite young; they have been backpacking across Asia to Kathmandu, Bangkok, Rishikesh, in search of adventures or enlightenment and have heard about Rajneesh. Most are in their late twenties or thirties or forties; they are, in general, resourceful, sophisticated, adventurous, independent, and educated. I know that one of the brightest people in my medical school class at Harvard and one of my most talented psychiatric supervisors during my residency have become sannyasins.

In some ways, I realize, these sannyasins are not unlike those who do est or meditate with Swami Muktananda or Chogyam Trungpa. But by coming to India and, once there, becoming Rajneesh's disciples—accepting the name he has given them, putting on orange clothes and the mala—they are taking a far larger chance with their lives and making a very different kind of commitment. They have undergone a change as great as the one embraced by college-age Moonies and Krishnas.

Most of the Westerners, like the Indian sannyasins, have come to Rajneesh when things are going well, when they have achieved many of the material and interpersonal goals they set for themselves as adolescents and young adults. They are, I discover, well-to-do if not wealthy and, in many cases, established in a craft or profession or way of life. They have wives and husbands and lovers with whom they get along and, often, children whom they love and care for. But, they tell me, they also feel the need for an experience of meaning, a relaxed self-acceptance, a joyfulness, a coherence in their lives and a deeper connection between themselves and the world around them.

As a psychiatrist I recognize that these are men and women in the throes of the midlife crisis, which has recently become so much a feature of life in the industrialized West, particularly in the lives of people entering psychotherapy. Most of them have the edgy discomfort of the seeker, the itch of the rebellious and unfulfilled, the apprehensive self-absorption of the narcissistic, but not the fixed anxiety of the neurotic or the stubborn inertia of the chronically depressed. They are also, I cannot fail to notice, in many ways like me.

During my weeks in Poona and over the next seven years, I would ask many of the hundreds of people I met what drew them to Rajneesh and why they came at the time they did. At first I was looking for some traumatic event, a dramatic, Pauline turning point. Sannyasins sometimes had dramatic stories to tell, but more often their journeys to Rajneesh seemed inevitable, as if he were a magnet insistently pulling on them. Yet these were not passive people, certainly not helpless victims. They had been attracted at a time in their lives when they had reached the limit in terms of character and work and social role, at a time when growth and change now required dissolution and re-formation. These successful men and women, then, had come to Poona to begin the second half of their life cycle, to undergo transformation from youths who gird themselves to act on the world to elders who live in effortless harmony with it.

There was also, and equally importantly a fit between their need for change and the qualities and teachings of the man who seemed to promise it. Jung had described this fit, this relationship, as "synchronistic": the events—the potential disciple's needs, the particular teacher's availability—were connected not by causality but by mutual participation in a given moment in time. The East put the matter simply: when the disciple is ready, the guru arrives.

Though these were valid ways of describing the fit between Master and disciple, they were not exhaustive. Each person had different experiences, needs, and aspirations. Each responded to different aspects of the protean and prolific Rajneesh. Each one found a particular aspect of his words or meditations or persona to be uniquely appealing, reassuring, or illuminating. And always in this response there was a mixture of clear perception, idealization, and unacknowledged projection; of fervent desire and wariness; of hope and fear.

Like Laxmi and Sheela, a number of Westerners were first attracted by Rajneesh's face, most particularly, his eyes. Even in the pictures on the covers of his books they were extraordinary. They were not serene and empty as are the eyes of the statues of Buddha or sad as in the depictions of Christ. They were not fiery like Gurdjieff's or merry like Meher Baba's. Occasionally they were absurd and comic, as protuberant as Ping-Pong balls. But most often, they were deep and liquid, like the darkest, sweetest honey, and inviting. "Come to me," they seemed to say, "with all your fears and neuroses and all your secrets. You can tell me anything. Nothing will shock me or surprise me, I have seen it all." And, more subtly still, almost subliminally, those eyes carried a reminder and a warning. "I will also not be touched or disturbed by anything you say or do or by anything that happens to you. There may be compassion in me, but there is no pity. You may see honey, but if you interfere with me or challenge me, you will feel steel."

Others were drawn to Rajneesh by what they heard or read about his attitude toward sex and the communal indulgence that he encouraged. There were at least three arrows in Rajneesh's sexual quiver. Some people had heard about what Shiva called "the feast of fucking" that was under way in Poona and rushed off to indulge in it. Others hoped that under Rajneesh's guidance they could free themselves once and for all from the inhibitions and frustrations that, in spite of their participation in the sexual revolution, still plagued them. Perhaps he could help them overcome the fears of intimacy that seemed inevitably to spoil even the freest of sexual relationships. Still others had already tasted what Rajneesh seemed to know so well: the experience of self-transcendence in sexuality, the disappearance of physical boundaries, the stilling of the chattering of the mind, the merging with the other in orgasm. Rajneesh was the Tantric Master who could teach them to make sex their meditation. Most often these motives — the sybaritic, the therapeutic, and the transcendental — were mixed.

A number of people, including many psychiatrists and psychologists, were drawn by the experience of Dynamic Meditation. Like me, they were eager to find new ways of dealing with the persistent self-destructive patterns, the resistance to change, that they found every day in their patients — and in themselves. Their first experience of Dynamic, in a workshop at a humanistic psychology convention or at the home of a friend, was often profound. Dynamic cut through the words they used to describe and defend themselves, the daily stratagems for getting smart and getting ahead. It cut through to the bone of feelings and revealed capacities for activity and observation as well as sadness, joy, and anger that they had never realized.

Andy Ferber, my former psychiatric supervisor, told me that during Dynamic he had discovered "a reservoir of energy in myself that made me wonder if I had been depressed every day of my life." Robert Birnbaum, a psychologist, in an article in the *Journal of Humanistic Psychology*, recalled coming unexpectedly into a room where people were in the last stage of Dynamic. He felt "a profound shock. . . . I dropped to sitting cross-legged, closed my eyes, wept silently and sank effortlessly into peacefulness."

Some disciples were first attracted by the collections of Rajneesh's discourses that began to appear on the shelves of bookstores. Sometimes his interpretation of the tradition in which they had been raised gave it new life. Jews like me, who felt no connection with the perfunctory religious observance or the fervent Zionism of their parents or indeed the ceremonies and strangeness of contemporary orthodoxy, were touched by Rajneesh's commentaries on Hasidic tales and Hasidism. "Hasidism," he explained, "is the core of Judaism, its heart, just as Zen was the core of Buddhism. Hasidism says that if a man starts living a natural life, one day suddenly love of God arises as naturally as love for the woman or love for the man arises . . . as naturally as breathing after birth." Romanticizing, poeticizing, he seemed able to help us to participate in, celebrate, our own tradition.

Others were touched by a single discourse or even a few lines that reinterpreted and reframed experiences that had seemed shameful, damning, inexplicable. Mahadeva, a large, charming, handsome man from the Bronx, who once played college football, had been a heroin addict during the 1960s. He joined a therapeutic community in New York, stayed to become a staff member, and eventually became a social worker. In 1975 Mahadeva read a passage from *The Mustard Seed*, Rajneesh's commentary on the Gnostic Gospel of Thomas. "I remember," he told me, "Bhagwan said that being good because you are afraid of being bad wasn't really good. That only someone who has really sinned can choose to be good. Otherwise you haven't experienced both sides. Your goodness may just be hypocrisy. And all of a sudden these things that I'm so ashamed of made sense. There was a pattern. I had gone all the way in one direction. I was a junkie and I was rebelling, but actually I was looking for an answer. I didn't find it in lying, hustling, and drugs. Now I was changing, moving the other way."

Again and again sannyasins told me that in reading Rajneesh they had the sense that he was telling them what they already knew, confirming the fleeting thoughts, perceptions, or feelings that they had suppressed or been too timid to trust. His writings helped them to experience what had just been an idea, to see clearly what they had only glimpsed: that prayer was an ugly form of barter; that men were afraid of women and the power of their sexuality; that there was a difference between the calm of aloneness and the pain of loneliness; that possessiveness was a cancer eating away at their relationships; that organized religion was little better than organized crime.

Even when Rajneesh's words caused his readers pain, probing their most cherished beliefs and prodding their unexamined prejudices, his understanding was reassuring. He spoke calmly, easily, of their most secret fears, of insecurities they had learned to camouflage with displays of sexual prowess or saintliness, success, expertise, or erudition.

People like Deeksha who had been active in the radical political movements of the sixties and early seventies found themselves agreeing with Rajneesh's critiques of politics. They had been disheartened by the way their emotional limitations—the insecurity, competitiveness, and aggressiveness—had restricted their effectiveness; by the difficulties of changing a system that continually threatened to overwhelm or co-opt them; by the inherent superficiality of politics itself. When Rajneesh compared politicians to criminals or declared that "politics is ambition . . . ego . . . aggression," they could not help agreeing. Even those who still wanted to change society felt the need for an internal change, a sureness, a peacefulness, a detachment that would protect them from the temptations to egotism and hypocrisy that political activity would inevitably bring.

Antiwar and antinuclear activists, community organizers, socialists, and Marxists responded to his message, sometimes grudgingly but gratefully. Even feminists like Anna Forbes, who had studied and taught women's history and had been vice president of her university's chapter of the National Organization of Women, were attracted. Forbes read and felt in Rajneesh's books a truth that transcended and trivialized ideology. She loved the meditations, she told me, and, almost in spite of herself, Rajneesh.

Forbes was recently divorced and living in Mexico teaching English when she first heard of Rajneesh. She "wasn't crazy about wearing orange or a man's picture around my neck," and she was scared and repelled by stories of violence in the Poona therapy groups. But she saw sannyas as a necessary device, a way to move ever more deeply into meditation.

Some people met and were attracted to Rajneesh's sannyasins before they read his words or did Dynamic. These disciples in their funny orange clothes had a certain quality they hadn't found among their friends. "They were," one woman told me, "so open and sweet, sexy yet not aggressive; so full of life with their dancing and singing, so much in love with Bhagwan, that it was infectious."

Others were drawn not so much by Rajneesh's words or meditations or by his physical characteristics or his sannyasins as by some quality that was part of but apart from all of these. Yashen, a young British mathematician, a sweet, chubby, shy man, tried to describe it to me: "I was looking for intellectual answers to my questions, who I was and what my place in the universe was. I felt, 'I'm fine, thank you very much, but if anything can help, great.' I wanted to collect skills. I had been reading Wittgenstein—I think the *Blue and Brown Books*. He was teaching so brilliantly, so logically. But then, I remember, he said something like 'There are some things that we can never know, and more so, some things that can never be known, ideas we can only dream about.' That rang a bell for me. I saw he was right. I remembered that Gödel says very much the same kind of thing mathematically.

"I had thought I would like to be happy like my mother and father, get married and have two point two kids, and do business and marriage and sex. But now it seemed there was an emptiness, and I very much felt that I had questions and wanted solutions. I wanted a little bit of wildness too. Philosophy and mathematics weren't going to get me there. I got the *Tibetan Book of the Dead*. I never read very much of it, it wasn't for me. Then I read Ram Dass and he was clever and I kept on reading. I was meeting sannyasins and I still looked on them as if they were doomed. They were nice and they danced and sang and they had a good time. But they didn't see how important it was that you followed your own way and didn't surrender. Once you did that, you were lost. I certainly didn't want a guru.

"One day I bought one of Bhagwan's books on Zen. I left it lying on the shelf for three or four months and then I picked it up and read a few pages, and I thought, 'This man's alive.' Bhagwan was explaining a Zen haiku. I don't remember the haiku, but he was saying that what's being communicated by the haiku is that we just have to come back to ourselves, we have everything we need.

"This wasn't new. It was a bit of a cliché, but somehow he was saying it in an alive way. I had read many other books. I had been looking for answers in Wittgenstein and Russell and Whitehead, in Dostoyevski and Tolstoy. And I had been moved. But the person writing seemed like a dreamer. It wasn't as if he was living. Something inside me said that what this man Rajneesh wrote was already part of my experience. It opened the door to something that was already there. It was as if the words were dancing on the page, there was a sparkle in them. Reading him was like jumping on a merry-go-round, and I knew that someday I would have to go and see him. 'This man is alive and available,' I said, 'why miss this chance?' "

The potential sannyasin might initially have been attracted by one aspect of Rajneesh—his eyes or his meditations or his discourses. But soon—like a man returning to visit a favorite painting, or a new lover growing more intimate with his beloved's body—he was drawn to other details, other charms. Appreciation of Rajneesh's intelligence or the relevance of his words might pave the way for love of his appearance. Enchantment with his eyes made his words seem sweeter, more dear. And all these might be reinforced by increasing familiarity with texts and meditations, enriched by one's investment in them, and confirmed by the enthusiasm and the presence of others who were drawn to him. The story Robert Raines told me illustrated the fit between Rajneesh's appeal and one man's needs and aspirations, the way an initial attraction could quickly generalize and deepen.

Raines was the only child of middle-class parents. His father was a city tax assessor in Houston, his mother a homemaker. "I grew up Catholic, a straight-A student and a musician, literary and artistic." As a teenager he played the drums in Houston clubs with Mexican and black musicians. The experiences they described forced him to observe the inequities that minorities suffer. He had the sense then, in the mid-fifties, that he wanted to "help bring about significant social change," but his interests in music and art and literature were primary.

At St. Thomas University in Houston he met "liberal and radical priests and nuns," who encouraged him to see Jesus as a political as well as religious revolutionary and the church as a force for social justice. After graduation he went to the University of Delaware, where he received a Ph.D. in English literature. His thesis was on *The Duchess of Suffolk*, a Jacobean play about "the consolidation of Protestant power." He left the Catholic church after he heard a priest preach against the Beatles. "The Berrigans and Teilhard de Chardin notwithstanding, the organization wasn't going to work for me."

Raines married, had two children, and went to California to teach at the University of Santa Clara. He edited textbooks on art and social change, participated in theater workshops and encounter groups, and demonstrated against Nixon's offensive in Cambodia. Like so many others in the late sixties and early seventies, he'd begun to feel the intimate, often strained connection between his personal and professional life and his political convictions. Little by little he began to work out a synthesis that felt right to him. Education, he decided, meant "personal growth, new ways of living." He helped organize the experimental New College of California in Sausalito and started a theater group there. He quarreled with his colleagues and left. He and his wife separated.

In California Raines's experiences proliferated and intensified. He took mescaline. And, like many people before and after him, this restless, rebellious young man had glimpses through the newly cleansed "doors of perception." He saw something "far beyond emotions and intellect, a stillness, a special radiance in everyday life." He read Wilhelm Reich, whose work and courage seemed admirable and congenial. Freud and his loyal students talked about healing character, adjusting personality; Reich the apostate said character itself was pathological. Reich also indicated that there was a possibility for transcendence in sexuality. And Raines, who had experienced this annihilation of thought and loss of self in sex, adopted him as a guide and a teacher.

At the same time Raines began to recognize that he had unresolved problems. Sometimes while leading the theater group, sometimes on mescaline, he felt his "fear of others," his anger, his desire for power, his tendency to protect ideological positions. He perceived that in order to be an effective agent for social change, he had to change. He went to a psychotherapist, but she seemed as inhibited as he was and even less aware of it.

Raines began to cast around for some other kind of help. He wanted to drop the ego that was constraining him in the prison of character, but he didn't know how. Reich was dead, so he looked to the religious teachers who were also concerned with dissolving the armor of character and abolishing the ego. He checked out the spiritual groups that were available in California—Hare Krishnas, Sri Chinmoy, Muktananda, Maharishi Mahesh Yogi. And, like any good intellectual, he read their books and "Alan Watts and Ram Dass and lots of other texts—Zen, Tantra, Vedanta." Their teachings interested him, but except perhaps for Watts, who had died, their words ultimately seemed false: "I kept hearing the same voice of sexual repression." He wanted a teacher who understood the creative power of sexuality as well as the necessity for the abolition of character and the loss of ego; someone who saw the connection between personal goals and political change; someone who was available to help him find what he was looking for.

In 1974 he fell in love with a woman. "In her bedroom was a picture of an Indian man with liquid eyes. I said, 'Who is that, your guru?' She said, 'That's Bhagwan.' " She told him she had been in Poona with Rajneesh for six weeks but left because she was longing for the comforts and pleasures of home. Rajneesh had told her to go back to the West. "All desires," he said, "are innocent." Raines was smitten with the woman, with Rajneesh, and with the echoes of William Blake that he heard in Rajneesh's words to her.

The woman soon went back to India and left Raines her books. He read them all. "This man knew," he said, in a phrase I would hear from one sannyasin after another. "His words were coming from an unconditional source." Raines felt that "there was no ego, no character in this man. I had tasted the same flavor while inspecting a leaf in the forest and listening to a waterfall. Listening to Bhagwan was like listening to nature itself."

Sometime later Raines typed a six-page letter to Rajneesh, asking to become his sannyasin. He had, he wrote, been reading John Blofeld's descriptions of Tibetan Buddhism and had become fascinated by the Bodhisattva vow that Buddhists take. They refrain from the last stages of enlightenment in order to help "all sentient beings" achieve that state. He felt as though this statement was "the essence" of everything he had tried to achieve politically. It felt as if he might already have taken the vow. What did Rajneesh think?

A letter came back from Laxmi. "Be light. Enjoy yourself. Wear orange. Come to Poona as soon as possible." Raines's new name would be Swami Anand Bodhisattva. His friends would call him Bodhi.

Mahadeva, from the Bronx; Bodhi, from California; and several thousand others were mail-order sannyasins. Long before they went to India and saw or heard or met the man, they were wearing Rajneesh's picture and orange clothes. Though they didn't, couldn't, know what it would mean, they had decided that Rajneesh was their Master and they his disciples. It was only a matter of time—and for some, money—before they went to Poona. Many more people waited till they arrived at the ashram before taking sannyas.

For some the actual initiation seemed inevitable, the end of a long journey. Andy Ferber told me that for several years he had felt dissatisfied with his precocious success as a family therapist, in turmoil in his own family life, and, increasingly, concerned about the future of humanity. "Each field I'd gotten into—psychoanalysis, biochemistry, family therapy, naturalistic observation—I went to the point of developing research level competence. I knew the people who supposedly knew where it was really at—Larry Kubie in psychoanalysis, Birdwhistle and Shefflin, Carl Whittaker, Ivan Nagy, Nathan Ackerman in family therapy. There wasn't, alas, anybody I wanted to be like when I grew up.

"I read the *Report of the Club of Rome* and made five hundred copies and gave them to everybody. Here was the information about limits to growth. It looked like we only had twenty years left, but almost nobody got it. I spoke to Harold Lasswell, who was my mentor at the time, and to Gregory Bateson, and they were both stymied. They felt there was only faint hope for the species, though I think," he added, "Bateson became more optimistic later. These were intellectual giants, and it was becoming clear to me that the intellect was not the way, there had to be another way." Ferber took up Dynamic Meditation, read Rajneesh's books, and bargained with his wife over when it would be right to go to Poona. Over a year later the time came.

Sitting in front of Rajneesh, in darshan, he had a sense that his life was coming together, that whatever might happen to him or the world, this was where he should be now. "Here for the first time ever, I felt it was all over. There was a love so vast that everything I'd called love till then was nothing. When Bhagwan put the mala around my neck I felt a great burden lifted off my shoulders. 'Anybody connected with psychology, psychiatry, group therapy, is connected with me,' he said. 'They awaken a thirst that only I can satisfy.'" Rajneesh gave Ferber the name Bodhicitta.'

For others, taking sannyas was more of a struggle. Here is Robert Birnbaum's description from his article: "The day before my darshan appointment I ruminated over whether or not to take sannyas and came to the 'heady conclusion' that I would not. I was experiencing too much ambivalence and I didn't want to give up 'my independence.' My wife also expressed reservations.

"There were about ten of us for darshan. As we entered the marble porch and approached the chair where Bhagwan was sitting with several close disciples about him, he seemed to lean to one side, look through our approaching group, and reach to my wife and me with his eyes. He chuckled several times and, gesturing, said, 'Come here both of you. I have been waiting for you a long time. First you take sannyas, then we talk. I have your new names all ready.'

"My knees weakened," Birnbaum wrote. "I doubted whether my legs would take me the rest of the way to his feet. My wife began laughing out loud. We were being swept up like the underbelly of a wave, crashed down into something new. I felt loved, wedded, honeymooned . . . and a little shanghaied." Robert Birnbaum, a well-to-do hip Berkeley psychologist and father of four, became Swami Prem Amitabh and his wife Ma Prem Anupama.

Many of those who arrived in Poona, were, like me, curious rather than committed. Most, perhaps the majority, who had taken the trouble to travel from the West, eventually took sannyas. Some, like Brian Gibb, a Scot who had been in the British diplomatic service in Brussels, held back for months.

Gibb went to Poona with an intellectual interest, to see and to learn, as he said to me some years later, "from someone who had pulled so many strands together, the political, psychological, literary. . . . Bhagwan seemed very practical," even as Gibb himself was. Gibb had "no desire at all to be anyone's disciple," but in Poona he "kept feeling that something had happened to the people around me." The sannyasins seemed "freer, happier than any collection of people I had seen. I sensed that in order to experience what was going on, to see if it worked, you had to be committed." He became Swami Prem Pramod, the Joy of Love.

Others, like the young woman from New England, Krishna Gopa, were far less cautious. They came to their first darshan with Rajneesh a few days or a week after their arrival. Even in groups of fifty his presence, his wordless attention, seemed to absorb their thoughts, obliterate doubts. Their hesitations seemed absurd and counterproductive, a resistance not to the domination and control they feared but to life itself. "What about you?" Rajneesh said to Gopa, turning toward her. She came forward, bent her head, and received her new name and her mala. Sometimes there would be more dialogue. He might, perhaps sensing ambivalence, tell a wavering visitor to come back in a few days or not to worry about taking sannyas at all.

Rajneesh understood all the reservations that anyone might have about becoming his disciple. But he seemed supremely confident that these reservations — at least in those who had come so far and were now so close — were creatures of fear, not intelligence. He neither condemned nor dismissed them. They were simply the last gasp of an ego that was a protective device and, ultimately, an illusion. "There are those," he said knowingly, "who are skeptical . . . not yet finished with their ego, who still hope the mind is going to deliver some paradise, some happiness, some bliss to them."

During my stay in Poona, initiations are taking place at evening darshan in Chuang-tzu Auditorium, behind Lao-tzu, Rajneesh's house. In the early years almost all of Rajneesh's disciples could attend darshan every evening. Now, with six thousand sannyasins in Poona—and one hundred and fifty places—admission is highly prized. A few particularly favored disciples are there each night. All others come only when they are being initiated, arriving in or departing from Poona, ending a therapy group, or presenting an especially pressing petition.

I attend twice, carefully washed and shampooed with odorless soap—the sniffers who guard this gate are far more strict than those at morning discourse. The first time I am in the company of others who have just arrived in Poona. We are silent but excited as we take our places to the rear of the open amphitheater, behind motionless figures who are seated cross-legged or kneeling on the floor in their best orange gowns. In front of us is the chair that Rajneesh will occupy. When we are quite silent and still, he enters, sits, and inclines his head slightly to Laxmi.

For an hour Rajneesh answers questions that a succession of disciples coming to his feet ask. I strain to hear his English words but catch only emphasized phrases, the tail end of sibilants. Sannyasins closer to the front laugh gently and nod their heads. Then there is a pause and initiations begin. Those who are about to take sannyas go forward and sink to their knees. One weeping woman carries a baby. A proud couple hold the hands of a young son. As the new sannyasin settles in front of Rajneesh, he leans forward to slip the mala over his or her head. He touches him or her—or shines a small flashlight—on the third eye, the seat of insight and of esoteric powers, which is invisible on the forehead between and above the two sighted eyes.

The new sannyasin looks seriously at her Master or laughs or cries or throws her head back in blind ecstasy or raises her arms high, inclining toward Rajneesh like a flower to the sun. Rajneesh takes a pen in his hand and writes a new name. For each there is a little speech.

"This will be your new name," he tells a middle-aged English Protestant chaplain, "Swami Prem Chinmaya. Prem means 'love,' Chinmaya means 'consciousness.' Love and consciousness are the only two things worth having. Love for others and consciousness for oneself, and life is perfect." He goes on for several minutes, telling stories, quoting Buddha, warning that consciousness without love is dry, incomplete, "a failure," that love without consciousness can lead to the self-righteousness of the Christian missionary. "This is the whole man," he continues, "the holy man, and the future will depend on him."

To one side of Rajneesh is Shiva, the bodyguard, with his red ponytail and beard. Next to him is Maneesha, a dark-haired woman, who has a large notebook open on her lap. She edits Rajneesh's evening words and his sannyasins' questions into dozens of volumes of Darshan Diaries, which will later be published. On the other side, a scarf on her head, is bright-eyed Laxmi. Sometimes one can see Sheela, slumping a bit. Vivek is there, sitting a little to the side, shy, almost frightened. Her face, with its lovely long nose, is framed by her hair. She is holding her knees. Up close to Rajneesh in the center of the first row are Teertha and Arup.

When the initiations are over, the musicians tune up, the lights go off, and a half dozen long-haired women in loose gowns take their places in front of their Master.

Two women are kneeling, the others form a semicircle behind them and raise their hands. "Raise your arms," Rajneesh says to us. "Sway with the music." This is the beginning of Rajneesh's energy darshan. The women are his mediums. He reaches out and touches the third eye of the women who are kneeling. He is, I am told, transmitting the Shakti that rises in his body to them, causing their Shakti to rise; and they are amplifying it, transmitting it to the women around them, who in turn are sending it to us.

The music grows louder and louder. A strobe flickers on and off. At first I am resistant, immobile, but soon I sway with the bodies that are pressed against me. My arms ache and shake and move faster with the mass of orange men and women, and I begin involuntarily shouting and shaking, hopping on my ass, seized like some Holy Roller as the music rises and pulses over us and through us. I cry and writhe and shout, watching myself as I do, and finally laugh as if I have been released.

Abruptly the music stops and the lights come back on. Sannyasins around me are laughing, weeping, embracing one another, or sitting stone still. Rajneesh's chair is empty, and we are told softly, insistently, that it is time to go.

About a dozen non-sannyasins arrive in Poona at the same time as I. Most of us stay in the dormitory and hang out together at night, eating curry and chappatis and drinking lukewarm soda from the concessionaire on the porch. Seven will take sannyas in the month before I leave.

Anselm is the one I get to know first. He is in his early thirties, a redheaded artist who has come from New Zealand. He is independent, competent, smart, and handsome, the kind of friend I have made in faraway places before, someone with whom to travel and hang out and gossip. He is able to laugh at the discomforts we share and open enough to express his doubts about his life, his art, and sannyas. But once the mala is around his neck he seems different. There is a change, to use a phrase current in the ashram, "in his energy." Nothing seems to touch or bother him in quite the same way. It is as if the rough edges have been worn away. He moves now as if he were on roller skates. We see less and less of each other.

After I leave I hear that three more of my dormmates have become sannyasins: Therese, who came from the mental hospital; her boyfriend, Gilles, the engineer; and a scrappy young woman from Los Angeles ("I'm here to check it out," she said on many occasions, "not to follow some guy and kiss his feet"). Only one person besides me does not "take the leap," as the sannyasins describe initiation. She is widely known as the "woman in white." Blue-eyed, with fine, shining light brown hair, she is always perfectly turned out, even in the overpowering damp heat, a kind of debutante among the sweaty working-class seekers. She wears white dresses and, in the evenings, a white shawl. She floats through the ashram, smiling or crying or speaking with, it always seems, great and distant compassion. She has told me breathily that she already has another guru, another Master.

Simply by taking sannyas and being in Rajneesh's ashram and doing the daily meditations, the disciples began to experience changes. For some the work was slow and on the whole rather gentle. Here is what Yashen, the mathematician, told me: "Bhagwan's presence was so simple; there in the morning, nothing sophisticated; talk for two hours; there in the evening and people came and sat next to him. Somehow I could feel myself just changing.

"In the beginning I wasn't giving him any credit. 'I'm achieving this,' I said to myself. But it's like a vortex when I come close to him. I saw my whole vision and what I wanted was irrelevant. Not that it's wrong, just that it's irrelevant. I had been trying to switch trains on the subway when actually I needed an airplane. It wasn't the wrong way, but now I saw there were other possibilities for me. I touched a tree that was near Buddha Hall and I felt tingles in my arm and I was just there, no longer anything or anyone in particular, somehow just very alive."

For others the process was like a roller coaster or a whirlpool. Defenses were stripped away mercilessly. People found themselves regressing swiftly and sometimes uncontrollably. It reminded me of what I had seen in people who became acutely psychotic or were on a bad acid trip; what I had read in historical accounts of disciples and their gurus.

In his article Amitabh (Robert Birnbaum) described his experience in the weeks after he took sannyas: "I became more and more agitated. . . . As I went into each meditation a host of pyschological hangups from my past began erupting." Anxieties, which he had thought years of psychotherapy, a fruitful professional life, and a fulfilling marriage had laid to rest, overwhelmed him.

"Especially, I felt paralytic fears of abandonment, loss of identity and self-importance, and low self-esteem." Though he was terrified, Amitabh found he was also able to witness "the drama" of his disintegration. He saw that "there was no support to these notions," that his fears were not only neurotic but ultimately illusory. With the help his new Master gave him, he came to welcome the dissolution of what Rajneesh called his "man-made harmony." In time he came to feel far less restricted by his defenses, less dependent on his role or status, more intuitive and trusting, more loving and spontaneous—and far more effective as a psychotherapist.

Each evening during the first hour of darshan, Rajneesh provided personal guidance to several disciples, responding to the questions they had waited weeks or months to ask. This is not, as anyone who has done psychotherapy knows, easy work. But, according to thousands of pages of transcripts in the Darshan Diaries, he did it extraordinarily well, with wit and freshness. If he seemed to a casual observer too confident, too ready with a response, or too outrageous, he was not experienced this way by those who had posed the questions. Their responses clearly indicated that they felt understood.

Often Rajneesh was contradictory. In fact, he seemed to be tailoring his response to the particular needs of the person in front of him. He would tell one woman to witness her desires for men other than her husband but not to act on them: "Only children are interested in new things. . . . Love is a great adventure. . . . Let love be your meditation. . . . Each challenge is painful because each growth is painful." Some time later, when another woman with the same kinds of desires began to act on them, he advised her to follow her every itch: "Sex is simply innocent. You are not interested in [the man] himself . . . but in the masculine energy that is expressing itself through [him]."

He would tell one man to meditate more and the next that he meditated too much. People who craved structure were told to abandon it and those who fought against it were forced into it: "Do the same meditation," he advised one rebellious, disorganized man, "at the same hour in the same place every day." "Leave Poona and go back to the West," he told a disciple who had just settled in. "Stay here," he said to the one who could not wait to return.

Often Rajneesh urged people to move farther in the direction in which they were headed; and just as often he sensed that what they thought they wanted was not what they needed and advised something else or the opposite. Yet he never seemed to push too hard. When someone was at a breaking point, unable to bear the insights he was offering or the injunctions he was giving, he dropped them. He was not concerned with consistency or the elaboration of doctrine but with giving the appropriate response to the situation at hand. "Do I contradict myself?" he would ask rhetorically, quoting Whitman. "Very well then I contradict myself."

Contradiction, confusion, and continual change—Masters have always used these techniques with their disciples. They create receptivity, an openness to seeing things as they are, as they break habitual patterns. The Tibetan Marpa told his disciple, the black magician Milarepa, to build and then destroy house after house. Gurdjieff used to call meetings and then cancel them, to conceal nuggets of wisdom in acres of bombast. More recently, Western hypnotherapists like Milton Erickson have used confused stories as naturalistic trance inductions, and paradoxical injunctions—for example, "Be spontaneous"—to spring patients from neurotic binds.

If there were underlying principles and an operative technique at work in Rajneesh's counsel they were, in fact, contradiction, confusion, and continual change. "Confusion," he noted, in a lecture on Hasidic stories, "is my method. The moment I see you accumulating something, creating a philosophy or theology, I immediately jump on it and destroy it." And again, in a talk on the Master-disciple relationship: "The moment I see you attuned [to my rational discourse] I will push you into the irrational."

By 1979 it was much harder for Rajneesh's sannyasins to speak directly with him than it had been a few years before. There were thousands of them in Poona clamoring for their Master's attention, advice, and presence. He could only speak with a few each evening, and he could no longer say, even if he wished to, "Think about what we have discussed for twenty-four hours and come back." Old-timers, who formerly could "book a darshan" a few days in advance, now had to wait weeks or months.

Most of the communication to Rajneesh was through the letters that sannyasins would drop off in the box outside the office. He would respond to a few of the questions publicly in morning discourses. "Bhagwan," asked one disciple, "have we met in a past life?" "Chidvilas," Rajneesh answered, "we have not even met in this life. . . . I go on trying to meet you and you go on escaping. . . . If I say yes [we have met in a past life], your ego will be strengthened, you will start thinking yourself special. All I am going to say is 'Meet me now.' "

However, most communication from Rajneesh was in the form of typed replies. It was common knowledge around the ashram that Laxmi, Arup, and Sheela supplied the responses to the laboriously worded, passionately felt questions the sannyasins asked. This lack of personal contact between Rajneesh and his disciples didn't seem to diminish their connection with him. The questions he answered in morning discourse often seemed to be ones every disciple might have asked, the answers appropriate to each person's dilemma. Nor were sannyasins particularly concerned about the authorship of the written replies to their letters. Many simply believed, against all the odds of their numbers and his limited capacity, in spite of the persistent murmurs that it was not so, that he had personally replied to them. Others decided that since Laxmi—or Arup or Sheela—was "Bhagwan's vehicle," her reply was his.

Besides, the intimacy with their Master and his capacity to help them felt much deeper, more pervasive and powerful, than any specific interaction. In asking for and accepting initiation, the sannyasins manifested the kind of hopeful expectation that is the core of any therapeutic relationship. Placebos, pills that have no intrinsic pharmacological activity, can have remarkable pharmacological effects—if the patient believes in their efficacy. This belief derives in part from the authority of the person who prescribes the pill and the awesome qualities of the place—doctor's office or hospital—in which it is prescribed. Sannyasins, similarly, held the expectation that Rajneesh could help them to know and be themselves.

Rajneesh's claim to have achieved enlightenment was the basis for his authority. Tacitly or explicitly—it varied from discourse to discourse—he promised his sannyasins a similar kind of liberation, from the repetitive round of neurotic thought and behavior, from life-denying apprehensions, and from fear of both death and life. He could help them realize the "Buddha nature" which, he explained, lay dormant within each of them. Having primed themselves for transformation, having granted Rajneesh the authority to work on them, and being convinced that whatever he did was for their good, they were prepared to make maximum advantage of whatever opportunity he offered them. His discourses and darshans, his gestures and actions, even the actions and words of those who represented him or were closer to him, were used by his disciples as guides for living, signposts to wholeness.

This hopeful expectation was compounded by the love the sannyasins felt for their Master. In giving to this man who seemed now like a child, now like a parent, a god, or their own best self, they felt enriched, nourished. The more they gave to him and felt for him, the more they felt love in and for themselves. The more love they felt, the more they could give to him and to others. As St. Francis, Jesus, and other spiritual psychologists well knew, giving love is far more enriching than receiving love.

In surrendering to Rajneesh and becoming his disciples, sannyasins were not only evoking expectations and affirming their love but also creating a bond. They lowered the ordinary barriers that each of us erects to protect and differentiate ourselves from others and re-created the kind of symbiotic dependency that the infant has on its mother. There was a tendency to see him as the origin of the love they felt rising in themselves; to cede to this man, who seemed the source of goodness and wisdom, their own faculties of will, and judgment, and understanding. Though the sannyasins were physically capable of dissenting, disagreeing, leaving Poona, or renouncing Rajneesh, such actions came to feel less like separations and more like amputations.

Life in the Poona ashram reinforced the bond with Rajneesh in many ways. He was physically present in morning discourses and evening darshans, and visible in thousands of pictures, which filled every ashram wall. His face was close to the heart of every disciple, easily visible in the locket each sannyasin wore around his neck. A glance at him or the sound of his voice refreshed them. His words were available in hundreds of books, and his voice on thousands of tapes. Many sannyasins used his books as oracles the way some Christians do the Bible or the ancient Chinese did the *I Ching*. The words of the page to which they turned seemed, with the uncanny appropriateness of synchronicity, to match and illumine their situation. He was indeed like a second mother, both a real and comforting presence and an internalized source of nourishment and reassurance. In times of confusion or desperation, even when far from him, they could, like a child left alone, call on him in their imagination, evoke his image, feel his presence.

The surrender of many disciples to the same Master creates a powerful kinship among them. Members of some groups emphasize this connection by calling one another Brother and Sister. When thousands of sannyasins dressed in the same colors and wore the same man's picture around their necks, it created a subtle physical bond, a kind of sympathetic vibration, among them as well as between them and their Master. Their customs and rituals and life-style reinforced it. They called one another Ma and Swami, greeted their Master together in the morning, and gazed at his portrait during the day. They lived crammed together in rooms in or outside the ashram, voluntarily isolated from the world around them, constantly in each other's company and in and out of one another's beds. Everything they did continually reinforced the feeling of being on the same emotional and physical wavelength.

Even to many of the older, more sophisticated disciples, being a sannyasin seemed like joining a family. Not a family like the one they knew as children, a family folding in on its members with rules and expectations and recriminations, but a family out of a storybook, a kind of multinational, psychospiritual Swiss Family Robinson. Here they were living in a fertile oasis of seekers, under the benign guidance of a Master, free to, encouraged to, explore and develop every aspect of themselves. Though they might not speak publicly about it, many of them believed that they—Bhagwan's people—would be the model for the new Aquarian age of peace and harmony and enlightenment, the seed for its growth.

"Love is my message," Rajneesh told them, and many tried their best to live it out, to love him as they felt he loved them, to love themselves, and to love those who also loved him. In this protected community they let themselves trust where they might previously have retreated. They tried to be honest rather than, out of fear or kindness or convention, dissemble. "Even if the guy next to you is an asshole," Gopa told me, "there is a connection. He is here for the same reason you are, because he loves Bhagwan. And that makes a kind of trust."

This chosen family offered reassurance and closeness without the restrictive ties that normally accompany intimacy. For many it seemed a kind of eternal adolescence, the utopia of which they had always dreamed: thousands of men and women meeting each other again and again, loving and fighting, appearing and disappearing, in groups and meditations, at work and at play, like partners in a great dance. And every step in the dance, no matter how difficult or clumsy, was valuable. When one's lover left or an ugly side of one's personality surfaced, it could be regarded as an opportunity to learn about oneself. Recognizing one's frailties or dependencies could be a prelude to becoming free of them.

Many believed that even the diseases that plagued them in India—amebiasis, bacillary dysentery, hepatitis, herpes, gonorrhea—were, if not devices that Rajneesh engineered for their benefit, at least occasions for self-knowledge. Physical symptoms offered opportunities for increasing awareness; fevers produced visual hallucinations, mystical experiences. With Rajneesh's help they could learn from death itself, transmuting their fear to appreciation of its naturalness, its inevitability, even its beauty. When Vipassana, a lovely young Dutch musician who taught the ashram children, was dying of a brain tumor, Rajneesh urged his disciples "to sit with her, to taste her death, to allow her death to happen and then to celebrate it with her." When she died he said it was "time to sing and dance and give her a beautiful send-off."

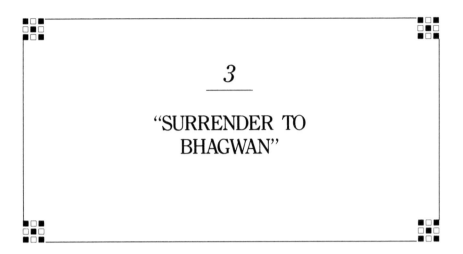

3

"SURRENDER TO BHAGWAN"

Rajneesh's discourses and meditations, his counsel, and above all his presence and his relationship to his disciples were the heart of life in Poona. But the therapies—the individual and particularly the group therapies—distinguished the Shree Rajneesh Ashram from all others. Rajneesh began groups in 1975 as another of his many "experiments" in changing his disciples' consciousness. They wanted to free themselves from fear and envy and insecurity, to find the peace that he and his meditations seemed to promise. Rajneesh wanted to find techniques to free people from their childhood conditioning and the habitual anguish and distractions that kept them from being always in the state of moment-to-moment awareness that is meditation. He had the vision. The many therapists who were becoming his sannyasins had the skills. The fit was a good one.

"My insistence [on groups]," Rajneesh told a questioner, "is very fundamental, these other ashrams in India have no notion of the modern mind. Buddha and his meditations . . . and Patanjali [the preeminent Master of Yoga] and his methods, are of immense value, but they cannot work directly on the modern mind. . . . Before you can do Vipassana or Zazen, you have to go through groups like encounter and primal therapy and Gestalt. They will take the poison out of you, out of your system, then you will be again primitive, innocent, childlike. Then Vipassana will work. Otherwise not." After one year in Poona there were seven groups. By 1977 there were thirty. When I arrived in 1979 there were somewhere between sixty and ninety each month.

The assumptions of these groups and the way they worked were in many ways congruent with, and derived from, the human potential movement. Freud had created a refined, careful methodology for making the unconscious conscious, for helping the ego to tame the id and restrain the superego. The modest goal of his "talking cure" was to turn "neurotic misery into ordinary unhappiness." The human potential movement was far more optimistic and less modest.

Abraham Maslow, a research psychologist at Brandeis University in the 1950s, was disturbed by Freud's perspective. From his point of view, psychoanalysis, which was based on a medical model of disease and cure, was deep, pessimistic, and narrow. Behaviorism, its chief psychological rival, offered a technology useful for eliminating some self-destructive behavior but was superficial. Maslow believed that a "third force," an alternative to and an improvement on the first and second forces (psychoanalysis and behaviorism), was necessary. He called it humanistic psychology.

Humanistic psychology was concerned with the higher aims and aspirations that both psychoanalysis (with the notable exception of Jungian analysis) and behaviorism seemed to ignore. Maslow postulated a "hierarchy of needs," proceeding from the basic ones of security and survival, to sexual, emotional, and intellectual satisfaction. At the top of the hierarchy was the need for what he called self-actualization. Maslow discovered that people who were leaders in their field—artists, scientists, statesmen, intellectuals—had certain common characteristics, among them spontaneity, joy, creativity, and altruism. These manifestations of the self-actualized person, he believed, were the therapeutic goals to which a humanistic psychology must aspire.

The second major figure in humanistic psychology was Carl Rogers. Rogers was a pioneer in the development of both nonmedical psychotherapy and group therapy. Trained in the ministry before he became a psychologist, Rogers, unlike Freud, saw human beings as basically good. "It has been my experience," he noted in *On Becoming a Person*, "that persons have a basically positive direction," a trajectory that unimpeded would lead them to a wholeness that was "both self-preserving and social." From this perspective neurosis was seen to be merely a mask for an underlying and as yet unrealized wholeness. The job of the Rogerian therapist was to provide the client (Rogers did away with the medical term "patient") with the "unconditional positive regard" in which this goodness, this sanity, could express itself. In encounter groups, which he also helped develop, Rogers and the therapists who studied with him tried to foster a community of positive regard.

Humanistic psychology originated in America, but it owed its optimistic, interactive, evolutionary, holistic perspective to the work of non-Americans: Jan Christian Smuts's biological holism; Kurt Goldstein's organismic theory; Wolfgang Kolher's work on "meaningfully structured wholes" in Gestalt psychology; the emphasis on subjectivity and present experience of European existentialists and phenomenologists, including Martin Heidegger, Edmund Husserl, and Jean-Paul Sartre; and, perhaps most important—at least so far as therapeutic practice is concerned—the radical, Freudian revisionism of Wilhelm Reich.

Early in his career Freud postulated the concept of the "actual neurosis," a state of anxiety produced by the damming up of sexual energy, or libido. Later Freud put the actual neurosis in the larger context of emotionally and cognitively induced psychoneuroses. However, Wilhelm Reich, one of his favorite students, made the biological concept of the actual neurosis the cornerstone of his theoretical and therapeutic system.

For Reich, whom Freud eventually disavowed, the goal of therapeutic work was freeing this dammed-up energy, thereby permitting and facilitating "orgastic potency."

For him this flow of energy ("orgone energy") in the body was primary; thoughts and feelings were related if not derivative phenomena. Instead of just sitting and listening to a patient and interpreting, Reich and the analysts who studied with him often stood and watched, gave instructions, touched the patient's nude body, and probed the "muscular armor" in which they believed psychological defenses were encysted. They used deep breathing and physical exercises to awaken the repressed energy.

The men and women who gathered at the Esalen Institute in Big Sur, California, in the 1960s elaborated and combined Maslovian, Rogerian, and Reichian perspectives. Will Schutz increased the emotional intensity in the encounter groups that Rogers had pioneered, encouraging physical as well as verbal confrontation. A host of Reichians and neo-Reichians systematized and expanded on their master's work. Some combined Reichian techniques with group therapy. Others, like Ida Rolf, used them as a basis for new kinds of individual work. Rolf, a former biochemist, created a system of body-oriented therapy—focusing on the tough fascial layers between muscle—which was designed to release emotional as well as physical "blocks." Charlotte Selver and Charles Brooks developed "sensory awareness," a meditationlike technique combining deep relaxation and phenomenological observation.

The quintessential Esalen therapist and, arguably, the most significant of the practitioners of humanistic psychology and the most profound influence on groups in Poona was, however, Frederick (Fritz) Perls. Perls was a European-trained psychiatrist who had been influenced by existentialism and had studied with both Kurt Goldstein and Reich. During his tenure at Esalen he turned Gestalt psychology from an academic approach to perception into a powerful therapeutic system. He expanded the concept of Gestalt formation to include perceptions of one's own feelings, thoughts, and bodily sensations. He created methods—confrontations, dialogues, dream enactments, psychodramas—to enable his patients to recognize, recall, reexperience, and reintegrate parts of themselves that they had, through unconscious repression or conscious suppression, split off from the whole. Once this was accomplished, the Gestalt, the meaningful whole, toward which the organism had been moving, could be formed and left behind. Now change, the natural condition of life, could proceed.

Perls worked primarily with the present contents of his patients' inner and outer worlds. He believed that much of psychoanalysis's retrospective orientation was misdirected, a perpetuation of the neurotic's need to hold onto past thoughts, feelings, and behavior. Toward the end of his life Perls became increasingly interested in the similarities between his approach and Eastern meditation techniques that were designed to increase present awareness. "Lose your mind," he counseled, "and come to your senses."

Perls made two other and related contributions to therapy that would shape, and to some degree skew, practice among his heirs in the West and in Poona. The first was in technique. Though he preferred to work with groups in intensive workshops, Perls's therapeutic process was, unlike that of Rogers and many other group therapies, a series of individual encounters between himself and a succession of patients. The patient sat in "the hot seat," Perls teased, probed, and pushed. Others in the group learned about themselves by watching the patient work with Perls.

Perls's attitude toward the therapeutic process was also novel. In psychotherapy there is a balance among engagement, empathy, and detachment. The psychoanalyst is the model for detached empathy, the Rogerian for engaged empathy. Perls seems to have been an advocate of what I call engaged detachment, in therapy and in life. It was he who formulated the Gestalt Prayer "You do your thing and I'll do mine," which has been cited as a justification for narcissism and mocked as an emblem of the Me Generation. In his last years Perls removed himself to Vancouver, where he started a commune, but for the most part he was, unlike Maslow and Rogers, a laissez-faire individualist, a kind of Adam Smith of psychotherapy. This aspect of his work no doubt encouraged sannyasins who were turning their backs on the world in search of their own psychological and spiritual salvation.

During the 1970s humanistic psychology expanded in many directions. Hypnosis, which Freud had abandoned, was revived and widely taught. Relaxation and meditation techniques and guided visual imagery were explored as adjuncts to psychotherapy. Large group experiences like est, Lifespring, and Actualizations became popular. Body-oriented therapies from the East, such as acupuncture and shiatzu, Tai Chi and Yoga, were included in the curriculum at Esalen and the "growth centers" that opened around the United States and in Europe.

Many of the therapists who came to Rajneesh had trained at Esalen and the growth centers that it had inspired or with the creators of the various humanistic therapies. Some, like Robert Birnbaum (Amitabh), had all of the proper establishment credentials; others like Paul Lowe (Teertha), had no advanced degrees. In Poona they found themselves in the company of hundreds of other innovative therapists. Some of these people, like Mahadeva, had been involved in the tightly structured therapeutic communities that were becoming the treatment of choice for people with refractory character disorders and problems with drug and alcohol abuse, programs such as Synanon, Phoenix House, and Odyssey. Others, like Michael Barnett (Somendra) and Andy Ferber (Bodhicitta), had been leaders in fields like community psychiatry and family therapy. They were experts in understanding how the familial and social context could create and shape the mental lives — including the "mental illnesses" — of those who lived in them. Still others had worked with or been influenced by R. D. Laing and David Cooper, Richard Alpert (Ram Dass), and John Perry. They had explored the transformative power of psychotic episodes and psychedelic drugs.

Many of these therapists had the sense, before they came to Poona, that Rajneesh was at least a master therapist, that his work might represent the next step in the evolution of psychotherapy. He seemed to have an intuitive grasp of traditional psychoanalysis and humanistic psychology, of the familial and social factors that produced disturbed individuals, and of the therapeutic factors — intuition and understanding, recollection, catharsis, awareness and humor, intimacy and community — that might alleviate their suffering. In Poona he was combining these therapeutic approaches with meditation to create the world's largest therapeutic community and growth center.

Some of the therapists, including highly skilled people like Bodhicitta, never practiced their profession in Poona. They participated in therapy groups and paid their money — 600 rupees ($80) for a five- to seven-day group was about average — like everyone else. Others, like Teertha and Amitabh, never took groups themselves but quickly moved into positions as group leaders and received free room and board.

All the therapists, leaders and participants, acknowledged Rajneesh as their Master and accorded him the role of both ultimate therapist and supervisor. He accepted them more lovingly, knew them more deeply, and worked on them faster and more powerfully than any analyst or therapist they had ever met or heard of. He reminded many of them of Perls, but he seemed free of Fritz's hangups—the ego, the apprehensions and pretensions. To others Rajneesh recalled Milton Erickson, the brilliant American psychiatrist and medical hypnotist. Like Erickson, Rajneesh seemed able to work with people speedily, with great but loving detachment; he could induce hypnotic trance in virtually unobservable ways, by the cadence of his speech, the quality of his narrative, the use of his hands and eyes; and, like Erickson, he had an uncanny knack for creating paradoxical situations, binds, from which his listeners felt they could only flee into greater freedom and sanity.

In Poona Rajneesh encouraged therapists to use in groups techniques that had been developed for individuals, to mix dance and bioenergetics, Gestalt and hypnotherapy, encounter and sensory awareness. He created dozens of new and hybrid groups and named them: Enlightenment Intensive, Centering, Samarpan (Surrender), Anatta (No Self), Leela (Play), and Urga (Energy). He pushed therapists beyond any ideas they might have about what could or should be done or avoided. They were to trust their intuition. If they were stymied they were to relax, breathe deeply, touch their mala, or summon up their Master's image. He would be there, with the appropriate response, working through them. They had the technical knowledge, but he was ultimately responsible. It was, they discovered, enormously freeing.

The groups in Poona had many formal characteristics in common with therapy groups in the West. They began by encouraging each member to accept a role as a patient (or client), someone permitted to recognize and experience the emotional suffering against which he had defended himself and to undergo change. They held out the prospect of an understanding that might increase awareness, and of emotional experiences that might help correct past traumas and distortions. They encouraged members to be honest about their feelings about themselves and others. They offered a variety of opportunities to display and explore these feelings, in interactions with the leaders and other participants; to observe the destructive patterns they may have transferred from previous experiences with parents, other authority figures, and friends; to distinguish these old patterns from their present evolving relationships with the group leaders and group members.

In Poona, as in the West, the members of the group were able to offer one another multiple perspectives on behavior and a supportive context within which they could accept themselves and one another with all their frailties. At the same time, the leader encouraged cohesion in the group and individual internalization of the developing group norm.

The assumption in Poona, as in most humanistic psychology groups, was that intelligence and creativity were inherent in humans but had been frustrated and distorted by conditioning. In the freer, more loving, and creative environment of the groups, these qualities would appear, be nurtured, and grow. The more fully people expressed themselves, the more quickly they would shed their deforming defenses. They would then recover their natural sanity and achieve the integration that was their birthright.

There were, however, important differences between the groups at the Shree Rajneesh Ashram and most of those elsewhere. In the West people participated in therapy groups according to their interest and the group's availability. In Poona they were often guided through a particular sequence of groups, chosen from a wider selection than was available anywhere else.

At first one usually took the Enlightenment Intensive or Centering group. These were large — a hundred people was not uncommon — and emphasized awareness of one's thoughts, feelings, and bodily sensations. Interpersonal confrontation was discouraged. From then on, each person had a path that Rajneesh — or Arup — believed, usually after a brief meeting, to be the appropriate one. Generally speaking the "hard cases" — the most angry and repressed people — were quickly assigned to the tough, confrontational groups: Teertha's Encounter, Primal, and Samarpan. Those who were more emotionally vulnerable or simply less defended, like Therese, were given gentler groups at first — Gestalt, Let Go, Art Therapy. In between these extremes were groups that combined some elements of confrontation with meditation, like Tao, Leela, or Tantra. In the last, participants were encouraged to explore — and act out — every conceivable kind of sexual relationship. Ten days of "hypnotherapy" might be assigned to someone who needed an intensive introspective experience and ten days of Vipassana or Zen to someone who had just done several confrontative, cathartic groups.

In Delhi and Bombay, prior to going to Poona, I had heard cautionary tales from American diplomats and Indian doctors. Many people were sent to mental hospitals from the Shree Rajneesh Ashram, they said. Others were put on planes to families and physicians in America and Europe. There were many suicides.

"Many" may have been an exaggeration. Still, I did meet a few people who had been hospitalized in Poona and Bombay, and heard about a dozen others. Later, back in the States, I treated one man who had returned from Poona in a manic state. I heard definitive reports from sannyasins of two suicides and rumors of several others.

Critics of the ashram said that the people who became psychotic and killed themselves were carelessly permitted — or encouraged — to participate in cathartic therapy groups for which they were emotionally unprepared. When they became panicked or despondent, the ashram administration washed its hands of them. The administration maintained that these people were deeply disturbed before they came to Poona. The ashram staff had, by their lights ("We're not their parents you know"), done their best to be of help.

There seemed to be some truth on both sides. These people were all adults. No one had — like the Moonies, who advertise workshops on "world peace" or "homeopathic medicine" and deliver endless lectures on *The Divine Principle* and eighteen-hour days of flower selling — lured them to Poona or promised them anything other than what they found. On the other hand, the ashram administration often tended to be cavalier if not careless. The selection process, even for the most violent and confrontative groups, was sketchy at best. The follow-up, except by accident or if the disciple was wealthy or related to a longtime sannyasin, nonexistent. "Seeker beware," seemed to be the motto.

One of the curiosities of the ashram was the relative absence of Indians in the groups. When I asked about it, I was offered, singly and in combination, several explanations. Indians were capable of surrendering to Rajneesh directly, without the purging that Westerners (and Japanese) required. Or they were unsuitable for groups: having been so repressed for so long they were too likely to become sexually aggressive. Or they just couldn't make good use of such alien techniques.

In Poona the ordinary limitations of therapy groups everywhere else were breached and extended. The extreme geographical separation from one's ordinary life; the long hours of each day; the many days of each group and the succession of groups; the relentless pressure — insults, taunts, physical provocations — that some group leaders used on people who they felt were resisting; the way the leaders would mobilize the entire group to second their efforts; and the group's encouragement to live out, act out, whatever had been repressed: all combined to force group members to drop their habitual defenses and behaviors, to produce situations in which they came face to face, in the group, with whatever had been buried most deeply in their psyche.

In these groups any of the traumas of childhood might be evoked — the infant's loss of maternal security, the four-year-old's lust for his mother, the young girl's rape by an adult male. As feelings arose, the group members were encouraged to express them and act them out. Sometimes a leader would discover that virtually everyone in the group shared common and unexpected problems. "Here were these people," Kaveesha, who led the Tantra group, told me, "who had been through the sexual revolution, through psychotherapy, even through sex therapy, and they still had deep repressions, deep fears of sex. In America the people I worked with in clinics and private practice were clothed. Here I could let them take off their clothes and reexperience all their misconceptions and fears. For example, I did some hypnosis, regressed them all to childhood and asked them to look at each other's genitals. It turned out they were all totally terrified. They experienced all their fears, all their misconceptions, and cleaned them out. Afterward they seemed so joyous and so open. Sex had become beautiful and simple again."

Often it turned out that group members had complementary problems. The girl who had been raped had her counterpart in the man who feared and hated and humiliated women. The leaders of the more confrontative groups, believing that catharsis was curative, orchestrated confrontations that replicated or even intensified the original traumatic situation. A woman might be mocked, seduced, and on occasion actually raped by a man who was just like the one who had seduced her as a child. A terrified man might be told to sleep with the domineering woman who reminded him of his mother. Competitive men put on boxing gloves and slugged it out until, bloody and barely conscious, they could no longer lift their arms. Two women escalated a minor disagreement into a frantic screaming, punching, hair-pulling bloodletting. Afterward, one of them, Mudra, a fifty-year-old psychologist, told me, "I saw that she was like my sister and I said, 'You stop,' and she said, 'You first.' I said, 'Let's count to three,' and we did. And it was such a relief. Such laughter came. Then we played together and hugged one another."

In ordinary psychotherapy these situations are dealt with verbally and symbolically. In behavioral therapy a phobic object or situation may be approached in carefully graded steps — a picture of the feared rat, then a rat in a cage at a distance, and so forth. Even in encounter groups in the West, strict limits are almost always placed on sex and violence. Wrestling may be allowed but not boxing. Sexual contact may be permitted but only with clothes; or if, as it rarely is, intercourse is permitted, any coercion is forbidden. At Poona impulses were acted on, primitive fears deliberately aroused, often with incredible intensity. Anxiety and even panic were precipitated over and over. A claustrophobic man was repeatedly buried under mattresses. In one group snakes were loosed among blindfolded people.

At times it seemed and looked like a Dantean *Inferno*, where the sins of the damned are exaggerated and replayed—Paolo and Francesca, the illicit lovers, bound suffocatingly together in a whirlwind of their passion. But in Dante's Hell there was no surcease. In Poona the reliving of traumas and fears was limited. Almost all with whom I talked found it therapeutic, healing.

The emotional charge was drained from the ancient and unexamined fear. Where there had once been unconscious reaction ("I hate you, but I don't know why"), there was now awareness and observation ("I see I am reacting to you as if you were my brutal father"). For some, anger exploded, leaving compassion for parents and lost lovers. Unendurable fears dissolved into acceptance. In almost every case, sannyasins felt reassured. They had experienced the worst they could imagine and survived.

In Poona every group, even the most confrontational, was combined with meditative techniques. This meant, at a minimum, doing Dynamic for an hour in the morning and Kundalini for an hour in the evening. Sometimes Dynamic dredged up new material to work on in group or helped relieve the anger or anxiety that the previous day had evoked. Kundalini tended to foster relaxation and awareness, even as the group evoked catharsis. Both contributed to a calm detachment that helped group members deal with the stress that was being evoked and assimilate the information that was being recovered, even as they created a new model for dealing with future stressful situations. Relive past traumas, they were told. Reenact neurotic patterns and watch them unfold; the very act of watching will keep you from being overwhelmed or confined by them. Act out and be aware.

In the West groups are a part of the participant's life, a weekly session or a brief retreat, a weekend, or a few days away. In Poona they were a way of life. Participants moved from one group to another, often with only a day or two's rest or a ten-day meditation camp intervening, week after week, month after month. Many people told me that at some point in the process something "changed" in them, and with this change a new kind of peacefulness, in which there was acceptance but not inertia or slavishness, came. "At a certain point," Yashen, the mathematician, noted, "you just give up. It may be the first day of the first group or the tenth day of the tenth group. There's just no point in fighting anymore. It doesn't work. My mind had been geared so that anything new I didn't want. If it hurt, I definitely didn't want it. I always felt like I was hanging on. But when I finally said OK and let go, I found I didn't have to change. Whatever I was hanging onto simply was gone."

Finally, in Poona therapy groups functioned tacitly or explicitly to deepen the participants' connection to Rajneesh. Group members were working on themselves and one another, but they were also being encouraged to work their way toward Rajneesh and into a more intimate relationship with the community of his sannyasins. In this context giving up the defenses that distorted one's interpersonal relations included relinquishing the self-protectiveness that had kept one from a deeper "surrender to Bhagwan."

Every group was regularly punctuated by Rajneesh's presence. Sometimes the group began with a story of how or why Rajneesh created it. Each morning group members attended his discourses. Often there were readings from his books. Stories of advice he had given to others in similar situations were used as teaching devices. Sometimes during a period of group confusion or after a particularly cathartic confrontation — when, in short, they were most vulnerable — group members were told to "look at the picture of Bhagwan, into his eyes." "Surrender more deeply to the group and the group leader," they were reminded when they seemed resistant. The leaders were "manifestations of Bhagwan," "vehicles for his energy."

In every therapeutic group one must deal with the group leader's authority. He or she may quickly come to represent all previous authorities — parents, teachers, bosses — as well as one's own punitive superego. Irrational transferential fears and angers arise; so do the regressive desire to submit to the leader and the complementary impulse to annihilate him or her. In the West these feelings are pointed out and probed. Experiencing them provides an opportunity for examining and then jettisoning what one has preserved, irrationally, unnecessarily, from childhood. Letting go of this feared and overvalued parental authority is a step toward reclaiming one's own authority.

In groups in Poona this opportunity for autonomy was compromised. Elsewhere one came to see that one's attributions of omnipotence or omniscience, malevolence or beneficence, to the group leader are fantasies, transferential phenomena, projections. In Poona group members were told, time and again, that Rajneesh actually *did* know more, see more, feel more, and love more than anyone else. His authority was of an altogether different and indefinable order than one's own. Since he had chosen the group leaders and they were explicitly "vehicles for Bhagwan's energy," their authority also could not be demystified. One might work through one's neurotic dependence on, or rebellion against, previous authorities; but one wound up being more dependent on, more grateful to, present authority. *They* were not omnipotent, omniscient, and inerrant. Bhagwan really is.

This connection was enhanced by the way the groups were structured and the way Rajneesh's presence and authority were invoked in them. Achieving freedom from the constraints and neuroses of one's past was of course a good thing, but it derived its greatest importance as a necessary precondition for surrendering to Rajneesh. Becoming more completely oneself meant becoming more completely a seeker of enlightenment, more completely a sannyasin of Bhagwan. At the end of each group, leaders and members went together to Rajneesh's evening darshan.

Because I have arrived during a ten-day meditation camp, I have free time before my first group begins. I spend much of it with sannyasins who have completed four to eight months of therapy groups and are now simply hanging out. They go to morning discourses, perhaps drop in to sing and dance at an evening music group, and spend the rest of the day in or around the ashram. Some of these people seem sweet and open, nonjudgmental and playful. I don't know what they were like before they came to Poona, but it occurs to me that all that catharsis, all those risks taken and survived in groups, have made a difference.

As I sit with them, eating in the ashram snack bar, or drinking beer in the Blue Diamond, I recall the delights of being in Paris during a college summer. Everything seems new and exciting. Each day offers the opportunity for self-discovery and each meeting a chance to compare notes with others who are learning simultaneously to observe themselves and experience their lives more fully. We talk of our fears and pleasures, our discoveries and longings, as unself-consciously as the oldest of friends.

Others who live on the fringe of ashram life are as monstrously self-absorbed as the sannyasins I first met in the United States. They have latched onto their new identities as liberated sannyasins in a way that, I imagine, is as limiting as their old patterns, and probably far more obnoxious. They use their common discipleship to establish a binding, exclusive, and defensive solidarity with one another, to bludgeon outsiders. Acting out seems to eclipse awareness. They are rude and arrogant in the ashram; they feel one another up on the streets of Poona and leer at Indians who seem embarrassed or offended. They are often insensitive to the fact that economic privilege has allowed them the leisure to travel to India and spend months with their guru, and contemptuous of those who have not seen the light of the man they breathlessly call Bhagwan. Though they do Dynamic and sing and dance and make love with apparent abandon, they remind me less of Zorba the Buddha than of some of the hippies I knew in the dying days of Haight-Ashbury—the kind of people who rummage unasked through your closet and refrigerator while they mumble about peace and love.

Most of the Westerners live on money they have saved in their home country or inherited. Some make money with skills they have brought with them or learned in Poona: a coterie of massage therapists, foot reflexologists, and tarot readers live like gypsies on the periphery of the ashram. Others have set up small concessions for the export of clothing or wall hangings, stone boxes and shawls from Kashmir, ivory bracelets, and teak animals, all the tsatskes of the subcontinent. Shiva takes photographs for Western publications. Bodhi sells peanut butter to sannyasins.

Some women who have run out of money and want to stay in India with Rajneesh support themselves by prostituting with wealthy Indian and Arab businessmen in Bombay. Two of them tell me they are highly prized as sexual partners: "We are," one well-bred English woman explains, "after all, white, and rather rare commodities. Sometimes they pay more if you wear your mala," she adds. When I ask whether Rajneesh and the ashram administration know about the prostitution, I am told that he and they do. When she and several other women asked Laxmi if it was all right to prostitute themselves the answer came back: "Do what you feel to do."

Other sannyasins buy and smuggle drugs, mostly hashish. Later some will be arrested in the Orient and Europe. In France two women, hoping to escape jail, will plead that they have been "brainwashed" into their illegal activity "by Bhagwan and his group therapy." Many people trade currency on the ubiquitous Indian black market. I understand that a number of the sannyasins who have stayed are evading immigration restrictions by marrying British Commonwealth nationals, who are allowed to stay in India indefinitely.

Most of the people I meet are not involved in illegal activity. They come and go regularly from Poona, commuting on vacations from the jobs they still hold in the West—as professors or doctors or therapists or lawyers or craftspeople or business-people. Some have been sent back by Rajneesh to start meditation centers. Others have given up on or suspended careers. When they go back to their own country they pick up work where they can, making money as carpenters or construction workers, as physicians in hospital emergency rooms, as waitresses or waiters or massage therapists.

In the West, they tell me, it is not easy to be a sannyasin. Rajneesh has explained that sannyas will be "one of my greatest devices," a powerful tool for forcing disciples to make a break with the past and all the roles they have played. The orange clothes and the mala reinforce the difference. They make what Gurdjieff called "friction" between the sannyasins and anyone else. Old friends may mock them as mindless dupes; strangers stare and ask questions. A lawyer who pleads cases in an orange three-piece suit and a mala tells me he keeps wondering "what the hell the judge and jury think of me and how it affects the verdict." All sannyasins have to come to terms at every moment with who and what they are and how they appear to others.

"You feel like a freak," Mahadeva later tells me. "All my life I'd been an individual, a rebel. Now I'm wearing an orange uniform with some guy's picture around my neck. I used to go to discos in New York and hang out at Elaine's. People, even some of my old friends, would look at me like I was crazy. I was very uncomfortable, very self-conscious. Then, after a while, I decided, 'Fuck it. I'm a sannyasin, I'll flaunt it.' I got more and more outrageous: 'You think I'm weird, well take a look at this!' Then I saw that either way I was dependent on other people's reactions. Finally, I just accepted it. This is me. This is what I'm wearing."

Sannyasins living in the West tend to gravitate toward one another, informally at first and then in the centers that Rajneesh has instructed them to set up. Whatever the differences among them, here are other people who have committed themselves to the same Master, the same vision, the same way of living and looking at the world. They wear the same clothes and the same man's picture around their neck. If they feel weird or on guard with others, they can at least be comfortable and relaxed with one another. When they return to Poona the sannyasins embrace their Master and his community with all the ardor of beached fish returning to water.

Though they are devoted to Rajneesh, most of the sannyasins I meet in Poona have moments when they wonder what they can possibly be doing with their lives and with him. During my month at the ashram, I spend many hours with Anand Moses. Moses, who is a large man with long, black hair and a full beard, was a senior health planner with a large firm in New York City, but right now he is mostly concerned with planning his own future. We walk around the ashram together or sit with Dar-shan—who always seems patient and sympathetic—at the gate while he debates, Hamlet-like, the virtues of going back to the West or "blending in" with the commune. Every few days he sends a note to Rajneesh to ask for guidance. And every time he receives a response—usually it is cryptic—he pores over it, searching for clues about his future.

Moses lives well in the States. He has an interesting job, a nice apartment in Manhattan, friends. He eats good food, smokes "good dope," and goes "to the nicest places for vacations." Several years ago he did Dynamic and "found the place inside myself, which was most near, most dear to me." He decided "I have to see the man who created this meditation." In Poona he barely gets along and is growing increasingly puzzled by how dependent he is becoming. "For thirty-five years, since I was eight, I've never asked anyone to help me make a decision. And here I am . . ." he gestures to yet another question he is asking his Master. Still, Moses loves Rajneesh and the ashram—"Where else could I laugh so much and love so much and cry so much? Besides," he adds, "wouldn't you feel stupid if Buddha or Jesus or Lao-tzu were here on earth and you could be with him and you chose not to?"

While they stay, while they wait, while they make up their minds about what to do, Moses and the other sannyasins drift through a continually changing round of emotions. They take groups, or hustle for a living, or hang out. They fall in and out of love—with other people, themselves, and Rajneesh.

The ashram staff is set apart from the rest of the sannyasins. They have done the meditations and therapies until Rajneesh has decided they are free enough of their past conditioning, "surrendered" enough to him, to become part of his commune. They have given up their practices, closed their shops, sold their cars and houses in Europe and America. They and their families are "with Bhagwan," in Poona, for the duration. They have highly prized canteen passes for food. They wait in shorter lines for morning discourses and sit at the front of Buddha Hall.

Just as he "works on" new arrivals through meditations and groups, so Rajneesh works on the ashram staff through their work. He teaches them by insisting they accept and embrace the situations—cleaning toilets, chopping vegetables, editing books, teaching the ashram children, or treating sick people—in which he places them. In making work assignments Rajneesh has combined his own observations with Gurdjieffian principles. The doctor whose identity depends on caring for others may be given menial work to do, while the man who is desperate to escape his profession may well be assigned to the clinic. Others who are experienced, capable, and willing, like Anna Forbes, the feminist, who has become Ma Anand Nandan, and Ma Prem Karuna, who was once an educational psychologist named Wendy Wyatt, are quickly moved into positions of authority. After six months of bookkeeping, Nandan is assigned, with Shiva, to direct Rajneesh's and the ashram's guards, the Samurais; Karuna is put in charge of a "Rajneesh University" that is about to open, a place to train people in therapy and meditation.

In any case, the attitude sannyasins are encouraged to adopt insures that something will be learned. All jobs, even and perhaps particularly the most boring, are opportunities to develop one's capacity for witnessing, for meditation. If the department head is a tyrant—Rajneesh calls loud-voiced Deeksha, who supervises 230 workers in the ashram kitchen, his "dragon master"—so be it. The tyranny is to be embraced, because Bhagwan, their Master, has arranged it for their learning. "Anyone," he has said, "who is in a position of authority to you, you have to surrender to. Sometimes you may be more right and the other person wrong, often it will happen that way, but still you have to surrender. Only if you are ready to drop your ego, your judgments, your rationality, your intellect, only if you are ready to allow me to cut off your head will you be able to understand what is happening here."

Pramod, the former diplomat Brian Gibb, was initially assigned to the ashram print shop. There he silk-screened jackets for Rajneesh's books: "It was an incredibly boring, repetitive job. You pour paint on the screen, pull a squeegee over the screen. You do it hundreds, thousands of times a day. In the West, of course, it's done by machine.

"I have a lot of mental energy, and there I am standing there with the paint and the squeegee. The first two weeks were hell. I was thinking, 'Why am I doing this, why don't I have a more important job?' " He thought maybe it was a mistake. "I got kind of concerned with the games my mind played. Then I got into the rhythm of it and I focused. I said to myself, 'I am doing this and only this. Why worry about tomorrow? Why worry whether it's a mistake?' I got into a meditative state. I felt calm and slowed down. It didn't matter what I was doing. It was the way I was doing it that was important." And finally he told himself, " 'That's the reason why I'm doing this job, to see the way my mind works.' "

This kind of adjustment is not permanent. Just when an ashramite begins to pride himself on being receptive and meditative, his job is changed. The boring work one has learned to love, the security that one has embraced, is taken away. Now there is another challenge to another, as yet unexamined, aspect of one's psyche. The man who has learned to enjoy doing mindless work that requires little responsibility, who is finally pleased to slave under Deeksha's direction, must now become her doctor and take responsibility for her health.

There are some people who are more or less exempt from the oscillations and buffeting of ashram life. Rajneesh may "hit" them—point out their blind spots or "reduce their egos" by mocking them—but they are all but impervious to the rest of the sannyasins. The group leaders, demi-Bhagwans, move like gods among mortals. When Teertha, tall, long-haired, gray, and slightly stooped, walks by, conversations stop. The darshan mediums are regarded with the kind of awe that Greeks once reserved for sibyls and oracles. The men and women who live in Lao-tzu House with their Master are said to partake more fully of his "vibrations"; places next to them at darshan or in their beds are coveted.

Indeed, something seems to have happened to some of those who have been with Rajneesh, doing his work for years. Darshan, Krishna Prem, Amitabh, Arup, Karuna, Gopa, and Laxmi all seem, at least in my meetings with them, direct without being judgmental, devoted but not overly dogmatic, loving but not terribly sentimental, optimistic, relaxed, confident, and joyous but not self-congratulatory or offensive. "Enlightenment," Amitabh says to me, "I don't know anything about that jazz, but when Bhagwan speaks, his words reflect a silence, an emptiness, a kind of eternal, endless now." Their ordinary courtesy and playful humor are as welcome amidst the self-indulgence and sometimes obsessive self-examination of the ashram as the evening breeze after a stifling day.

There is, however, something eerie and unnerving about the depth of their surrender. They have, to a large degree, succeeded in dropping the self-protective mind, dissolving the rigid bones of convention and the tense muscles of habit that once inhibited their movement. At times, though, they seem too pliable, too dependent, too devoid of independent critical thought, as they sway with the winds of their Master's words, the changes of ashram life. "I know," says Karuna, who has a Ph.D. in education and directs the ashram therapy training program, "that he knows better than any of us. The longer I am here, the fewer questions I have."

About ten days after I arrive at the ashram I begin my first group, the Enlightenment Intensive. The technique is a simple one, borrowed from the Indian sage Ramana Maharshi. Ramana advised his disciples to sit silently in vichara, or inquiry, asking themselves, "Who am I?" We do the exercise in pairs, sitting on a stone floor facing one another, almost but not quite touching. "Tell me who you are," I say, and then for five minutes my partner speaks. Then a bell rings and my partner asks me, and for five minutes I speak. We have four rounds of this and then we change partners and start again. We do this for fourteen or sixteen hours a day for three days.

Twice each day we do meditations with the rest of the ashram, Dynamic in the morning, Kundalini in the evening. Twice each day we walk in silence for forty minutes. We eat our meals together in silence, take bathroom breaks two or three times a day, and sleep for five or six hours at night on mattresses on the same roof on which we sit and eat.

We speak in English or as close to it as non-English-speaking Japanese, Italians, and Germans can come. Each of us says whatever comes to his or her mind. "I am Gregor," my first partner begins. "I am twenty-three. I am angry. There has been anger all my life. I am German. My father was an SS." He hisses the letters. "I like to fuck little boys." The bell rings and Gregor says, "Tell me who are you," and I begin. "I am Jim. I am an American. I am a Jew. I am a doctor. I am shaking."

While listening, we are supposed to remain silent, impassive. It is difficult not to react while listening to Gregor describe in detail his hate for "Jews and niggers" and indeed everyone, including himself. And it is hard, I find, not to project my own expectations and prejudices on him or my other partners.

Late in the first day one woman looks at me with cold fury. She speaks with contempt, in what I am sure is yet another German accent, of the weakness of men in general and intellectuals in particular. When it is my turn, I speak my own hate and fear of mindless fascism. Two days later, after the group is over, we talk, and I discover she is Italian, not German, that her family were partisans, not collaborators.

Knowing it is a game, that I am really only watching my own mind—my fears and hates and projections—I still feel troubled by the emotions that are coming up. Sometimes—all the while recognizing my transference—I glance up at the group leaders, wanting some kind of relief, some support. Two of them are stone-faced. The third, a large man named Vimalkirti, who is, I later learn, Prince Welf of Hannover, seems kindly.

By the beginning of the second day, demographic and biographic information has given way, first to accusation, then to confession; each revelation deepens the next. Laughter erupts around me, the sound of sobs rises above the susurrus of confidences. "Tell me who you are," says an Australian man, and memories flood me. "My dog is dying." I describe his body in my arms, the smell of his rotting leg. I see him, innocent and devoted, and feel, bone-deep, my failure to save him. I think about all the times when I haven't let myself love enough. I begin to sob like a child. Tears pour onto my shirt. I want to hold my partner. "Change," intones the leader, and my partner begins: "The day my grandfather died. . . ."

The process wears away the edges of our artifice, peels our masks and dodges. The meditations we do—particularly Dynamic—keep raising the stakes, bringing what has been suppressed to the surface. Two or three times a day in the "group bathroom," we are forced to drop another layer of self-protection.

The toilets, without seats or doors, face the sinks and showers. I don't ordinarily care much for privacy, but I do like to be alone when I shit. I sit and stare myopically at silent people, brushing their teeth and inserting Tampax and showering. In the corner near the shower a couple seems to be struggling. After a moment I see that her legs are wrapped around his waist. The bathroom cleaner is mopping, apparently oblivious, three feet away. The door opens and closes; other eyes glance up and drop. When the woman moves away, I notice that she is the tidy, quiet, fiftyish librarian who sleeps not far from me on the dormitory porch.

Toward the end of each evening all the ashram lights go out. We turn from one another to face Lao-tzu House and Chuang-tzu Auditorium, where Rajneesh has finished answering questions and initiating new sannyasins. Now he is beginning the energy darshan. A frantic hum rises from that direction. In the darkness, above the sounds from Chuang-tzu, I can hear the people in the nightly music group in Buddha Hall. The rock and roll and the Indian music are over for now. They are singing simple sweet devotional songs that are like the bedtime prayers of small children. "You can go with the flow," they sing, "Be whoever you are. Just be total": *toe-tell*, it sounds like. And "Bhagwan, I love you, love. I love you love, I love you love," over and over again.

The feeling of devotion, bhakti the Indians call it, is powerful and infectious. I do not know exactly how I feel about Rajneesh, but I silently, happily, join in this sannyasin song just as when I was a child I sang with equal pleasure Jewish psalms and Christian hymns. Why not go with this flow? Why not thank—indeed love—someone who has helped make it possible to feel this sweetness and joy?

On the third day of the group everyone's mind begins to grind down. We are reduced to groaning our boredom, complaining of flies, reciting the aches in our bodies. My Japanese partner repeats himself over and over: "My back hurt," he moans, and then, "Japanese noodles," and then something incomprehensible, and then, "My back hurt," his mouth wide in a grin, and "Japanese noodles."

Then it is my turn. I laugh wildly, my body exploding with unexpressed energy. "Be quiet. Go in," Vimalkirti whispers in my ear. For a moment there is light in my head. No pains, no flies on my nose, no thought, only a feeling of great peace and enormous well-being as I slowly breathe in and out. "This is who I am," I think. The bell rings. "Change."

The affectionate, dependent feelings I have for my group leader, the desire to go with the flow of devotion to Rajneesh, are familiar to me from my time as a patient in psychoanalysis, my work as a psychiatrist. I have genuine respect for Rajneesh's writings and meditations, a growing if puzzled and wary appreciation of and affection for this powerful and insightful man. I can feel that the strange transforming power that seems to be in the air in Poona in some way emanates from him. In my feelings and in those of the sannyasins I have been observing, I can see that there are aspects of transference—the transfer of my own childlike dependency and love, my need for a protective and powerful person, to Rajneesh and his group leaders. I know too that these feelings are heightened by the veneration that thousands are daily showing Rajneesh and by our collective isolation in this ashram far from the familiar landmarks of my life, the moorings of my friends and family and work.

For me these are aspects of my relationship to Rajneesh, of my time in Poona. Poona and the ashram are places I am passing through, not ones I plan to make my home. Rajneesh is a teacher for me and someone whom I am studying, not my guru. I am a non-sannyasin, my dependence is relatively small. My openness to him and his sannyasins is, however, a precondition for learning from the ashram experience, for using each aspect of daily life as an occasion for self-knowledge, a mirror and a magnifying glass.

Over the next weeks I feel myself slowly shedding the cloak of analytic detachment that I realize I have put on long before I ever became a psychiatrist. Why do I need to hold myself back? I'm not here just to write about the experience, I'm also here for me. Besides, that's the only way I'll really know what Rajneesh has to teach.

Images of childhood arise as I walk on the path past Indian children playing in the dust, back to the dormitory—I am a small boy standing at the edge of a baseball field pounding my glove, afraid to ask if I can play. Another time, while listening to an ashram guard berate a sannyasin who has entered where she is forbidden, my mind shifts again. I am in my parents' apartment. My father is arguing with me, telling me he knows what is best for me, that I am "destroying" myself by disagreeing. The air seems to leave the room. I want to shout, to hit him to make him stop, but I can't.

In and out of groups and individual sessions, I see other childhood fears and hopes emerging. I watch too, sometimes with horror and sometimes with amusement, as the quirks of my present character become caricatures—as, on the stage of the Shree Rajneesh Ashram, my inner life becomes living theater.

My experience with women in Poona is painfully, comically illustrative. Never have I been with so many attractive women, and never have I felt so strangely frustrated and puzzled by my relationships with them. Some of this, no doubt, is because I am not a sannyasin. I am of the world and they are of Bhagwan. I have doubts and they do not, or at least seem not to. It is as if we are speaking different languages, or indeed need to breathe a different kind of air.

This is by no means the only problem. In Poona I am exquisitely aware of the mutability of my attractions and disaffections. I'm turned on one minute and off the next. The woman to whom I've been eagerly talking for twenty minutes suddenly leaves me cold. My mind and my genitals are at war. She is beautiful but suddenly, inexplicably, I don't want her. I find myself thinking about the woman at the next table, who has just looked over at me. But if I go with her, I won't be able to be with the one who is sitting with me.

The women who interest me most prefer me as a friend. The ones who seek me out turn me off. I can never quite get it together with the one woman with whom there is a powerful and continuing mutual attraction. When she is ready, there is no place to go. When I am, she is in bed with dysentery. When we both are, I'm in a group and cannot leave. Finally, passion cools and we find ourselves squabbling. Amidst this "feast of fucking" I am hungrier than I've been since early adolescence.

One night I find myself, after one of Rajneesh's darshans, weeping like an abandoned baby. I sit on a rock outside of Lao-tzu House and hope for someone to comfort me. Hundreds of people pass by. No one stops or seems to notice. I feel still more alone, invisible. Time passes and I have to leave. The ashram is about to close for the night. I walk behind couples who have their arms around each other, past the cleaners with their brooms and mops, toward the gate, lost in the feeling of being lost.

Outside the gate, where the ashramites smoke cigarettes, Mona, a lovely woman whom I haven't seen for days, appears. She comes up to me, puts her arms around me, holds me close. I feel her heart beating against my chest, her breasts warming me. She asks me to come back to her hut. I am empty, ready to be filled. Then my mood changes again. It's good to see her, to hug her, but I'm not sure I want to make love to her. Then I want to. As I walk home with her, I'm laughing as hard as I cried a few minutes before. My moods and their changes all seem so ridiculous.

The next day over tea I tell my dormmates about my evening. Anselm nods. "That's the ashram. That's Bhagwan," he says. "First you lose your cool, then you never know what's coming next. You can walk around one corner and start crying, or fall in love or fall down. But after a while," he flicks at the flies that have gathered on the edge of his cup, "you see that life is not about making or being something, it is about flow and change."

"This place," adds Gilles, "is a paradise for one who would know himself."

Now, relaxing, I move more into the flow of ashram life. I come to see how my expectations and my demands limit my experience. When I expect something to happen in a group, an interview, a liaison, it doesn't. When I relax and act simply and without expectations — Wu Wei, effortless effort, the Taoists have called it — the road smooths out in front of me.

I find that good feelings held too long or too tightly grow stale. Unhappiness accepted, disappears. This, I realize, is the way life is. I feel like I have been asleep. Accepting all aspects of my personality, all my thoughts and feelings, learning to be their witness — this of course is the essence of Rajneesh's meditation, of the ashram's teaching.

Aside from his twice daily appearances and occasional visits to his parents (who had taken sannyas and come to live in the ashram) and to seriously ill disciples, Rajneesh remained in his room. What he did there was a matter of intense interest and debate and the subject of considerable gossip in the ashram.

Rajneesh was a vegetarian — not for religious but "aesthetic" reasons — and generally kept to the diabetic diet his doctors had prescribed. At one time, I was told, he drank. In the early days Laxmi wrote to disciples who were coming from the West: "Bring the best French brandy for Bhagwan." There were rumors that in Bombay Rajneesh drank bhang lassi, a sweet concoction of yogurt, almonds, and hashish that is consumed at Indian feasts and religious ceremonies. Now there are rumors that he uses other drugs—Valium and Quaaludes furnished by his doctor, Devaraj, and nitrous oxide (laughing gas) administered by his dentist, Devageet.

With the exception of Laxmi, only those who cared for him saw him regularly: Vivek, Devaraj, Devageet, his cook and cleaners. At night, however, a number of sannyasin women had "private darshans" with the Master. Many years later Rajneesh would claim that he had "had more women than any man in history."

During the time he was still in Bombay, these experiences were widely discussed and compared. Rajneesh loved the gossip and the consternation his sexuality aroused in traditional Indians who believed that holy men, like Catholic priests, should be celibate. He told Satya Bharti, one of his early Western disciples, that she should tell her curious friends he had "shared his energy" with her—even though he hadn't. It would be funny and confuse people even more.

In Poona many sannyasins believed that Rajneesh had "dropped sex" at twenty-one, when he became enlightened; others said he no longer had intercourse, only blow jobs, because of his asthma, his allergies, his diabetes, and his bad back; still others said he had two women every night. The women who had private darshans were told not to speak about them, not because Rajneesh was concerned about gossip, but because it would change the experience for them. Most of them, even those who later became disillusioned with Rajneesh, would not talk about it.

Years later, after he became Hugh Milne again, Shiva said that several women told him Rajneesh was not much of a lover—a lot of voyeurism, a couple minutes on top, and then it was over. One woman I spoke with who had been his lover in Bombay agreed. He liked to look and touch, she said, but she never had an orgasm with him. There were "energy feelings" similar to ones she had experienced in meditation. Another had a very different version. It was, she told me rather vaguely, both like and not like having other lovers. He was with her but also distant and unattached, loving but also not really sexual. His energy seemed to surround her, to fill her—like, I supposed, Zeus coming to Danaë in a shower of golden rain.

Ma Prem Radha (not her real name, which she is reluctant to use), a psychotherapist and a psychic, told me years later of a physical relationship with her Master that was more instrumental than sexual. Before she came to Poona, Radha had taught languages and had been trained as a therapist. In 1974 she went from London, where she was practicing, to Poona. Soon she was leading a group and living in Rajneesh's house. "I could see," she told me, "I was becoming a medium for Bhagwan's energy. I felt I was one of the chosen ones, very special." In the evenings she would go to his room. "It was ice cold. I took off my clothes and knelt before him, facing Vivek—I think he used me to 'charge' Vivek. He would manipulate my genitals, masturbate me, but it was also as if he was rewiring my circuits. He was moving the energy in the lower centers, and I was trying hard to raise it, to transform it. I could feel he was charging me, making me a magnet so I could communicate his energy to large numbers of people at evening energy darshan. I began to feel my own powers, to see past lives. He told us not to talk about our experiences."

At evening darshans she was again kneeling in front of Rajneesh. "When the lights were out, he sometimes touched our genitals, our breasts, stimulating our lower chakras." She was one of those who "pumped out energy" to me and the others in evening darshan. During this time she felt "a tremendous release" in herself. Sometimes

Rajneesh would tell her, and the five or six other mediums, to "lose our boundaries, to melt . . . to go into the pot, become a stew . . . the energies would rise higher." She couldn't tell if her Master was "getting his jollies" out of touching them, but she knew that he was "orchestrating" their energies. At the time, she hoped that the energy would be illuminating, that the power and sexuality she felt would be transformed to love and wisdom. It was only some years later, after she became disillusioned with the organization around her Master, that she began to feel that his intimate attentions may have been a form of control, a means Rajneesh was coldly using to bind her and his other disciples to him.

Rajneesh spent most of the remainder of his time, twelve or more hours a day, reading, mostly in English but also in Hindi. He read continuously—the texts he was using for his lectures and commentaries on them, religion, philosophy, psychology, biology, physics, fiction, poetry, history, linguistics, criticism, biography, geography. His disciples, basking, I suppose, in their Master's reflected glory, told me there were some 150,000 volumes in Rajneesh's library and that he read as many as ten, fifteen, twenty books a day (years later Deeksha, disgruntled, would say the actual number was four to seven and they weren't read in their entirety).

Sometimes one could find hints of what Rajneesh was currently reading in his lectures, a few references to Walt Whitman's *Leaves of Grass* clustered together, or several attempts to draw parallels between the discontinuities and paradoxes of subatomic physics and those that one experienced in meditation. More often his readings ran like a deep vein through his lectures. References popped up in odd places—Wittgenstein's *Tractatus Logico-Philosophicus* in the same talk with Stephen Potter's *Gamesmanship* and Kahlil Gibran's *The Prophet*.

Though he lived quite apart from ashram life, Rajneesh claimed total knowledge of, involvement with, and control over it. "Nothing happens in this ashram without my knowing it," he said in 1977. "I never go to the ashram to see what is happening. Sitting in my room," he added, hinting at extraordinary psychic powers, "I am watching everything that is going on." He was not only all-seeing but all-powerful as well. "This is not a democracy," he reminded a disciple who objected to the rough treatment an Indian sannyasin received at the gate. "Whatsoever is happening here," he announced when a sannyasin questioned the physical violence in the Encounter group "is happening with my knowledge."

Each day Rajneesh would speak at length with Laxmi. She would tell him who was working where; what plans were being made for a new ashram department; what the financial situation was; how the search for a new, larger rural commune was proceeding. He asked questions about her narrative and what he had heard in darshan the night before and whether she had carried out the previous day's instructions. He gave directions and made decisions about everything from individual job changes to the location of the new commune. Laxmi did what he told her.

In the early years in Poona Rajneesh was intimately, directly involved in his disciples' lives. The Darshan Diaries are filled with detailed counsel to individuals about their relationships and their attitudes toward work. There were dialogues with group leaders about the conduct of therapy and with ashram administrators about the rivalries springing up among them. By 1979 there was far less of this. Laxmi was the conduit for his orders, and sannyasins believed that she and the department heads to whom she passed them on had their Master's authority. Rajneesh himself seemed increasingly distant and powerful, more and more like a god, less and less like a man.

The elaborate morning arrivals and departures, the sound and lights of the energy darshans, the allergies that restricted contact with him and the illnesses that threatened to end his life, the injunctions to secrecy—all served to increase Rajneesh's remoteness from his disciples; to embellish and heighten his authority; to encourage ashramites to value him more, treat him more lovingly; and to frustrate any kind of critical feedback from sannyasins to their Master. Moreover, everything that was happening at the Shree Rajneesh Ashram was, he explained, according to a plan for collective evolution that he alone had devised and to which he alone was privy. Sannyasins, he reminded them, might be coming to Poona to relieve their personal problems, but he was "cooking something else."

Little by little increasing numbers of sannyasins renounced any standards that originated outside the ashram gates. In their attempt to divest themselves of the repetitive, self-defeating minds that had frustrated their efforts at change and transcendence, many also dropped critical thought. For example, instead of reading the book on which Rajneesh was commenting, the vast majority simply waited like baby birds for their Master to feed them predigested texts. They knew Bhagwan on the *Isa Upanishad*, the stories of the Hasidim, and Buddha's *Diamond Sutra*, but they did not know the originals. Nor were they interested.

Though Rajneesh continued to urge them to be themselves, to doubt, this message became, amidst the realities of ashram life, ever more faint. Most sannyasins refrained from criticizing ashram rules and policies, the behavior of group leaders, or their work assignments. Everything became a device to increase awareness, to deepen surrender and their connection to their Master.

The results of this collective uncritical trust were sometimes funny. What began as one of Rajneesh's innumerable and contradictory opinions might be enshrined as unquestioned authority by the time it reached a kitchen worker or boutique salesperson. Alternately, when a message was transmitted from Rajneesh to Laxmi to a department head to the individual sannyasin, distortion was inevitable. Accordingly, fads supposedly based on Rajneesh's preference—in clothing and language and attitude and music—would sweep the ashram and then disappear again when it turned out he had been misunderstood or had changed his mind.

Sometimes there was an unpleasant, coercive aspect to this conformity with the Master's direction. Arup told me a story: Several years before, Rajneesh had told her to lead Enlightenment Intensive. She didn't want to, but reluctantly agreed. Three times a month, before each group began, she developed severe headaches. After three months Rajneesh told her, "You can stop leading the group now. Next time, don't say no. Just say yes to it."

Arup wasn't sure exactly why she had the headaches. Perhaps she was bringing them on herself by doing a group she didn't want to do. Perhaps she was so closely identified with Rajneesh that resisting him was a kind of self-betrayal. Or, perhaps the subtle forces that emanated from Rajneesh, that he seemed to exercise for his disciples' good, could also be used like black magic—I had spent enough time in India not to be too skeptical—or voodoo to bring them back into line, to punish them. I told her it sounded sinister, like the means the Devil was reputed to use to enforce a bargain.

"Yes," she said, laughing a bit, "I know about that. I was brought up Catholic and believed in the Devil. But all I can say is, if the Devil can bring so much joy, then I would go with the Devil. Krishna Prem," she went on, referring to the head of ashram public relations, "says that if Bhagwan is a hoax, and it's all a joke, he'll say, 'Fine, it's been beautiful.' "

The more sannyasins assented to Rajneesh's self-proclaimed omniscience and the more deeply they allowed themselves to fall in love with him—to "surrender" to his "orange whirlpool"—the more profoundly he could "work on" them. Such surrender is a powerful traditional way to establish receptivity, a precondition for dissolving old patterns of behavior, a vehicle for transmitting a new, more meditative and joyous approach to life. But it is also, particularly as an organization's needs for expansion and order take on a life of their own, increasingly vulnerable to perversion.

At Poona the concept of surrender could be, and sometimes was, used to coerce doubters and dissenters into obedience; to justify self-indulgent actions that administrators, group leaders, and supervisors chose not to question; to reinforce the unexamined arrogance of the true believer. Since everything that happened happened with Rajneesh's knowledge and at his direction, and since Rajneesh was an Enlightened Master, then everything—unless and until he personally corrected it—was just as it should be.

To me the two most striking examples of unexamined surrender—and the seeds for the further development of an uncritical authoritarian group mind—were the sterilization program and the violence in some of the ashram groups. Both troubled me greatly while I was in Poona and made me uneasy about the man from whom I was learning so much and a movement that seemed in many ways sensible and attractive.

Since the early 1970s Rajneesh, who was always a staunch advocate of birth control, had actively discouraged his disciples from having more children. It wasn't that he had an animus against children. He enjoyed the ones his disciples brought to Poona. Their unfettered expressions of emotion, their injudicious queries, probably reminded him of himself as a child, of the childlike playfulness and provocativeness that were still so much a part of him. On the other hand, he believed that most people were unfit to have children; that there were already far too many of them; and that caring for children would divert his sannyasins from the work on themselves they had come to him to do.

"For twenty years," he announced, much to the horror of orthodox Hindus, "there should be an absolute worldwide moratorium on childbirth. It is the only way to deal with the world's food and population problems." "Eugenics," he later went on in a vein that recalled the "stirpiculture" of Noyes's Oneida Community but could not help raising the specter of Nazism and a master race, "should be instituted. Scientists should choose the healthiest, most intelligent people to donate their germ cells to produce future generations."

At Rajneesh's direction the ashram inaugurated a program of sterilization: tubal ligations and vasectomies were available to all. He reportedly suggested that all the women who were closest to him—Vivek, Sheela, Deeksha, and Ma Yoga Vidya, another ashram administrator—should be sterilized. Some others he advised against it, but generally he was very much in favor of these procedures. Sterilization was not a condition for staying in Poona, and the vast majority of sannyasins did not have the operations. Still, a climate developed in which tubal ligations and, later, vasectomies were seen as signs of "commitment to Bhagwan." Pressure was applied by heads of ashram departments who, not altogether jokingly, spoke of "quotas."

"Arup would call," Deeksha related to me years later, "and say, 'The clinic has room for two women and three men,' and I would call my workers together and say, 'Bhagwan says it is better for the community not to have children. Who feels to go to the clinic?' "

For sannyasins in their thirties and forties—many of whom already had children or knew that they didn't want them—sterilization seemed a reasonable and reasoned alternative. But some women in their early twenties, and a few girls as young as fourteen, felt so strongly about being close to their Master, about conforming their lives to fit his teachings, that all other considerations, including the possibility that they might later change their minds, were obliterated. Hundreds of sannyasins had the operation.

Not everyone succumbed to the pressure. Gopa, for example, agreed to have the operation then had second thoughts. "The whole thing was kind of a fad. I knew that I wanted to do it to show how total, how committed I was to Bhagwan. A woman gynecologist made it clear that it was irreversible and I needed to look long and hard." Gopa was "terrified," but she made an appointment at Ajit Saraswati's clinic. "The evening before the operation I remember thinking, 'Damn it, I don't have to prove anything to anybody. I just want to learn to be me. I don't know if I want babies or if fertility has anything to do with my femaleness.' Then I realized for the first time since about age twelve, that I wanted to be female." The next morning she called to cancel the surgery. It was, she assured me, a decision anyone could have made. Still, many people ignored their second thoughts and went ahead with the irreversible operation. Later some, including Nandan, the feminist, bitterly regretted it.

I had heard about the physical violence that took place in the "therapy chambers" long before the U.S. embassy warned me. While still in America I had visions of the Marabar Caves that Forster described in *Passage to India*, of sweaty bodies beating and buggering one another in a dank, dark, airless space.

Before I left the United States I spoke with Richard Price, a Gestalt therapist who was one of the cofounders of the Esalen Institute. I knew that he had taken sannyas by mail, and I had heard that he had become disillusioned after visiting Poona in 1977. I had met him before and liked and trusted him.

Price told me that on his arrival at the ashram he had taken the ten-day meditation camp and had loved it. He felt alive, alert, happy, "incredibly grateful to Bhagwan," and at home with the sannyasins. Then, at the insistence of ashram administrators who were eager to show him "Bhagwan's version" of the therapy that Esalen had done so much to develop and disseminate, he did the Encounter group.

"There were," he told me, "eighteen fights in the first two days alone, then I stopped counting." He watched one woman break another's arm. Once he tried to stop a young man from physically attacking a sixty-year-old woman and was harangued by Teertha. In the last three days of the group, when the violence had subsided, he said, Teertha spent his time "working on" the three members who were not yet sannyasins, trying to get them to "join Bhagwan's order." Price thought the violence and coercion might just be specific to Teertha's group. Then he met a woman whose leg was broken in the Primal group. Price was disgusted.

After leaving Poona he sent his mala back and wrote a letter to Krishna Prem, whom he regarded as a friend. In it he described Teertha's "autocratic, coercive, life-negating style of leadership, a style re-enforcing violence and sexual acting out of the most unfeeling kind." When *Time* did a story about the ashram ("God Sir at Esalen East"), he wrote to the magazine, praising Rajneesh's lectures and meditations and condemning the Encounter group: "It owes more to the SS than to Esalen." Finally he wrote to Rajneesh, "Is what you say and *what you are*, so shallow, that such means are necessary?"

Neither Price's observations nor his sense of betrayal were unique. In a January 1980 article, "Violence in Therapy," which appeared in the journal *Energy and Character*, David Boadella, a well-known British Reichian therapist and former sannyasin, recounted several episodes of violence in Poona, including one presented by Eva Renzi, a German actress, in the pages of *Stern*, a popular German magazine: "At the end of the first day, the leader demanded that each of us should seek a partner that was not acceptable to us. The pairs that had formed must spend the evening and also the night together." The next day, according to Renzi's account, the man with whom she was paired (a well-known Dutch psychiatrist and author) "sprang up, pulled me up and began uninhibitedly beating me. 'You whore, you humiliated me, you cursed woman, I'll kill you.' " Then a man and two women grabbed her, then the whole group. "What happened next was like an evil dream. They shouted, 'Fight, fight with us you coward, don't you play holy, you whore.' They punched, scratched, kicked me and pulled my hair. They tore my blouse and pants off my body. I was stark naked." Renzi ran from the room.

In January 1979, just two months after the murder-suicides at Jonestown, Rajneesh issued "instructions" to all group leaders to "no longer allow participants to use fighting as a means of discharging repressed emotions or for any other purpose." Violence, according to Krishna Prem's press release, "had fulfilled its function within the overall context of the ashram as an evolving spiritual commune."

So the violence had ended by the time I got to Poona, and neither I nor anyone else was, in Rajneesh's words, "required to go into it." But it still bothered me. It wasn't that I was against fighting in groups. I knew from years of psychiatric work and my own two years' experience in an encounter group that the potential for destructiveness was present in all of us, that some kind of controlled release coupled with awareness could be therapeutic — indeed, had been therapeutic for me. In Poona the vast majority of the people I met had, like me, been terrified before, and during, groups where violence was common. In retrospect, however, most of them, like Mudra, the fifty-year-old psychiatrist, believed that the violent confrontations — even their own bad bruises and broken limbs — had been a small and necessary price to pay for the freedom they now felt from past traumas and inhibitions, for the perspective they had gained on their own sadism and masochism.

I could also see that violence in a few groups might in some way have helped to exorcise the community's latent collective violence. I knew too that spiritual teachers—Marpa with his disciple Milarepa, Gurdjieff, and many Zen Masters—had sometimes used violence as a device to break down disciples' arrogance and resistance to change, to get them to see reality, including themselves, as they were. In this context, incitement to violence or acts of violence were just another aspect of what the Tibetan Buddhists called ati yana, the crazy wisdom of spontaneous and inexplicable but appropriate action.

From Rajneesh's point of view it all worked: "Nothing is out of my hands—whatsoever is going on. I give enough rope. It seems everything is completely free, it is not so . . . just that the rope is long enough. . . . Danger happens only when there is repression, in freedom there is no danger."

His ashram was, he told his disciples, like the fabled Sufi school in Isfahan, "a temple of total ruin." In the past, he explained, there had been small, secret schools where a few seekers experimented with their psychological and physical limits. Now he was creating a huge "open university" to which anyone who was ready to "die and be reborn" could come. The size and availability, the intensity of the groups and meditations, the riskiness and visibility of the experiment, were all necessary. This was not a time for cautious secrecy or unnecessary exclusiveness: "Humanity is at a dangerous crossroads. . . . If man cannot be taught to be free and yet sane then there is no future for humanity. . . . To teach man I have to devise and use all sorts of mad games, so that the accumulated madness could be acted out, catharted out, thrown out." Just as in Dynamic Meditation, so in the ashram, activity was necessary before calm, catharsis before awareness.

Still, I had my doubts about the value of violence in the groups. It was true that even with the hospitalizations and the two suicides, far fewer people were adversely affected than I would have expected with such powerful techniques used on so many thousands of unscreened participants. But I wasn't sure what I attributed this to, or how much of what Rajneesh was saying was a rationalization after the fact or an attempt to give coherence where carelessness had reigned.

In my own experience in America, violence had been controlled and contained, whereas in Poona it had, according to Price and others, often been self-indulgent. There was a kind of smugness, indeed a stupidity, about some of the pronouncements that surrounded it. "Experiences like those of Frau Renzi belong to the normal phenomena of encounter groups all over the world," Teertha wrote. "Nobody freaked out or was killed," he told me, though the former was certainly debatable. "Besides," he added blithely, "all of us were protected by Bhagwan's energy."

Nor were the historical parallels altogether applicable either. These had been intimate relationships between individuals in which the Master was dispassionately deploying extraordinary means designed for a particular disciple. The men—the male leaders seemed to encourage far more violence than the women—who led the groups in Poona were themselves disciples, still dealing with their own problems. "The violence," Teertha admitted several years later, was "as much for group leaders as for the members, so we could see it work itself out." Only then, he implied, when they were more comfortable with more extreme violence, could they choose not to use it.

Committing violence on others so that one might learn: it reminded me of the most callous aspects of a medical education in which we "learned" on our poor, often black, clinic patients, not the strategy of an enlightened spiritual Master. Why hadn't Rajneesh worked with the group leaders to get out their violence, their sadism, before allowing them what he described as "complete freedom with others." What, I asked for the first but not the last time, was his hurry? Did he know what he was doing?

Ultimately, what troubled me far more than the violence itself was the pattern of which it and the sterilizations—and, to a lesser degree, the tacit approval if not encouragement of prostitution and drug dealing and offensive behavior toward local Indians—seemed to be a part. They were said to be demonstrations of the "complete freedom" that Rajneesh felt his disciples needed in order to discover all aspects of themselves, or the "mad games" a Master might play to increase awareness. Perhaps, I thought. But there were also common and unacknowledged characteristics that portended control rather than freedom, craftiness not madness.

Staying "with Bhagwan" in Poona, providing the ashram with money, had become far more important than the means by which one stayed. Following the group leader's directions or the ashram's directives with unquestioning obedience, "blending in" to the commune, were far more highly valued than personal doubts and individual intelligence. There was the same scent of coerciveness and conformity I had deplored in the Moonies and Scientologists, and in the stories I had heard about Jim Jones and the People's Temple. It seemed stupid and shortsighted, as well as arrogant and potentially dangerous. And, perhaps most important to one who was a seeker as well as an observer, it seemed subversive of the freedom and individuality that Rajneesh said he wanted to promote, antithetical to his picture of the Master as "a catalytic agent . . . a sun encouraging a flower to open but in a very delicate way."

Several days before I leave Poona, while I am still sifting through my concerns and reservations, I have a session of rebirthing. I am skeptical about the technique and particularly about the hype that surrounds it, but I am also curious, and particularly anxious to see what the combination of Rajneesh and rebirthing will be like.

Rebirthers follow the theory of the psychoanalyst Otto Rank and the practice of Leonard Orr. They believe that only by reexperiencing the primal trauma of birth— having, I suppose, a corrective experience of it—can one undo the harm, the emotional and physical constriction, the fear and rage, that result from the abrupt transition from intrauterine peace to the cold, noisy, bright lights of the delivery room and the larger world.

The technique is, I discover, remarkably simple. I am instructed to lie naked on a mat (sometimes rebirthing is done in water) and breathe deeply, in and out, through my mouth. In Poona, to my surprise, my rebirther, a beautiful, rather distant Danish blonde, takes off her clothes as well. She sits behind me, naked except for her mala, on a mattress.

After a while my breathing begins to feel hoarse and raspy and my body begins to rock and flail. I know I am hyperventilating. The oxygen is accumulating and the carbon dioxide in my blood is decreasing. As a result my fingers bend toward my wrists, as if I were spastic. I feel strange pains in my head and body. The woman touches me gently from time to time on my chest, to encourage me to breathe more deeply, or on my head, reassuring me. She is gentle but impersonal.

I am aware of some sort of raw force not exactly in her, but coming through her. It feels—I wonder if I am oxygen-intoxicated, imagining it—like Rajneesh. "Breathe more deeply. Open your mouth," she says. Now it is as if she is hardly there, a hollow reed, an instrument that Rajneesh is playing.

My head feels terrible, constricted as if it is being crushed in a vice. I can barely breathe. I panic for a moment, feeling like I am going to suffocate, remembering the fear that haunted the moments before childhood sleep. My God, am I imagining this? Or is this really some bodily memory, a replay of my descent through the birth canal. There is agony in my right shoulder. It is being crushed toward my chest, tearing at my upper back in the place where tension always produces pain. I am terrified. Air is rushing in as if my mouth were a vacuum. I'm shrieking now, an unearthly sound I have never consciously made before, crying, screaming. I am flailing on the mat, squalling like a newborn, feeling my mouth open, hearing the sound and marveling, as if at the first glimpse of an ancient relic.

Suddenly I realize I feel free and yet vulnerable. It must be ninety degrees in Poona, but the air is cool on my sweating body. My skin feels alive, tingling as if ice or wintergreen oil were on it. A few gasps and now the breath comes deeply. Then I—really it is my body—feel the urge to move.

Yoga positions begin to happen to my body. It is clear that I am not initiating them. "Relax, let it happen," I tell myself. Stretches and shoulder stands, the plow and the cat. I am beginning to pick up speed, to move like one of those wooden men who flips over a bar, folding and unfolding. New postures happen, ones I have seen in books but never dared attempt. I unbend from the plow on my back, legs over my head. My toes touch the ground and I rise to a standing position, gracefully, like the dancer and gymnast I never was.

The positions are becoming more and more improbable. My head folds down between my knees. I tumble forward. Now comes the headstand. Never have I even attempted it. Slowly my legs come down in a backward bend, and I arch up into a high bridge, flipping over onto my feet. All the while my mind is working. I am remembering the first part of Dynamic when my effort some-times disappears and my breathing takes over my body; then the story of Swami Muktananda, who while he was a wandering saddhu had a similar experience with yoga postures and howled like a wild beast; then the legend that says yoga postures were originally positions in which sages became enlightened.

I get scared and try to stop it, and pain fills every joint. For the first time I see Rajneesh's picture above my head on the wall. He seems to be laughing, not kindly, drumming his fingers on the arms of his chair. I relax and the movement picks up, like a car accelerating on the bend of a roller coaster. My rebirther leaves. I cry like a baby for a moment, then laugh at my fear of being alone. Nature is unfolding in me with enormous power and confidence. I *need only trust. The light is fading from the room.*

The movement continues. Several times when it seems to be over I start to drag myself to my clothes and I am seized by laughter and motion. Finally, after another hour, I am spent. By the time I gather myself and rise for dinner, it is dark. There is no pain in the knees that have bothered me for years. Even my aching lower back is straighter than any osteopath has ever made it. My eyes, when I look at them in a mirror, are as clear as a baby's.

I look up now, away from my own face to Rajneesh's. He is looking down at me, smiling, impish, knowing. I feel a pull toward him, insistent, threatening, exciting, like the undertow of surf. I feel that he has made this experience possible, kicked my energy like some sluggish electron into a more excited, active, higher state. I feel gratitude and love, not so general now as in groups, but focused on Rajneesh, on his—what to call it—generosity. I feel clean, blissful, and—yes, I have to admit it—reborn. That's why they call it rebirthing. I giggle to myself.

Why not continue like this in groups and in therapies, clearing out all the old worries and suspicions, yielding up the physical blocks in my body and my breathing, letting myself change, becoming as natural, as easy with myself, as I now am? Images come to me. I see myself living without effort or self-consciousness, like a Zen monk or a young hunter or a great natural athlete, or indeed like myself when I am, as a doctor or a friend or a lover, at my very best. Only that is an occasional thing, alternating with ambition, self-consciousness, petty hassles, and even more petty fear. I see myself tending a garden, making food, leading groups, responsible to and focused on the task at hand, free from others' expectations, and, especially, my own.

I am, I imagine, part of the kind of community that my friends and I created in the hours of a campus demonstration, the weeks of a political project, or the months on a hospital ward—but never sustained. I remember Moses' words: "Wouldn't you feel stupid if Buddha or Jesus or Lao-tzu were here on earth and you could be with him, and you chose not to?" For the first time I think seriously about taking sannyas. I imagine myself moving from loved work and friends to loving glance and embrace, part of, enfolded in, Rajneesh's orange whirlpool—at home.

Over the next several days the intensity of my feeling fades. I do not change my reservations back to the West or become a sannyasin. There are things I want to do in the world, ambitions and desires to fulfill, people I love, more things to discover. It seems absurd to wear orange, unnecessary or even foolish to subordinate myself to the ashram discipline that I do not trust. I feel Rajneesh is a great teacher, but I can continue to learn from him and his meditations and his books without surrendering. And besides, and most important, I feel a nagging suspicion. Amidst all the beauty and intelligence and sensitivity, there is a love of power in Rajneesh, a cruelty that he does not acknowledge. It makes me mistrust him, and fear him. It may just be the protection of my ego, which I know is certainly alive and kicking, but I don't think so.

Still, on my last day in Poona, as I am saying good-bye, I have second thoughts. Many of the friends I have made gather around me. They want me to stay, to relax with them here in this place. There seems to be so much love in them. It would be such a blessing to forget about my career, the records and résumés I have made acceptable, the conventional wisdom of my parents, my ways of getting on and along in life, and, most of all, my habitual weighing and balancing of doubts and reservations and alternatives. After all, what I want most is what Rajneesh and countless other Masters have urged: to die to the past and the future, to ideas and ideologies, expectations and conventions; to die to all this and live totally, fully—now as peaceful and compassionate as Buddha, now celebrating, dancing like a Hasid—in the timeless, eternal present.

4

NEWS FROM
POONA

Not long after I returned from Poona, I began to use Dynamic Meditation in my therapy with individual patients and groups. I was still working at NIMH, but I had moved from the country to Washington, D.C., and was seeing more private patients. Dynamic seemed to help some of these people express their conflicts, to decrease the controlling power of thoughts and behaviors that had baffled conventional talking therapies. It also gave them a way to work on themselves apart from the hours of therapy. Dynamic wasn't for everyone. It was too strenuous for most older people, and others just didn't want to suffer the pain of so much physical effort. But those who did it regularly for several weeks seemed calmer and yet more energetic than before. They were, in general, more detached from their problems, more open to me and to psychotherapy, more confident in their ability to help themselves.

I tried some of Rajneesh's other meditations with my patients as well—Kundalini and Nadabrahma, a relaxing yet enlivening Tibetan humming exercise. I began to prescribe some Tantric techniques as an adjunct to psychotherapy: "Talk nonsense in a mirror," I might say to someone who obliviously talked nonsense all day. "Sit together, look into each other's eyes, unblinking, every night," I advised some couples who were angrily building walls with words. "See what happens."

Twice a year I spent time with Shyam. Sometimes he came to work with me in Washington. Sometimes I visited him in London and at Suryodaya, the rural clinic and meditation center he had set up in Suffolk. I studied acupuncture with him and tried to develop in my life and work the meditative, intuitive approach in which the techniques of Oriental medicine are grounded. When I saw Shyam he would tell me the news from Poona, as it had been relayed to him by sannyasins who had visited him on their return.

Apparently, sannyasins in India were feeling under siege. In May, 1980, a Hindu extremist threw a knife at Rajneesh during a morning discourse: "You are insulting our religions," he had shouted. The knife fell short, but it was a sign of the increasing tension between the ashram and the other inhabitants of Poona. Instead of simply sniffing attendees at morning discourse, guards began to pat them down. An armored Rolls-Royce and a metal detector—like the ones at airports—were on order. Sannyasins were being beaten up on the streets of Poona.

Partly as a result of this external pressure, the ashram's organizational structure, which had been subject to continual improvisation, was becoming solid, if not rigid. Boundaries between the sannyasin community and the external world were less permeable. Rules had been formulated for official Rajneesh meditation centers in the West. Sannyasins' behavior was being examined for deviation from orthodoxy.

When I saw Shyam in London in late 1980 he told me that he had received a letter from Laxmi. She began by reminding him that he did not always wear orange clothes and the mala, and went on to inform him that he was on an "ego trip" and was no longer "doing Bhagwan's work." Laxmi told him to send back his mala. Shyam was unimpressed. "Bureaucracy," he snorted. "Idiots!" He believed Rajneesh had ceded too much authority to an organization of which he was becoming the captive. Shyam tacked the notice of his excommunication to the door of a rest room in one of his offices and sent a note back to Laxmi: "If Bhagwan wants the mala, tell him to come get it." He continued to wear his Master's picture when he wanted, and to direct a now unofficial Rajneesh Meditation Center.

At home in Washington I would go every few weeks to the Devadeep Rajneesh Meditation Center. I liked doing Dynamic with other people, and the music and dancing that came afterward; and of course there was my research, which included periodic interviews with sannyasins about themselves, their Master, and their movement. Devadeep was one of several hundred meditation centers around the world that Rajneesh had encouraged his disciples to open. In small cities the center might be just a single family or a few friends living together. Devadeep, like Paras, a center I visited in San Francisco, and Suryodaya, was a minicommune of ten to twenty sannyasins.

The Deep, as its inhabitants called it, was in many ways a refreshing change from Poona. There were some highly privileged people living there—Ashir, a young Austrian physician, and Pranama, the son of a high Reagan administration official, who was on leave of absence from college. But they, like the other inhabitants, lived modestly and worked hard. The center leader, Swami Prem Deben, a former seminarian and youth counselor, and about half the people who stayed at Devadeep and came to the meditations were black. "Bhagwan," Deben had asked on a visit to Poona, "how can I bring more Afro-Americans to you?"

"You tell them I am a black man," Rajneesh had answered.

Most of the sannyasins had jobs as secretaries or therapists, X-ray technicians or bureaucrats. The time they spent in the regular working world and, perhaps, their unavoidable status as members of a racial minority seemed to provide a kind of counterbalance to the self-importance that in Poona often accompanied spiritual aspiration and effort.

The center was friendly, crowded, and disorganized. Every few weeks, with the arrival of traveling sannyasins or "news about Bhagwan," the emotional climate of the house shifted from depression to exultation and back again. Deben, always overworked and sometimes overearnest, ran groups—Anger group on Tuesdays, Hugging group on Wednesdays, Rebirthing, Relationships, and Healing on Saturdays and Sundays. Until the neighbors complained, several sannyasins were plying the therapeutic massage trade they had learned in Poona. Periodically, center businesses would appear and disappear: the Orange Broom, a cleaning service, in which both Ashir and Pranama worked; an isolation tank rented by the hour; and a company that sold, among other items, a blanket made according to the specifications of a Reichian orgone box. On weekends, while their middle-class neighbors went to church, the sannyasins, their friends, and anyone who was curious about Rajneesh did Dynamic, played Afro-Indian jazz, watched old videos of Rajneesh, danced madly, and traded gossip. Some of them came to see me as patients, and some of my most lonely patients found friends there.

I heard from the people at Devadeep that the search for a new commune, far larger and more self-sufficient than the Poona ashram, had intensified after I left India. In 1980 Rajneesh announced a plan to establish a sannyasin city of 50,000 or 100,000 (he then claimed 500,000 disciples, though the figure seemed inflated by at least tenfold) in Kutch, in northwestern India. It was to be like the sanghas, the communes that formed around Buddha and Mahavira. But Rajneesh's city would be larger, more potent, less parochial. Its influence would be amplified by the power of mass communication.

In his morning discourses Rajneesh was now repeatedly proclaiming the urgent need for a "new humanity": "If we cannot create the new man in the coming twenty years . . . then humanity has no future." The commune would be the womb for the new man, "a place where [my sannyasins] are not distracted by the world." There the "energy field" that emanated from him—he now called it, with customary modesty, "the Buddhafield"—would catalyze transformation in those who came to live and work. "Infinite energy" would be available.

"The new commune," he said (sounding, I thought, a bit like the young and utopian Karl Marx or Friedrich Engels or the Herbert Marcuse of *Eros and Civilization*), "will be on a big scale . . . sannyasins living together as one body, one being. Everybody is going to live as comfortably, as richly as we can manage. But nobody will possess anything. Not only will things not be possessed but persons will also not be possessed in the new commune. If you love a woman—live with her—out of sheer love, sheer joy, but don't become her husband. You can't. Don't become a wife. To become a wife or a husband is ugly because it brings ownership and then the other is reduced to property.

"The new commune is going to transform work into play, transform life into love and laughter. Remember the motto again: To hallow the earth, to make everything sacred, to transform the ordinary mundane things into extraordinary spiritual things." Eventually, he predicted on another occasion, the sannyasins who had been transformed would disperse, bringing the energy, "the aroma of enlightenment, of love, of prayer," everywhere they went.

Rajneesh was confident, but from what I understood the new commune wasn't about to happen. I heard that Laxmi, now accompanied by Ma Prem Isabel, a Chilean woman who had previously done public relations for Tahiti, was frantically canvassing India for a site. She had been given a deadline, early in the spring of 1981.

Previously, efforts to move from the overcrowded quarters in Poona had been stymied by the government of Rajneesh's enemy and perennial discourse whipping boy Morarji Desai. The Desai government, directly or through the state governments, frustrated the plan to establish a commune in Kutch, and a more modest proposal for Maharashtra, the state in which Poona was located. Now Indira Gandhi was making matters difficult.

After Gandhi's reelection in January 1980, Laxmi, with her strong Congress party connections, had been optimistic. Gandhi had once been interested enough in Rajneesh to read some of his discourses and meet with him. After the meeting he had praised her "intelligence." "She is," he said, "flexible, open, brave, vulnerable, ready to see anything new, ready to understand anything happening in the modern world." The newly reelected prime minister was courteous but not helpful. The controversies and scandals that surrounded the ashram and its therapies could only be a liability for her new government. The necessary permission was not forthcoming.

In early 1981, while Laxmi was desperately trying to make Rajneesh's dream a reality, the day-to-day administration of the ashram fell to her secretary, Sheela. This arrangement would become permanent. Rajneesh was impatient with Laxmi's inability to find a site for the new commune. The need for this was preeminent and Sheela, who apparently was urging Rajneesh to move to America, now seemed to be the one who could make it happen. While Laxmi and Isabel were still in Kashmir looking at yet another possible site, Sheela, I later found out, called a secret meeting of forty sannyasins. "Bhagwan," she told them, "wants to go to America." They were to prepare for the journey.

In March 1981 I learned that Rajneesh had stopped speaking in public, that, like the twentieth-century Indian teachers Meher Baba and Baba Hari Das, he had "entered silence." I was told that he said this was to be "the ultimate stage" of his work. He had used his words to draw people, to wake them up; now silence would "deepen the communion" with those who had committed themselves to him. It would be, he said, "a transmission beyond words . . . a quantum leap from a lit lamp to an unlit lamp." I wondered if Rajneesh, who looked in recent pictures increasingly frail, was readying his disciples for his death.

And then, just a few weeks later, Rajneesh was in America, at the Chidvilas Rajneesh Center in New Jersey, which Sheela and Chinmaya had established in the early seventies. He was staying in a ten-bedroom house called the Castle, which the sannyasins had recently bought and which Deeksha and a crew of carpenters, electricians, and plumbers had renovated.

The official word was that Sheela had wanted Rajneesh to come to America for his health. His diabetes and asthma and allergies were out of control. His coughing supposedly aggravated his back condition, perhaps causing a disc to herniate. Several specialists had attended Rajneesh in India, including Dr. James Cyriax, whom Devaraj had flown in from London. Sannyasins were told publicly by Sheela, not Cyriax, that Rajneesh might have died if he had stayed in India. In America, he would find the specialized care he needed. Rajneesh would, sannyasins were told, return to

Poona in three or four months, perhaps after he had undergone an operation.

The ashram was in chaos. Some had known, others suspected, that the move would happen, but most of the six thousand sannyasins jammed into Poona were taken by surprise. There were tears and anger and bewilderment. Some believed that Rajneesh, who had only been granted a temporary visa—for reasons of health—would return as soon as his back was better. Most were skeptical. They had heard the rumors that "Bhagwan has said, 'India is finished.' "

At any rate, without Rajneesh there, almost all of the Western sannyasins were preparing to leave India. They were selling their possessions—motorcycles, clothes, stereos—to raise money for their return to the West. Those who had rooms in the ashram, recently and dearly purchased "for life," were trying their best to be philosophical about the loss of their investment. Some Westerners, including Nandan and Veena, and many Indians were staying in Poona. Under the direction of Ma Yoga Vidya, a former computer specialist and present assistant to Sheela, they were dismantling the ashram. The rest were dispersing to Europe, America, and Australia, where they would soon be told to create and live in self-sufficient communes.

Before and after her departure Sheela had explained that the real reasons for leaving India were far more complex than Rajneesh's health. In private meetings with small numbers of sannyasins she told of the dangers to Rajneesh—and his sannyasins—from "enemies." The Indian government was harassing and persecuting the ashram—it had revoked the tax-exempt status of the Rajneesh Foundation, Ltd. (incorporated in 1978 as the successor to the Jeevan Jagruti Kendra), and was moving ahead, though with typical Indian lethargy, to collect $4 million in income taxes and several hundred thousand dollars in sales, import, property, and export taxes. She spoke of the government's refusal to allow Rajneesh to purchase a site for the new commune in India. She reminded sannyasins of the knife-throwing in 1980, and of the assaults on them; of two episodes of arson in 1981, a costly one against the book warehouse and another at the health center. According to her account, the sannyasins' landlord in Saswad, where a small rural commune had been established, had been harassing his tenants. She said that he also tried on one occasion to rape a young sannyasin while riding in a car with her. Finally, Sheela confided information that the Poona police were preparing to arrest Rajneesh for "inciting religious rioting."

As I began to look at these stories more clearly, another version began to emerge, one in many ways at variance with the official sannyasin line—the danger to Rajneesh's health—and even with the private version. Some of the events that had precipitated or justified the departure might well have been staged by the sannyasins themselves. The Poona police suspected that sannyasins had set the fires in the warehouse and medical center, to recover insurance on the books (only books in Hindi and Marathi, of little use after a move to America, were burned) and to make themselves appear the victims of persecution. The landlord accused of having tried to rape the sannyasin was in turn accusing her of fabricating the story. Even the Hindu extremist who threw the knife was said by some to have been paid by sannyasins to do it.

I also learned from sannyasin patients who were troubled by the deception that Rajneesh and Sheela had been discussing a new commune in the United States—not just a visit for medical purposes—as early as late 1980, long before the alleged arrest was imminent. In the spring of 1981 sannyasins were being sent to look for large, isolated parcels of land in the American West and South. Considerable but never disclosed sums of money—millions, perhaps tens of millions of dollars that the ashram had made on donations, therapy groups, discourse admissions, the sale of food and rooms, books and tapes—were being moved illegally out of India. There were Swiss bank accounts in Sheela's name. Gold had been melted down by ashram jewelers and refashioned to resemble cheap bronze bangles that could be smuggled out of the country.

At the same time personnel were being readied for a large-scale, long-term move. Ashramites who would be essential to a new commune—carpenters, electricians, businesspeople—were dispatched from Poona in twos and threes. They were told to have their hair and beards cut before presenting themselves for U.S. visas. At the instruction of the ashram hierarchy, marriages with British Commonwealth citizens, which had been made to circumvent Indian immigration law, were dissolved and new unions with American disciples, to circumvent U.S. immigration law, were formed. Some group leaders were dispatched to the West "to share Bhagwan's message"—at the "March Event," a series of brief groups and meditations attended by a thousand people, which Poonam organized in London. Others traveled to other cities in Europe, the United States, and Australia. Meanwhile, center leaders who had been planning to visit India were told to wait.

PART II

RAJNEESHPURAM

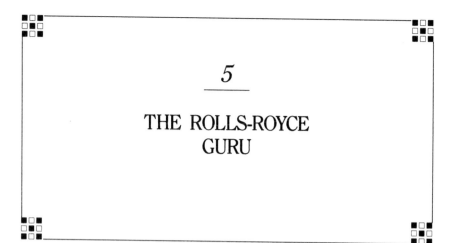

5

THE ROLLS-ROYCE
GURU

The sannyasins came to Oregon in the summer of 1981. Sheela and her second husband, Swami Prem Jayananda—formerly John Shelfer, a New Jersey businessman—selected the site over half a dozen alternatives. (Chinmaya, her first husband, had died in June 1980 of Hodgkin's disease.) The ranch was, as Rajneesh had wanted it, arid, large, and isolated—19 hard miles from the nearest tiny town, Antelope, 150 miles from Portland, on the eastern side of the Cascade Mountains. The site, which included land in both Wasco and Jefferson counties, was, sannyasins confided, relatively protected if nuclear war came.

If overpriced, it was not overly expensive: $5.75 million for 64,229 acres of deeded land and 17,000 acres leased from the federal Bureau of Land Management. The land was beautiful but an ecological disaster. The cliffs and outcroppings of rock, the gouged canyons and the sandy colors, were more like those of Utah than the lush Pacific coast across the mountains. Over the years it had been carelessly managed, badly overgrazed, and eroded by floods from the John Day River, which ran through it. In fact, it was known locally as the Big Muddy Ranch. Hollywood westerns, including one starring John Wayne, had been made there.

The sannyasins came to the Big Muddy with enthusiasm, confidence, unspecified but very large sums of money, and a plan to "make Bhagwan's vision real," to give full scope to his "Buddhafield," to serve as the birthplace for the "new man." On the 6 acres of the Shree Rajneesh ashram in Poona, the emphasis was on transforming people through therapeutic and meditative techniques. Here on the 64,000 acres of "Rancho Rajneesh" sannyasins would reclaim and transform the earth itself. Work would be their meditation and learning to work together, their group. In their commune sannyasins would live productively, in harmony with their own natures and the natural world around them.

In the first year they brought in mobile homes for themselves, planted trees to control erosion, installed new irrigation systems, dug wells, cleared land, built a dairy barn, put in crops and fruit trees. Though they initially announced that they wanted only to develop a communal farm, they were already preparing an official Comprehensive Plan for a city of several thousand—"Sannyasins move fast," I was told.

I heard that Rajneesh had flown from New Jersey to Oregon in July 1981. To avoid arousing the ire of the U.S. Immigration and Naturalization Service, he was described as a "guest" on the ranch. He had a lovely if not luxurious house, and plans were under way for him to reside permanently in Oregon. A few months later I learned that "Bhagwan's health is improving daily." Because he loved greenery the sannyasins had sodded the bone-dry land in front of his house and planted trees. They installed an indoor swimming pool for his pleasure and brought in the first of the Rolls-Royces they would buy for him. During that first year they spent, on their land and their Master, between $20 million and $30 million. Already the ranch was one of the largest, most developed, and richest communal experiments in America.

I heard a great deal about the ranch before I went there. The sannyasins at Deva-deep spoke of it with all the wonder and fervor of Jews contemplating the Promised Land. "In the new commune," they would say, echoing Rajneesh, or "On the ranch," and then go on to describe how it would be when it was completed, or what projects were already under way.

In Washington they worked at jobs that paid poorly. At Devadeep they economized by living crowded together, two or three to a room. But from the fall of 1981 almost all of them sent a sizable portion of their earnings—15 to 30 percent was not uncommon—to the ranch. At one point when they were asked, like Zionists in the forties, to contribute $100 each to plant a tree in Oregon, they did their best to comply.

Though some of the Devadeep sannyasins had doubts about leaving their families or their jobs, many believed they would ultimately live out their lives on the ranch. They would go as soon as there was enough housing, when their skills were needed. Meanwhile they were saving to go for the First World Festival. This would be in July 1982, on Guru Poornima Day, when Indians traditionally gather with their Master.

Periodically someone from the ranch came east to bring news and answer questions and raise more money. In the pictures they showed sannyasins and their guests, they pointed out administrative trailers and barns in the valley, housing trailers on the sides of the hills. Men and women were shown eating outside what looked to be the original ranch house. They were bundled up in red and orange down jackets with cowboy hats over their eyes. Snow was on the ground. They looked happy.

In the winter of 1981 I saw Laxmi at Mahadeva's apartment in Manhattan. She had come east with Ma Prem Chetna to raise money for the ranch. She perched on Mahadeva's couch, a bright bird in orange, surrounded by half a dozen men in red and orange jumpsuits and jeans, silk shirts and scarves. One of them, Jaipal, was explaining that he would introduce her to someone who had made millions creating the first computerized dating service. "He has read Bhagwan and is interested in the ranch." Jaipal himself had made millions in arbitrage, but it didn't interest him much anymore. He told me that he got more satisfaction from sweeping up Vrindavan Cafeteria in Poona than from any of his big money deals. He was thinking about living on the ranch but wasn't sure about the loss of privacy, the long-term commitment to manual labor that would be necessary. He often flew his own plane; that day he was chauffeuring Laxmi around Manhattan.

In Washington a few days later I saw Laxmi again. She was in the basement meditation room at Devadeep, in front of a group of sannyasins. She was pacing back and forth rubbing her fingers together. "Vitamin M," she said gleefully. "The ranch is beautiful but it needs to grow, it needs an injection of money, of vitamin M."

When I talked with her privately, she was, as always, ebullient. Still, when I asked whether it had not been hard to lose her position to Sheela, her denial was forced. "Sheela," she said, "has the burden of running the ranch. She is a good administrator, and," turning on her grin, "Laxmi is free—to travel and raise money. Besides, it is fitting. Sheela knows America better than Laxmi. Laxmi is also serving him." When I asked if her distance from Rajneesh pained her, she dismissed the question. "He is here," she said, touching her heart, "with Laxmi."

Eight months later, in August 1982, I am driving from Portland toward the ranch; over the Cascades, so I can see Mount Hood, and out onto the plains, past Maupin and east and south again, to Antelope, where sannyasins live in several of the town's houses. They have recently bought the Antelope Café and General Store with its gas pumps and renamed it the Zorba the Buddha Café.

A mile or two outside Antelope, there is a sign just like all the other green county signs that say Madras and The Dalles, Antelope and Shaniko, Clarno and Fossil. Only this one says, even more improbably, Rajneeshpuram.

The entrance to the ranch is about nine miles from Antelope. Two marble pillars mark it. Lines are engraved on them from Buddha's first sermon. One version is in the original Pali, the other in English. *Buddham Sharanam Gachchhami*—I go to the feet of the Awakened One. *Sangham Sharanam Gachchhami*—I go to the feet of the Commune of the Awakened One. *Dhammam Sharanam Gachchhami*—I go to the feet of the Ultimate Truth of the Awakened One. Not far away is a guardhouse. Two men in lavender and plum work clothes—the sannyasins have gradually been expanding the colors of their wardrobe along the spectrum from orange to pink to red, to violet and purple—wave at me.

I wind slowly up and down and up again through the shadows, from the near desert of central Oregon. I drive on, climbing more steeply for a few miles, then leveling off, then rising once more around a bend, and there is a valley. Arriving on this ledge at dusk on the dirt road from Antelope, along the rim of the hills that embrace the ranch, I find it easy to see why Sheela and Jayananda bought the place.

Light still falls in layers of orange and purple across the shelves of rock. The air is clean and still, cooling fast. My eyes, relaxing, reach far away over the dry streambeds toward where the bottomland disappears in more hills that eventually slope down to the John Day River. There is an acrid smell of sagebrush. In spring the Big Muddy must race through the valley, but now the bed is cracked and dry. Juniper trees are brown with dust near the road, gray-green higher up on the side of the hills.

Arriving on the ranch I feel uncertain about my role. In Poona I was primarily a seeker, embracing the experiences of the ashram as best I could, only intermittently a scholar and a writer stepping back to puzzle over, to analyze them. Here I'm not sure. There are meditations to be done on the ranch and even, by this time, a few therapy groups. But they are not the heart of life. Here working on oneself is an aspect of doing work to build a community. Visitors like me are regarded not as seekers or potential sannyasins, but as representatives of an external world with which the ranch is maintaining an uneasy truce, toward which it is trying to turn its best face.

In Poona I went to the press office only in the last days of my stay. Laxmi thought that it would be fun for me to talk with Krishna Prem and that he could, incidentally, introduce me to anyone I hadn't yet had the chance to meet. In Rajneeshpuram I am greeted by a cadre of women whose job it is to guide visitors around the ranch and to arrange interviews for those who are covering its activities for the news media. Since I am writing a book about new religions — Rajneesh and his sannyasins are to occupy a chapter — I am "a journalist" and considered part of the media.

These women, at first called hostesses and later, for obvious reasons, nicknamed Twinkies, are the only ranch residents whom most casual visitors, and the vast majority of journalists, get to know. One or another of them is almost always at a visitor's side, cheerfully offering statistics on production and land reclamation, arranging and limiting interviews and access to activities on the ranch, presenting the ranch positions on controversial issues. Ma Prem Isabel, who accompanied Laxmi on her fruitless search for a site for the new commune in India, is the head Twinkie. She is a remarkably attractive and efficient French woman who grew up among Chile's upper class.

I have a strange, continually changing, sometimes warm, often uneasy relationship with Isabel and most of the other Twinkies. Their refusal to be critical of anything that happens on the ranch, their quickness to justify any and all of Rajneesh's and Sheela's words and deeds, and, in time, their lies, make me uneasy. I am a strange case to them as well. I have known about Rajneesh, have done his meditations and read his books, for so long. I am in many ways so sympathetic to him and to their way of life, so close to so many sannyasins, yet I haven't put on the colors and the mala. Sometimes they seem to be more suspicious of me than of obviously hostile or ignorant journalists. During my first visit I think they may have realized that I know too much to believe some of their explanations. Much later it will occur to me that I — with my reservations and my journalist's role — might personify doubts they do not care to express or even admit to themselves.

Sometimes the Twinkies treat me with the courteous but firm correctness they reserve for the press. Sometimes we fight about what I will be allowed to see or do. I want to visit a friend at her house. Isabel says I can't. I ask why not. She says it will "intrude on others in the house." "I will ask them," I say. "They'll feel obligated to say yes," she says. "Isabel, they're adults," I say. "Visitors are not" — her jaw is tightening now — "allowed in sannyasins' houses." "Isabel, that's a crazy rule, or else you're hiding something in the houses." Eventually Isabel allows me far more freedom than other visitors, but there are always arbitrary — and to me, suspect — limits against which I strain.

Sometimes I suggest to Isabel and the others that they are being evasive and rigid.

Isabel tells me on more than one occasion that I am impolite and deliberately provocative. At other times, at the end of a long day or after a particularly touching interview or a pleasant meal with mutual friends, Isabel or another of my Twinkie escorts and I hug with genuine affection. Though these women are my age or younger, they remind me, at least in their role as Twinkies, of matrons in the movie houses I visited as a child, or big sisters, unsure of their authority but determined to enforce it on an obstreperous younger brother.

Ultimately I simply accept the role in which I am cast. I am a journalist and psychiatrist. My job is to find out what is happening on the ranch and how it is affecting the people who are living there; how it is or is not fulfilling Rajneesh's vision of communal harmony. No matter how much I may enjoy the people, I have to remember, just as I would in a clinical situation, to ask the hard questions that nobody particularly wants to answer; to listen to the responses they evoke; to pay attention to the discomfort that evasion or self-deception will inevitably produce in me. I am not there to be a group member or a solitary meditator. Nor is it my concern to be liked or accepted or included. Just as the sannyasins are learning to focus on and relax with their work—their road construction or city planning or cooking—to use it as their meditation, so I will use my own work of questioning, analyzing, reporting.

I take a tour of Rajneeshpuram (the City of the Lord of the Full Moon), the tiny, dusty town the sannyasins have incorporated on the ranch. The mayor, a tall, dark, handsome bearded man named Swami Krishna Deva—K.D.—is my guide. K.D., formerly David Knapp, was a marriage and family therapist and a real estate broker in California before he became a group leader in Poona. He tells me he was elected mayor partly because he knew about land use planning. He had worked in residential programs for delinquents, and just before he went to Poona he was preparing to buy land in Southern California for a hospice.

"What we are doing," K.D. says, as we step out of his trailer office into the heat, "is taking people who are basically successful, saying, 'Here is a new challenge.' We're finding out what we can do, pooling our energies, our financial resources, our creativity. A family may work for forty years on a plot of ground and we"—he gestures toward the newly planted fields—"can transform it in a week. When I used to be in private practice," he goes on, "I worked twenty-five hours a week. Then I worried about being burned out. In Poona I worked eight hours a day, seven days a week, and I was never tired. Here I work even more.

"There is so much love in the work," K.D. explains as we pass the sites where a shopping mall and a university will be constructed. "Look at the landscaping. Look at the details in the flower beds. You can see the aliveness and the love. But you have to have eyes to see. What we have here is the"—quoting Rajneesh now—" 'extraordinariness of ordinariness.' It's like we've graduated from one school to another and we've been given more responsibility. It's not the same kind of structure as in Poona. It's more relaxed and fun. There is more trust."

Indeed, the ranch seems in many ways idyllic and utopian, far less pressured and more homelike than Poona. Life is simple, its pleasures unmediated. Tasks that would be onerous and alienating in another context seem playful and fulfilling here. For many, the necessary physical labor to build and maintain a small town and till a large piece of land seems less a burden than a lesson, a pleasing change from the professional and administrative tasks for which they have been trained.

Early the next morning I chat with Punito, the slight, graying woman who is cleaning the trailer in which I'm staying. Born Maria Teresa (for Teresa of Avila) Camposarcone, she was a curious, devout, and imaginative child. As a girl she kept wondering who God was and what he looked like and why he made the world as he did. One day, nosing around her father's library, she happened on the writings of Dionysius the Areopagite. "I opened the book and it said something like 'The God who can be known is not God.' Somehow that satisfied me."

Punito tells me she became a musician and, in the late 1960s, made her living by teaching in Head Start programs in New York City. In the early seventies, after reading R. D. Laing's *Politics of Experience*, she had "some sort of breakdown." She went to London, where she met Laing and other psychiatrists who, it turns out, I also know. She recovered, studied for some time with Ravi Shankar, and headed to India to work with a teacher whom Shankar had recommended.

She arrived in Poona on her way to her new teacher and heard that a man named Rajneesh was telling his Western disciples to chant in the streets of India. "I thought, 'Far out, uptight English singing in India.' I went to him and he said, 'I'll be your music and singing teacher,' and he was right."

After Maria Teresa—now Ma Prem Punito—left India, she returned to the United States. She and her husband started a Rajneesh Meditation Center in Seattle. Later they went to Laguna Beach, California, where they began the Utsava Rajneesh Meditation Center. Utsava, she explains, was originally a Church of Divine Science. It became a Rajneesh center after the minister, who had visited her and her husband in Seattle and gone to India, became a sannyasin. When he changed his affiliation from Divine Science to Rajneesh, he took the congregation and its valuable property with him. Currently, litigation is under way between some of the former congregation and the present sannyasins who occupy Utsava. But that is no longer Punito's concern. "Now I'm cleaning the guest house."

While I do my morning stretches she sets a glass-topped table and a chair on the deck facing the brown-green hills. She brings two kinds of jam on a tray, and puts them in the refrigerator, tidies the counters and the shelves. She works without haste or hesitation and smiles with the deep, unaffected pleasure of a child playing.

"I like to keep the place pin-neat," she says. "I really like doing the laundry for you and the other people who stay here, and bringing fresh-baked bread, and making sure the plants stay healthy. After all those months of setting up centers and running them and dealing with everybody's problems and anticipating legal hassles, it's nice to do simple work well, to live in a beautiful place with my man and my son."

Punito's appreciation of quiet, basically monogamous domesticity is far more common on the ranch than it was in Poona. There is still a great deal of what the Oregonians outside Rajneeshpuram might call promiscuity. Two people who have enjoyed rock-and-rolling together at the evening music group may well spend the night together and then, the next evening, find other partners for both dancing and love-making. But the overall feeling, particularly among the sannyasins who have been selected to live as permanent residents, is far less sexually fervid than in Poona.

The work schedule—7:00 A.M. to 7:00 P.M., seven days a week—and the hard, physical labor limit their energies, even as the urgency of their task focuses attention that might otherwise be devoted to sexual experimentation. The overcrowding of the ranch—there are clearly more sannyasins per trailer than the statements of the Twinkies indicate—sets limits to privacy. And the distance between lodgings and lack of transportation restrict the sannyasins' access to one another. For many people it is easier and more comforting to have a steady and regularly available lover. In a way, I suppose, this degree of domesticity is predictable. Living in the country, working the land, and building a town, the sannyasins are coming to resemble other rural people in their morals as well as their activities.

In Rajneeshpuram, however, long-term relationships do not generally imply marriage, an institution which on various occasions Rajneesh—who has obviously boned up on Engels—has called "slavery," "idiocy," and "prostitution." There are some people who were married long before they became sannyasins, but most of the marriages on the ranch are legal fictions, concocted in Poona or in the United States to enable valued foreign sannyasins to remain in Oregon. Some of the matches are absurdly obvious, for example, Krishna Deva and the lovely but hardly compatible Indian woman he is soon to marry. Others are a bit more subtle—the ranch administrator and the lawyer. But anyone who knows the parties involved or observes which trailer they enter at the end of the day knows the truth.

When I ask about the marriages, K.D. and Sheela, Vidya and Isabel, all deny that they are anything but genuine. "Yes," I say, "I know you're worried about the Immigration and Naturalization Service and can't admit it, but I want to tell you that these arrangements are transparent. I know a number of sannyasins who have told me they have done it—with, as well as without, the ranch's instructions—to stay in the country."

"Jim," Isabel and K.D. say to me, in very similar words and with obviously counterfeit candor, "we're already attracting everybody's attention. We have to be very careful about breaking the law. We just wouldn't do something like that."

As I listen to them I am more puzzled by their arrogance and obtuseness than I am troubled by their commission of what is, after all, a victimless crime. It seems to me to reveal, even in this more relaxed setting, the same easy contempt for outsiders—their intelligence as well as their laws—that I have recently heard about in Poona. It also makes me wonder what other circumstances will prompt my hosts and hostesses to lie to me.

Though there are few genuine marriages, there are children here on the ranch. Their number is a fraction of what one might expect from people of childbearing age, but there are more than one would find in singles' enclaves and more than I had seen in Poona. Many of them have come with a parent who is part of the summer's temporary work crews.

The children are housed in quarters apart from their parents, with minimal adult supervision. Though this will later be justified as a strategy for breaking down the bonds and bondage of the nuclear family, as a way of making the children more the commune's, it seems at this time simply a matter of convenience. I see only one or two infants and a few toddlers—even summer workers have been strongly discouraged from bringing their young children, because they deflect too much attention from the task of building the community—but there are about forty or fifty kids who range from five to fourteen years old. During the day the younger ones—an attractive, brash, cheerful crew—play in groups under adult supervision or freely roam the ranch. Those who are eleven or more are integrated into the work life of the adult community.

I spend time with two thirteen-year-old girls, Madhu and Binu, while they put together brown bag lunches for farm and construction crews at Magdalena Cafeteria (as in Poona every building or area of the ranch is named after a spiritual teacher). Each is on the ranch for the summer with her mother and both their mothers are separated from their fathers. Madhu's father, who is not a sannyasin, has granted permission for her to stay. Binu's father, a psychologist, runs a Rajneesh Meditation Center in North Carolina. Madhu and Binu knew one another before they came to Oregon. Now they live together with a third girl in one part of a small trailer.

Both girls are cheerful and chatty and enthusiastic about the ranch and their life on it. There are advantages, Madhu, a chunky, open-faced girl, tells me, to living with her mother on the ranch and to living with her father outside. As she talks to me I notice that she lacks the self-consciousness and self-absorption that limit so many conversations that I have had with young adolescents. She not only believes that what she says is interesting but is interested in my opinions as well.

Madhu enjoys being with her mother here and working with adults and contributing to the well-being of others on the ranch. "Work is our play," she tells me, smiling. But she also likes being with her father in Brooklyn ("I'm getting closer to him now. It's not so easy if you're separated a lot") and going to school and "hanging out in the city," by which she means going shopping, visiting Manhattan, and going to concerts. "Bhagwan," she says simply, "is with me wherever I go." She regards him as her "best friend," a kind of beneficent and reassuring presence, at once grandfather and buddy, a loving support in her efforts to be "more open and loving with my friends, especially my dad."

I hang around Magdalena watching people chop vegetables for the evening meal. One group of men and women are listening to rock and roll on a cassette player while they work; occasionally one or two of them will get up and dance across the huge room. Older Indian women—one is Rajneesh's mother, Saraswati Jain—are gossiping as they snap beans. The light outside begins to go red and purple as people line up for the evening meal.

The sannyasins are clearly tired at the end of the day but seem for the most part fit and tan and happy as they sit down for dinner. During the day, they assure me, there has been time for tea breaks, personal crises—somebody is always leaving or being left by a lover—and chats with friends at work. Now they are laughing and hugging one another, telling stories about the work they have been doing and making dates for the night ahead. They are happily eating large portions of fried tofu and rice with creamy gravy, fresh green beans, salad with four kinds of dressing and seeds and raisins; bread that is still warm from the oven and apple cobbler and ice cream; glasses of iced tea, lemonade, and beer, light or dark.

The next morning I meet Veena, who was with Rajneesh in Bombay. In 1972 she and Shyam started a Rajneesh meditation center in London; in 1982 she is a Twinkie in Oregon. We are going up into the hills together to see the proposed sites for the "university city," hospital, and the new sewage recycling plant.

The middle-aged man who gasses up our four-wheel-drive vehicle tells me he was once a professor. "Twenty years of teaching, and even great works of art become stale. Enough," he said, "was enough."

While we're waiting Veena scolds a news photographer who is taking pictures of two sannyasins embracing. "There's so much beautiful work going on here. Why focus on sex? These people are on a tea break. It's absurd," she says, turning back to me. "We have press here all the time, and all they want to know about is sex and Bhagwan's eleven Rolls-Royces." We begin a discussion about Shyam. It turns out she hasn't spoken with him in years and is annoyed with him. "Such a beautiful man and such an ego trip. He doesn't give Bhagwan credit. He acts like he's the Master." I disagree. Shyam gives Rajneesh great credit and great love and still wears his picture around his neck. Meanwhile, the professor-mechanic is whistling a Mozart symphony while he cleans our windows and checks our oil and water, our points and plugs.

After our trip, I head for lunch with Sunshine, a dark-haired, bright-faced Twinkie who lives up to her name, and her boyfriend, Srajan, a carpenter. She used to run restaurants, he was a Zen monk in Asia for years before he met Rajneesh.

On the way we give a lift to a small, fast-talking, grinning man whom I'm sure I've met before. He turns out to be Swami Prem Siddha, a psychiatrist from Southern California, who, under his given name, Leonard Zunin, wrote a popular best-seller called *Contact: The First Four Minutes.* Siddha, who is a few years older than I, treats me as if I were a first-year psychiatric resident on the ward where he is chief. "So," he says, even while we're introducing ourselves, "what do you think of us? Pretty amazing kind of therapeutic community!"

Sitting in the original farmhouse, which has been converted to a restaurant, Siddha proceeds, freely combining interrogation and narrative. He was working in Southern California, consulting with NIMH and the Veterans Administration about the problems of the wives of Vietnam veterans, and doing a private practice, making lots of money. Then he heard about Rajneesh. "He was so clearly the next step beyond psychiatry. He made what I was doing seem like child's play. I thought I helped people. It wasn't that I was wrong. It was just so small."

He knew as soon as he got to Poona that he would become a sannyasin. "Bhagwan," he explains, "was talking about the psychology of the Buddhas, not the psychopathology of Freud. He revealed the shortcomings even in the humanistic psychology of Maslow and Fromm. They are still trying to change the mind. Bhagwan says mind itself is the problem. You have to look at your consciousness, without analyzing, dividing, or qualifying. His is basically the psychology of no mind. You understand what I am saying. I can see it." Siddha is noisy, active, and helpful, and he reminds me of Hanuman, the divine monkey servant in the Hindu play the *Ramayana.* "How come you never became a sannyasin?" His enthusiasm is infectious and I find myself laughing.

Later that day I continue my tour. Children are working with adults in Magdalena, baking dozens of loaves of bread; a nurse and a social worker are lining up seedlings in the Paul Reps Greenhouse; crews of men and women in red jeans and lavender jumpsuits are smoothing gravel behind a dump truck. As I go from one site to another, watching this, I am reminded of musicians in an orchestra, or, more precisely, players in a jazz group. There is an overall conception in Rajneesh's vision — living communally in the Master's Buddhafield, working meditatively, hallowing the earth — and there is the melodic line of the particular task at hand. But the texture comes from improvisation, playfulness, continual change. When, sometime later, the hotel has to be finished for an upcoming celebration, crews work twenty-four hours a day; earlier that summer warm weather prompted landscapers to direct their attention to one of the lakes where people might soon want to swim.

Some of the new settlers have come to the ranch with experience in construction and agriculture. Swami Anand Neehar, who has a Ph.D. in philosophy and coordinates agricultural projects on the ranch, was a dryland farmer in Australia. Swami Deva Wadud, the city planner, was trained at the Harvard Graduate School of Design before he became a psychic, a sannyasin, and a group leader. But most of the sannyasins, like Punito, the professor-mechanic, and Siddha, are highly educated, city-born, Poona-trained amateurs. A survey that Norman Sundberg of the University of Oregon will take a year later will indicate that 64 percent of the ranch's population have bachelor's degrees, 36 percent have advanced degrees, including 12 percent who have doctorates. Twenty-two percent of the population have "graduate or undergraduate degrees in psychology or psychiatry."

These people, long accustomed to learning, and to learning how to learn, have hired the teachers they need — ecologists and agronomists, soil chemists and experts in insulation. They trust that in "Bhagwan's Buddhafield" they will be able to do what needs to be done, that everything will work out. Of all the people operating the dozens of pieces of heavy equipment, only one has ever done so before he came to the ranch. "It's far out," a New York advertising man who now drives a front-loader tells me. "This whole trip is to wake us up. It's the most amazing meditation, and if you're not aware, you're in big trouble."

Everything has to be done fast, K.D. assures me when we meet later in my stay. If humanity is, as Rajneesh has said, at a crossroads, if we are in immediate danger of destroying ourselves, his attempt to create "a new man" and a conscious community must be accomplished as soon as possible. It might be of vital importance not only to people who live on the ranch but to humanity.

Others feel the same sense of urgency but also preserve a certain playful detachment. At lunch one day, Swami Anand Yatri, who has edited a number of Rajneesh's books, gestures toward the newly planted fields and the hills. "This may all be a device. Sannyas means 'wanderer.' This is not permanent. Each thing is not what it seems. Bhagwan wants a road so he can drive out to the forest, and that road is made far more beautifully than if it were an ordinary road. And then more work is done with the forest. Trees are planted and workshops spring up and there may be chickens. So a simple thing becomes very different. And it's all done because he wanted a nice place to drive."

"It is," adds Ganda, a Swedish Twinkie who is with us, "like sitting on a lovely carpet and having it pulled out from under you, little by little."

At two o'clock all work on the ranch stops. It is time for the daily darshan with

Rajneesh, only here in Oregon, it is called a drive-by, not a darshan. Sannyasins do not talk to him or sit in silence with him. They stand on the side of the dirt road, in their red and orange and purple work clothes and their boots, silent in namaste, or swaying, dancing to some inner rhythm. Their Master, wrapped in a long gown and sparkly cap, a diamond watch on the wrist that rests on the steering wheel, drives slowly past them, in one of his Rolls-Royces.

On my first day I find the performance ridiculous and vulgar. This is the kind of display I would expect from an Indian maharaja or an obtuse Catholic prelate in an underdeveloped country, not from a Master who mocks pretension. What kind of intimate relationship is this? I feel like the boy who saw that the emperor had no clothes.

However, by the third day of my visit I feel a surprising change as Rajneesh's car comes closer to me. Thoughts about the disparity between the meretriciousness of the Master and the disciples' humble labor, and the disagreements I have just had with Isabel, and the phone call I need to make, dissolve. My mind becomes as quiet as it ever has in meditation. I feel a heavy wind blow through my bones. The car passes. Rajneesh looks at me, in my eyes. I find myself laughing like a child, embracing men and women I have never met. There are, for no reason I can discern, tears of gratitude in my eyes. I do not know why this has happened to me — or even what has happened. It feels like Rajneesh's presence has lowered the center of my being from my head to my torso, as if the responses now arising in my heart and my gut are unalloyed, unimpeded by the reservations and qualifications of thought. It occurs to me that what I am experiencing is the wordless transformational power of the Buddhafield.

During this visit I spend two days with Sheela in Jesus Grove, where she lives and works in a sprawling prefabricated house. She is a small woman whose large dark eyes are her most striking feature. Even on the ranch she, like her Master, favors unexpectedly luxurious clothes — silk and satin in the midst of sannyasin denim. There is a brittleness and an edge of sarcasm in her voice, a tendency to pontificate that almost never leaves her, except when she speaks of Rajneesh. Then her voice grows young and breathy and she sounds like an adoring daughter. Sheela can be kind, ordering cookies — "I'm bribing them," she stage-whispers to me — or a face wash for a child who wanders in, praising an aide for good decisions. More often, she is sharp and vulgar, if not mean, scolding a woman who is making too much noise chopping food, mocking a coordinator who says he needs more people for his crew.

Sometimes her comments strike me as peculiar, unnecessarily aggressive, even a bit paranoid. "D.P.," she asks the dogged, obviously exhausted construction supervisor Deva Prem, "who would know about the Comprehensive Plan [for the city of Rajneeshpuram] if you died?" She seems to emphasize the failures of her coordinators to share information and authority, while she herself hoards information, only to drop it, unwanted, on the already overburdened. Amidst her concern for her coordinators' problems, there are gratuitous insults to the state and county officials with whom they have to deal. When Videh, who is in charge of the water system, talks about his collaboration with state and county governments on matters related to purification, she interrupts, "No wonder you're polluting." She seduces and wheedles and bullies, sometimes all of them at once. "I'm just saying, goddamn it, D.P., spend some time with me. I want to know your department."

Sheela is president of the Rajneesh Foundation International. This is the tax-exempt American counterpart of India's Rajneesh Foundation, Ltd., and the religious teaching arm of the expanding international sannyasin empire. Sheela is also Rajneesh's personal secretary. These dual roles, comparable in the sannyasin world to premier and first secretary of the Communist party in the Soviet Union, give her virtually total control over the policies and plans that affect sannyasins at the centers around the world as well as on the ranch.

Rajneesh is, of course, the unquestioned source of Sheela's power. Though he continues to maintain his public silence, he is, according to Sheela, the guiding force behind all the major decisions she makes and all the directives she gives. During their daily two-hour meetings he advises her, as he once advised Laxmi, on everything, from her dealings with department coordinators to her attitudes toward Oregonian neighbors. "Bhagwan is always telling me," she tells me, " 'Be more assertive.' " Apart from Vivek, who continues to care for Rajneesh, Devaraj, his doctor, and Devageet, his dentist, Sheela is the only one with direct and regular access to him.

Sheela brings to Rajneesh news of the ranch and the international network of large communes and small centers; questions that sannyasins have submitted to him; and her own queries about administration, political tactics, and public relations. She is also the only conduit for his replies. At meetings of the coordinators of the ranch departments that I attend, she offers anecdotes about Rajneesh's behavior and observations as if they were her own precious jewels. He is "really enjoying his swimming pool"—or the newly paved road—she tells them. When Rajneesh has something to say to "the world at large," it is Sheela who calls the press conference and reads his words.

From morning until late at night, a steady stream of sannyasins come to sit in front of Sheela. I watch as they perch at the other end of the sofa on which she lies, curled like a cat. I listen to requests for approval of expenditures for heavy equipment; reports on farm production; an update on income from the First World Festival, recently held at the ranch; intelligence from the Oregon Legislative Assembly in Salem, where there are already rumblings of anti-Rajneesh feelings; descriptions of the Rolls-Royces available for purchase from American dealerships; complaints from or about workers.

On each of the days I am with Sheela, she calls a meeting of the coordinators of all the ranch departments. They pack her living room, people covering every inch of couch and chair and floor space. Sheela clearly relishes these meetings. As she issues directives and responds to queries from the motor pool, construction workers, the architects, the medical clinic, she resembles a great hitter, say Rod Carew, taking batting practice. She sends the ball sharply in every direction and rarely misses.

During one of these meetings Sheela and I have a curious interchange. "Jim," she says, "Jay"—she gestures toward her husband without turning her head—"thinks you may be from the CIA." I am flabbergasted. "I told him," she continues, "who cares? Are you?"

"How," I ask Sheela, "did you come up with that idea?" The explanation has something to do with my having used a piece of government identification in some transaction. I explain that the identification is from NIMH, not the CIA.

"If you wanted to come and not have sannyasins know who you are," she continues, as if she hadn't heard, "I could have given you red clothes and a mala. The CIA doesn't bother me," she concludes, and returns to the business at hand.

Sheela appears to know as much about who is sleeping with whom—and whether or not it is good—as she does about which crews are overworked and where infighting and power plays are affecting production. Nothing seems too small or too personal for her notice. Often, by the time coordinators of farming or public relations or construction bring a problem to her, she already has it under study. She has, she says mysteriously—and, I think, a bit menacingly—her sources. I am reminded as I watch her in these meetings of the potentate of a small kingdom, or a Mafia don, or the autocratic matriarch of an extremely large Indian joint family, images that in later years will seem particularly vivid and appropriate.

Jayananda, Sheela's graying, rumpled second husband, is often at her side. She uses him as a foil, alternately consulting with him and commenting on his frailties as if he weren't there. "Jay is not very assertive," she will say, or "Jay is worried about the cost of the Hotel Rajneesh in Portland. But I'm not. Jay doesn't like the hits I give him." Jay counsels Sheela about financial matters, calls time at press conferences, makes sure plane connections are met, and suffers Sheela's public hits in pained silence.

Jayananda and K.D., whom Sheela treats with only slightly more respect than her husband, are the only men in the inner circle of ranch administrators. Rajneesh has always put women in leadership positions. He has said that men, preoccupied with wars and dominance, have "utterly failed." So he has given women "a chance." I remember that he said they were better adminstrators, better leaders, because they acted not through logic but "through the heart." Their functioning, he elaborated, "is graceful and insightful, loving and compassionate."

While I sit in Sheela's living room the women who lead the commune drift in and out, like students in a sorority, from the back bedrooms where they sleep, from the sites on the ranch where they supervise work. They deliver their news, order omelets from Sheela's kitchen, and stand at the edge of the ongoing meetings. They are a chorus commenting on the reports that coordinators present, praising Sheela's perceptions or embellishing a point she has made.

In public at least, Vidya, who closed the ashram in Poona, seems first among equals. She is a tidy blond mathematician and computer scientist. Born Jewish in South Africa, she is now president of the Rajneesh Neo-Sannyas International Commune, the organization founded to "put Bhagwan's vision into practice." The others include Ma Prem Padma, a chunky American who directs Magdalena Cafeteria; Ma Anand Puja, the Philippine-born nurse-practitioner whom Sheela selected to care for her dying first husband, Chinmaya, and who is secretary-treasurer of the Rajneesh Medical Corporation; Ma Shanti Bhadra, a small, dark Australian woman who will become treasurer of the Rajneesh Foundation International and vice president of the Rajneesh Medical Corporation; and Ma Prem Savita, a British chartered accountant who, as managing director of Rajneesh Services International, oversees the financial affairs of all of the Rajneesh entities in Oregon and around the world.

When Sheela travels the ranch in her Mercedes, she takes one or more of these women with her. They follow at her heels when she checks a work site, sit with heads inclined toward her in the restaurant for lunch. Though Sheela and Savita and the ranch's lawyers have created a bewildering variety of legally separate entities, it is clear that the same small group of people—under Rajneesh's general guidance and Sheela's direction—run every aspect of life on the ranch.

I visited Rajneeshpuram five more times during the next three years, and growth and change were visible all around. Trailers, barns, greenhouses, warehouses, A-frames, townhouses, construction shacks, recycling yards, tents on platforms, cafeterias, and cultivated fields spread across the valley and up into the ravines—brown, green, tan, white—like cells multiplying in time-lapse photography. Old buildings had new functions: the restaurant where Siddha and I ate on my first visit became the newspaper office, then the city hall. Structures were moved to make way for fields, and what had once been grazing land was built up.

By the spring of 1985 a small city of some twenty-five hundred residents—part frontier town, part hip fantasy, part bureaucratic concoction, and all sannyasin— was in place. K.D. and the rest of the ranch officialdom—Rajneesh Legal Services, the Rajneesh Investment Corporation, the weekly *Rajneesh Times*, and the Rajneesh Modern Car Trust (which held title to the Rolls-Royces that Rajneesh drove)—now had their offices "downtown" on the second floor of Devateerth Shopping Mall (Deva- teerth Bharti was the sannyas name of Rajneesh's merchant father, Babulal Jain). Downstairs was the restaurant named, like all sannyasin eateries around the world, the Zorba the Buddha Rajneesh restaurant. It served good vegetarian food—pasta, soy-based "chicken brie burgers," vegetarian sushi—as well as beer, wine, and liquor. The Noah's Ark Boutique sold jeans and shirts, socks and sweaters, silk dresses and down parkas, all in the approved sannyasin shades of red and purple, pink and violet. There was a "religious" bookstore that offered only Rajneesh's books and tapes, a stereo store, a beauty parlor, and a deli.

The overall effect of the shopping mall was at once precious and funny, claustropho- bic and comforting: sannyasins selling Rajneesh's world to other sannyasins, a com- pany town isolated from the surrounding world by geography, customs, and, most particularly, design. Magazines and newspapers were supposedly available in the deli as well as wine and beer, cheese and nuts, but I never saw a copy of *Time, Newsweek,* the *New York Times,* or the *Oregonian,* the state's largest newspaper. "We only have ten copies of each," I was told, "and they sell out immediately." *Harper's Bazaar, Vogue,* and a variety of sports magazines always seemed to be on the shelves. Because of the hills, radio and TV reception was impossible, except at Jesus Grove, where Sheela had installed a satellite dish.

At night, sannyasins would hang out in or around the mall. Some ate and drank in the restaurant or pizza parlor, others sat around on the benches and steps outside the stores. A few hundred yards away was a disco. The sannyasins, like the Oregonians with whom they were increasingly feuding, drank beer and danced to disco music.

Some of them played at the blackjack tables that the disco, with Sheela's enthusiastic support, had installed. Some went to the no-smoking, no-alcohol "Kids' Disco," which the ranch's teenagers managed.

By the time I made my second trip, in early 1984, all visitors were entering at Mirdad, the reception area (Mirdad was a Sufi mystic). There we registered and received plastic bracelets of the kind patients wear in hospitals. The different colors of the bracelets indicated the different housing accommodations we had and our purpose in being on the ranch: permanent resident, participant in group or training, tourist, and many more. They also revealed to bus drivers and ranch security what areas of the ranch we had access to and how long we were entitled to stay.

On the road between the reception area and the center of town were metal and carpentry shops, garages and warehouses, where sannyasins worked. A little farther along was the Rajneesh International Meditation University (RIMU), the descendant of the Poona university that Karuna had directed. At RIMU extended training in counseling and bodywork as well as group and individual therapies and four daily meditations were available. These were led by the former Poona group leaders, who were now described as spiritual therapists. Nearby, at the airport the sannyasins had built, sat half a dozen "Air Rajneesh" planes—Douglas DC-3's, a Convair 240, a helicopter.

Two hundred yards on the other side of town was the Hotel Rajneesh. Visitors, primarily wealthy sannyasins, their parents, and reporters, could stay for $90 a day for a single, $110 for a double, three cafeteria meals included. Just down the road was Rajneesh Mandir, the 2.2 acre equivalent of Buddha Hall, where several hundred sannyasins did Dynamic Meditation each morning and fifteen thousand people gathered during the annual summer festival for darshan with their Master.

The only private cars allowed were those of a few favored sannyasins, Sheela and Teertha among them. But there were dozens of buses—Rajneeshpuram eventually had one of the largest mass transportation systems in Oregon—plying the roads. From before six in the morning till after eleven at night, they took sannyasins from the trailers and townhouses where they lived in the hills to their work sites, from work sites to cafeterias, Rajneesh Mandir, and the mall. The buses were free to ranch dwellers and to visitors staying on the ranch.

Some 2,000 acres outside the city were under dryland cultivation. There were 60 acres of organic vegetables; 1,800 square feet of greenhouses full of flowers, plants, and sprouts; a vineyard that Neehar, the agricultural coordinator, predicted would produce 20,000 bottles of wine by 1986. There were chickens—2,800 of them—100 beehives producing wildflower honey, and, a bit incongruously, 550 head of grazing beef cattle, which the sannyasins, who maintained a vegetarian diet, would sell.

The sannyasins built a huge earthen dam—Gurdjieff Dam—on which flowers were planted in the form of their new logo: two birds in flight, overlapping, the larger one the Master, the smaller, the disciple. They constructed 140 check dams, reshaped streambeds, and planted thousands of trees to help stop flooding and erosion and to irrigate their crops. All their farming was organic; sewage was biologically treated and purified for irrigation; and 70 percent of everything they used was being recycled. Birds and animals that had fled the ranch years before were returning. I saw a kingfisher and a red-tailed hawk near a stream, and, in the evening, not far from town, some deer.

Just outside the limits of the city of Rajneeshpuram was Rajneesh's house, named Lao-tzu here as in Poona. It was clearly visible from the air but was omitted—for security reasons—from the tourist maps that were handed out at the hotel. In front of the house was a new and ever-expanding complex of garages that were filled to overflowing with Rolls-Royces. Over the years the number of cars increased from 1 to 11 to 23, from 44 to 74. Eventually there would be 93. Some of the cars were standard Silver Spur models, in blue or maroon or green; others were custom-painted with gold flecks or flames, thunderclouds or wild geese. There were several stretch models and an elongated armor-plated one.

As it grew and developed, the ranch received a good deal of press, particularly in Oregon. Its programs of water conservation, its recycling projects, its mass transit system, its organic farming methods, and the energy and intelligence of the sannyasins who had created all this were favorably reported for several years. But these achievements were eclipsed, slowly but inevitably, by the growing fleet of Rolls-Royces. Whenever I told friends or patients that I was going to Rajneeshpuram or to see Bhagwan Shree Rajneesh, it was the Rolls-Royces that came to their minds.

In India Rajneesh had been known as the sex guru, in America he was becoming known as the Rolls-Royce guru. He had always liked good and expensive cars and certainly he must have enjoyed the way the Rolls drove, the comfort and elegance of the interior. But I was sure he enjoyed even more the notoriety and confusion, the anger and envy, that his possession of so many—so absurdly, unnecessarily, outrageously many—of them aroused. Just as he enjoyed provoking the Gandhiites and ascetics in India, so he loved sticking it to America's puritans.

In displaying his wealth so conspicuously, in ignoring accusations of selfishness, Rajneesh was mocking the preconceptions of his New World audience, who—particularly the Christians—tended to associate spirituality with poverty, modesty, charity. He was telling them they were deluded, that wealth was "immensely spiritual," a precondition for spirituality. Poverty was worse than useless, and voluntary poverty an inverted form of pride. He would, some time later, declare himself "the rich man's guru" and condemn charity as a tool for enslaving the poor and a salve for the guilty consciences of the rich.

It seemed to me that at the same time Rajneesh was, a bit more subtly, putting us on. His display of wealth was a lampoon of the far greater wealth and power of the Pope and many of America's TV evangelists. They acted humble, if not poor, kissing the earth and praising the impoverished, emphasizing their own humble beginnings. In so doing, he seemed to be saying, they showed themselves to be hypocrites. Rajneesh was, he would have us believe, at least honest. He praised the wealth he enjoyed, condemned the poverty he avoided. A popular ranch bumper sticker read: "Jesus Saves. Moses Invests. Bhagwan Spends."

Since Rajneesh was unavailable for comment, reporters always asked sannyasins why he had the Rolls-Royces and how they felt about them. None of the sannyasins were sure why their Master liked the Rolls-Royces. In fact, their various answers seemed more like a projective psychological test, more a reflection of their states of mind than of Rajneesh's. Some said the cars were a demonstration of the "great love of Bhagwan's disciples"; others that they exemplified Rajneesh's scorn for the aspirations of the middle class; others, particularly businesspeople, indicated that they were quite a good investment; and a fourth group noted their unmatched value for obtaining publicity. Gopa told me Rajneesh once said privately that he had so many so that when people's mouths were open he could "shove in the truth."

Some sannyasins were annoyed at questions about the Rolls-Royces, but most who cared to comment publicly seemed delighted. One morning when there were already sixty-seven of the cars on the ranch, I watched two grown women and three men ooh and ahhh and laugh and embrace as seven more Rolls-Royces were unloaded from the trailers that had brought them up from California.

I found that my reactions to the cars were always changing as well. Initially I was repulsed—why waste money that could be used for the whole community on idiotic and useless luxury? Later, in an analytic frame of mind, I classified Rajneesh's collecting as a symptom that had existed since childhood. I remembered reading that when he was a boy his mother had sewn extra pockets in his pants so that he could collect more stones from a nearby beach; he had filled his room with them. Later he collected books, then fountain pens, then hats and towels, then watches, each one more expensive and ornate than the last, and now, finally, cars. Always the best and most expensive.

It was, I concluded, a fixation. The prepubescent boy's obsessive collecting—a kind of sublimated, anxiety-ridden greed—was preserved in the middle-aged man. I could only hope he was taking it to its limits, acting it out as one did in the second, cathartic, stage of Dynamic, so that it might lose its hold on him. The stones had lost their meaning and been dumped. He gave away the books and pens. When he was satiated, perhaps the watches and cars would lose their meaning too.

One morning I awakened and imagined a beneficent Bhagwan accumulating Rolls-Royces to show people that infinite wealth was available. All we had to do was live like the lilies in the field, trust existence in each moment, and everything would be given. The Rolls-Royces were simply symbols that those of us too stupid to get the message of the Sermon on the Mount might understand.

Another time I focused on Rajneesh's ethnicity. How many Indian men had I seen who lavished more attention on their Rolex than on their wife? Rolls-Royces? Every maharaja worth the name had owned at least one. The motor car that was the pride of the colonizing British was the ultimate status symbol for the colonized. Rajneesh was simply one-upping all of them.

Then, on another occasion, it hit me that the Rolls-Royces didn't mean anything at all. All the meanings that we were attributing to them were only reflections of our psyches. The cars were what Indians call a leela, a play. Their showy presence was merely a clever reminder that the whole of existence is just a play.

By the summer of 1985 Rancho Rajneesh was the largest and by far the most heavily capitalized, best-known, and most closely observed communal experiment in America. The twenty-five hundred permanent residents were divided according to several administrative categories but united in their devotion to Rajneesh, in their commitment to live out his vision.

Fifteen hundred of them were members of the commune, the Rajneesh Neo-Sannyas International Commune (RNSIC), a religious communal organization whose individual members, like Shakers, paid federal and state taxes on a prorated share of the commune's income. Some commune members "worshiped" as the sannyasins had come to call work, as therapists and teachers at the Rajneesh International Meditation University. Others prepared food in the cafeteria and restaurants, cleaned rooms, maintained roads, and landscaped the grounds. They received free food and lodging, clothes, laundry service, and a small allowance for incidentals.

Most of the other one thousand permanent residents worked in one or another of the tax-paying corporations that did business on the ranch: Rajneesh Travel Inc., Rajneesh Medical Corporation (RMC), Rajneesh Legal Services, and so on. They received a stipend—Siddha, the psychiatrist, for example, was paid $435 a month by his principal employer, RMC—most of which they, in turn, paid to the commune, which provided the same services for them as for its members.

During 1984 and 1985 there were also as many as two thousand long-term visitors, the vast majority sannyasins, on the ranch at any given time. Some were taking courses and workshops at RIMU, doing meditations and receiving training—for weeks or months—in, for example, Rajneesh Rebalancing (an eclectic therapeutic massage) and Rajneesh Counseling. At the university they could participate in groups and have individual counseling sessions with Teertha and Siddha, among two dozen others. Siddha, who still volunteered some time in Security and worked at the Rajneesh Medical Clinic, was also the university's vice chancellor. In addition to his duties as group leader and individual counselor, Teertha was now Rajneesh's surrogate. At Sunday night darshan he would sit in a chair and lean forward placing malas around the necks of new disciples, giving them their sannyas names, as his Master once had done. Later he would answer questions and give advice to visitors and permanent residents alike.

There were many other visitors on the ranch as well. Most were work-study participants in the Rajneesh Humanities Trust (RHT). The RHT people came for three months and paid $400 a month for room and board to live and work alongside commune members in the Buddhafield. They were usually assigned the same kind of simple, physical chores that one might engage in on a retreat at a Zen or Catholic monastery.

The relationship among these entities—RNSIC, RHT, RIMU, RMC, etc., etc.— was complicated enough so that even after several briefings I was still quite confused. Ma Prem Savita (the accountant) and the lawyers had created an incredibly complex structure of corporations, organizations, trusts, and so forth, to enable the sannyasins to create the kind of community they wanted; to conform with state and federal laws and licensing requirements; and to achieve the necessary appearance (if not the substance) of separation of church and state. Thus, Rajneesh Foundation International (RFI), which bought the ranch, transferred it to Rajneesh Investment Corporation (RIC), a for-profit corporation, when it became clear that other than religious functions would take place on the ranch. Similarly, when Rajneesh's desire for Rolls-Royces exceeded the ordinary need for transportation that a religious leader might be supposed to have, an entity separate from the church (RFI), called the Rajneesh Modern Car Trust, was created to hold title to them. And so it went—not according to some grand scheme but rather in adaptive, expedient, ad hoc fashion.

By 1985 more than $130 million and an extraordinary amount of free labor had been invested in the ranch. Some wealthy disciples had given hundreds of thousands, even millions, in cash and securities or Rolls-Royces and jewelry. They had also lent money to the commune, the corporations, the car and jewelry trusts, perhaps as much as $35 million altogether. Working sannyasins, including those who lived at Devadeep, still gave what they could and then some. The sense of urgency continued. Periodically, anxiety-provoking announcements about Rajneesh's frail health were made. The scope of his vision was large. And the threat of nuclear war was not diminishing. Sannyasins wanted to make the ranch as rich as possible as soon as possible, "for Bhagwan"—and, when and if they could go, for themselves.

In Poona, giving had been strongly encouraged. Laxmi and her assistants said it was a sign of "commitment to Bhagwan" and of nonattachment to material things. Wealthy disciples were often given favored treatment—private darshans with Rajneesh, living space in the ashram. But there had also been instances when Laxmi had turned away money. "Keep it child," she might say to an eager donor. "When Laxmi needs it, she will ask." Fund-raising at the ranch, under Sheela's direction, was a highly organized, high-pressure affair. Poona had been a relatively small operation. Costs were low, profits high. The ranch at first produced no money and required enormous sums—for the start-up costs of construction and agriculture, for the maintenance of the workers and the comfort of their Master.

In the early years in Oregon, Ma Yoga Sushila, who had once been a social worker at the Jewish Community Center in Chicago, was the chief fund-raiser. She wined and dined wealthy disciples on the ranch and in Europe, and promised important positions "close to Bhagwan" to large donors. Pleas for the urgency of the cause were liberally spiced with guilt-inducing warnings of disastrous consequences should money not be forthcoming: Bhagwan's health might suffer; the ranch might go under; the new man would have no place to be born. Some sannyasins were reportedly asked to sign over their inheritances, their homes, and their jewelry, or to contact parents from whom they had been estranged to ask for money for "emergencies." It had about it the sound of the least attractive tactics that organized religions had used and then some.

After the first year the ranch itself began to generate money. Perhaps the single largest source of income was the four yearly festivals. There were three smaller festivals—celebrating Rajneesh's enlightenment day in March, his birthday in December, and the enlightenment day of his father (and of all disciples) in September. Each of these attracted several thousand sannyasins to the ranch. The largest celebration, on Master's Day, Guru Poornima, in July, was labeled the Annual World Festival.

For sannyasins everywhere the Annual World Festival quickly became the highlight of the calendar. Like pilgrims heading for Mecca, they saved their money. The ranch encouraged attendance with brochures advertising therapy groups and extended training sessions—in ecology and administration as well as in counseling and bodywork. There were pictures of sannyasins riding horses in the hills and swimming in Krishnamurti Lake and, most important, sitting or dancing in Rajneesh's presence. The ranch also applied more direct pressure. European centers that had been consolidated into large communes were instructed to send and pay for all their members.

Minimum admission for the seven-day festival was $509 for a place in a four-person tent ($796 for three-to-a-tent accommodations, $1,804 for two-to-a-room in the hotel), three cafeteria meals a day, and a seat in Mandir in Rajneesh's presence on several mornings. Therapy groups, food and drink in the restaurant, and souvenirs were extra. The ranch estimated that in 1984 fifteen thousand people came and spent in excess of $10 million.

The sale of Rajneesh's books—there were now more than 350 published collections of his discourses and personal darshans with his disciples in English and Hindi—brought in perhaps $1 million a year. The tapes of his talks and of the original music that had been played at festivals also sold well.

By 1985 the ranch claimed—it was hard to be sure because figures were not infrequently inflated—that some thirty thousand people a year were paying for courses and training programs at RIMU, some of which cost as much as several thousand dollars a month including room and board. Several thousand more people were contributing up to $400 a month to participate in the RHT program. In 1984 the Rajneeshpuram Chamber of Commerce said it took 100,000 mostly curious, sometimes hostile visitors on tours of the ranch at $2 a head. All of these people spent money in the shops and restaurants of Devateerth Mall.

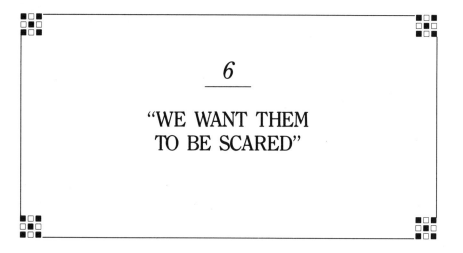

6

"WE WANT THEM TO BE SCARED"

Fed by the energy and money of Rajneesh's disciples, the ranch grew and developed at an incredible pace. Thousands of sannyasins from all over the world wanted to drop "life outside," to do anything necessary to "come home," to "be with Bhagwan," in the healing, enlivening energy of his Buddhafield. When word came that large numbers of Americans would be accepted in the fall 1984 RHT work-study program, that if they worked out they could stay "forever," almost everyone at Devadeep was ready. They quit their jobs, sold or stored their belongings, and gave up their places in the house. Single mothers readied their children for school in Rajneeshpuram. On the ranch they would embrace their "worship" as cleaners or counselors or construction workers and hope for the word that would confirm their status as permanent residents.

The ranch was growing and prospering materially, but so too was another aspect of life at Rajneeshpuram. By early 1984, when I visited for the second time, I could easily see coercion of sannyasins along with the cooperation among them, fear as well as celebration, hostility toward, as well as wariness of, the outside world and outsiders.

Everyday life was, as before, a pleasure. Clerks in the hotel, waiters in the restaurant, men and women tending plants or working construction or driving buses did their jobs with economy, ease, pleasure, and, in many cases, great friendliness. In ordinary intercourse they were relaxed and so was I as I made my way around the ranch, talking with people, catching up with old friends who had recently become commune members, arranging interviews, watching the drive-bys, and hanging out with the adults and children.

On the other hand, the ranch's leaders—Sheela, Vidya, Puja, Karuna, Savita, K.D.—seemed isolated and beleaguered. When we talked privately I felt that they were touchy and defensive, sometimes even belligerent. When they looked directly at me their eyes were like walls. Often I knew that they were lying—to me and to the mass of people in the commune.

Anyone who knew both the sannyasins and the political and social scene in economically depressed, rural central Oregon could have predicted that there would be problems. Those who claim new and superior religious revelations, assemble large numbers of followers in one place, and threaten conventional theological doctrine and sexual mores almost always arouse fear and anger. When they elect, as they often do, to establish their communities in conservative rural areas, the risk is even higher.

When the first sannyasins drove through Antelope in the summer of 1981 on their way to the Big Muddy, there were thirty-nine people in residence in the town. Most were retirees who had been drawn to Antelope by the quiet, the isolation, and the low taxes. Many were born-again Christians. There was a post office and a combined general store and gas station, and an elementary school to which the children of ranchers from the surrounding area went. The few commercial buildings were unused, and many of the homes were for sale.

What the town residents had heard about "the Bhagwan," as they called him, and the sannyasins made them nervous: an Indian guru with hundreds of thousands of disciples and millions of dollars was coming. In short order they were told, apparently by opponents from elsewhere, about the sex and violence in the therapy groups in Poona. Many of them were deeply offended. They were Christians who didn't believe in premarital sex, to say nothing of group orgies. Articles were circulated in which former members and "cult experts" were quoted as saying that the group, like the Chinese communists in Korea in the fifties, used techniques of brainwashing. Some of the older men remembered Korea and what had happened to the prisoners of war there quite well. They also heard that "the Rajneesh," as they called them, might be preparing for "another Jonestown."

Still, the sannyasins and the Oregonians who lived in the area before they came—retired people and ranchers—later insisted that they had initially met each other with good will. "We had nothing against them," Sheela told me. "They had a dream," Bill Dickson, the Antelope postmaster, recalled. "We thought maybe they could make a go of the Muddy." However, when I talked to them, I discovered that most of the leaders in each camp had believed from the beginning that the other barely concealed its malice and secretly harbored prejudice.

When the disciples arrived, they tried at first to allay their neighbors' fears. They wore ordinary clothes without their malas and called themselves by their given names: Sheela Silverman (this was her first husband's family name), John Shelfer, and David Knapp, not Ma Anand Sheela, Swami Prem Jayananda, and Swami Krishna Deva. They gave a party at the Grange in Clarno and invited all the local people. They had a band and there was catered food. They wanted to be good neighbors, they said.

The party impressed some, but it made others, particularly those who stayed late, uneasy. According to Fred Christensen, a nearby rancher, the sannyasins "got so drunk and so free. . . . Sheela sat in my lap . . . guys were dancing with guys . . . one girl took off her blouse. . . . It was," he concluded, "the kind of party I might

Rajneesh at age thirteen (left) in Gadarwara, India, 1944; at twenty (bottom left), in the year before his enlightenment, in Jabalpur, India, 1952; and at twenty-one (bottom right), after his enlightenment, Jabalpur, 1953. (Rajneesh Foundation Europe)

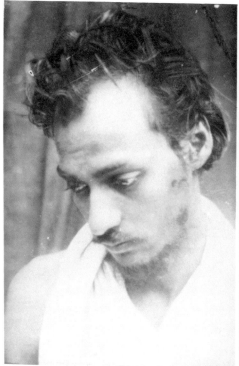

Rajneesh in Bombay with Ma Prem Veena (left) and Shyam Singha
(right), 1972. (Shyam Singha and Rajneesh Foundation Europe)

The gate to the Shree Rajneesh Ashram, Poona. (Howard Josepher)

Rajneesh and Ma Yoga Vivek in the ashram garden, Poona, 1975.
(Rajneesh Foundation Europe)

Ma Krishna Gopa (left) receiving her sannyas name, at the Poona
ashram, 1975. (Rajneesh Foundation Europe)

Swami Anand Bodhisattva (Bodhi) with Ma
Prem Madhuri, who introduced him to
Bhagwan Shree Rajneesh, Poona, 1975.
(Bodhi Raines)

Scene at Laxmi Vilas, typical of the places
sannyasins lived at in Poona. About 1976.
(Bodhi Raines and Rajneesh Foundation
Europe)

Therapy group, Shree Rajneesh Ashram, Poona, about 1977. (Rajneesh Foundation Europe)

Rajneesh at darshan, Poona, spring 1975. (Rajneesh Foundation Europe)

Bhagwan Shree Rajneesh greeting his sannyasins on his birthday,
Buddha Hall, Poona, 1977. (Rajneesh Foundation Europe)

A sannyasin cleans Buddha Hall, Shree Rajneesh Ashram, about 1979.
(Rajneesh Foundation Europe)

Ma Yoga Laxmi (center), Ma Prem Arup (left), and Ma Anand Sheela (right) conducting ashram business in Krishna House, Shree Rajneesh Ashram, about 1978. (Rajneesh Foundation Europe)

Dancing at Devadeep Rajneesh Meditation Center, Washington, D.C. Swami Prem Deben is at right, with shirt off. About 1980. (Devadeep Rajneesh Meditation Center)

Energy darshan, Poona, 1979: Rajneesh touching the third eye of sannyasins. Swami Prem Mahadeva is in lower foreground; Laxmi is at far right. (Rajneesh Foundation Europe)

Energy darshan, Poona, 1979: Bhagwan Shree Rajneesh touches the third eye of sannyasins. His right hand is on the head of Ma Anand Nandan. Laxmi is in background. (Rajneesh Foundation Europe)

Rajneesh arriving on Lear jet in Redmond, Oregon, Ma Yoga Vivek at his right. Summer 1981. (Rajneesh Foundation Europe)

Cultivated fields, vineyards, and Rabiya dairy. Rancho Rajneesh, 1982. (Rajneesh Foundation Europe)

Bhagwan Shree Rajneesh arrives at Gurdjieff Dam with Ma Anand Sheela on his fifty-first birthday, December 11, 1982. (Rajneesh Foundation Europe)

Devateerth Mall, Rajneeshpuram, Oregon, July 1983. (Rajneesh Foundation Europe)

Swami Krishna Deva (left), the mayor of Rajneeshpuram, with Rajneeshpuram security guard. Oregon, 1984. (William Byron Miller, *The Oregonian*)

Scene at drive-by, 1984. Flower-strewn Rolls-Royce with Rajneesh at the wheel, accompanied by security guards. Tents for World Festival are arrayed in front of Rajneesh Mandir. (*The Oregonian*)

Rajneesh greeting the "chosen few" at evening discourse at Lao-tzu House. Ma Anand Sheela is to his right. In front row (front to back) are Swami Ananda Teertha, Swami Satya Vedant, Ma Prem Mukta. Rajneeshpuram, winter 1984. (*The Oregonian*)

Magic takes a break from sweeping up in front of Magdalena Cafeteria. Rajneeshpuram, spring 1985. (James S. Gordon)

Scene at drive-by, June 1985. Bhagwan Shree Rajneesh is in the Rolls-Royce, clapping. White-bearded Bapuji dances with finger cymbals; Ma Yoga Vidya (with dark glasses) walks beside the car. (James S. Gordon)

Bhagwan Shree Rajneesh giving morning discourse at Rajneesh Mandir after Sheela left the ranch. Fall 1985, Rajneeshpuram. (*The Oregonian*)

Rajneesh Times reporters Ma Mary Catherine and Swami Anand Subhuti (left) at a press briefing given by Lieutenant Dean Renfrow of the Oregon State Police and Ma Deva Barkha of the Rajneeshpuram Peace Force. At right is Swami Prem Niren, the new mayor of Rajneeshpuram. Oregon, fall 1985. (Rajneesh Foundation Europe)

Ma Prem Hasya and Swami Dhyan John on the deck at Sanai Grove. Rajneeshpuram, September 1985. (James S. Gordon)

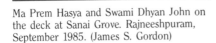

Bhagwan Shree Rajneesh on his way to evening press conference at Sanai Grove, fall 1985, dancing with the twin sons of Ma Prem Mangala (right), Chandan and Kundan. Swami Prem Bodhen is in background. Rajneeshpuram, Oregon. (Rajneesh Foundation Europe)

Jon Bowerman, his wife, Candy, and daughters, Becky and Elizabeth, on their property across the John Day River from Rancho Rajneesh. The Bowermans' house is at left rear. Winter 1986–87. (Allene Hawkins, *Madras Pioneer*)

Bhagwan Shree Rajneesh in police custody at the Athens airport, early morning, March 5, 1986. Swami Devaraj is behind him at his right, Ma Anando at his left. (James S. Gordon)

Bhagwan Shree Rajneesh giving discourse in Bombay, winter 1986. (Rajneesh Foundation Europe)

have gone to early in college," but not one to which he would bring his wife and young children, as he had. He couldn't imagine "what kind of religious group" would throw a party like that.

At the party and in the following weeks, Sheela explained why she and her coreligionists were there in Oregon: "All we want to do on the ranch," she told reporters and townspeople, "is create a lovely farm. We have no therapy programs and no meditation center here. There will be forty people or so on the ranch." The sannyasins said they wanted to use the town of Antelope simply as a reception area and a center for communications until they developed their ranch. By August they had bought two commercial lots and two houses that were for sale. At the same time they began to develop the ranch, obtaining trailer permits from Wasco and Jefferson counties.

By the fall of 1981 the townspeople were becoming increasingly skeptical. These people clearly weren't farmers or ranchers. Why did doctors and lawyers and businessmen—smart, successful people by the look of them—want to farm in such an unpromising place? If they liked Oregon and farming, there was much better land available. And hadn't Sheela said there would only be forty people? Already they heard there were several hundred. And why were so many of them going to settle on a ranch which one or two families and a few hired hands could work? It didn't make sense.

Only months after the sannyasins' arrival, 1000 Friends of Oregon, a public interest group concerned with land use issues, became involved, tying the sannyasin-Antelope issue together with the growing controversy over the ranch itself. If need be, 1000 Friends informed the ranch, it would go to court to oppose the establishment of "nonfarm services" there, and advised the sannyasins to locate the "facilities and services" they needed inside the "urban growth boundary of Antelope."

The 1000 Friends organization had been founded in 1975 with the backing of the late governor Tom McCall. According to some longtime observers of the Oregon political scene, its purpose, like its name, was admirable. The group was concerned with restricting and regulating development, with setting aside large portions of Oregon's countryside for recreational use, with preserving the state's natural beauty. In other areas of the state it had been helpful to farmers whose land had been threatened by uncontrolled development. In Antelope the organization's intervention was more problematic. Because 1000 Friends opposed development of the ranch so vigorously, it made the conflict between the sannyasins and the Antelopians all but inevitable.

By the end of September the sannyasins had purchased a total of nine lots in Antelope. In October, in line with 1000 Friends' "advice," they asked for remodeling and construction permits from the Antelope City Council so that they could build a printing plant and office complex in town.

The purchases and applications escalated the Antelopians' anxieties. What did a printing plant have to do with "a lovely farm"? What else were these people going to spring on them? Could they be trusted at all? The townspeople were also, more concretely, worried about the water needs of the printing plant and office complex and the possible tax increase they might entail. They had moved to Antelope to escape the complexities and economic burdens of urban life that the sannyasins were now threatening to impose on them. The townspeople did their best to delay and frustrate the permit applications.

Tempers ran high. The townspeople and the ranchers felt threatened by the sannyasins' money and power and the phalanx of lawyers they were able, on a moment's notice, to deploy. Some of them became vocal in their criticism to the press, close-mouthed with the sannyasins. No, the sannyasins hadn't done anything illegal — yet — but there was something wrong about them. They had lied. They didn't seem to care about anyone but themselves. They were, well, dangerous.

During this time, more local people began to feel that the sannyasins were treating them in a condescending and contemptuous way. Jon Bowerman, a rancher with property bordering on Rancho Rajneesh, traced his negative feelings to a Regional Planning Council meeting in late 1981. Bowerman, the son of Nike track shoes founder Bill Bowerman, was an independent sort, a part-time poet and saddle bronc rider who had once coached the U.S. women's Olympic ski team. He preferred to live and let live. After years of traveling he now wanted to make his home on a ranch near the land his family had settled a hundred years before.

When some people — neighbors and friends of his, including Fred Christensen and his wife, Ruth — asked Jon Bowerman to sign a petition they had drawn up against the incorporation of a city on Rancho Rajneesh, he refused. He liked John Shelfer, whom he had met several times and said he wasn't concerned about the "red people" (they had begun to wear their sannyasin clothes) and their religion. The Planning Council meeting changed all that.

"The Rajneesh came first," he told me, "maybe a hundred of them. They filled all the seats." The local residents, mostly older people, "were forced to stand." According to Bowerman, when they tried to speak, the sannyasins ridiculed them. After the meeting Bowerman was angry at "the Rajneesh," angry at their bad manners, particularly toward older people, angry at their lack of neighborliness.

By this time the sannyasins were also exasperated. Why, they asked, were these people resisting what were, after all, routine requests for building permits? They didn't have designs on Antelope. In fact, they were seeking permission to incorporate a city on the ranch, to move all their facilities there; but, particularly given the opposition of 1000 Friends, that would take time. Compromises were suggested, attempted, and broke down. The sannyasins took legal action and in April 1982 the Wasco County Circuit Court, agreeing with their contentions, ordered the Antelope council to issue the permits.

Meanwhile, the council had set an April 15, 1982, date for holding an election to disincorporate the city of Antelope. If nothing else worked, this would frustrate the sannyasins' intentions. If Antelope wasn't legally a city, then it couldn't be an appropriate, urban, location for the kind of buildings the sannyasins wanted.

As they prepared for the disincorporation election, the townspeople became more combative. They condemned the sannyasins to the newspaper and TV reporters who had begun to flock to the town, and they said they believed it was "better to be dead than red." The sannyasins, with the law and money and city sophistication on their side, pushed ahead. They bought the Antelope General Store, refurbished it, and renamed it the Zorba the Buddha Café. And they bought more houses: "We'll buy up all the town we need," Sheela reportedly said. More sannyasins moved into Antelope, thereby confirming the fears of those who had believed all along that they planned to take over. And on April 15, 1982, the sannyasins, by then a majority of the Antelope citizenry, defeated the disincorporation proposal 55 to 42.

At the same time that the opponents were lining up in Antelope there was another battle taking place that focused on the ranch itself. The sannyasins should seek exceptions from the land use laws, 1000 Friends had maintained, for any nonrural building they wanted to do on the ranch. The sannyasins didn't want to go through the exception process; it was untried and potentially long and complicated. The exceptions might not be granted, and, if granted, could be challenged. Instead they decided, with the advice of their own land use experts, to go ahead with their plans to incorporate a city on the ranch. Then they could issue permits for whatever structures the community decided on.

In October 1981 the sannyasins asked the Wasco County Court/Commission to allow them to hold an election to incorporate 2,135 acres of their poorest farmland as a city. A letter was sent by 1000 Friends to the Court/Commission, opposing the incorporation. By a two-to-one vote the commission granted the sannyasins' petition in November. The decision was questioned after it turned out that one of the commissioners who had voted in favor of the petition, Rick Cantrell, had made a favorable cattle deal with the sannyasins. After an investigation by an ethics commission, Cantrell was cleared of conflict-of-interest charges. On May 18, 1982, the new settlers voted 154 to 0 to incorporate the city, to be known as Rajneeshpuram.

Now 1000 Friends moved to the state level. At the group's urging the Oregon Land Conservation and Development Commission adopted an administrative rule: "A new city must comply with land use laws; if that city is on farm or forest land, an exception must be made." The rule was retroactive to August 1981, three months before the sannyasins' petition to incorporate was approved, and only affected the city of Rajneeshpuram.

The Land Use Board of Appeals then declared that the Wasco County Court/Commission had acted improperly in approving the incorporation of Rajneeshpuram, even though it had been done in accordance with the operative laws. At 1000 Friends' petition, a Wasco County Court judge restrained Rajneeshpuram from issuing any more building permits. Anticipating these moves, the city had issued all the permits it would need for some time. The struggle over incorporation continued as each side appealed decisions that went against it. In the summer of 1985 the Oregon Supreme Court ruled that state land use laws did not prohibit incorporation. Other issues involving annexation of land to Rajneeshpuram and a legal challenge to the Cantrell ruling were not resolved.

Meanwhile, by fall 1982 the sannyasins had taken over the Antelope city government. Initially they intended to elect only a majority to the city council and not to challenge the older residents' candidate for mayor. They changed their minds about the mayoral election when the other candidate, Don Smith, said he thought he would represent only the views of the older residents.

Karuna, the educator who had organized the university program in Poona, was elected mayor of Antelope. When, after the election, two of the three non-sannyasin council members refused to serve, the sannyasins found themselves in total control. The city council was now composed of five sannyasins and John Silvertooth Stewart. Silvertooth Stewart was a young descendant of the John Silvertooth who ran a bar in Antelope when it was a stop on the stagecoach run between The Dalles and Canyon City. He thought of himself as an open-minded man and was willing to act as a "mediator between the old-timers and the Rajneesh." Initially he felt that "people were picking on" the sannyasins.

Not long after his election Silvertooth Stewart went through the trash in the city dump. "I was," he told me cryptically, "looking for clues about what was going on in Antelope." He found minutes of coordinators' meetings in Rajneeshpuram in which Rajneesh had reportedly said sannyasins might need to be "brutal" with former ranch employee Bob Harvey, a non-sannyasin. "I may be a dumb Oregonian, but I know what 'brutal' means." After eight months on the council listening, watching, and waiting, he quit.

During this time, the council granted sannyasin corporations the building permits they had asked for. Later it would contract with the Rajneeshpuram Peace Force (police force) for protection, and levy sizable taxes, reportedly up to $1200 per year per household, to cover the improvements that were being made. The remaining local residents objected strenuously. "Used to be if we wanted something done," Jim Opray, a retired sheetmetal worker recalled, "we'd just get together, chip in, and do it."

One evening in early 1984 I go with Subhuti, a reporter for the *Rajneesh Times*, to a now all-sannyasin council meeting. The meeting begins with a bad joke (jokes, not necessarily bad ones, are now apparently required to begin and end city council meetings). The main business that evening is a proposal to change the names of the streets in Antelope. The familiar names of ranchers, Indian fighters, and timber barons are to be supplanted by names of saints and sages: Mevlana Bhagwan, Kabir Road, and Gurdjieff-Bennett Drive.

"No one around here knows those people," one old woman complains, and then plaintively, "What's the matter with the old names?" Karuna, whom I knew in Poona as soft and gentle, swiftly gavels her into silence, as if she were a small child. (A few months later the council would change the name of the town itself. Antelope would henceforth be Rajneesh.)

After the meeting, back in Rajneeshpuram, I tell Subhuti that the sannyasins' behavior seemed petty and ugly. I am ashamed for them and angry with them. Subhuti, who in pre-sannyasin days was a political reporter in England, says he can see my point. On the other hand, I simply haven't been through what the sannyasins have. The locals have fought them every step of the way and have refused attempts at compromise, even though what the sannyasins are doing is legal. Besides, so many of those people have chosen to leave that the sannyasins are now 80 percent of the population. Why shouldn't they change the names?

I say that's not the point at all. It is the smugness that bothers me, the absence of grace in victory, the lack of any kind of self-critical check on their childish vengefulness. On top of that, the behavior seems so counterproductive and self-defeating. Any local person who was at that meeting or who hears about it afterward will not easily forgive. The rest of the state, already inflamed by the sannyasins' high-handed tactics in Antelope, will simply take the name changes as yet another gratuitous insult. What is the point? Subhuti doesn't, he confesses, really have an answer.

The next day K.D. does. The sannyasins, he explains, are simply "a mirror" to the local people, forcing them to see the aggression that they ordinarily conceal with politeness and politics. The sannyasins are acting spontaneously, responding to the situation, refusing to play the hypocrite's game of conciliation and cooperation. I suggest to K.D. that he is casting the sannyasins in the role of therapist, or indeed Master, with the locals as patients or disciples. It is an encounter group, but they have never signed up. He goes on, ignoring me: "The kinds of things we're going to provoke in people are going to shake them to their roots. It's the birth of another religion, but the impact of Jesus or Buddha is nothing compared to what the media can create."

Though it might seem insensitive to me, the sannyasins, he concludes, are actually being more respectful, more compassionate, than their opponents. "Bhagwan says, 'If someone hits you on the cheek, don't turn the other. Weakness is masochistic. Hit him back on both and maybe that will end it.' " As I listen I am reminded both of Rajneesh's debt to Nietzsche—"A little revenge is more human than no revenge"—and of the increasingly mindless way in which sannyasins appear to be parroting their Master. The assumption seems to be that Rajneesh and his sannyasins are the sole possessors of the truth, that their actions are by definition unquestionable, as empty of motive and neurosis as the mirror to which K.D. has compared them. It seems to me that at this point it makes just as much sense to see the townspeople's reactions—the fear and anger and outrage—as reasonable responses to the sannyasins' aggressive and deceptive behavior.

Yet another point of contention involved the school in Antelope. This battle was as complicated as the struggle for Antelope itself and even more filled with misunderstanding, overreaction, and venom. When it ended, in 1983, sannyasins were fully in charge of the local school, which was expanded to include all grades from kindergarten to twelfth and renamed the Lincoln School. The non-sannyasins in the Antelope school district had not wanted their children to be taught by "followers of the Bhagwan" and had withdrawn their children. They now bused them to Madras, more than forty-five minutes away. Meanwhile, the sannyasins had, on a technicality, taken control of the school board's administration of funds. Angry at the ranchers' delay in negotiating a compromise, they refused to use any of the $50,000 in carryover funds to help them offset the busing and tuition costs.

These actions troubled many Oregonians, among them Attorney General Dave Frohnmayer, even more than the Antelope takeover. Once again the sannyasins were playing hardball, squeezing everything that the law would let them out of the situation. Only this time there were children, not just adults, involved. The fact that the sannyasins felt aggrieved by the county and state cut no ice with most Oregonians.

By this time local people were being harassed by sannyasins from the ranch and by the Peace Force, in the city of Rajneesh and on their own property. A number, including Margaret Hill, the former mayor of Antelope, complained of frequent and disturbing nighttime patrols by the Peace Force, of sannyasins who would park outside their houses and film them and their visitors. Jon Bowerman said, and several of his neighbors confirmed it, that sannyasins had on a number of occasions and for no apparent reason shined spotlights on his home from across the John Day River at two or three in the morning. On Memorial Day, when local people floated down-river on rafts and inner tubes, sannyasins overflew them in helicopters; during the ranch's own summer festival, armed guards patrolled the borders of the ranch. And one of the local people, Jim Opray, had been arrested by sannyasin officers in his own home on a minor charge that was quickly thrown out of the local county court.

As the legal and procedural struggles escalated, they brought out ugliness in almost everybody involved. By focusing on the letter of land use planning law, for example, 1000 Friends seemed to be going counter to the concern the organization had for the spirit of the law, at least as it applied to the ecological experiment on which the sannyasins were embarked.

The sannyasins reacted to the continuing challenge to their city with personal attacks on the 1000 Friends' staff. When lawyer Mark Greenfield and Paul Gerhardt, a land use planner, went to Rajneeshpuram in June 1983 to look at documents, a raucous, jeering demonstration was held against them. According to an affidavit filed by Gerhardt, at least one angry sannyasin made anti-Semitic remarks to Greenfield: "Are you Jewish? Jews are cheap. We burned Jews in Germany." Both Wadud, the city planner who was showing them the permits they requested, and Sheela later dismissed the remarks as "a joke."

In fact, inflammatory rhetoric—engendered by fear, fed by the sannyasins' bullying, and fanned by the perceived political advantage of opposing "the Bhagwan" and his sannyasins—had marked every step of the controversy. Early in the dispute, Donna Quick, a former Antelope City Council member, called the sannyasins "criminal" in a letter to a Beaverton, Oregon, paper and suggested that they be "slaughtered." Even experienced politicians were not immune to what amounted to Rajneeshophobia. Oregon governor Victor Atiyeh suggested early in their stay that "if old-time Ore-gonians don't like them, they [sannyasins] should leave the state." And the state's senior U.S. senator, Mark Hatfield (who concurred with the decision of the Antelope council to seek disincorporation), assured a correspondent, "We'll continue to do everything appropriate to make sure that the Bhagwan and the Rajneesh community are scrutinized to the fullest extent of the law."

At every opportunity Sheela upped the rhetorical ante. Sometimes she spluttered and blustered incoherently. In interviews with the press and on local and network television, she attacked anyone who disagreed with her, called them all "bigots," "racists," and "fascists." Questioned about it, she said, "Well, they are, aren't they?" In one interview on ABC's "Nightline," while an embarrassed Ted Koppel tried vainly to keep some semblance of order, Sheela shouted down local Oregon state representative Wayne Fawbush. She called him "Mr. Fascist" and told him that he was "full of shit." The media happily recorded Sheela's pronouncements. Popular antagonism escalated, and new attacks, verbal and legal, were launched against both her and the people she represented. When I was in Oregon in the spring of 1985, a song titled "Shut Up Sheela" was receiving considerable airplay.

By 1985 most of the older residents had left the town of Antelope. Those who remained, and many of the ranchers in the surrounding countryside, were fearful and bitter. Sheela, and by extension the sannyasins, had shown their contempt for everything these people held dear: Christianity, the sanctity of the family, local tradition, sexual modesty, and a quiet, rural way of life. Both Jon Bowerman's wife, Candy, and Ruth Christensen told me how disturbed they were by the ranch's policy of separating children at age five from their natural parents: "The children aren't allowed to live with their parents because they want them communalized." "The Bhagwan," Ruth Christensen went on, "encouraged his sannyasins to allow their children to have sex and to watch them make love."

Virtually all the local people regarded the sannyasins as unscrupulous and untrustworthy. "In the past three years," Fred Christensen noted, "every time they talked, it turned out to be a lie. They didn't want Antelope and now they run it. They said they wanted a farm and now they have a city." Area residents were uneasy about the arms the sannyasins had begun to brandish—"not hunting rifles, semiautomatic weapons"—and the ideology their leaders purveyed.

In October 1983, at the request of the legislature, the Oregon attorney general, Dave Frohnmayer, issued an "advisory opinion" concerning the "religious nature" of Rajneeshpuram. The city, he maintained, violated both the state and federal constitutions' guarantee of the separation of church and state. There was a "total fusion of government and religious functions." Therefore, "this city is fundamentally incapable of behaving as a city."

Although the opinion did not have the force of law, the attorney general acted on it. He recommended that Governor Atiyeh sign a 1983 bill that withheld revenue-sharing funds from Rajneeshpuram. He denied the Rajneeshpuram Peace Force access to the computer banks of the Oregon Law Enforcement Data System, which would in turn prevent the Peace Force from obtaining information from the FBI's National Crime Information Center.

While the state was concerned about "the pervasive and unavoidable" influence of religion on Rajneeshpuram, the U.S. Immigration and Naturalization Service (INS) was denying Rajneesh preferential status as a religious worker. The INS maintained that even if he was one, his poor health and public silence kept him from acting in this capacity. At the same time, the INS refused to change his status from the visitor's visa that he was initially granted (for medical reasons) to permanent resident status.

In the spring of 1984, after receiving thousands of pages of supporting documents, including hundreds of letters of recommendation, many from prominent non-sannyasins, the INS granted Rajneesh preferential status as a religious worker. It didn't rule on his residence application. According to one highly placed official with whom I spoke at the time, the agency had doubts about whether Rajneesh's medical condition actually justified his initial visa. The INS was waiting for a grand jury investigation to determine whether Rajneesh had made false statements on his application in India and America in 1981, and in a subsequent interview, in 1982, with the Portland INS office. An indictment would forestall the need to act on his residency application.

Since 1981 the INS had also been investigating the status of foreign sannyasins and the marriages—perhaps as many as six hundred—that had taken place between sannyasins who were U.S. citizens and those who weren't.

The investigation apparently began with Edwin Meese, who was then counselor to President Reagan. Meese forwarded to the INS a letter that he had received from the father of a sannyasin. It urged an investigation of sannyasins' applications for residency permits. Like most other federal agencies, the INS is quite responsive to the interests of senior White House officials. The INS was in any case disposed to be skeptical of what appeared to be a large number of convenient marriages by followers of a teacher who had repeatedly condemned marriage.

The investigation the service undertook was in many ways clumsy, inadequate, and shortsighted. For a long time the Portland office assigned only one full-time agent, Tom Casey, to the sannyasins' case. The sannyasins, meanwhile, had orchestrated a complex strategy to enable disciples to remain in the country. When Casey came to the ranch in search of people who were in the country illegally, they were hidden on remote corners of the property. Sannyasins who wanted to extend their visas—and who wanted to avoid close scrutiny of their applications, which would reveal they were workers in Rajneeshpuram, not tourists—applied through the INS's Houston office. Some—particularly visible members of the ranch's leadership, like Arup, Krishna Deva, Isabel, and Swami Prem Niren (probably the ranch's most skillful attorney)—were married amidst great fanfare in Rajneeshpuram. But most sannyasins were, at the ranch administration's direction, flying all over the country. In St. Louis and Albany, Boston and Seattle, they took off their malas and their colors and participated in quiet ceremonies designed to link Americans with foreigners who were deemed important to the ranch.

As Casey, who knew he was being outflanked, became more frustrated, he became excessively zealous, even threatening. Potential witnesses were allegedly intimidated: a frail and ailing Laxmi reported having been pushed around by INS agents; according to a well-documented story in the *Oregonian*, attempts were made to persuade the New Mexico Board of Medical Examiners to deny ex-sannyasin physician Trevor Hawkins his license until he testified against the ranch. Later, a ranch Freedom of Information request unearthed an internal INS memo of April 8, 1983, which confirmed the sannyasins' charges of prejudice. "Perhaps this is wishful thinking," the memo read, "but there is speculation that possibly the pressure applied by the Service to the immigration situation of the [Rajneesh] organization may cause them to pick up stakes and leave the United States."

During his three-and-one-half-year "silence" Rajneesh was still very much the center of life on the ranch that had been created to put his vision into practice. His drive-bys were as much the high point and pivot of each day as his morning discourses and evening darshans had been in Poona. Four celebrations focusing on Rajneesh or commemorating events in his life highlighted the sannyasin calendar. At these times disciples from all over the world came for silent communion with him.

Rajneesh also continued to communicate verbally with his sannyasins. He did this primarily through daily conferences with Sheela. And of course there were conversations with those who cared for him, among them Vivek, Devaraj, and Devageet. Vivek, his long-suffering caretaker and sometime lover, was closest to him and most protective of him. Devaraj, the handsome, wild-eyed British doctor, weighed and measured the food for his diabetic diet, prescribed and regulated his considerable intake of medicines for back pain, diabetes, asthma. Devageet, the dentist, administered nitrous oxide to his Master and listened lovingly to his rambling, gas induced monologues.

Rajneesh called Vivek by the name Gudia, which was his nickname for his childhood girlfriend, Shashi. He had given the doctor and dentist—a quick, goofy pair whose humor was halfway between Abbott and Costello and "Monty Python"—the surname Bharti, the same as his father's. Gudia, Raj Bharti, and Geet Bharti. With them Rajneesh could relax.

There were also meetings and talks with other disciples, most frequently, according to several sannyasins, with women with whom he had a sexual relationship and with wealthy donors. Occasionally he saw a non-sannyasin visitor. Among them were Kirk Braun, a sympathetic Oregon journalist who subsequently wrote a highly favorable book on ranch life, and Bob Davis, who had been executive assistant to Governor Tom McCall and was for a while retained by the sannyasins as a lobbyist and public relations consultant.

According to Sheela, and to Davis, Rajneesh was kept apprised, at least in general terms, of both the ranch's development and its enlarging struggles with the Oregonians. Nor does he seem to have been a passive participant in this process. In my first meeting with her on the ranch, Sheela said that he had repeatedly urged her, and other ranch spokespersons, to be more "assertive" in their dealings with the authorities. In the minutes of the January 9, 1983, coordinators' meeting, there was a note that "Bhagwan called Jay [Jayananda] and Isabel to tell them 'we have to be 100% supportive and because we are a minority we have to be assertive and very together to survive.' " On a number of occasions Rajneesh was the final arbiter of important ranch positions and decisions: he decided to terminate Davis's contract, because he disagreed with the lobbyist's policy of accommodation; when Sheela's power was challenged by Laxmi and Deeksha he supported her; and when Frohnmayer later brought a suit claiming that the establishment of Rajneeshpuram violated the separation of church and state, Rajneesh told the lawyers who would defend the ranch that the attorney general was correct, there was "no separation of church and state" in Rajneeshpuram.

Through Sheela, Rajneesh also offered the kind of personal advice he had given in darshans in Poona: "Bhagwan," read the minutes of the November 14, 1982, coordinators' meeting, "said it was not good for lovers to work together all day, especially if the woman is the coordinator." And several times he conveyed messages—some mocking and angry, some kindly—to sannyasins who had left the ranch and criticized him and his movement.

On at least three occasions Rajneesh asked Sheela to make public statements on his behalf. Each was urgent, dramatic, and disturbing. All were circulated to sannyasins around the world and widely reported in the American, European, and Indian presses. All had a powerful effect on his disciples and the shape of his movement. And though they addressed several different and apparently unrelated issues, each had the effect of reinforcing the other.

The first of these pronouncements came late in 1981, when Rajneesh, through Sheela, announced the formation of the "religion of Rajneeshism," a religion that was later described in a small book, *An Introduction to Rajneeshism*, which combined fragments of Rajneesh's discourses and interviews. It was, according to Karuna, who worked on it, written with his "general guidance." It detailed the tenets of the new religion and its structure. There were to be three categories of ministers — acharyas, arihantas, and siddhas — specific requirements and duties for each, and a mantra to be said while bowing down at the beginning and end of each day. The mantra, first used by members of Buddha's sangha, was called a Gachchhami. It was the inscription one read on the marble pillars at the entrance to the ranch. (*Buddham Sharanam Gachchhami; Sangham Sharanam Gachchhami; Dhammam Sharanam Gachchhami* — I go to the feet of the Awakened One; I go to the feet of the Commune of the Awakened One; I go to the feet of the Ultimate Truth of the Awakened One.)

Many of the sannyasins — who could henceforth be called Rajneeshees — initially felt baffled and betrayed. Above all else, Rajneesh had inveighed against the deadness and hypocrisy of organized religions, their dogmas and prayers and priests. Sannyasins had been drawn to him, in part, because of his iconoclasm. Now he was establishing a structure — complete with prayers, dogma, and several categories of priests — that was as restrictive as any they had grown up in. Sannyasins imagined that legal considerations to which they were not privy must have forced him to turn his communion with them into a religion. Most gagged on the word *Rajneeshee* and many would refuse to use it.

Previously Rajneesh had contrasted "religiousness" with "religion." The former was what he was catalyzing in his disciples. It "happened only when a Buddha or a Krishna or a Mahavira or a Christ is alive." It was a love affair, liberating, shattering, transformative. One could not possess it but was "possessed by it," as a dervish was by dance or a lover by his beloved. Religion, by contrast, was "born . . . when religiousness dies." It was a "corpse" that the believer could manipulate to suit himself. But now Rajneesh was reversing himself, creating a religion — a corpse — of his own. And of course there were reasons. Creating a religion would, he said, give him the opportunity to establish a structure that would enlarge and outlive his relationship with his disciples. Unlike Jesus and Buddha, he noted, he would shape his religion and its organization before he died.

"Rajneeshism," Rajneesh elaborated in an August 1983 interview that was included in *An Introduction to Rajneeshism*, "would be a kind of religiousness, not a dogma, a cult or creed but only a quality of love, silence, meditation and prayerfulness." It was a "religionless religion." He had, he matter-of-factly added, an advantage over the other great spiritual teachers — Jesus, Buddha, Lao-tzu, Krishna — a perspective they lacked. They were unaware of each other. He had come afterward and had learned from their mistakes. His religion, grounded in an understanding of history, would for the first time unite the meditativeness of the Eastern traditions with the activism of the West. It would be available to everyone. All other religions, he announced, "will disappear into Rajneeshism as all the rivers disappear into the ocean."

The creation of a religion was not, it turned out, necessary for immigration or tax purposes. The Rajneesh Foundation International was already classified as a "religious teaching organization." No additional benefits were gained by calling it a religion. Their Master's "religionless religion" was, the sannyasins were forced to conclude, just another contradiction, another device. He had said that at this crucial point in history there were only "two alternatives—suicide or a quantum leap in consciousness which Nietzsche called Superman." Perhaps the religionless religion would somehow help them make this leap.

In September 1983, Rajneesh, through Sheela, "spoke" again. This time he sounded a more apocalyptic note, as he reworded predictions of the sixteenth-century French astrologer and physician Michel Nostradamus: "The period of crisis will be between 1984 and 1999. . . . There will be every kind of destruction on earth including natural catastrophes and man-manufactured autosuicidal efforts. . . . The holocaust is going to be global. . . . There will be floods which have never been known since the time of Noah . . ." The only refuge, Rajneesh explained, hammering home the theme of the Superman, would be within a "Noah's Ark of consciousness." Even if they survived physically, only people with meditative minds would be able to endure the chaos that would follow nuclear war. Each week for months the warning was printed in the pages of the *Rajneesh Times*.

Meanwhile, sannyasins worked to turn the ranch into a literal Noah's Ark. They accelerated their efforts at self-sufficiency, began to fashion—according to K.D.—shelters and caves in the hills, where they could preserve their Master, his books, and themselves in the event of nuclear war. Sannyasins in California, having heard Rajneesh predict the destruction of Los Angeles and San Francisco, closed all but one of the Rajneesh meditation centers there. Many who left flocked to the ranch, though few were allowed to stay for more than several months.

Then, on March 5, 1984, Sheela again issued a statement on Rajneesh's behalf, about AIDS. It was, he said, the "disease with no name" that Nostradamus had predicted. Before the end of the century it could wipe out "two thirds of the world's population." He counseled his sannyasins to take precautions against it: "If a person is ready and can drop sex altogether through understanding and without repression, this is the safest protection from the disease. Or remain with the same partner moving more and more into intimacy and less into sexual activity."

Almost immediately Puja, acting for the Rajneesh Medical Corporation, presented the community with specific guidelines: even those who were monogamous should use rubber surgical gloves for foreplay and condoms for intercourse; there was to be no oral or anal sex; "scrupulous washing after sexual exposure" was mandatory. When, soon after, new research showed that the AIDS virus might be transmitted by saliva, kissing too was prohibited. The feast of fucking was over. The time for fasting had come.

After the initial shock and grumbling, sannyasins at the ranch and around the world went along with the program. Soon there were more precautions: phones and toilet seats were to be sprayed with alcohol before use, as were hands before dining; neither stamps nor thread were to be licked. When the sannyasins left Rajneeshpuram or the other communes and centers, they took their precautions—and their unaccustomed cautiousness—with them. Like orthodox Jews or Hindus, many found it unacceptable to eat out. In their families' and friends' homes they rinsed dishes in bleach and sprayed the toilet seats with alcohol. Many avoided any sexual contact with non-sannyasins.

Rajneesh's communications to his disciples had a function that transcended their immediate messages. Taken together they, and the actions that they precipitated, served to deepen the sannyasins' connection to their Master; to bind them more closely to one another; to separate them from the world outside, which seemed increasingly polluted and threatening.

The issues that Rajneesh focused on and the imagery that he used made me uneasy, in many ways. I agreed that there was a real danger we might, as a species, very soon destroy ourselves and that some change in consciousness, some increased intelligence and compassion, some quantum leap out of greed and fear, nationalism and the old us-them pattern, was necessary to keep us from doing it. And, even in 1984, I was convinced that AIDS was an extraordinarily dangerous disease. Its virus captured the very immune system that was meant to protect us; it was, if not a symptom, at least a metaphor for the destructiveness we were inflicting on ourselves. So far Rajneesh seemed painfully close to the mark.

On the other hand, in prescribing the cure he was in danger of perpetuating the disease. We are about to destroy ourselves as a collectivity, I thought, precisely because we do not recognize how inextricably connected we are to one another; because we believe that it is better to die, even as a species, than to compromise our principles; because we are sure that *we*—communists or capitalists, Muslims or Jews, Catholics or Protestants—are better, more human than *they*; because we have, in Erik Erikson's words, created a "pseudo-speciation." *We* are human and *they* are not.

And here was Rajneesh, making the correct diagnosis but prescribing yet another kind of elitism, another kind of division between *us* and *them*, between the Superman and the herd, between the human and the not-human. We—the Rajneeshees— might "survive the holocaust. . . . The remaining will be monkeys or commit suicide. . . . The remaining don't matter."

The statements about AIDS raised another specter. In this case Rajneesh was far more prescient about the dangers it posed to heterosexuals, as well as homosexuals, than anyone else who was then speaking publicly about it. But the excessive and fearful response of his sannyasins, especially when combined with the doctrine of separatism and supremacy, could produce a dangerous and paranoid mindset: The evil, the disease, is out there. We, who are to be the new humanity, must keep ourselves pure, away from it and them.

In Sheela's hands Rajneesh's words became tools to justify the tactics she had used to establish and enlarge the ranch, the extraordinary measures she would take to protect it from illegal attacks and legal challenges from without and dissent and doubt from within. If the ranch and the other communes were the womb of the new man, the Nietzschean Superman on whom the future of humanity depended, if Rajneesh was his midwife, then any and all measures to insure his and their survival and well-being were justified. The atmosphere of self-protectiveness and secrecy thickened each month. The demands for physical and ideological purity became ever more intense. In time, the ranch became an armed camp with a siege mentality, the "religionless religion" as totalitarian and suppressive as any "cult" I had visited.

Initially Rajneesh had been protected in his house and on his rides in the Rolls-Royces by Bob Harvey, the Big Muddy foreman who had stayed on to help the new settlers; by Jayananda, who also had a gun permit; and by a few unarmed sannyasins.

Sheriff's deputies were deployed and private security hired for the First World Festival in the summer of 1982. In October 1982 the by then incorporated city of Rajneeshpuram created an armed police force, which it called the Peace Force. On July 29, 1983, a bomb exploded at the Hotel Rajneesh in Portland. The explosion caused $180,000 in damage at the Rajneesh Investment Corporation–owned hotel and injured only the suspected bomber, but it caused sannyasins, who feared religious persecution, to increase security exponentially, at both the accessible downtown hotel and the ranch.

By 1984, vehicles on their way to and from the ranch were observed from several guardposts on the road from Antelope (now named Rajneesh). Visitors' cars, clothes, and luggage were sniffed by dogs trained to detect drugs—the sannyasins were wary of agents provocateurs as well as dealers and users—and thoroughly searched.

The Rajneeshpuram Peace Force became a visible and sometimes oppressive presence, on the ranch and in the city of Rajneesh. There were sixteen regular officers and thirty reserves, well trained and increasingly well equipped with pistols, rifles, shotguns, and at least twenty-eight semiautomatic weapons—Uzis, Galil assault rifles, M-1s, riot guns. There were also more than one hundred part-time sannyasin volunteers—like Siddha and Bodhi—in Rajneesh Security, the ranch's "neighborhood watch group." When I first visited the ranch, in August 1982, I saw one man riding shotgun in a car behind Rajneesh. By the fall of 1984, security was far greater and tighter than anything I was accustomed to around the president in Washington, D.C.

When I asked if the display of hardware at drive-bys and near Rajneesh's house wasn't excessive—at once provocative of outsiders and intrusive on the sannyasins' communion with their Master—I was told that it was necessary and judicious to "protect our Master." There had been dozens of written and phoned threats on Rajneesh's life. When I asked to see them Isabel told me I couldn't—Sheela believed that any report about them would simply provoke more. Still, Isabel and K.D. and Vidya and Sheela assured me that they existed. People, they said, had been spotted on the road from Rajneesh with guns. Sannyasins had been beaten up in bars, harassed on the street, and then there was the bombing of the Portland hotel.

Initially most sannyasins had been horrified by the weapons. These were for the most part nonviolent people—antiwar protestors, aging hippies, environmentalists. They did not eat meat and forbade hunting or fishing on their land. They had always believed and been encouraged to believe, by their Master, that he was not subject to harm by his antagonists. The knife in Poona had fallen short. No one had ever hurt him. It was almost an article of faith: "There's such divinity doth hedge a king." But they knew that "people hate Bhagwan and his sannyasins," and they believed that their continued growth and success—and his assault on hypocrisy and mediocrity—might well bring more violence.

That was the way individuals had responded in therapy groups in Poona, the way the larger society reacted in India and now in Oregon. Defenses probed long enough produced explosions of angry resistance. Perhaps, the sannyasins concluded, the guns were necessary. "After a while," several of them assured me, "you hardly notice the Swamis with the automatic weapons." "We want them [potential attackers]," a grim K.D. said, "to know that if any violence is expressed toward us we will defend ourselves. We want them to be scared."

The protectiveness extended to every aspect of life in the commune. Once visitors were on the ranch, their actions were closely scrutinized. Any deviation from customary practice, even walking along the county road, was noted. "Can I help you?" I was asked on many occasions when I needed no assistance. Violations of the rules—taking a picture on private property (virtually everything in Rajneeshpuram except the area in front of Devateerth Mall) or visiting sannyasins in their homes—were swiftly reported to Security. A number of areas that were once routinely accessible to visitors were declared off limits to all but a few.

At times the protectiveness skirted or exceeded the bounds of legality. By mid-1984 some Rajneeshpuram residents were telling me they believed their incoming and outgoing mail was being intercepted, read, and in some cases destroyed. I heard that there was an elite special security team originally composed of twenty-four sannyasins in place; all were ready to "take the law into [their] own hands" if the authorities tried to arrest their Master, to give their lives to protect Rajneesh.

I know that I began to feel myself under scrutiny. I suspected that my calls from the hotel were being monitored, and occasionally I felt uneasy about my physical safety. These people might know how to handle weapons—there had been an impressive and highly publicized display of sannyasin discipline and marksmanship—but I had spent enough time in the West to know that you only carried a gun if you meant to use it. Life on the ranch had begun to take on a deeply paranoid cast, and guns in the hands of paranoid people—or people responsible to paranoid leaders—were very dangerous indeed.

By 1984, Sheela and the others in positions of leadership were acting as if the dangers they perceived from the outside world were also threatening from within. The people whom Sheela trusted or needed were treated with indulgence, allowed to change their jobs when they wished. Others who had happily devoted their lives—working twelve hours a day—to make Rajneesh's vision come true, were treated as potential traitors, subjected to psychological intimidation and verbal assaults. Sannyasins who requested a change of work were routinely accused of "negativity" and often assigned to tasks they liked even less. Those who questioned arbitrary policies on the commune or the aggressiveness toward the Oregonians were told they were being disloyal to the ranch and to Bhagwan.

At the beginning of the fall 1984 RHT program, Sheela called twenty people who had talked among themselves about their concerns to the front of a mass meeting. They were told to pack their bags and leave the ranch that evening. She warned the other RHT participants that they would face the same fate if they too threatened the ranch's "unity."

Everyone on the ranch was now *required* to line up for Rajneesh's daily drive-by and to be, or appear to be, smiling and happy while there. Cleaners were told to report sannyasins who were in their rooms when they should have been working. Sannyasins were expected to report anyone they heard being "negative"—critical of the ranch's policies or Sheela, doubtful of Rajneesh's authority—no matter what the circumstances. People were expected to turn in roommates who didn't use the AIDS precautions.

The independently incorporated *Rajneesh Times* was subjected to continual and sometimes bizarre censorship from Sheela and her confidante, Shanti Bhadra, the RFI treasurer, neither of whom had a statutory relationship to the paper. The paper—its motto was "Positive journalism direct from the source"—continually compared the blissfulness and perfection of ranch life with the banality and degradation of the world outside. Its editorial cartoons depicted the sinister forces arrayed against sannyasins: Attorney General Frohnmayer was a goose-stepping führer; Mark Greenfield, the 1000 Friends attorney, an evil-looking caricature of a Jew; Rajneeshees, distinguished by their malas and casual attitude, were innocent bystanders or victims of these aggressors. On the other hand, nothing critical of the ranch or potentially favorable to its opponents was to be printed; only smiling faces were allowed in photographs; no news briefs on terrorism in the Middle East were allowed for fear of "giving ideas to Oregonians"; the word *hierarchy* was not to be used (even a translation of a Rilke poem about "the hierarchy of angels" was suspect) because there was supposed to be no hierarchy on the ranch.

Everywhere on the ranch language was altered, to make oppression seem like spiritual discipline, coercion a form of caring, and discipleship a kind of permanent second childhood. Work had become "worship" and departments "temples." Coordinators metamorphosed to "moms" who made all decisions for those they supervised and provided them with emotional succor and parental discipline. Sheela was the "big mom." To promote "unity"—and to discourage individual, and potentially critical, thinking—sannyasins were told not to speak of others, particularly decision-makers, in the third person. It was always "we": "When we saw the need to arm ourselves," or, "We decided that all children over five should live apart from their parents." I was reminded of psychiatrist Robert Lifton's description of the "loading of language" in Chinese thought reform, of the party slogans from Orwell's *1984*: "War is Peace. Freedom is Slavery. Ignorance is Strength." In Guyana, Jim Jones was called Dad and his wife was Mom.

Meanwhile, it looked to me as if Sheela was falling apart. At a school board meeting (I wasn't there but later saw the video) in the fall of 1983 at Rajneeshpuram, she seemed out of control. Though she wasn't on the agenda, she had showed up and demanded to speak. She spat out her words with a rage that far exceeded any offense given and demolished adversaries who no longer had any real power to affect, let alone injure, her or the commune. She began by attacking Margaret Hill, the former mayor of Antelope: "Margaret Hill was a teacher," Sheela said. "Look at her face now. She looks retarded." Then she turned, like a gunner looking for a new target, and spotted Marcia Wichelman, whose husband had recently died in a hunting accident, and her two sons. "He [Mr. Wichelman]," Sheela began, "shot himself because she was screwing around with another man." The camera panned to Mrs. Wichelman, whose face and body crumpled as if she herself had been shot. "She might," Sheela went on, as Mrs. Wichelman, supported by her sons, rose to leave, "tell her children the honest truth."

In late 1983 sannyasins told me that Sheela was "really giving hits to the Oregonians." When I arrived on the ranch in February 1984, I expected to find a slightly more aggressive, self-righteous, and paranoid version of the woman I had met a year and a half before. I wasn't prepared for the ailing, obviously drugged person whom I ran into in the Hotel Rajneesh. She clearly belonged in bed—if not in the hospital—but was dragging herself around, inspecting the all but identical decor of the hotel's comfortable but unremarkable rooms—the round bed, bench, armchair, closed circuit television set. Though she wasn't touching them, she looked to me to be drawing strength from the physical presence of Padma and Puja, who accompanied her.

We talked for a while. Sheela told me she had just had a bout of thrombophlebitis, a recurring affliction. We agreed that she was too tired for a formal interview on this trip. I found myself taking on the role of physician, feeling compassion for her, beginning in my mind to formulate a kind of "differential diagnosis." Had she been taking drugs? I wondered. Amphetamines could have been responsible for the paranoid aggressiveness of the Marcia Wichelman episode, and tranquilizers or painkillers might produce the picture I now saw. Or was she caught in some kind of strange psychosomatic cycle? I could eaily imagine that after long periods of intense control on the ranch and unremitting hostility to those outside it, she would go into a state of psychophysiologic exhaustion in which she would be vulnerable to depression—aggression turned inward—and physical illness. Or perhaps it was some combination of drugs and character, the pressures of being a dictatorial leader and the conflict with the outside world.

7

THE SHARE-A-HOME
CAMPAIGN

The tension between the sannyasins and the Oregonians — between what some people were calling the Reds and the Whites — built higher and higher during the heat of the summer of 1984. Compromise and mutual understanding seemed all but impossible. The state and the federal authorities were behaving as if the very existence of the ranch were an affront and a threat to the sovereignty of government and its laws. The ranch, with its assault rifles and its helicopters, was acting as if the physical survival of its inhabitants and not merely of the city of Rajneeshpuram were at stake. Heightening or, depending on one's point of view, parodying the confrontation was the U.S. Navy. During the summer, jets from the Oak Harbor, Washington, Naval Air Station made many low, noisy, and vaguely threatening flights over the ranch.

The Whites were mounting a legal invasion. In the preceding months their advance forces had won small victories. The county commissioners had denied tax-exempt status to Rajneesh Mandir (which the sannyasins said they had originally planned as a greenhouse but later turned into a meeting hall); delayed the permit for the July festival; and voted to repeal Rajneeshpuram's Comprehensive Plan. State and federal authorities had also been stepping up the pressure on the ranch. In May, 1984, the INS referred a criminal case report alleging marriage fraud to the U.S. attorney for Oregon, Charles Turner. In July and August, Turner, acting for the INS, asked for a stay of the immigration cases against sannyasins. He said that the criminal investigation of possible marriage and visa fraud might well result in the presentation of evidence to a federal grand jury. Meanwhile Attorney General Frohnmayer was pressing the church-state case.

The sannyasins, the Reds, for their part had been parrying the administrative threats and preparing a massive legal offensive, against the county, the INS, and the attorney general. They had also been fighting a series of guerrilla actions. Previously they hid sannyasins when county officials were checking on the number of people in residence, and sent foreigners to the hills when INS agent Tom Casey appeared. Now it seemed that they were escalating from passive resistance to obstruction and perhaps, though no one could prove it, from obstruction to criminal aggression.

When Dan Durow, the Wasco County planner, arrived for an inspection of the ranch during the summer, he found the road blocked with heavy equipment that just happened to have broken down there. On August 19, when the three Wasco County commissioners visited Rajneeshpuram, a series of mishaps befell them. First their car had a flat tire. While the men waited for ranch mechanics to find them a suitable substitute, Isabel offered the men water, which Puja, the nurse, brought out for them. Shortly afterward two of the men — Wasco County judge William Hulse, who had been an outspoken opponent of the ranch, and County Commissioner Raymond Matthew, another opponent — became ill, Hulse dangerously so. At the hospital poisoning was suspected but never proved.

Then, from September ninth to twenty-sixth, 751 people in The Dalles came down with poisoning from salmonella typhimurium. The state health office traced bacterial contamination to ten different restaurants. Dr. Larry Foster, the assistant state epidemiologist who headed the investigation, concluded, "The outbreak [in The Dalles] resulted from a low-level outbreak affecting several different food handlers and establishments."

The fact that food handlers became ill before patrons and that patrons contracted the disease on days on which ill food handlers worked seemed to confirm this hypothesis. But it didn't make sense to anyone who examined the facts carefully. Why ten restaurants at the same time, and how could so many food handlers have become ill? If they lived together communally or if there had been a food handlers' picnic it might have fit together. But they didn't and there hadn't been a get-together. The Wasco County Sheriff's Department, the state police, and even the FBI were called in to investigate. None of the agencies found evidence of "tampering," but they did learn that two sannyasins were seen in one of the restaurants just before the outbreak. I found it almost inconceivable that the sannyasins could have been responsible for the poisoning, but many local people were sure that "somehow the Rajneesh did it."

The conflict between the ranch and the outside world, the Reds and the Whites, came to a climax with the Share-A-Home program. Between September 2 and October 12, 1984, the Rajneesh Humanities Trust brought thirty-seven hundred "street people" to the ranch, to "share our homes." Sheela described this massive effort — recruiters and buses were dispatched to forty-one cities across the country — as "humanitarian," but there was clearly another motive. The sannyasins wanted to elect a candidate to the Wasco County Court/Commission, the body that decided issues — most particularly the land use question — that might well determine whether Rajneeshpuram remained a city and the ranch a viable entity.

A few months before, the ranch stipulated that fall participants in the RHT's work program should be American citizens. Aggressive recruiting took place. Scholarships were offered for those who could not pay the regular monthly fee. Hints were given that after three months the RHT participants would be able to stay on the ranch "forever."

Now the ranch, with uncharacteristic beneficence, was bringing in the homeless, "sharing our abundance" with them. When I discovered that they were accepting only homeless people who were over eighteen and American citizens and without a record of felonies, everything fell into place. These homeless, as well as the RHT participants, were potential voters. They would swell the numbers of loyalists in the November election: under Oregon's liberal registration law only a twenty-day residency was required to qualify to vote.

At first I was amazed at the grandiosity and impracticality of the scheme. The sannyasins would need at least five thousand voters in addition to the permanent residents and RHT people to affect the election. How could they possibly accommodate so many and such potentially unruly people? What made them think that once these people were on the ranch they would want to stay?

Later, as I watched the first TV news footage of sannyasins approaching street people in Portland, I was alternately fascinated and angered by the program's bizarre mixture of cynicism and generosity. The sannyasins were so obviously using the street people, treating them as if they were cattle to be moved, numbers to be toted up, unwitting soldiers to be thrown in the face of the enemy Oregonians. On the other hand, the ranch was also, inevitably, giving them an opportunity. It seemed to me that in trying to accommodate these people the sannyasins would have to offer them some productive role in life on the ranch. Perhaps some of them really would find a home there. And maybe they in turn would be good for the ranch. The presence of these poor people, many of them black and brown, would add leaven to a self-satisfied, over-privileged community, and challenge the sannyasins' insularity.

━━━━━━━━━━━━━━■□━━━━━━━━━━━━
□■

When the Share-A-Home recruiters come to Washington, D.C., I arrange to spend a day with two of them, Anado and Mitzi. Anado is a stocky blond man with glasses and a full beard. He grew up in Oklahoma, where his father was a physician. He tells me he left home for the Haight-Ashbury district in San Francisco in 1967 during the "Summer of Love." He slept in crash pads and in the park and took drugs and went to parties. I try to imagine him then, a twenty-year-old aspiring poet, a middle-class hippie, sitting on the cushions in the waiting room of the Haight Ashbury Free Clinic, where I worked as a volunteer physician. Anado found the Haight a place where you could "do and be anything," a world larger and more various than the one in which he had grown up. Until that summer, he tells me, he never "sat at the table with a black person," except for his maid.

When the scene in the Haight fell apart, Anado moved to New York's Lower East Side. He drove a cab for seven and a half years, went to Poona in late 1978, "just after Jonestown," and from there to the ranch. He worked in the kitchen at Magdalena Cafeteria for a year and a half, "preparing food for people you love, with love." "It's celebration, it's everything," he says, including me with his eyes, "I—and probably you too—had always hoped for in the Haight."

Mitzi nods her head while Anado talks. She "was an idealist too," "a Jewish city girl" who had worked for the B'nai Brith Anti-Defamation League but became dissatisfied: "I was *talking* about brotherhood. This—being on the ranch, bringing in the street people—is *living* it." Her recruiting reminds her of what she has read about the civil rights movement of the early sixties, people standing up for themselves, creating and sharing a community that is politically active, morally responsible.

It does feel a bit like those heady early days of the civil rights movement, I think, when those of us who had too much privilege saw how our fate was connected to those who had so little, and acted on it. We *knew* we were right. And it felt good. Even the situation—rich and poor people, black and white—is reminiscent. Wait a minute! I feel like I'm dreaming. In the South we were helping black people with *their* struggle. These sannyasins are hustling the street people, moving them out to Oregon for their own purposes.

When I point this out, Anado and Mitzi earnestly deny that they are interested in the votes of the street people. I wonder if they have swallowed the party line and conned themselves so they can believe they are acting selflessly.

I go with them as they make the rounds of parks where homeless men and women "chill out," the churches and shelters where they eat and sleep. As I go from place to place with Anado and Mitzi, I have the sense that I am traveling with missionaries. They are out to claim bodies, not to save souls, but the fervor is very similar. "It's a crime-free, drug-free city, man," Anado announces to the raggedly dressed, half-stoned black men who are waiting for lunch at the Zacchaeus Mission in Northwest D.C. "We want you to come to a city where Martin Luther King's dream is coming true. We give you food, a place to stay, a pack of cigarettes a day, and two beers at night, and we give you the chance to make a life with us."

"That sounds like slave labor," one grizzled old man offers.

"No slaves there, man," Anado is slipping into street talk. "Three regular meals, three people to a room."

"You must be some kind of goddamn religious charity."

"No way," says Anado sincerely, omitting, I notice, the recent creation of Rajneeshism the religion. "We're the Rajneesh Humanities Trust. We want people to take responsibility for themselves." He shows pictures of sannyasins building Gurdjieff Dam and putting up A-frames and eating at Magdalena. A few men put their names on forms and take information about where and when to meet the buses that will go to Oregon. We move on.

We stop at a storefront where food and clothing are being handed out. Anado and Mitzi each pitches to groups of two or three.

"Do you have to work?" a reasonably fit young man asks.

"No way," Anado answers, "only if you want to."

"What about—you know—pussy?"

"Yeah," says Anado, a bit exasperated but still trying to please, "that too, if the ladies want it—all you can handle."

A young woman comes out of the building to shoo us away. "These people don't want to hear about your ranch. I saw pictures of your group in India, the sex and violence. You don't care about these people. You're going to use them to vote and throw them out." Anado begins to protest.

"I heard you don't even give them return tickets." The sannyasins have stopped giving return tickets on September 23, because they say that street people are taking the trip out to the ranch as a lark. "What are they going to do if they don't fit in?"

"Same thing," Anado says, "as they do any other place, figure out how to get where they want to go."

Another young man, a stocking cap pulled down almost over his eyes, steps forward. "Do you supply everything?" he says softly.

"Yes," Anado answers, "clothes, food, a place to stay, cigarettes. . . ."

"Everything?" with a gap-toothed grin.

"Yes, everything."

"Yeah, I got you," he says, and gives Anado a soft, backhanded rap on his upper arm.

We drive back to Devadeep, where Anado and Mitzi will meet the other recruiters who have been in D.C. Anado has just read and taken comfort from Sheela's statement in the *Los Angeles Times*. She has said, "If the state harms one of my people, I will have fifteen of their heads." He is trying to explain why it means so much to him. "Sheela is like a spark to all of us, like a mom. There are so many moms on the ranch, so much female energy and nourishment. It brings out the men's female energy, it brings out our softness. When you finish work at the end of the day," he tells me, grinning, "you come back and your room is spotlessly clean and clothes are laid out on your bed, folded. You feel the care." There is about Anado the quality of a child who finally feels safe and wants to stay that way. "We have to protect ourselves from those who call themselves Christians, the ones who warn the street people against us, who threaten to bomb our homes and kill us. We have to stand up to them."

The street people going to Oregon remind her, Mitzi says, of "the story in the Bible of the Master asking the beggars to a feast."

Anado disagrees. "Bhagwan's not asking, this is not religious."

Mitzi persists. "This story is one of Bhagwan's favorites," she begins, then changes the image. The street people boarding the bus on a few hours' notice, leaving behind the streets, the drugs, the crime, remind her of herself, of middle-class Americans leaving their jobs and homes, clothes and names, putting on red and a mala, becoming sannyasins.

Anado concurs. "The bottom end of the social scale," he concludes, "is about as savory as the upper end. These people are ready, eager, and ripe for a new way. They know this one hasn't worked, no matter how they may have tried."

It turns out that a number of the "new friends" whom the sannyasins recruit are not actually street people or homeless. Most of those who will end up staying on the ranch for more than a few weeks are working poor, unemployed, underemployed, or temporarily down and out. But, as Anado suggests, they are all dissatisfied with their lives, vulnerable to violence on the street or in their neighborhood, and lonely. If the sannyasins are, as Krishna Deva has said, "dropouts from the top of the social ladder," the new friends have barely been holding on to its bottom rungs.

When push comes to shove, each of the recruits decides he (almost all of them are men) is ready to try something new. While I watch and listen, they brush aside the worries of some of the people who run the shelters they stay in, the specter of Jonestown that is continually raised. "Shit," one young street dude says to me, "this is Oregon, not Guyana jungle. They got roads there." "Maybe, just maybe," another says, as we stand together watching Anado tell about the drug-free, crime-free city, "these people are for real."

Two days later I am in Lafayette Park, across from the White House, flanked by antinuclear signs and the tents that the Community for Creative Non-Violence, Mitch Snyder's organization, has set up to protest budget cuts that affect the poor and homeless. The men we've talked to are leaving on the rented Trailways bus that evening, along with some of the sannyasins from Devadeep. They will stop in Pittsburgh, Cleveland, Denver, Salt Lake City, and Boise before they arrive at Rajneeshpuram.

Some of the men have obviously made an effort to clean up. There are small touches, a clean shirt, a face freshly nicked from shaving, hair slicked down. Some men have bedrolls. A few are muttering to themselves, and a few more are shaking badly. One black man in his forties tells me he hasn't worked for months. Another, who claims to be his brother, is more foggy; he just doesn't know when he last worked. They are all making an effort to sober up or taper down, to get themselves together. And they are clearly nervous.

I talk with the men. Some believe that they are getting a round-trip ticket, though they have signed papers that state this isn't so. Others aren't quite sure where they're going. Anado avoids me this evening. He paces nervously while I talk to the men and refuses to let me look at the form they have signed. "I've got no extra copies," he says. I tell him I don't want to keep it, but he mumbles and walks away.

Another sannyasin, a man I haven't seen before who seems to be in charge, walks over. I have the strange sense that he is measuring me as if preparing for a fight. He asks me to leave.

"You're making these people nervous."

"These people are nervous about going. I've talked to them before, with Anado and Mitzi. You and Anado are more nervous than they are. Besides, this is Lafayette Park!"

The man starts up again.

Deben, the Devadeep leader, who is going on the bus, comes over and cools things out, explains that I am a friend.

The man apologizes, "I was an asshole," he says. But his defensiveness is still palpable.

"Why not show the form to someone who asks? Why act so suspicious?"

"We don't care what people think," he says, not responding to the question. "At first we bent over backwards in Oregon. People kicked us. Now we stand up straight and tell people off. I sometimes shake my head when I hear Sheela on TV, but I know she's doing it to protect us. I'd do anything to protect the commune. It's my life." Pause. "Short of breaking the law. I'm secure," he goes on, though I haven't suggested he isn't. "I don't care about publicity or what anyone says, I don't need it to live my life, it does nothing for me."

He is protesting too much, far too aggressively. It makes me sad. It's clear that anyone who is not totally with him, who has any questions, including me, is, at least in his mind, against him. I can only guess that he's so defensive because he feels forced to defend behavior that he knows to be dishonest.

The Share-A-Home program, which for a few weeks attracts nightly attention on television and radio, deeply disturbs many of the ranch's neighbors. They *know* that there is no other reason for "the rich Reds to love the poor blacks" than the elections. "These people," one cowboy tells me over a beer, "are the most selfish creatures on God's earth." And the local people can add. If all the ranch residents and all the sannyasin participants in the RHT program and all the "new friends" vote as a bloc for a candidate of their own, they may well elect that person to the Wasco County Court/Commission. "The Rajneesh" may also, if they bring in enough people, influence races for state representative and U.S. Congress.

A few of the Oregonians I speak with during late October, when I visit for ten days, are only mildly concerned. One older woman at a bar in Madras, the Jefferson County seat, tells me she has lived through many administrations and "many crooked politicians," and she doubts that "the Rajneesh" would be any worse than most. However, many nearby Oregonians fear that the coming of the street people is part of "the Bhagwan's" larger design for "taking over." "First Antelope," one woman tells me, "and then Wasco County, then Oregon, then the whole country."

As I drive around I discover that many are couching their fears in apocalyptic terms. A college graduate who is on his way to law school has read one of Rajneesh's books, and it reminded him of Hitler: "The same old song of the Master race." The proprietor of a Christian bookstore in Madras, a generally pleasant and kindly woman, tells me that one day when Rajneesh stopped on his daily drive from the ranch to Madras, she "looked into the Bhagwan's eyes and saw evil." Many Christians, she tells me, including some ministers, believe that "the Bhagwan" may well be the Antichrist. She tells me that Mardo Jimenez, a local minister and a "real patriot," has been holding rallies and vigils "for Christians and Americans" and "against the Bhagwan" for months. She says she is "terrified," but as she speaks I have more the sense of a soldier girding for battle than a civilian awaiting destruction.

In Maupin, slightly farther away, I hear rumors from a number of people that "the Rajneesh have Russian-made tanks and antiaircraft guns" on the Big Muddy. They don't hedge either in attributing September's salmonella poisonings to the Rajneeshees. "My sister-in-law and her husband both got poisoned," one man confides. "There's no question they did it. Look what happened to Bill Hulse and Ray Matthew."

Five hours away, in Canyon City, a judge has just given up on impaneling an impartial jury in a trial involving a sannyasin suit. Surveys have shown a "92% negative feeling" toward "the Rajneeshees" in central and eastern Oregon, and courtroom questioning seems to confirm the results. Throughout the central and eastern parts of the state bumper stickers with slogans like "Better Dead than Red" and T-shirts with a picture of Rajneesh's Rolls-Royce in the center of a gunsight are selling well.

People in nearby Albany have just decided they will register in Wasco County to offset any sannyasin advantage. Though no major incidents of violence by local people have occurred, threats are being made against the street people and the sannyasins. Sheela's response "If the state harms one of my people, I will have fifteen of their heads" seemed a sign of warm support to Anado and Mitzi in Washington. It sounds like a declaration of war to the nearby Oregonians.

Throughout the Share-A-Home program, the visible ranch leadership—Sheela, Vidya, and K.D.—maintains, against all common sense and in contrast to some sannyasins who are embarrassed by the hypocrisy, that there is no political motivation.

There is "absolutely no connection," a tight-jawed Vidya tells me, between the Share-A-Home program and the election. The fact that the last bus arrived precisely twenty days before the election is merely "coincidence."

Reports of a large shipment of Haldol, a powerful tranquilizer used primarily in treating psychotic people, Puja assures me, are "absurd." Of course, she says in the confidential tones of one professional to another, a few of these men need the drug to function. "Ours," K.D. sanctimoniously concludes, is "solely a humanitarian effort. . . . Before, we were accused of selfishness and frivolousness, of caring only for ourselves and putting all our money into Bhagwan's Rolls-Royces. Now we're being accused of sharing with others."

Even before I arrive, however, the sannyasins have decided that voting might be a good idea. They hadn't thought of it, they said, but now that some Oregonians had suggested it . . . if these people wanted to vote, it was, of course, their right as Americans. The only grace note came from Swami Anand Devalaya, a Rajneesh Investment Corporation official, who waved a paintbrush on statewide television: "We're going to paint Oregon red," he proclaimed with manic glee.

Meanwhile the state administrative apparatus has gone into high gear. Attorney General Frohnmayer has tried to convince the U.S. Justice Department that the importation of so many people for the express purpose of voting may be a violation of civil rights laws, but he has been rebuffed in Washington. The Oregon Secretary of State, Norma Paulus, has taken a different tack. Voting requirements will be stringent for the sannyasins, the Share-A-Home people, and those who have planned to move for a day from Albany to Wasco County. She has called for hearings in The Dalles, the Wasco County seat, one hundred miles away from Rajneeshpuram. The state's lawyers can review the registration of each voter who has changed his or her place of residence in the past year. People who have moved from one house to another on the ranch, as well as migrants from the streets of New York and commuters from the next county, are all asked to appear.

The sannyasin lawyers go to court, first to protest the hearings, and then to ask for their relocation: a two-hundred-mile round-trip is an expensive and excessive hardship; they have a place on the ranch where hearings can easily be held. Sheela calls a press conference. I watch her, stiff and trembling with rage in the floodlights, as she compares Oregon officials to the KGB. "I thought," she says, "such things only happened in Soviet Russia." Her mala is made of pearls. In the middle of the day she wears a satin gown with a cape and hood. She reminds me now of a malign popess from some imaginary tarot deck. My God, I think, she really is bonkers.

The Share-A-Home program has continued amidst the accusations and denials. In the last weeks before the October 12 deadline for meeting residency requirements, even the minimal screening procedures for candidates were widely ignored. In Washington in September people were strongly encouraged to rid their systems of drugs and alcohol before getting on the bus. Psychotics and obviously dangerous men were generally told not to come. But by the first days of October men were hallucinating, shooting drugs, and going into DT's on the buses.

Perhaps three times as many people as the ranch could successfully accommodate were bused in. Significant numbers of them were violent and seriously disturbed. Fights erupted, possessions were stolen, and threats abounded. Many were asked to leave almost immediately, I am told. Large numbers of others were, I later find out, without their knowledge or consent, given Haldol—which has potentially dangerous and permanent side effects—in their evening beer and in mashed potatoes.

By the last days of October, when I arrived in Rajneeshpuram, more than half the Share-A-Home people who have been bused in are already off the ranch. Most of the others will soon be on their way. While I am there the sannyasins decide to boycott the election. They say they are outraged at being asked to go to The Dalles to register to vote. It is too expensive, in time and money, they say, echoing their lawyers. More to the point, it is clear they no longer have the numbers to influence the election.

The first Share-A-Home people were given guaranteed return tickets to their point of origin, or indeed anywhere else in the country. Later the sannyasins stopped giving out round-trip tickets. Now when the Share-A-Home people leave or are asked to leave, the ranch simply drops them off in groups in nearby cities: Madras, The Dalles, Portland. The townspeople I talk to in late October are furious about this. How are they to deal with so many people, many of whom have no resources, suddenly dropped into their midst? And why should they take responsibility for people whom "the Rajneesh" have thrust on them? They all fear crime, and the smaller cities simply don't have the facilities to shelter and feed them. The ranch is cavalier: We at least "tried" to help the street people, K.D. and Vidya smugly tell me.

Some of the Share-A-Home people feel betrayed by the sannyasins who have promised them a new home. "They said we wouldn't have to work," one man reminds me, "and now they're telling us we have to 'worship' "—he spits as he says the word— "twelve hours a day, seven days a week, no pay. Sheeit."

A few people, undeterred by Puja's denials and the derision of Vidya, complain that they have been unwillingly drugged. One man dies, apparently of an overdose of a prescription medicine he had taken for some time, while on his way toward Portland. Four, infected perhaps by the endemic litigiousness, file a multimillion-dollar lawsuit against the sannyasins for failing to provide return transportation (the sannyasins say they didn't promise it to these people and that they have the papers to prove it) or give them back their own clothes.

Many Share-A-Home people are told to leave because they aren't "in tune" with the program, because they have fought over women in the disco, because they have "sloped" at worship or stolen from their dormmates or generally had a "negative" attitude. Many agree with these assessments of their behavior, but others are hurt and angry. They want to stay and are willing to change, and so far as they can tell they haven't given the ranch reason to expel them. Others leave on their own. They have felt as confined by the walls of the valley and the rules of life in Rajneeshpuram as they had by the regimentation of a family and job outside.

Amidst all this exploitation and lying and injustice, I find some Share-A-Home people who thrive. Even among those leaving early, like Bob, a twenty-nine-year-old unemployed warehouseman from Seattle, there are a number who feel they have gained something from their stay. "This is an all right place," Bob tells me, "but it's not for me." He "got rid of a lot of negativity" by doing Dynamic in the morning and has decided that it was his fault he was fired from his last two jobs. "I got Bhagwan's message: I'm responsible."

The men I talk to who are planning to stay seem, as a group, more self-sufficient and less disturbed than those who have elected to leave or been kicked out. Some, like David and "Magic," are young and vulnerable. Magic has, not so many months before, returned from Lebanon, where two hundred of his Marine buddies were blown up. David is, like me, from D.C. "A home boy," he says, grinning shyly. He has had trouble holding a job, finding a grip on things. They both "love" their worship and the feeling of safety on the ranch. They feel physically healthy and enjoy the groups the sannyasins have created to help them "get to know ourselves," and "get out [our] anger." There are fights in Rajneeshpuram; David admits, but nothing much. "Have you ever lived on the street?" he asks me.

There are also hip young dudes who have been hustling a living outside. Andre, from D.C., boasts of living off women on both coasts. "Mergatroyd," who bops and breakdances his way around the ranch, tells me he headed a gang that made a living selling slizzem (fake gold jewelry) on the streets of Philadelphia. They seem to thrive on the ranch, enjoying the long nights in the disco and the "European ladies who can't get enough black energy." The groups are "interesting," and the worship isn't too hard.

Most of the "new friends" are older. Vincent, who is black, had some college and sold coke on New York's Upper West Side; Richard, a Chicano, was once a nurse's aide in Los Angeles but lost his license. They know how to get by, have done it for years, but are tired of the life they have lived outside. Just as the younger men resemble the idealistic and adventurous hippies who found their way to Rajneesh in Bombay and Poona, so these guys remind me of the upper middle-class men and women who saw Rajneesh as a guide for—and life in Poona as the resolution of—their mid-life crisis. In fact, Vincent, a handsome dark-skinned man who makes his ranch-issue jeans and sweatshirt seem like the finest silk and gabardine, sees his quandary in much the same way Shiva and Teertha and Bodhicitta saw theirs a dozen years before. "It was all repetition. Make money, spend money, make some more, worry about getting caught or getting knocked off."

Vincent is working on a landscaping crew and clearly loving it. He had thought he had it together. " 'I'm not fucked up,' I said to myself. 'I just need a change.' But I found out I was more fucked up than these guys," he gestures toward some of the older men, who have obviously put in hard years on the street, and maybe in prison. "At least they knew it. . . . I may go back," he says. "I owe something to my daughter. But I want to die in the Buddhafield."

Life on the ranch is affected as profoundly by the new friends as they have been by it. In many ways it has been a wonderful, galvanizing change. Sannyasins have had to exercise the capacities for quick and direct responses that they have presumably been learning in "Bhagwan's open university." People who were content to do menial jobs, to care only for themselves, now have to supervise and help meet the material and emotional needs of others. Men and women who were able to avoid the realities of urban life "in the world"—inequity, street crime, hostility—now have to deal with it in their own home.

Some have found themselves unequal to the task and have retreated. Others, while becoming aware of their fears and prejudices, have risen to the occasion. I watch one morning as Arpana, a German potter, gentles down the men in her landscaping crew, encouraging some to work harder, showing them how to pack the earth at the base of the seedlings; allowing others to slope; breaking up potential fights; and offering advice about their home lives to the men who sit next to her.

At first she was "terrified" of these men who leered and whistled and shouted and stood too close to her and seemed always on the edge of violence. Then some of them left and it was a little easier. She now speaks directly to anyone who harasses her and is no longer afraid. "I'm incredibly thankful for this program," she says. "Landscaping brings out the 'outside part' of me, coordinating, the 'mothering part.' "

Over at Paul Reps Greenhouse, Mahadeva, who has come on the fall RHT program, is also enjoying himself. He seems huge in a yellow slicker and black rubber boots, standing in mud at the edge of the greenhouse. "It cracks me up. I leave New York, where I counseled junkies for fifteen years, to come here and live on the ranch so I can work with my hands, get out of my mind. I work here in the greenhouse for a few weeks, really digging it. And then these guys come along. And what am I supposed to do, turn my back on them? Turn my back on my training? So, I'm working with junkies again. I've got ten of them here. Not all of them work hard or well, but they're beautiful, they're all a part of it.

"And I tell you, some of these young women are incredible! This old guy does a job, and one of them comes along and says, 'You did a beautiful job,' and this guy's just done a little bit and she could have just as easily said it was a shitty job, but he's so pleased. Nobody's said anything nice to him for twenty years, and he works twice as hard.

"I just try to keep them laughing, tell stories, work with them, and we're having a great time. That guy—Bhagwan—he's done it again."

Others on the ranch are also using their training. Puja describes the health program for venereal disease, hepatitis, tuberculosis, crabs, scabies. Medical and psychiatric histories are taken. Special attention is paid to possible symptoms of AIDS—generalized lymphadenopathy, Kaposi's sarcoma, persistent lung infections. There is a "seizure clinic" and one for intravenous drug users. All the new friends are quarantined sexually for ten days. Men with suspected cases of AIDS are sent to San Francisco. Medical and psychiatric treatment are available to all. The "moms" in the various departments serve as a kind of informal referral service. If a man seems disturbed or ill, they call the clinic for an evaluation.

Puja is angry at the Oregon Psychiatric Association, which has criticized the ranch for attempting to care for so many severely disturbed people. She is angry at the press for criticizing the ranch for having Haldol. She quotes the national figures on psychosis among street people, reassures me that she has only forty-eight bottles of Haldol, enough for twenty-four psychotic patients for two weeks. Of course, she says, nobody is drugged against his will. She offers to show the order slips and the inventory to me.

Siddha, the psychiatrist, is also angry at the Oregon Psychiatric Association. He and the other therapists have created groups that provide "a safe atmosphere where the men can express their opinion, voice their questions about the ranch." They are also offering longer sessions that focus on "inner growth." There the men, like sannyasins before them, can talk about their problems, work out their conflicts. These groups are, he assures me, "amazing. . . . These men have so much pain and anger. They are so ready to come off it . . ."

The men are also encouraged to do Dynamic and Kundalini and to dance at night. They are not forced to do anything. "These are independent people. We respect their dignity." Siddha is very impressed with the Share-A-Home program as a whole. "After World War Two, some countries welcomed the homeless but they never guaranteed they would take care of them." The president of the Oregon Psychiatric Association is another story: "He asked if people were being held against their will. This is implicit accusation."

I tell Siddha that I understand his point. Psychiatry's record for dealing with the desperately needy and the homeless has been dismal. I can understand questioning the program and especially wanting to learn from it, but accusations made without evidence have a hollow ring. The program, in spite of its inequities and exploitativeness, does seem a great improvement over what these men have been offered in city and state mental hospitals and shelters. Those who stay are functioning, useful members of a loving community. They seem to have a real opportunity to change. Still, I do have some questions. What about the men who have complained of being drugged? Siddha cuts me off. "People came on meds," he says. "Here they're actually on lower doses."

When I return to the ranch in March 1985, there are at most several hundred of the Share-A-Home people still in residence. Two months later there will be perhaps 100 or 150. Though they have "blended in" to ranch life, living and working alongside the other residents, they also offer a certain contrast. Many are black and have obviously worked with their hands for a living. Some are quiet and dignified as they ride the early morning buses to and from their work; others enliven sannyasin gatherings and Rajneeshpuram life with the sharp questions and cadences of street jive and the sound of bongo drums. Most wear red—and a number have on the sannyasin's mala—but there are some who have kept their beat-up lumber jackets and worn Levi's.

Some of the men are still ecstatic about life on the ranch. As I move around from department to department, talking to those who have stayed, I hear similar stories from them. In their first days and weeks, they carried the ways and the wariness of the street with them. Then something happened—"Bhagwan," "Dynamic," the kindness of the sannyasins—and they began to relax, to give themselves up to the work and the people around them. Now they feel at home.

At Magdalena one day for lunch, I run into Magic. "Outside," he tells me, "I used to be rough and ready, big and bad. Then I saw my buddies die in Lebanon and I wondered what was going on. 'Hey, man,' I thought, 'this is stupid.' " He pauses, pushes the broom on the porch outside Magdalena for a few moments, and begins again. "I went back to Philly and worked as an apprentice pressman, but I didn't like that much either. You have to keep your hands in your pockets and watch your ass. Then I came here and I saw I didn't need to be like that. You work *with* people here, not *for* them. You come closer and closer. If you feel like crying, you cry. If you feel like dancing, you dance. It's a family. Then," a bit shy now, "there is Bhagwan. When I look at him it's like being"—he takes his hands off the broom—"in love with a girl. You can feel it," touching his heart with his fingers, "through your body."

For others the place has lost its first paradisiacal glow. Now they offer more sober but still favorable estimates. "It's a beautiful life," Swami Prem Anashwar tells me, "but not an easy life."

Anashwar is a former part-time cook from Portland, where he lived alone and lonely for four years after his wife died. When I first saw him in the fall of 1984, Anashwar was still Vernon Gentile. He was wearing street clothes, carrying a tape recorder, and interviewing people for the *Rajneesh Times*. He was thin and worn and gray and had about him an apologetic eagerness. He acted as if he had just been or were just about to be, hit.

Now he looks five years younger. He has put on some weight and his color is good. His eyes, clear now, don't dart away when he looks at me. He took sannyas and then left the ranch during the winter. He wanted to go off by himself without ever saying good-bye, without the red clothes and the mala, to decide if the sannyasins had somehow seduced him into becoming one of them. After six weeks away, working as a cook on a boat off Hawaii ("It was real nice"), he came "home."

He recalls, relaxed now, his first days on the ranch the previous September. "There I was, standing around waiting for some Indian guru in a Rolls-Royce to drive by. It seemed totally crazy. I kept looking for the man with the butterfly net." On the second day he saw Rajneesh, he found himself crying for no reason. "You better have some kind of wonderment when that happens." A few days later he did Dynamic. During the second stage he started screaming all the thoughts he had never let come to consciousness. He heard "pure, unadulterated hate" come out of his mouth.

He did Dynamic every day after that and spoke with Siddha and some of the other "spiritual therapists" who were offering their services to the newcomers. When, in late October, Rajneesh began to speak to a small group of disciples, inveighing against the spiritual Masters he had lovingly explicated years before, Anashwar went to the videotaped reruns of the discourses. "Everything he was saying was common sense. Jesus was neurotic. Otherwise why would he want to be crucified. There is no God; there is just us. It's up to us." His first worship was hard to take. Outside he had been a cook; here he was assigned to be a dishwasher. He resented the loss of status. After a while, with help from his sannyasin friends, he understood that these were his "ego games. The man worshipping at the sink next to me used to be a doctor with his own practice."

Slowly, he began to trust other people and talk to them, even to touch them and hug them. He felt for the first time since his wife's death that he had come alive. Sometimes he got bored. Working twelve hours a day, seven days a week, was not easy. Being in the same place was difficult for someone used to wandering. But the amazing thing, he confesses, was that he "loved these people"; most of the time he "actually enjoyed the worship."

When I return in the fall of 1985, Anashwar isn't there. "He left without saying good-bye," one woman tells me. "I think it was just too much worship and not enough freedom."

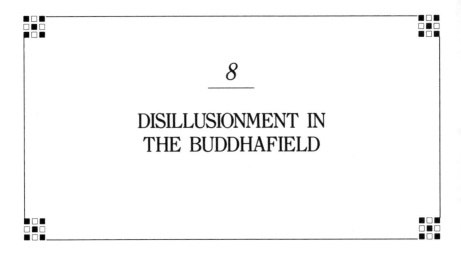

8

DISILLUSIONMENT IN
THE BUDDHAFIELD

No one really seems to know how many people ever took sannyas, received a name from Rajneesh, put on the mala and the colors. The organization's declared figures followed Rajneesh's pronouncements rather than any totals actually recorded. During the late seventies the figures periodically increased by increments of 50,000. At various times Sheela cited totals of 300,000, 350,000 and 400,000. In 1984 Rajneesh said he had "half a million" disciples, and in 1985 he claimed "one million."

According to several sannyasins who had access to mailing lists, there were probably never more than 40,000 initiated sannyasins worldwide, of whom 10,000 or 15,000 had probably dropped sannyas by the time the ranch was established. The inflation of figures (which is common to many groups, including virtually all new religions) was variously denied, ignored, said to include hundreds of thousands of "white sannyasins" (Indians who didn't wear the mala or colors), attributed to some esoteric understanding of sannyas that Rajneesh had, or rationalized—perhaps accurately—as the total number of people who had a "connection to Bhagwan."

While Rajneesh and his sannyasins were still in Poona, even before Sheela became his secretary and long before Rajneeshism was a religion, some of the sannyasins had taken off their orange clothes and their malas. A few, like Richard Price, were angry and disillusioned, disturbed by the shortcomings they had found in Rajneesh and in the ashram in Poona. Others weren't so much disillusioned as puzzled. Once back in the West, they didn't feel the desire to maintain the commitment they had made or were unsure about why they had made it in the first place. Back in their ordinary lives, out of the orbit of Rajneesh's influence, away from the tight support of a community of sannyasins, confronted with hostile questions, they found that it all seemed a bit like a dream.

Many others wore the clothes for years and then, apart from their Master and the intensity of his presence, cut off by his silence, and absorbed in lives that included other sannyasins only incidentally, they felt their commitment diminish. "Sannyas just began to drop," Mudra, the psychologist from Florida, told me. "I found that I wanted to wear other clothes. That I was no longer prepared to play the Master-disciple game." She, like almost all the other former sannyasins I spoke with in the late seventies, felt profound gratitude to Rajneesh and appreciation of the experiences she had had in Poona: "I was only half a person when I went to Poona. It was easily the most important experience of my life."

Even though many people left the movement, there were not, until the establishment of the ranch, professional ex-sannyasins, people who devoted a significant part of their life to opposing Rajneesh and his group, the way ex-Moonies, ex-Hare Krishnas and ex-Scientologists often did. The single notable exception was Eckart Floether, a visible, vocal German ex-sannyasin and current born-again Christian who spread word of Rajneesh's anti-Christian teachings to Oregonians. Most of those who dropped sannyas before the move to America seemed to feel, like Mudra, that they had benefited from their experience.

There were some who were angrier. One woman who in 1972, at Rajneesh's urging, had left her children in the West so she could pursue her spiritual life, was now furious at "the sadistic, controlling, sociopathic son of a bitch." But neither she nor anyone else I met during the seventies was actively fighting Rajneesh or his movement. Why spend energy being against something that was freely chosen? And they had learned enough from their time with Rajneesh, or on their own, not to dwell excessively on the past.

There were other reasons dissatisfied sannyasins didn't attack what they had once embraced. They were never aggressively and deceptively recruited the way members of other groups were, nor were there any restrictions on leaving. The very idea of sannyas was that of being a wanderer, of coming and going from India to the West, from one living situation to another. Some were told, and many feared, that dropping sannyas, being away from Rajneesh's influence, would preclude enlightenment or spiritual advancement. But they were not generally threatened that eternal damnation or insanity would follow their apostasy, as were members of some groups. Since they had not been threatened or coerced, there was less impetus to strike back.

Similarly, though there was some pressure to give money, there was not, as in some groups, the insistence that one had to give all or devote one's life to raising money. Giving was a sign of surrender, of good discipleship — but so were many other things. If one didn't have to give everything — indeed anything — then one was unlikely to feel cheated later on.

Finally, all those who took sannyas in the seventies had been told again and again that the Master-disciple relationship and all the groups and all the ashram work that were part of it were ultimately a game. You played because you wanted to, at your own risk, from moment to moment, and for exactly as long as you wanted. All aspects of the game could be instructive. Because it was a game, because Rajneesh had promised nothing except a game, because he had always said he would change the rules at his pleasure, it seemed absurd to complain about the way he had played it or the results.

During the last months in Poona the nature of sannyas changed, and with it the potential for disillusionment and the impetus for taking revenge. The game became serious. The concealment of the move to America from the majority of sannyasins, as well as from Indian and U.S. authorities, created a sense that deception and betrayal within the movement were possible. The potential danger of being arrested or deported for the illegal transfer of money and goods to America, for the marriages of convenience, and for the concealed plan to relocate Rajneesh permanently, changed the structure of the community: the benign dictatorship cum anarchy of Poona was replaced by a more tightly knit authoritarian structure, capable of acting swiftly, decisively, and secretly. The move to America, the purchase of the Oregon ranch, the speed and extravagance of the new commune's development, and the lavishness of Rajneesh's and Sheela's life-styles reinforced the structure — and created a shortage of sannyasin money and commitment, which previously had been more than ample.

Once in America, and particularly with Rajneesh maintaining silence, the centralized power structure tended to institutionalize and perpetuate itself. Rajneesh put pressure on Sheela to move quickly and efficiently. Sheela, unwilling to listen to alternate points of view, became increasingly authoritarian toward and demanding of those below her in the hierarchy. All power flowed from Rajneesh to Sheela and from her to the rest of the sannyasins. The desires and prejudices and limitations of the Master and his personal secretary became the unquestioned standards for sannyasins. Elaborated in the policies of those who were close to Sheela — Vidya, Puja, Savita, and others — they came to shape the entire movement.

In India sannyasins had been free to involve themselves to whatever degree they wanted. They could drop in and out of Poona, live on the fringes of the ashram while they were there, take groups, or make a total commitment to "Bhagwan's work." In any case it was understood that they were there for themselves, that Rajneesh's sole purpose was to work on them. In America there was a subtle shift. There was pressure on everyone to direct all their energies, all their resources, to the ranch, to make "Bhagwan's vision" real. Their development, their "flowering," was secondary.

Many people — convinced of Rajneesh's wisdom, of the preeminent importance of his work, of the urgent need to create the new man now, before the holocaust came — acceded. "Bhagwan chose Sheela," so they would take her direction. Besides, they were on the ranch — or looking forward to it — with their Master and so many of their friends.

For others, adjusting to the change was more difficult. In Poona they had enjoyed an intimacy with Rajneesh or an authority in the ashram that Sheela no longer permitted them. If she thought they threatened her hegemony or if they incurred her wrath, she was likely to take revenge. The jobs she gave them, the way she treated them, served to subdue and exclude and demean them rather than to make use of their talents. Often enough this treatment was described as a device for "reducing the ego." Some people accepted this. Others, like Laxmi, Deeksha, and Shiva, had been around long enough and knew Sheela well enough to distrust her intentions and question her interpretations of their Master's wishes. They tried to get around Sheela, to change the policy and the situation for themselves by going directly to Rajneesh or asking Vivek to intercede. When this ultimately proved impossible, when it seemed, finally, that Rajneesh himself provided the authorization for, if not the direction of Sheela's policy, they felt they had no choice but to leave.

Not long after I saw her in New York in late 1981, Laxmi had returned to the ranch. When she came back east a few months later, she would say only that she had left the ranch again because of immigration problems ("Laxmi wouldn't marry an American") and that she was living happily in Woodstock, New York. She was the guest of a Zen monastery there and hoped to get a green card allowing her to remain in the country as a "religious worker," a teacher of Zen. Meanwhile she was making a living selling curry and chappatis from the back of a bus in the town and at rock and country and western concerts. Other sannyasins said there had been a confrontation between Laxmi and Sheela and Rajneesh had thrown his weight behind Sheela. When word came from the ranch that Laxmi was "negative" and that sannyasins should avoid her and Deeksha, who had also left, she laughed. "Bhagwan is just testing Laxmi."

I saw Laxmi a number of times over the next three years, at Devadeep, where she sometimes gave workshops, and at her apartment when she moved to Washington. She told me about her ongoing struggles with the INS. She said that in Portland agents had held her incommunicado and threatened her; they promised her a green card if she would incriminate Rajneesh. In New York, she said, she had been roughed up. She asked for my help in finding a specialist when she found she had ovarian cancer. We had dinner together several times and laughed and drank a few glasses of champagne. I didn't forget to bring her chocolates.

We talked for hours, but I could feel her holding back. She was bitter toward Sheela, but she never expressed any doubts about her Master. I wondered, unavoidably, if somehow suppressed doubt and anger and loss had made her vulnerable to cancer. When I told her about my growing uneasiness about the ranch—I described the ways in which the people around Rajneesh were being increasingly deceptive and paranoid—she counseled detachment. "Disciples are disciples. Never worry about them. Trust your experience of him."

Laxmi never left her Master, but after months of agony, Shiva did. In Poona, Shiva had worked hard, as Rajneesh's bodyguard during his twice daily appearances; as head—with Nandan—of the Samurais, who provided all the ashram security; and as a photographer. But there were great rewards. He felt the reassurance and nourishment of his "psychic connection" with his Master, the satisfaction of serving someone he loved and responding swiftly to his unspoken needs. He sat at his Master's side in evening darshan, had "prestige" in the ashram, a "beautiful private room," and lovely women. It was, he told me some time after he left, "like Christmas every day."

In New Jersey right after Rajneesh came to America, Shiva worked at construction, roomed with other people, and was cut off from direct contact with Rajneesh. After he went to Oregon his disillusionment and his resentment increased in tandem. Though he was still favored in many ways—allowed to live in Rajneesh's house and to possess a motorcycle, for example—he resented his twelve hours a day driving heavy equipment and his lack of access to his Master. He was distressed by Sheela's high-handed treatment of Laxmi and the local people, her capricious and vengeful behavior toward those who displeased her, and the ranch's high-pressure fund-raising tactics.

At first Shiva saw Rajneesh as Sheela's victim. He described his Master's abandoning the idea of making the ranch more democratic — Rajneesh originally wanted the commune to have a governing body of seven Monitors as Buddha's sangha did — because of Sheela's opposition. Later he heard accounts that made him believe that Rajneesh was the source of the ranch's problems. Rajneesh had, Shiva learned, turned his back on those, like Laxmi, who had been most loyal. "In Poona," Shiva said Rajneesh told an unnamed sannyasin, "the wrong people were in charge. They were cunning and deceitful." Rajneesh seemed to his former bodyguard to have become a spiritually impoverished man relying on drugs to stay high and filling his inner emptiness with material wealth. "Every week," Shiva said Rajneesh told Sheela, Jayananda, and Isabel, "I will be needing more Rolls-Royces."

Shiva left the ranch, returned, and in the fall of 1982 left for good. Unlike Laxmi, who remained loyal and kept a low profile in exile, he denounced Rajneesh publicly, to *Stern*. The ranch, he said, was "a prison run by a ruthless despot." Shiva became increasingly anxious, depressed, and fearful for his physical safety. He knew the ranch was aware that he was talking to representatives of the INS and had dispatched sannyasins to follow and photograph him. He said he feared that Sheela would try to kill him. In 1983 he made a suicide attempt and was hospitalized. Several months before, in the winter of 1982–83 Shiva had met with Deeksha, who was in Zurich.

Deeksha had actually left the ranch before Shiva and Laxmi, but the circumstances of her departure were shrouded in contrary rumors and her whereabouts were unknown. When I asked about her in Oregon in 1982, I was told that she was upset about Laxmi's loss of power and angry at Sheela, that she had stolen money, and — as if this explained it all — that she was Italian.

When I finally met with Deeksha, long after she had spoken to Shiva, she seemed eager to talk but more anxious about the construction I would put on her words than any of the other sannyasins or ex-sannyasins I had interviewed. She was fearful and wondered if I could be trusted, and inevitably, I wondered the same about her. She told her story in the smooth accents of one who, in repeating it many times, had rubbed away the rough edges of doubt and ambiguity.

At some point in the years since she had left Rajneesh, Deeksha had reevaluated him and redefined her relationship to him. Characteristics she had regarded as harmless, even endearing, foibles in a man she loved, now seemed evidence of a vanity and deceit that contradicted his claim of enlightenment, early signs of a corruption that confirmed her present negative evaluation of him: Rajneesh was proud that a Brahmin woman — of a higher caste than he — cooked for him; he didn't read all of the books that he took from his library, only selected chapters or passages that he marked; he ordered photographs to be taken from angles that minimized the size of his nose and used a cream so that the sun would not darken his skin; he had his gowns designed to emphasize his height and the width of his shoulders.

Deeksha told me that already in 1980 in Poona she had had some misgivings — about her role there, in particular the sterilizations that she promoted, and about her guru. She still believed then that "Bhagwan would help us bring about a spiritual revolution, that we would become enlightened, transcend greed and jealousy." But she sensed that "the balance between the just things and the ugly things" in the ashram was shifting. In retrospect it now seemed to her that Rajneesh was becoming increasingly violent, coercive, and deceitful.

There was a plan in Poona, she told me, for Rajneesh's guards and sannyasins in the first rows at discourse to form a "human wall" to protect their Master from physical attack. She told me Rajneesh permitted and encouraged "everything," including most particularly prostitution and "even drug dealing," as long as it brought money to him. Deeksha claimed she had seen Rajneesh beat Vivek badly. She said she knew that the ashram hierarchy had instigated the fires at the warehouse and the clinic and the knife-throwing incident.

Deeksha said she began to have strange dreams in late 1979. In one, the ashram was "empty and decaying," the gardens overgrown. In another, which recurred, she sensed "a great danger looming over the ashram." In the dream, she ran to tell Rajneesh, entered his room, saw him sitting in front of her, looked in his eyes, and knew that "he was the danger."

In New Jersey, at the Castle, Deeksha became more troubled. She felt guilty when she was paired with Sheela to replace Laxmi. And, more important, she was horrified by the glimpses of her guru that her twice daily private meetings with him gave her. She "saw his real face" and found it as frightening and dangerous as in her dream. Often, she said, he was high on Valium and incoherent. At times, he seemed to her to be praising Hitler, whom he called "a genius," and Goebbels, whom he declared the "greatest practitioner of mass persuasion."

When he was lucid, he taught her and Sheela to "maneuver" people, to create "buffers" — "little Sheelas, little Deekshas" — so that harsh commands that they gave would seem to come from subordinates. Deeksha realized that Rajneesh was using her and Sheela as his buffers, and she felt that they were being tied more closely to him by complicity in or knowledge of criminal activity.

Still Deeksha stayed. She had, she said, invested ten years of her life in and donated large sums of her money to Rajneesh and his community. All her friends were there; even her mother was a sannyasin. Perhaps, she thought, things would "be better" in Oregon, perhaps she could help bring about changes. Within a month she realized that Rajneesh was "bored" with helping people to live the spiritual life that they had come to him to find and "excited only by power and money." She felt that "things would never change. The door to meditation was closed, the door to corruption open." It was time for her to leave. "Remember that if you create trouble," she claimed Sheela warned her on her departure, "I can take care of you in twenty-four hours."

When Shiva met with her, Deeksha was in hiding. Rumors had reached her that people at the ranch had "cursed" her, said that she had cancer and was crazy, and that she had stolen hundreds of thousands of dollars from a Swiss bank account of Sheela's on which she had been a signatory. She said she had received early-morning anonymous phone calls, and non-sannyasin friends with whom she was staying had been threatened. Sannyasins "walked across the street" to avoid her.

Deeksha believed that Sheela feared that she would divulge secrets about Sheela's Swiss bank accounts, the fires in Poona, and other illegal activities and episodes of violence done or contemplated. Deeksha told Shiva about her experiences and the fear and confusion and isolation she felt. She said that in her distress she had gone to Krishnamurti for help. Krishnamurti, she said, had told her that "what [Rajneesh] is doing in the name of spirituality is criminal. . . . You have made a great mistake in giving him the power over your life."

Commitment to a movement is strengthened when it is shared. So too is disaffection. Though they didn't cause others to leave, the departures of Deeksha and Shiva, both of whom had been so close to Rajneesh for so long, and Shiva's public denunciation of Rajneesh inevitably affected all sannyasins. Some were quite ready to accept Sheela's characterization of Deeksha as a sick woman and a thief, of Shiva as a disappointed power-seeker, "a Judas" whose "negativity" had led him to cooperate with the INS and endanger both Rajneesh and his movement. Shutting Deeksha and Shiva out was for these people reasonable and a matter of loyalty.

Their departure and the ranch's condemnation of them had a different effect on long-term disciples and close friends, some of whom shared their knowledge of the details of Sheela's tyranny. They now recalled earlier instances when they were troubled by or suspicious of Sheela's or Rajneesh's actions or when they themselves participated in activities that seemed questionable to them. Pramod and Nandan and others began to reevaluate their commitment to their Master and his movement.

During the last year in Poona, Pramod, the former British diplomat, had lived in the ashram and acted as head of the "translation department." He enjoyed Laxmi's administration: "She liked to play games, play jokes on people, but basically she was selfless. . . . She did what Bhagwan wanted her to do, what seemed to be necessary." And he liked Arup: "She was level-headed, logical, clear with people who supervised her work." Pramod, who had resisted discipleship, became "totally devoted to Bhagwan. I would go wherever he wanted to go, or do whatever he wanted to do. I believed that he was essentially good and valuable, that he had a special quality, a lucidity, a beauty, that wasn't physical. I believed that here, in front of me, was a man like Buddha or Jesus or Lao-tzu."

When Rajneesh left Poona, Pramod wanted to go with him, but Sheela asked him to go back to Brussels to run the Rajneesh Meditation Center that he had founded. Money could be made there, and money would be needed. For a year Pramod ran the center. Twenty-four people lived there. They had therapy groups, teams of people doing house cleaning and construction, a restaurant. Pramod enjoyed the work, and they did make money, but he always wanted to go to Oregon, "to be with Bhagwan." In June 1982, while his friend Shiva was trying to decide whether or not to leave, "I was finally told I could come."

The ranch was a disappointment. "On Bhagwan's first drive-by I experienced nothing except flatness, sadness. I didn't resonate with him. 'This man,' I thought, 'is empty.' In a sense he was always empty, but before it was non-ego, without personality or desires, the emptiness of a Buddha. Now it was nothing, or rather something missing.

"I didn't care about the Rolls-Royces—he'd had two Rolls-Royces in Poona—but I wasn't interested in watching a man drive past in a car."

After so many years of devotion Pramod was "panicky" about his reaction. He was intimidated by the "taboo against negativity" and didn't talk to anyone else about his feelings. He soon discovered he didn't like life on the ranch either. Twelve hours of construction work seemed to him both unremitting and "goal-oriented." In Poona, where he once silk-screened endless jackets of Rajneesh's books, "we lived in the here and now. In Oregon it was 'Finish by such and such a date.' " He tried to use the work as a Gurdjieffian device. Perhaps if he "pushed hard enough" he would break through to another level of energy, but it didn't work.

Soon Pramod was transferred to the *Rajneesh Times*. From this vantage he had a clear view of the ranch. All around him he saw the proliferation of desire, the swelling of egos. Sheela wanted to exalt herself, to raise ever more money, to spend and build without restraint. Rajneesh seemed possessed by his own material needs, and devious. Both seemed contemptuous of the Oregonians they offended and the sannyasins they exploited. In Poona, Rajneesh had seemed "clear, appealing. There was something flowing through him." When he had been provocative, it had seemed to Pramod to be "intelligent and witty." Now it seemed only self-aggrandizing and counterproductive.

After Shiva left in the fall and sannyasins were told to shun him, Pramod became more alienated. He could see that his friend's exile might be a device for Shiva, but it was also part of a pattern. At the First World Festival in July, Somendra, a therapy group leader; Prageet, a massage therapist who had started a popular center in France; and Chetna, who had been with Rajneesh in Bombay and Laxmi in New York, had been told to turn in their malas. Somendra, who had been specifically asked to come to the festival to give sannyas to new disciples, was publicly admonished for his hunger for power. Prageet was told that he "shouldn't have talked to Deeksha," and Chetna was simply ordered to leave.

Pramod tried to speak to Sheela about the expulsions and the treatment of the local people. His experience as a diplomat made him well aware of "the element of rightness in the local people's position and in ours." But Sheela was unwilling to see it. "It was 'We're under siege. They're rednecks. We're a spiritual community and they should acquiesce. We're creating a new man and everything is justified.' . . . 'Compromise' was a dirty word to Sheela."

When he and Subhuti wanted to publish a news account of a speech by Mark Hatfield in which the senator denied doing anything adverse to the ranch, Sheela axed the article. When they appealed, Sheela presented their position to Rajneesh. "The newspaper," he told them, through her, "is not meant to be a newspaper but propaganda." In April 1983, ten months after he arrived, Pramod left, disillusioned with the ranch, but still wearing the colors and the mala with his Master's picture.

Like Pramod, Nandan had had time away from Rajneesh before she came to the ranch. She had helped Vidya close the ashram in Poona but had been—she was not quite sure why—"crossed off the list" for New Jersey and Oregon. Instead she went to the Himalayas and then, in April 1982, to California. There she met Shiva, who had left the ranch for the first time. "He told me that the ranch was like a concentration camp. Laxmi had been kicked out, and no criticism was allowed." Nandan "loved Shiva, but I didn't want to believe what he said."

On the ranch Nandan quickly moved into a position of authority. She put together contracts with publishers for Rajneesh's writings; helped Arup deal with foreign Rajneesh meditation centers; orchestrated worldwide demonstrations on behalf of Rajneesh's immigration petition; and served on the Antelope City Council. A crisp, efficient woman, she enjoyed the challenges of the work but came to resent the lies and coerciveness that touched almost every task.

Leaders of Rajneesh centers around the world thought their Master was advising Nandan in her dealings with them, giving their centers names and responding to their problems; in fact, she told me, she was acting on her own and with Arup's supervision. When she called to urge center members to come to the summer festival, she "told sannyasins who couldn't afford to come that 'this may be Bhagwan's last festival.' I had them in tears and Bhagwan was perfectly healthy." She also told me that, in contravention of the supposed separation of church and state, she had been picked for the Antelope City Council by Rajneesh himself. Once on the council, she felt uncomfortable raising taxes and shutting the older residents up.

She quit the city council to take care of sannyasin children in Antelope. She loved the work and being with her friends and her lover but was saddened by the young children's separation from their parents. Meanwhile, she found the organization increasingly repugnant — "Sheela's harangues and the 'We are great' mentality." Then her "best friend turned me in for saying negative things." Nandan spoke with Sheela, who relayed the conversation to Rajneesh. He told Nandan, " 'If you see Arup and Sheela misusing power, it is up to you to correct them.' But when I did, Arup told me not to let Bhagwan's message go to my head."

Finally, in April 1984, she began to doubt Rajneesh as well. She knew he was taking large doses of Valium and inhaling nitrous oxide, sometimes twice daily, and it troubled her. How could someone who used drugs to get high be enlightened?

She began to recall other things that had bothered her. In Poona even before she took sannyas she had dreams in which Rajneesh was violent, sexually abusive, demonic. At the time Teertha and others had told her "it was 'just my ego,' that I was 'afraid of surrendering.' " Now she was wondering if these dreams were communications not from "the voice of ego but from the voice of clarity." She remembered reports from ashram guards who had seen Rajneesh hit Vivek with his hands and kick her. At the time she had dismissed the actions as devices; now they seemed simply brutal. She began to feel disturbed that she had undergone sterilization.

Perhaps under other circumstances these concerns would have passed or could have been rationalized or dwarfed by her appreciation of her Master and his work. But when she looked around his Oregon commune, she saw continuing repression. "He taught us to be spiritual rebels who could find their own truths, and here we were being punished for it."

In April 1984 she left the commune and took off her mala. "Somewhere I had a mechanism, some part saying, 'Watch out.' Finally the voice came back, and I listened."

Radha, who had been a medium in Poona, stayed on the ranch until early 1985 as a respected spiritual therapist. Although she was one of the few sannyasins allowed to spend time in Rajneesh's presence, she felt uneasy, unsatisfied. "The energy, the light were gone. There was no more teaching to be received. He was just an ordinary, sweet, jolly, sometimes brilliant, often tedious Indian."

If Rajneesh no longer moved her as he had, his organization now repelled and frightened her. Sheela and the others were "so power-hungry and violent." In meetings with the therapists Sheela, "lying down in an expensive negligee . . . would talk to us about not controlling and not manipulating, while people were waiting on her hand and foot, cowering around her. There was a total disconnection between Rajneesh's teaching and the practice. No one was allowed to question. There were spies everywhere. It was a police state . . . no longer a place for religious work on myself.

"It took me a while to realize I was still hooked on loyalty to him as my father-lover figure, still in a kind of hypnotic trance. I felt grateful to him too—I still feel grateful for what I learned—and I couldn't believe that he was responsible for what was happening on the ranch. But I had to get away—from the manipulation and the violence—to find myself. And it was only after I got away that I made the connections. He was responsible. Sheela was only an extension of him."

During this time some disciples who lived "in the world" also dropped sannyas. Many were responding to the increasing—and increasingly arbitrary—control the ranch was exercising over sannyasins and their centers. A professor I knew set up a marriage of convenience at the ranch's request and then felt uneasy about his role in it and stopped wearing his mala. A nurse who lived in California found herself continually resisting her local center leader's pressure to marry a foreigner and move into the center and send more of her paycheck to Oregon. Eventually she dropped sannyas. And so for a while did Mahadeva, who became fed up with what he considered ranch mismanagement of the New York center he was helping to run.

In 1984 when the ranch ordered all the American centers closed, save Utsava, in Laguna Beach, and all the others around the world consolidated, more people left. It didn't make sense to them. The hundreds of local centers in the United States and Europe, Australia and Asia, had been an expression of particular communities' needs and vitality. Perhaps the ranch needed more "energy" and more money, but how could you feed the branches if you killed the roots?

An earlier consolidation in 1982 did produce some exciting ventures—large discos and restaurants, successful businesses in the nine European and three Australian communes—but more standardization and control followed. Communes in Europe were told to pattern their decor on the ranch's, to plan the same menus on the same days, no matter the price of staples or the availability of commodities. Centers that didn't fit the ranch mold were pulled and tugged into the "proper" shape. Many sannyasins who had invested their time and money in creating their kind of commune were angered and saddened. In time even some of the oldest and most loyal disciples, like Poonam, became alienated. When I spoke with her in 1986 in London Poonam traced her growing disaffection, painfully, reluctantly, the way a patient might recall the toll that a chronic illness has taken on a previously healthy and happy life.

Shortly after Rajneesh arrived in America in 1981, Poonam, who was then in England, had received a message from her Master. "I want every country to have a Rajneesh city," he had said, "and I want you to found the first one—Medina." Excited, competent, and eager to oblige, she discovered "an amazing place in Suffolk." She asked the people who wanted to live there to sell their houses and buy debentures, stock in the house, for which the enormous manor house would be equity. She bought the building for £300,000 and promised that anyone who chose to leave would be repaid in a matter of months.

In addition to the kinds of therapy groups that she and Teertha had run in Quaesitor and in Poona, she started businesses: a construction firm, which grew out of the remodeling that was done on Medina; a design and printing business; an advertising agency; a computer business. Later she and the other sannyasins bought a health club in Belsize Park, near Hampstead in London. They remodeled it and renamed it the Rajneesh Body Center. It had five squash courts and offered aerobics, physical fitness, and body therapies and had a restaurant, bar, and disco. Two hundred sannyasins came to live in Medina, and it and the Body Center prospered.

Within a year Poonam felt interference from the ranch: directives to run or decorate Medina, and later the Body Center, in ways that seemed stupid, counterproductive, ugly, or uneconomical; orders to keep sannyasins away from Shyam and Shiva (now Hugh Milne again); instructions to disrupt the public meetings of other spiritual teachers and to follow Tom Casey of the INS, who had come to England to interview Milne.

She believed "everything came from Bhagwan" and wanted to do precisely what he said. I had "such trust in him. He had guided me for so many years, and only amazing things had happened when I went along with his suggestions." She didn't like Sheela. "She was stupid in many ways, and I found it ugly." But she put aside the doubts that were rising in her. "Surely," she thought, "Bhagwan must know this, he sees her every day. There must be something about her that he sees that I don't. This is all for his greater vision." She said to herself, "I have a small window and he has a much larger one."

At the World Festival in 1984 she was "told to stay in Oregon. I was made to feel like I'd fucked up in England," even though she knew her ventures had been successful. "I pushed down my own inner feelings. I was following my Master, I trusted my Master." She stayed in Oregon for six months until November, and participated in the Share-A-Home program. She remembered that the men were "so abused, they were sent off the ranch in droves. I took their warm clothes. I did it. I just can't believe I did it. I betrayed my integrity, and I did it from fear. Here were these guys shivering with cold, hopping around, saying, 'Please, ma'am, give me that jacket.' There was Shanti B saying, 'No, these guys have abused the place.'

"All I wanted was to be with Bhagwan. My life was the commune, in Poona, here in England, in Oregon. They could make my life uncomfortable. I was dependent on them for every little bit of my life—the clothes I wore, what kind of job I did, whether or not I'd be scrubbing floors all day. If I was a good girl I wouldn't be punished." Remembering, retelling it a year later, this fifty-year-old woman looked for a moment like a scared schoolgirl.

She sent a letter to Rajneesh. The reply came back. "Everything is being done for your ego. Drop all ideas of ever going back to England."

"I tried to get to Bhagwan through Vidya. She used to look after my kids when they were babies. But I couldn't." Finally, desperate, she left the ranch and "did all the things I thought he had told me not to. I lived on my own and started my own therapy practice and saw who I wanted. After a month of guilt and remorse for leaving my Master, I was really happy."

Directives from the ranch to centers and sannyasins around the world followed in the wake of these expulsions and departures. Poonam was no longer to be regarded as an authority. The ranch would not look kindly on, might even expel, sannyasins who did groups with Somendra or received acupuncture from Shyam. Don't talk with Shiva or Laxmi or Deeksha, Nandan or Pramod, Prageet or Chetna, sannyasins were told. "They're negative." For a while sannyasins were ordered to shun some of these people as if their disagreements and dissent were an infection. They were to be known as "the late sannyasins" and treated like "ghosts." Their names were no longer included in official sannyasin histories, and their images were expunged from group pictures.

Most sannyasins tried to understand these policies in the light of the Master-disciple relationship, as devices whose nature they could only guess. Maybe it was time for Shiva and Laxmi, Deeksha, Somendra and Shyam, to achieve enlightenment or simply be on their own. This was their Master's way of forcing them to drop their dependency on him, a cruel kindness. Some recalled that Gurdjieff suddenly and inexplicably sent away his longtime disciples Thomas and Olga de Hartmann.

Others saw these actions as part of Sheela's ongoing need to obliterate all potential rivals for Rajneesh's affection and organizational control. In this scenario, Rajneesh had two possible roles. Either he was isolated and insulated, Sheela's unwitting dupe, or indeed her prisoner; or he was simply biding his time, letting Sheela play out her "power trip." At the right moment Rajneesh, the Master, would confront Sheela, the disciple, with her behavior and everything would change.

Many of the people who left the ranch, like Shiva, Deeksha, Nandan, and Pramod, were coming to the painful conclusion that Rajneesh was not, or was no longer, enlightened. They believed he was now choosing Sheela, and the temporal power and material well-being she provided, over spiritual power and a selfless relationship with devoted disciples.

Most of those who remained sannyasins, in or out of the communes around the world, on or off the ranch, bounced from one possibility to another, wondering and weighing each. Ultimately they gave up the task of determining "the truth" and accepted each possibility as itself a device that Rajneesh had fashioned to reveal their own minds to them. It was not their concern anyway. They were sannyasins for their own development, for their relationship with their Master, not to question or evaluate the way he dealt with his other disciples. It was as fruitless to reflect on why these people left or had been expelled or why Rajneesh kept Sheela in power as it was to wonder why the guard at the gate in Poona had been told to keep a particular Indian sannyasin out of the ashram.

9

CAUGHT IN A
DOUBLE BIND

On October 30, 1984, in the last week before the election that the sannyasins once hoped to control, Bhagwan Shree Rajneesh began to speak again. In the first of his discourses his voice seemed rusty, as if from disuse. It soon became fluid. Each night, in a small bare room in his house, he addressed twenty or twenty-five sannyasins. Sheela and Vidya were there, and Teertha and Siddha and Kaveesha, leader of the Tantra group; Mukta, the Greek heiress, and Krishna Prem, the Canadian PR man, were also present. Some of the select audience were old Indian disciples, and some were newer, wealthy American ones, including Devaraj's wife, Ma Prem Hasya, and her close friend Swami Dhyan John. Hasya was a French-born Jew who spent a year in a Nazi labor camp as a child before she emigrated to Israel and then the United States. As Françoise Ruddy, she had collaborated with her previous husband, Albert, to coproduce *The Godfather.* John, an emergency room physician from Kansas City, had made millions by contracting with hospitals to provide medical staff. These were, Rajneesh said, "the chosen few . . . the messengers of Rajneeshism to the world at large."

Now and then a visitor was present. One evening in early November it was my turn. Sitting with his sannyasins, a few feet from Rajneesh on the floor in front of his chair, I had the sense of a man telling stories to children, stories about his own childhood, the books he had read and the thoughts he had had. He was teaching, sharing himself with pupils who were eager to learn what he knew. At the same time I felt him drawing sustenance from the rapt attention of his audience.

He looked older but more substantial than he did in Poona, as if he had been invigorated by the Oregon climate and nourished by his three-and-a-half-year "silence." His presence was calming, his speech elegantly paced, his voice soft, engaging. His eyes seemed to linger on, to search, each person. We had all been invited to resonate with Rajneesh, and so far as I could tell, we were all in that state of heightened suggestibility and calm alertness that is the hallmark of trance. I saw his images with him, heard as well as felt his words, fell backward in time as he gave us a little history lesson. He was adding, he had said, "a few touches to the portrait" he had been painting for twenty-five years.

During the first weeks of these discourses Rajneesh returned again and again to certain themes. He was an "ordinary man" and "ordinariness is blessed." If there was any difference between him and his listeners, it was "not of quality, it is only of knowing. I know myself, you don't know yourself." Following someone else was idiotic. Anyone could, like him, find the truth for himself. All contradictions were complementary. Life and death should both be celebrated.

"All the religions," Rajneesh said, "are based on fear. They are antilife. No religion has accepted a sense of humor as a quality of religiousness. . . . My religion is the first religion which accepts man whole as he is." "There is no God," he told his listeners. In the past, he said, he had used Buddha, Krishna, and Christ as "jumping boards" to reach people, but they were not God or gods. "The people who believe in God are really the people who cannot trust in themselves. They need a father figure, a Big Daddy." The extreme asceticism of Jainism was "ugly." Krishna was a "male chauvinist," and Buddha, "antilife." Jesus, who believed he was "the only begotten son of God," was "neurotic," the victim of a "hallucination." Their followers were deluded. Pope John Paul II ("Pope the Polack," Rajneesh called him) and Mother Teresa were "criminals." Their stand against birth control helped create the orphans for whom Mother Teresa—to worldwide acclaim—cared.

Rajneesh said that he was, by contrast, scientific and flexible. "I have not given you any beliefs, I have only given you methods . . . one hundred and twelve methods of meditation." "The Judeo-Christian Bible is a closed system, a collection of violent and pornographic tales. *The Rajneesh Bible*," as he called this series of lectures, "is an open system." His was really "the first and last religion."

Seeing Rajneesh in person, watching videotaped reruns with several thousand sannyasins the next night on the big screens in Rajneesh Mandir, I had an eerie feeling. He skillfully dissected religious pretention and hypocrisy, lampooned rigid and authoritarian political structures, but he was all the while permitting if not promoting what he attacked. "To be rebellious is to be religious," he said, but the day-to-day life of those who listened was becoming more and more conformist, increasingly constricted by ritual and ceremony, dogma, rules and regulations, and priests. At night, Rajneesh in his discourses celebrated the rebelliousness of his own childhood. By day, the omnipresent "moms" smothered doubt with reassurance and stifled the slightest signs of independence with admonitions to "be positive," "blend in," "surrender." His commune was protected by guardposts and semiautomatic weapons and ruled by a woman who grew more papal every day. But nobody, not Rajneesh nor his "rebellious" disciples, seemed to notice or comment on the absurdly obvious way his deeds and their own denied his words and their beliefs.

This was the kind of unacknowledged contradiction that the anthropologist Gregory Bateson and his colleagues described as a "double bind." In their classic example, a mother lovingly called her child to her. When the child was almost in her arms she turned away—or otherwise signaled nonverbally that she was not receptive. The message, the call, was contradicted by the action, the turning away; there was, in addition, an injunction, explicit or implicit, not to notice or comment on the contradiction; and, finally, there was no way for the still dependent child to escape from the situation.

Bateson believed that this kind of confused and confusing interaction, if repeated often enough over a long enough period of time, could be internalized by the child. He hypothesized that many of the signs of schizophrenia—excessively concrete thinking, inappropriate use of metaphors, marked ambivalence and confusion, and self-preoccupation and withdrawal—might be responses to this bind. They were ways of achieving communication without risk of blame for its content, intrapsychic reflections of interpersonal disorder, and strategies for avoiding criticism or punishment. Bateson was aware that similar binds were a traditional teaching device, used by Zen Masters, among others. The Zen Masters devised contradictory and apparently inescapable situations to force their pupils to find spontaneous, novel solutions. The distinction between the pathological and the pedagogic bind was, Bateson wrote, in the "aims and intentions" and "awareness" of the one who created the bind, in the quality of "caring in the relationship," and in the element of "choice" that the child or disciple could exercise. The outcome was also different. The Master's disciples might gain a wider perspective, more freedom; the victims of a destructive bind would only become more fearful and constricted, more vulnerable to the confusions, distortions, and mood changes of psychopathological states.

And indeed, when I returned in March and June of 1985, there was a kind of madness abroad on the ranch, complete with all the traditional signs and symptoms that one might see in paranoid and schizoid patients—withdrawal and isolation; excessive preoccupation with concrete tasks or personal well-being; denial of one's own thoughts and feelings, and projection of them onto others. People on the ranch were learning not only to shut up but to shut down their critical faculties and turn off their awareness. They suppressed the anger and doubt and rebelliousness that Rajneesh continued to urge on them. With an intensity born of increasing desperation, they focused instead on the pleasure they felt in doing their work well, in living with so many friends and lovers, and in being with their Master.

At times the denial and projection were so exaggerated and generalized that there were certain delusional elements about them. Many sannyasins refused to acknowledge their own exploitativeness, their own anger at and contempt for their neighbors, their own responsibility for the Oregonians' opposition and enmity. Instead they saw only the baseless, implacable hatred of know-nothing rednecks and their opportunistic political allies. The conclusion: we—Rajneesh and the ranch—are innocent; the Oregonians and the U.S. government are in a conspiracy against us.

The ranch leadership encouraged sannyasins to direct their attention outward toward the threatening Oregonians and inward to their own psychological and spiritual development. The disciples were kept from breaking the enchantment of the bind, from leaving the situation, by their love for their Master, their dependency on the community, and their conviction, developed over many years of discipleship, that the bind itself might well be of Rajneesh's conscious design, for their own good.

Not all were equally caught in the grip of the double bind. Those most removed from the vagaries and tyrannies of the ranch power structure, least involved in the requirements and confusions of discipleship, and most openly grateful for the material and emotional security of the ranch—the children and the Share-A-Home people—were least susceptible. For them life on the ranch was more pleasurable, richer, more instructive, and even, in most ways, less restrictive than it was outside.

When I visit the ranch in March I talk again with Madhu. She is sixteen now, taller and slimmer, not as childlike as when I first saw her, but just as direct. After our last meeting, in Magdalena Cafeteria in the summer of 1982, she spent two years with her father in Brooklyn. She was an honor student at Franklin Delano Roosevelt High School and played in the band. As she had hoped, she got to know her father better and went to the rock concerts she enjoyed—Ozzy Osbourne and Van Halen. She hung out with her friends and generally lived the life of a middle-class teenager, "in the world." This year she felt she had, at least for the time being, "finished up outside." She wanted to be on the ranch "with my mother and Bhagwan."

She liked her school in Brooklyn, but she likes school on the ranch even more. "Out there, there is separation—you learn things in the classroom but they don't apply to your life. Here in the School Without Walls [part of the Lincoln School] everything fits together." She takes math class and learns to apply math in the accounting department of the Rajneesh Medical Corporation. She agrees that her current reading, one of Ken Follett's books, is not challenging for a bright eleventh grader, but she tells me she keeps a journal where she sometimes practices the Spanish she learned in high school in Brooklyn. On vacations she works as a "junior flight attendant" on one of the Air Rajneesh DC-3s that flies daily between Portland and Rajneeshpuram. She is thinking about becoming a pilot herself and has written to the FAA for information on how to go about it.

Madhu is content with life on the ranch and is bothered only by the pressures that come from "the people that hate us." Recently, she tells me, local people have accused sannyasins of "child abuse," a charge she finds ugly and absurd. She is upset too that the state superintendent of schools and the attorney general have taken the state's money away from their school. She thinks it may have something to do with the fact that the teachers are "wearing religious dress," or that she and the other children are participating in religious activities, including commune-run businesses. The details of the technical violations don't seem terribly important to her. She's angry and impatient. She knows she is going to "a good school." Why, apart from prejudice and malice, would Oregonians take its money away?

Like Anashwar, the other Share-A-Home people who remain on the ranch are generally content. Most of them work in Surdas (the truck farm), Rabiya (the dairy), Gorach (the recycling yard), or Magdalena or Hasid Cafeteria. There are many blacks, some Chicanos, and a few Native Americans as well as whites.

The differences among them are striking but there is a certain consistency in their comments. They remind me a bit of elderly Chinese peasants who consider every present hardship in the light of life before the revolution. Always they come back to the contrast between the violence and drugs in the world and the peacefulness on the ranch, the loneliness and defensiveness that are endemic outside and the friendliness and respect of the sannyasins. Some, like Magic, are still simply, deeply touched by the presence of "that beautiful guy, Bhagwan." Others, like Dave, a muscular forty-nine-year-old, part Sioux, are equally impressed by Rajneesh's words.

While he scrubs huge pots with unflagging energy, Dave tells me what he has learned: "I was a Christian when I came, but I'm agnostic now." He speaks methodically, powerfully, as if his words were dismantling piece by piece the structure that missionaries gave his people. "People say God is there in the darkest moments, but the other day I was thinking of the Jews in the boxcar from Warsaw to Auschwitz. After twenty-seven days the SS opened the door. There was silence. And they tell me Jesus Christ suffered. Where was God then? Bhagwan is right. People believe in Satan because they don't want to accept responsibility for bad things. Anyone who says, 'Follow me' is dangerous. And then there's the theory of creation. I look at the Grand Canyon. It took a lot more than ten thousand years to make that." Dave looks at the "Christians" as well. They want to force Rajneesh out of America, or even kill him, and Dave wonders: "Is that Christian charity?"

Others who have avoided positions of authority, or have been shunted from them, have made a separate peace with the ranch. They have accepted the leadership's definition of reality, retreated within its rigid structures, and embraced a meditative life. In Poona, Bodhi, English professor and Reichian, edited and designed Rajneesh's books. In Oregon he has had a variety of jobs. He did landscaping and farming, occasionally wrote for the paper, and played in a band. For a year and a half, during 1984 and 1985, while the ranch was filling up with fear, he has worked "in Security, standing in a booth for hours on end."

It has been for him a kind of Vipassana, a process of moment-to-moment awareness of thought and feelings. His job seems necessary. He believes, he tells me, that "the outside world was becoming increasingly brutal, through no fault of ours." In the local papers he read about "the right-wing groups who wanted to incinerate us." When during the Share-A-Home program Attorney General Frohnmayer met with law enforcement people to discuss the situation in Rajneeshpuram and excluded the Rajneeshpuram Peace Force, it helped confirm Bodhi's belief in a "government conspiracy." He sees no reason to question Sheela's actions or the ranch's protectiveness. From where he stands, "Sheela's shrillness and arming ourselves and having all this security, were obviously necessary to protect Bhagwan."

Like Bodhi, there are many others who simply avoid any questions that challenge the ranch or the authority of its leaders. A clerk in the hotel tells me she is not allowed to leave for a week to go to her sister's wedding because she is "badly needed." When I act surprised, she says she thinks it might be good discipline for her, a way of affirming her commitment. I point out that others, more highly placed and far more vital to the commune's functioning, travel freely and for less good reasons. She thinks for a moment: "Well, they're already committed."

Some people I know better are more uneasy and often more open about their doubts, and especially their fears. A forty-year-old psychotherapist and social worker whom I know from Poona motions me over to her table on the patio outside Magdalena. She glances around, leans toward me, and speaks softly. She says she has had a serious physical illness and it has been difficult for her to get a job assignment that is not too strenuous.

"Why are we whispering?" I ask.

"If someone hears what we're talking about, I may be reported to Ramakrishna, and then they'll yell at me and change my job."

"What's Ramakrishna?"

"Ramakrishna is where you go to get yelled at. It's the personnel temple."

She tells me that she and her friends only talk about their problems with the ranch administration late at night and outside. People have been told to report one another for being "negative." There are rumors that some trailers are bugged.

"Why would you lose your job?"

"Because," she says, sounding like a little girl who has learned a lesson, "I've been negative."

"Why do you put up with this shit?"

"I'm a commune member," she says, fingering the golden metal band stamped with Rajneesh's signature that circles her mala and signifies her status. "I want to be with Bhagwan." She makes me promise that if I write about her, I won't use her name.

Many old-timers have been pushed out of the positions of power they held in Poona, lavishly abused for job performances that seem perfectly adequate or better. Some, like Shiva, Nandan, and Pramod, have already left. Some, like Arup, try to see the "element of truth" in the accusations that Sheela, Vidya, and the others have leveled at her. "We are here on the ranch," she tells me, "for our own growth, to see our own frailties, our greed, our jealousy, our egotism." When Sheela accuses her of greed or sloth or any of the other sins, she can always find some portion of them in herself. For a while she too, once second in command to Laxmi, retreats—to the Hotel Rajneesh in Portland, where she works as a waitress.

Ma Mary Catherine, the editor of the *Rajneesh Times*, and Ma Deva Sarito, who had once edited *New Left Notes*—former community organizers, and kind, sincere, intelligent women—are troubled by Sheela's shabby treatment of the local people. But they too rationalize it. Mary Catherine, who has a Ph.D. in political science from Yale and worked for ten years with neighborhood groups in Portland, wrote a detailed analysis of Attorney General Frohnmayer's opinion on the church-state issue and of the role that grandstanding and bigotry and Rajneesh-baiting played in Oregon politics. It was clear to her, as early as Frohnmayer's fall 1983 opinion, that he "makes judgments first and then asks for facts later." Now when we talk about Sheela and the ranch's posture, she comes back to Frohnmayer and 1000 Friends and the INS and the U.S. attorney. They clearly "want Bhagwan out of the country" and the ranch dismantled. Sheela is only parrying their attacks, defending the ranch.

"She has to be hard to deal with politics," Sarito adds sadly, almost plaintively. "I know that I'm glad I don't have to. Besides, maybe it is all necessary for the protection of the commune. There are people out there, lots of them, who *do* want to get us." And again, both of them say, as if this made it all right, "Bhagwan appointed Sheela."

The closer I get to the center of the ranch power structure, the more strained people seem, the stranger their justifications for what is happening. When I tell

Siddha, the psychiatrist, about the clerk's obedience and my old friend's fear, he is thoughtful. "Obviously, there are fearful people on the ranch. Bhagwan is merely mirroring their fear." Siddha says he has never felt any problem making suggestions or even criticisms, but in any event he tries always to see the positive: "We believe," he explains, "that what we nourish grows. If you nourish the positive, that grows and it becomes a way of life." I understand that, I tell him, but he is in a powerful position. He is a significant person in the community and has been invited to help give shape to important aspects of ranch life. He has the freedom to move from job to job, the opportunity to take time off, the money to eat or drink in the restaurant. "Everyone," he rejoins, against the evidence of my eyes and ears, "has the opportunity."

Later that day, as if to illustrate Siddha's point, Isabel tells me about Prabodhi, a former high school teacher from Washington State who took sannyas only a few years before and has risen swiftly to become commune treasurer and the recorder of the city of Rajneeshpuram. "She was willing to do whatever was needed, to shop, cook, order food, clean tables. Being 'higher up' only means having more responsibility and working harder."

Vidya, who is president of the commune and in Sheela's absence conducts the coordinators' meetings, picks up on the same theme. "Remember," she says, "this is a 'horizontal hierarchy.' I'm no higher than anybody cleaning toilets. She treats cleaning toilets as worship. I treat my work the same way." Three years before, I listened carefully to words like these and hoped that they might presage the kind of participatory democracy that many political groups and therapeutic communities in the late 1960s had tried to create. Now, as I watch what is happening on the ranch, they have a hollow ring to them.

Vidya is an efficient administrator. She has an eye for detail and even, in many instances, a real concern for the people whose lives she is affecting: "Make sure," she says at a coordinators' meeting I attend, "that there are Japanese and Italian translators at Reception. People are coming to Enlightenment Day from all over the world. We want them to feel at home." But this is no horizontal hierarchy. Nobody was consulted about the Share-A-Home Program or the attacks on Oregonians in which Vidya eagerly seconded Sheela or the summary dismissal of sannyasins from the ranch or the authoritarian structure of work. Still, I am not sure if Vidya is lying to me, the way she did about the Share-A-Home Program, or deluding herself.

I understand from people who work in the medical center that both Vidya and Sheela have been frequently ill. In March Vidya, whose back is troubling her, conducts the coordinators' meeting lying down. In late spring, when Sheela returns, she looks ghastly. Apparently the thrombophlebitis has recurred. I am told by the people at the medical clinic that Vidya is taking muscle relaxants and analgesics, that Sheela is on amphetamines, analgesics, and tranquilizers.

One morning Siddha introduces me to Ambalal Patel, Bapuji, Sheela's father and Rajneesh's godfather. Bapuji is a bald, white-bearded, rascally man who cuddles girls and winks conspiratorially at the men. He wears a traditional Indian costume, a lunghi, a long shirt with a short vest over it—all, surprisingly, in red and pink—and a mala. While we talk, a ten-year-old boy comes over to tug at Bapuji's cane and at his attention. Another boy hovers at the edge of the conversation. Bapuji, whom

Rajneesh calls "the oldest hippie," is an object of fascination on the ranch. Interestingly, he looks a bit like the prodigal brother of Rajneesh's father, Babulal Jain.

While we sit together in the Zorba the Buddha restaurant, Bapuji repeats the story of his "adoption" of Rajneesh, a tale that seems to me like something out of an Indian *Tom Jones*. "Babulal Jain," he begins, "was to me, like a brother, a goodhearted, generous man. The adoption was done," he goes on, "when Rajneesh was very young, about three or four years old," to accommodate an astrological prediction that Rajneesh would survive his childhood only if he were adopted. The fact that Bapuji never mentioned this to anyone—not even Vasant Joshi, his son-in-law and Rajneesh's biographer—for forty-eight years is not, to him, surprising. "There was no need," he says. Now that he is old, it is time "to reveal it to the world." Bapuji, it turns out, is a naturalized U.S. citizen. As his adopted son, Rajneesh would automatically qualify for the permanent residency status that the INS is blocking.

The story is wonderful but absurd. The adoption claim, first made in February 1984, was withdrawn almost as soon as it was advanced, and the original document disappeared when the authorities asked to examine it. Still, it is interesting to talk to Bapuji. I can see how his example may have encouraged Sheela's cunning and chutzpah. Bapuji seems devoted to Rajneesh. He considers him "far greater" than Gandhi, whom he followed as a young man. "The eyes, the depth of them, they have not changed since he was three or four. I tell you," he says, leaning toward me, "centuries and centuries haven't produced such a man."

The same day that I speak with Bapuji, late in the afternoon, there is an emergency meeting between the Rajneeshpuram School Board and Ronald Burge, Oregon's deputy superintendent of education, and a representative of the attorney general's office. It takes place in the new town hall, which was the original farmhouse and then the restaurant and most recently the newspaper.

A few days ago, after consultation with the attorney general, Superintendent of Schools Verne Duncan called a press conference to announce that he was taking state funds away from the sannyasins' Lincoln School. Duncan said he believed the school was violating the separation of church and state in several ways: children and teachers used the religious form of address "Beloved"; teachers wore religious garb, red clothes and malas; finally, a religious organization, the commune, benefited from the children's labor in the School Without Walls program.

Today K.D., the mayor of Rajneeshpuram, sits at one table with the members of the school board. Wadud, the city planner, is the chairman. The other two members are women—Pathika, who has a master's degree in education from Harvard, and Rabiya, an older black woman, who has taught music for more than twenty-five years. The representatives of the state sit at another table. The sannyasins look fit and relaxed and rather smart in their bright clothes. The state representatives are stiff, uncomfortable, in business suits. Both groups are warmed by floodlights: every moment is being recorded by the ranch's video equipment and a Portland TV station.

At the beginning of the meeting I am quite sympathetic to the ranch. Ordinarily money is not summarily taken away from a school district. A board is usually given ninety days to remedy the infractions. If it fails to do so, the district may be put on probation for a year. Instead of adhering to standard procedure, Duncan simply called a press conference to announce the cutoff of funds. This seems premature and unnecessary to me, a bit of grandstanding to harass sannyasins, who, according to the state's own inspection team, are doing a creditable job with their school.

Two hours later I find my sympathies wearing thin. It does seem that the state is discriminating against and mistreating the sannyasins, but they in turn are doing their best to mistreat and abuse their accusers. At the meeting I sit between Mary Catherine, who is covering the story for the *Rajneesh Times*, and Shanti Bhadra, one of Sheela's intimates, who is so angry she can barely sit still. Shanti B. has two children in the school, she tells me, a sixteen-year-old boy, Santosh, and a fourteen-year-old girl, Aruna. Santosh, she says, is precise and very good with video equipment, Aruna is more sensitive. Both have written intelligent letters to Superintendent Duncan, which she proudly shows me.

Aruna begins her letter with the salutation "Beloved Mr. Duncan." She goes on to complain to the superintendent that there is nothing wrong with addressing people as "Beloved," that it is an affectionate and not necessarily religious word. She reminds him that there are no gang fights, cliques, drugs, or graffiti in their school. "You should be proud," she concludes, "to have Lincoln School in your state."

Shanti B. and Mary Catherine and I watch as K.D. begins the meeting by calling for the resignation of "Vermin Verne Duncan." Afterward Wadud outlines the situation with the Lincoln School. It is clear to him that the state is not interested in the facts but only in depriving the sannyasins of what is their due. When the bureaucrats begin to ask questions, he interrupts: "Those are stupid questions."

"Yes, stupid," echoes Shanti Bhadra beside me.

I think, not for the first time, that though their children are rather grown up, the sannyasins themselves often behave like junior high school kids. They interrupt and shout nasty words and stand, at least figuratively, in the face of their opponents daring them to fight.

After the meeting, while the state people give a press conference, I talk with Subhan, the school board's lawyer, and Raja, a photographer for the *Rajneesh Times*. I tell them I understand that they are angry and that they need to fight for their rights. But they are clearly right and will certainly, with a few minor changes in school procedures, get the funds back. So why behave this way? "You have to speak up," Raja says, not quite hearing the question. There is a long history of prejudice and bigotry in Oregon, he reminds me. Indians were slaughtered. The Klan tried to keep Mormons and blacks and Catholics out. "Look at blacks in the South" — he is getting warmed up now — "Jews in Germany. If the Jews were not so polite, maybe six million wouldn't have been killed."

"Yes," I say, feeling a little academic in the face of so much fervor, "but the situation is different. It's not a question of killing. Also you have some power here and you happen to be right."

Shanti Bhadra is furious. "When they start on the kids it's despicable," she says, unconsciously echoing the sentiments of Oregonians about the original Antelope School District takeover by the sannyasins. The state people get up to leave and Shanti B. breaks away to follow them. She bends down toward the car window which is swiftly rolled up, and shouts through the glass at Deputy Superintendent Burge, "You're stupid, stupid, stupid."

I return to the ranch at the beginning of June. During the day I can go without a sweater or jacket. The hot tubs are bubbling in the courtyard of the hotel. There are tables outside on the deck of the restaurant. The spring rains have come and gone, and the ground is drying and warming. The battle between the local people and the ranch is heating up as well.

On my way to Rajneeshpuram I have spent an afternoon at Jon Bowerman's and an evening with him and his neighbors in the city of Rajneesh. Bowerman reviews the situation for me. There has been pain and dislocation. Only fifteen of the thirty-nine people who lived in Antelope when Sheela and Jay first came are presently there. But he is still quietly confident about the future. State and federal law enforcement authorities are gearing up to move on the ranch. There are rumors that a grand jury is about to be convened on the immigration charges against Rajneesh and the sannyasins. Frohnmayer is continuing to pursue the church-state case. On Sunday evening at the Antelope Community Church, Bill Dickson, the postmaster, speaks of what is going to come. He hints that the local people have held off on any direct physical action against the ranch because they believe that soon, in the courts, "the Rajneesh will get theirs."

Within hours after I arrive on the ranch I meet the members of the opposition. Almost everyone who has research and office skills who is not in an essential occupation is "worshipping" in Rajneesh Legal Services. Moses, the health planner, is the office manager. Sarito, the community organizer, and Gopa, who worked in the office in Poona, are there, and so are as many as four hundred other sannyasins, about one seventh of the ranch's permanent population. One Portland attorney who is opposing the ranch in a case tells me that Rajneesh Legal Services, with more lawyers and many more employees than any Oregon firm east of the Cascades, has "produced more paper than any firm I've ever litigated against."

Everyone on the ranch is working hard, but these people seem to be doing sixteen hours a day, every day. At the ranch airport in the morning and evening there are sannyasin lawyers and paralegals in their orange and red dresses and suits and shirts and ties, with briefcases in hand. They fly as regularly between Rajneeshpuram and Portland as suburban commuters.

Already they have filed eight to ten suits (it is hard for even a government office to keep track) against the U.S. attorney and almost as many against the Oregon attorney general. Presently they are preparing a brief against U.S. Attorney General Edwin Meese, Secretary of State George Shultz, and the INS, among others. The suit describes the INS's probe into sannyasin immigration practices as a "religion-based and discriminatory program of unlawful and intrusive monitoring" and asks for an injunction against its continuance.

Sitting on the terrace outside Zorba the Buddha with the sun pouring down on the new landscaping, drinking espresso as good as any in New York or Washington, eating croissants and Danish freshly baked in Magdalena, watching sannyasins replant the trees that have been undermined by the spring floods, I see no hint of the forces being mobilized off or on the ranch. Men and women on tea break walk past, laughing, holding hands.

On this visit I'm spending time catching up with people whom I haven't seen for a while or have wanted to meet. My first appointment is with Satya Vedant, who, under his original name, Vasant Joshi, authored the official biography of Rajneesh, *The Awakened One*. Vedant is an educated Indian, an academic who is married to Sheela's sister. He was once the dean of the California School of Asian Studies in San Francisco and is now the chancellor of the Rajneesh International Meditation University.

We relate easily to one another, as if we were classmates at Harvard or are serving together on a joint Indo-American Committee on New Religions. He is an alert and intelligent man who speaks with great reverence of Rajneesh. Much of our conversation is taken up with a comparison between Krishnamurti and Rajneesh. "Rajneesh," he says, "creates a wide circle. He has made everybody free to be whatever they want to be. He has touched them with many things. Here in America everybody writes about Rajneesh and sex, Rajneesh and money. But he has talked about many other things — meditation, the Master-disciple relationship, politics, ecology, the family, health. He has created a wide circle and whatever touches you, it is OK. Krishnamurti is by contrast a narrow circle.

"Bhagwan says Krishnamurti is one who has already reached the top of the ladder. Krishnamurti says people should right away jump up to it. Bhagwan says this is unnatural, not possible. Krishnamurti sees humanity as an abstraction. Bhagwan says there is no humanity, only individuals. His concern is more compassionate, he is ready to come down to your level. He makes no judgment. He says, 'I'm always there, in case you need my help.' He has given us" — Vedant looks around at the sannyasins who are filling in potholes, grading the road — "tremendous courage, tremendous strength. There is a possibility that we can get out of this misery. His is a pragmatic approach to life. He deals with realities as they are, even if it hurts. He doesn't care what his image is. He gives all of us the opportunity to try it out without condemnation or judgment."

Bapuji comes up to the table, shakes my hand, and speaks some words in Gujarati to his son-in-law. Bapuji moves off to join his wife, Maniben, who has stood several feet away. Vedant goes on, as if in answer to my unspoken question, "Sheela too has had an opportunity, just as we all have. I explore my writing on the newspaper and learn how to trust in my coordinator. If she makes a mistake, so what, we'll try again the next day. And all of us feel the same way about Sheela. She has the same opportunity we have. If she makes a mistake, she'll have another chance."

I indulge an urge to ask — or maybe needle is a better word — Vedant about the Rolls-Royces. He answers with the same grace he would devote to any other question. "Why are there so many Rolls-Royces? There is no reason, except that I can offer him something different every day. To watch him in the same car is boring. It gives him pleasure to have a new car. So here we are in the position to make available eighty Rolls-Royces. And tomorrow there may not be one. I'm not going to cry. Neither is Bhagwan."

Vedant leaves and soon my former psychiatric supervisor, Bodhicitta, and his girlfriend, Carolyn, arrive for lunch. He looks fit and tan, ten years younger and much happier than when I first met him fifteen years before. He parks his old bicycle nearby. While we eat and talk, he and Carolyn hold hands and gaze at one another like teenagers. They've been together for several years. I haven't seen Bodhicitta since early 1982. We didn't talk much then and we have a lot to catch up on.

"When I came back from Poona," he begins, "people thought I was hypnotized, brainwashed, or very batty." He was "in conflict—stay with the family or go off with Bhagwan. There was nothing left in my career. The ambition part had disappeared. Psychotherapy was an ego game, the therapist's teaching seemed to be cunning—there was no surrender in it, no love. I had found the source of love and happiness with Bhagwan, but none of my old teachers and colleagues were interested. They were miserable but they were looking for answers within the misery, in psychotherapy and intellectual analysis. I kept going back and forth to Poona and I kept asking Bhagwan if I should stay. And he kept saying, 'Go back, share my vision, it's not time yet, Bodhicitta.'

"I came to the first world celebration. I heard Bhagwan's prediction of the Third World War and it was like a bath of cold water. I wrote and I said, 'I will do anything I can do to make your vision come about,' to create the Noah's Ark of consciousness. I came out for the Counselor Training Course for three months. I went back and felt empty. People seemed so much more closed out there." Then, after years of agonizing about it, Bodhicitta left his wife and children. "Ninety percent of the people who hadn't dropped me after I became a sannyasin dropped me after I left [my wife] and the family."

He clearly loves being on the ranch and is, if not untroubled, at least not particularly concerned with the Oregon political situation. It seems unimportant compared to his own development and the dangers that the world faces. "There's a great steady river I am now. Sometimes I'm sad, sometimes I'm happy. Things that used to freak me out a lot now only make me upset for a few hours. There's a steady, continuing sense of well-being. My energy grows and grows."

I remember how flamboyant he was as a family therapist, how overbearing he could be as a teacher. There is still something excessive, self-absorbed about him. But he is sweet now. There is little tension in being with him, and I know that he does not arouse the same kind of competitiveness in me. Perhaps he has changed, and perhaps I have as well.

"The lovingness grows in me and confuses me sometimes," he goes on. "I still think about *The Limits to Growth*. I haven't seen anything that shows even a fraction of a response to the economic and ecological problems, let alone the problems of nuclear war and poverty." He has no answer either, but "at least I'm working on myself. This is a laboratory, a basic training in becoming aware and happy no matter what's coming down. And I have a sense that I'm not going to be a grunt all my life, that I'm going to be some modest kind of help to a lot of people. Still, I'd really be happy if there was nothing left to do except stay with Bhagwan and be in the commune. Life is so rich for me. I feel like I'm beginning to drop my lifelong sense of separateness."

It is one forty-five and Bodhicitta and Carolyn wander off to find a good spot for the drive-by. I get up too and go over to Torah Crossing, where I see Mary Catherine. We stand side by side. Pretty soon we're discussing politics again—the suit that the sannyasins have filed against Bob Harvey, the former ranch employee, claiming that he was accidentally overpaid ($1,000 a week instead of $1,000 a month), the rumors of the grand jury. I agree that the state is "after" Rajneesh and the ranch but point out that their use of the law is not very different from the sannyasins' in Antelope. There is bigotry, to be sure, but the ranch has been at least partly responsible for bringing down so much organized opposition. All those illegal marriages, the unnecessary abuse of local people, the takeover of Antelope, Sheela's insults, the behavior of sannyasins at the school board meeting a couple of months ago, even the suit against Bob Harvey—what's the point? Can't she see their responsibility? Mary Catherine begins her rebuttal: the sannyasins wanted simply to build an isolated community to be with their Master, to avoid politics. Suddenly, as if by agreement, we fall silent and begin to sway in time to the rising sound of guitars and drums.

It is precisely 2:00 P.M. and Rajneesh is guiding a Rolls-Royce down the long drive from Lao-tzu House. He is wearing a white robe and a white knit hat trimmed in blue. His long beard is almost as white as his robe. Today the Rolls is maroon. Vivek is in the seat next to him.

The Rolls passes through the iron gate toward the crossing named for Lieh-tzu, a Taoist Master. A heavyset middle-aged Indian woman, Taru, one of Rajneesh's early disciples, is twisting and turning, dancing to flutes and drums, cymbals and tambourines. Other sannyasins are singing the words of Indian devotional songs, bhajans, over and over.

A four-wheel-drive vehicle with two men in burgundy windbreakers precedes the Rolls. The men have sidearms and there is a shotgun in the rack of the cab. Behind the Rolls another man is walking. He is wearing black-rimmed goggles, carrying a semiautomatic weapon at the ready. Behind him are two men in a second four-wheel-drive. One is K.D. There is also a semiautomatic weapon in their vehicle. They are looking at the long curving line of sannyasins and at the hills behind them. Officers from the Rajneeshpuram Peace Force and Rajneesh Security are asking people to step back.

Overhead a tiny helicopter swoops and dives like a dragonfly. It hovers for a moment above the trees in Nirvana Grove, where there are small monuments to Rajneesh's father and Vimalkirti, my Poona group leader. He died in Poona of a ruptured cerebral aneurysm and was declared by Rajneesh to be enlightened. The helicopter moves off to check the sagebrush-and-juniper-covered hills behind Rajneesh's house. It darts ahead over the restaurants and stores of downtown Rajneeshpuram, over our heads to Torah Crossing and on to Zen Drive, where four thousand more people are waiting.

Rajneesh stops in front of a group of musicians. His eyes are large, dark brown, liquid. A handsome Indian man—a movie star from Bombay—is playing a drum. John and Hasya are side by side shaking tambourines. Not far from them are Anashwar and Magic. Rajneesh takes his hands from the wheel and raises them, palms up, in the air. The tempo and volume increase. Taru dances faster and faster.

The Rolls turns the corner and picks up speed as it heads down Zen Drive. The sannyasins he has passed turn toward one another, laughing, crying, embracing. Some gaze after the car and bow. Some gather around the musicians and continue their singing and dancing. Anashwar and Magic drift back to their work at Magdalena Cafeteria.

At the head of the next line Bapuji is dancing. Next to him is Siddha, and next to him, Vidya. Bodhicitta and Carolyn are standing near them—Bodhicitta has his hands in namaste—and nearby is Mona, who is now called Rafi, who took me home with her in Poona. Bapuji dances like a cross between an old bear and a young goat, keeping time with finger cymbals. Rajneesh stops in front of him, grins, and raises his hands. Vidya, the president of the commune, falls in step beside the car.

The Rolls glides slowly past commune members, Rajneeshpuram residents, and visitors, and passes in front of another group of musicians. Many of them are blacks from America's streets. Before they came, the sannyasins at the drive-by were silent and still. Now they explode with music and motion. There are saxophones, cornets, and guitars here as well as flutes, cymbals, drums, and tambourines. Everyone is singing, "Bhagwan is the Master of love and laughter." Rajneesh raises his hands again and smiles.

Rajneesh drives on, past the men and women who are worshipping at RIMU. Dozens of the people whom I have met over the years are on the line there. Puja and Krishna Prem, Karuna, Teertha and Gopa, Isabel and Moses, a few from Washington, and many more from Poona. As the car comes closer, they are jumping and clapping and laughing and singing, "Bhagwan is the Master of love and laughter."

Sheela is often visible at the drive-by, with Savita or Shanti B. or Puja, across the street from the line of sannyasins, a .357 magnum in a holster on her hip. Today I know she will not be there, for she is currently on one of her periodic trips to other sannyasin communities.

The Rolls passes by and turns onto the county road and heads along the rim of the valley toward the city of Rajneesh. Today, as he often does, Rajneesh will drive north to The Dalles, the largest town in Wasco County, a hundred miles away.

More and more, Sheela was absent from the ranch, traveling in Europe, Asia, and Australia, trying to speed up the process of consolidation that Rajneesh, since 1982, had repeatedly urged. On December 19, 1984, he explained—creating yet another double bind—that he was trying to "decentralize power," and that small centers were to be dissolved into bigger communes because small centers could be "crushed very easily." Each commune, he said, compounding the confusion, was "autonomous, but still they are all alike, exactly patterned like the commune here." He was sending Sheela "every month for three days to each commune . . . to see that the religious work is carried out according to my mission."

In practice, these contradictions—decentralizing by centralizing, autonomous communes "exactly patterned" on the ranch—and the fear of being "crushed" goaded Sheela to become more irrational, increasingly dictatorial toward the communes and provocative toward the communities in which they were located. Eventually she and Rajneesh and the ranch, with their incessant demands for money and personnel, for conformity within and confrontation without, produced precisely the dangers they meant to protect against.

This strange process of organizational self-destruction was most obvious in Sheela's trip to Australia in the spring of 1985. When she came to Perth in western Australia, the sannyasins there were an established and accepted part of the community. They ran profitable businesses and had a peaceful relationship with local people. A school was planned in Keri Valley. One local sannyasin owned a considerable portion of a major high-technology firm. Sheela arrived and blitzed local radio and television. Aping Rajneesh, and without apparent reason, she called the Pope an "idiot" and Mother Teresa "ugly," and she encouraged the sannyasin entrepreneur to attempt a takeover of his company.

In a few weeks she managed to alienate most of the people on the subcontinent, to poison many of the cordial relationships that local sannyasins had established, and to make it impossible for the sannyasin entrepreneur to remain with his own company. In one much-publicized photo session she smiled smugly and gave the finger to the camera and her Australian critics. When the Australian television's "60 Minutes" asked how she would feel "if the people of Australia did not want Rajneeshees in their community," she responded, "Tough titties."

In Australia, as elsewhere in the world, some sannyasins left the movement and some resisted or protested Sheela's actions; but most remained silent and acquiesced. On the ranch Sheela's visit, an obvious disaster, was hailed by the *Rajneesh Times* as a triumph. The paper printed a picture of a cake in the shape of a fist with the middle finger extended, with the legend "Tuff titties."

On and off the newspaper, sannyasins in Rajneeshpuram suppressed their anger and the doubt and rebelliousness that Rajneesh continued to urge them to express. Though they appeared as blithe and self-assured as ever, they had become passive and dependent, resigned and regressed, like small, vulnerable children whose parents had put them in a double bind. They remained trapped, unwilling to leave or to point out the destructive contradictions because they feared the loss of their secure position in the family of sannyasins, the deprivation of maternal, communal, love, and—most of all—exile from the presence of the father, Rajneesh, who had for so long been a source of strength and inspiration.

The process of denial and projection was also by now complete and reflexive. For all the subtlety of their argumentation, for all their intelligence, sannyasins now saw and interpreted the world in black and white terms. One party was right, the other wrong. Relative proximity to Bhagwan was the only compass for truth. This was true of their evaluations of both the ranch's relationship to the outside world and Rajneesh's with Sheela. What Sheela and the ranch did in relation to the world was always necessary and good; what was done to the ranch by the world was unnecessary, persecutory, malign.

The same principle held true in Sheela's dealings with the ranch. If Sheela acted toward other sannyasins in a way that seemed oppressive and destructive, this was because Rajneesh had told her to and knew that it was necessary; or because she was not telling him what she was doing; or because he was letting her, like a participant in a therapeutic group, play out the megalomaniacal side of her character. These differences were important to the sannyasins who had begun quietly to debate them. But the fundamental article of dogma remained unchanged: if there was wisdom it belonged to the source of wisdom, Bhagwan; if error or myopia, then it was Sheela's.

For many it was, as Siddha had said, a question of subjective experience, of simply "nourishing the positive" in one's experience of the ranch—and, presumably, eliminating the negative by starving it. Others, like Teertha, were inclined, at least publicly, to total trust. One morning at RIMU he looked deep into my eyes. "How, knowing

Bhagwan's work as you do, can you question?" Even those who were troubled by the authoritarian structure of ranch life, Sheela's destructive behavior, and the ranch's paranoia saw these as necessary steps in the commune's development. One had to accept the negative, go into it. "This," Sarito suggested, echoing a hopeful thought that I had once had, "is like Dynamic, with all the accusations and all the attacks and all the swearing and all the tantrums. We're in the cathartic stage now."

Perhaps it was all a device, many of them eventually concluded. Sooner or later, they believed, when the time was right, "Bhagwan will turn things around." Like children frozen in a double bind, like the fascists they accused the Oregonians of resembling, they waited for their leader to act.

In May 1985 the suit brought by Helen Byron, a wealthy ex-sannyasin in her sixties, against the Rajneesh Foundation International went to trial. In 1978, Byron, who was suffering from multiple sclerosis, was living in Maui with her daughter Barbara. Barbara went to Poona, took sannyas and the name Makima, and then encouraged her mother to come. On her fifth day in Poona Helen Byron donated $80,000 to the ashram. She became Ma Idam Shunyio and met Laxmi and Rajneesh. In June 1979 she was invited to live in the ashram. She was well cared for by sannyasin physicians and massage therapists, and her physical condition began to improve. That year she gave $113,000 to the ashram.

Helen Byron said that in 1980, at Sheela's request, she loaned $310,000 to the Rajneesh Foundation. She had kept the money in a Swiss bank account for "long-term medical needs." Her understanding was that the money was to be applied to the purchase of land in Gujarat and that she would be repaid. She did not ask for, nor was she given, a receipt for the loan. She trusted Sheela. She had also deposited $80,000 in the ashram bank. In June 1980, following the knife-throwing incident at the ashram, the $310,000 was transferred to a Chicago bank account. It was used to pay for the remodeling and armoring of a stretch Rolls-Royce, which was then shipped to India.

In 1981, on assignment from Sheela, Helen Byron went looking for land for the new commune in America. In June 1982, dissatisfied with Sheela's administration, she left the ranch and settled in Santa Fe, New Mexico, where she and her daughter Barbara and Barbara's husband, Trevor Hawkins—both of whom also dropped sannyas—still live. In January 1983 Byron asked Sheela for her money back; in July of that year Helen Byron was declared to be among the "enlightened ones." She asked for the money again, her request was denied, and she sued.

The trial brought angry ex-sannyasins—Helen and Barbara Byron, Trevor Hawkins, and Anna Forbes—into direct and public confrontation with Sheela and the ranch hierarchy. Testimony was presented by the defendant to discredit Helen Byron and by Byron to discredit Sheela.

The official ranch response to Byron's suit was exaggerated, unreflective, and unself-consciously ugly. The vitriol made me suspect even before I knew the facts of the case that Helen Byron was probably telling the truth. In a news story in the May 24 *Rajneesh Times* the headline read, "Vengeful Woman Sues RFI." It quoted an "unidentified court observer" who characterized the proceedings as "the vengeful crusade of a disenchanted old woman."

In the courtroom some thirty-five sannyasins—including many people who had been their closest friends—harassed Byron and her witnesses. The sannyasins stared at them in the courtroom, taunted them in the corridors, and crowded them in the courthouse elevator. Byron's lawyer, Mark Cushing, and several other witnesses told me that Siddha, the psychiatrist, seemed particularly venomous. Reportedly, he held his nose and complained of "the smell"; wondered aloud, "How much money are you getting for this?"; asked Barbara Byron, "How does it feel to be Judas?"; and called them all "traitors."

When all the legal dust had settled, one question remained for the jury: Who was telling the truth, Helen Byron or Sheela? The jury decided for Helen Byron and awarded her $1.7 million in compensation and punitive damages. (Eventually, to pay the judgment, Utsava, the sannyasins' Laguna Beach center, was sold.)

Several weeks afterward I tried to call Siddha at the ranch. I had felt that he was becoming more vehement, less coherent, in his defense of ranch policies, but the kind of behavior he'd shown at the trial seemed so ugly and childish, so unlike him. I wanted to hear his side of the story. He didn't return the call and I forgot about it for a while. I called again in July. Rosalie, the Twinkie who answered, told me that Siddha and Prabodhi, the commune treasurer and Rajneeshpuram's city recorder, had driven away in the middle of the night. No one knew where they were or when and if they were coming back.

I didn't know what Siddha's motivation was, but certainly the ranch and its leadership had been seriously threatened, both materially and psychologically, by Helen Byron's suit. She and Barbara were, I had learned, powerful and wealthy members of the sannyasin community. They were loved as well as respected. Their direct and unequivocal contradiction of Sheela's testimony had inevitably stirred up all the doubts—about Sheela and her honesty and the conduct of business on the ranch and around the world—that sannyasins, particularly those in a position to know or guess the truth, had tacitly agreed to ignore. Their open opposition to Sheela would steel others in their dissent. And finally, the Byrons' escape from the double bind, their willingness to tell the truth—about their confusion and acquiescence, and about the deception that was used on them and their own self-deception—would challenge the spell in which others, including those who attacked them, were still allowing themselves to be held.

PART III

BREAKUP

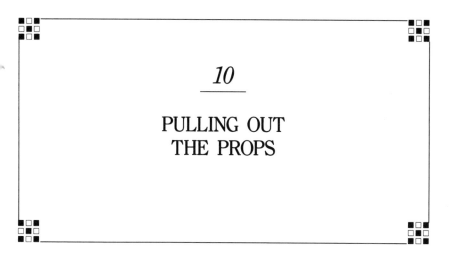

10

PULLING OUT
THE PROPS

On September 14 and 15, 1985, Sheela and nineteen others, including Vidya; Puja; K.D.; Shanti Bhadra; Homa, who had been the Rajneeshpuram municipal judge; Julian, an "electronics wizard" who was coordinator of the Edison Temple; and Su, who had worked with Vidya, left the ranch. In Europe some of them met up with Savita, who had directed the ranch's financial operations, and a Swiss sannyasin, Swami Dhyan Dipo, who had recently — after Sheela allegedly obtained a backdated Nepalese divorce from Jayananda — become Sheela's third husband.

On Monday, September 16, in the daily morning discourse he had begun a few months before, Rajneesh announced to the commune that Sheela had "resigned on her own . . . and taken those idiots she has put in powerful positions." "Sheela," he said, "turned my commune into a fascist concentration camp." He had begun, he said, to speak publicly when he realized this. Now he was revealing crimes of which he had only recently become aware.

Sheela and her "fascist gang" had poisoned the three people closest to him: Devaraj, Devageet, and Vivek. They had, he continued — without citing evidence — also poisoned Mike Sullivan, the Jefferson County district attorney (who was regarded as a potential threat to the ranch), and the water system in The Dalles. In addition, he suggested, they might have been involved in the salmonella outbreak in The Dalles the previous year, in a fire in the office of the Wasco County planning director, Dan Durow, and in sabotage of law enforcement vehicles. He demanded that state and federal authorities investigate his charges and bring "Sheela and her gang" back for trial.

Federal and state law enforcement officials were overwhelmed and overjoyed. They had been laboriously building immigration, land use, and church-state cases, which they believed were solid, against the sannyasins. But from what I had been able to discover from conversations with immigration and constitutional lawyers, none of them had the kind of "bulletproof case" that Attorney General Frohnmayer said he wanted. Even if indictments were handed down, trials held, and convictions obtained, the appeals could have gone on for years. It was by no means certain that they would ever reach the goals toward which their efforts seemed increasingly to be directed: the removal of Rajneesh from the country and dissolution of his Oregon commune.

And then, all at once, the man on whom they had set their sights had given them more ammunition than they had ever imagined available. The authorities, Oregon congressman Jim Weaver said, were looking for "a stool pigeon" and now "we got the biggest one of all, the Bhagwan himself." They quickly organized a task force that included representatives of the Oregon State Police, the sheriff's departments and district attorneys of Wasco and Jefferson counties, The Dalles city police, the attorney general's office, the FBI, and the Rajneeshpuram Peace Force.

Each day Rajneesh produced more "revelations." More than one hundred wiretaps and bugs had been placed in offices, hotel rooms, sannyasins' living rooms, Sheela's conference room, and Rajneesh's bedroom. There was a secret tunnel leading from Sheela's bathroom through hidden doors to an underground bunker that connected with a culvert which emerged above ground just beyond the fence around Jesus Grove. In the bunker books had been found. Among the titles were *Deadly Substances, The Perfect Crime and How to Commit It*, a photocopy of an article entitled "Poison Investigations" with sections and symptoms highlighted, and four volumes of a work entitled *How to Kill*.

There was also a secret laboratory, where Puja, the nurse, was experimenting with toxic bacteria and undetectable poisons. It seemed that Puja was also trying to culture the AIDS virus. It turned out that two sannyasins who did not have positive tests for AIDS antibodies—a woman named Zeno, who was a graphics designer, and Megha, a doctor—had been told by Puja they did and then sequestered far from the center of ranch life in Desiderata Canyon with eleven people who actually had positive tests. I was told that Zeno and Megha knew things about her activities that Sheela did not want revealed. Reporters were shown the bunker and books and bugs, and the laboratory, allegedly stripped before Sheela left, with its burned benches and gas masks.

Later, a hit list of potential targets for assassination was discovered. Attorney General Frohnmayer was on it, and so were U.S. Attorney Charles Turner, and Les Zaitz, a reporter who had co-authored a long and critical series of articles on the ranch for the *Oregonian*. Helen Byron and Laxmi and Vivek and Barbara Byron were scheduled to be "disabled."

From the first months on the ranch, Sheela had told sannyasins to conceal their intentions from prying eyes, to be careful in their phone conversations and correspondence. The enemy was everywhere. INS checks, she explained, might reveal the illegality of their visas; careful Wasco County monitoring might turn up more ranch residents than were permissible and uncover activities for which permits were necessary. The FBI and the CIA, she said, were intercepting mail and tapping phone lines to collect evidence. Later, sannyasins were advised to take care when eating off the ranch or to avoid sexual relations with those who had not been tested for AIDS. They were fed a steady diet of rumors about plots to attack and kill them and their Master.

Some of the accusations against others were accurate. Angry local people wanted the sannyasins to leave the ranch. County, state, and federal agencies were suspicious of sannyasins' activities, employed informers, and did, at least after a time, want to destroy the commune. "Even paranoids," as the poet Delmore Schwartz has noted, "have enemies." Still, the most outrageous accusations were not true. They were in fact projections of the fears and desires of the ranch leadership and descriptions of the ranch's own practices. They were also employed to heighten the sannyasins' fear, to bind them together against the outside world, and to cement Sheela's position of leadership. The sannyasins were the ones eavesdropping and poisoning, planning to spread AIDS and plotting to kill and maim.

These actions were not only criminal but grandiose and crazy, a textbook litany of paranoid acting-out consistent with what I had been observing but far exceeding my expectations and even the wildest rumors I had heard. The crimes Rajneesh listed in morning discourses were detailed with others in a document that Lieutenant Dean Renfrow of the state police compiled in late September from the testimony of dozens of sannyasins—the "Affidavit for Search Warrant of Rajneeshpuram." Though carefully and matter-of-factly worded, the affidavit made chilling reading. From early 1983 when, Renfrow's affidavit alleged, Jefferson County attorney Mike Sullivan was poisoned, through a July 6, 1985, attempt on Devaraj's life, the ranch leadership, under the guidance of Sheela and with Puja's expert help, adopted a policy of intimidating, disabling, and eliminating real or perceived enemies.

Sometimes, as in Sullivan's case, the poisoning seems to have been tactical, part of a carefully orchestrated campaign in which ingratiation and deception alternated with intimidation. Sometimes, as in the tranquilization of the Share-A-Home people, it was a crude, large-scale, all but indiscriminate pacification technique. Sometimes, as with Vivek, the motivation was mixed: envy and hatred went hand in hand with tactical advantage. In every instance, as I read, I could feel Sheela's fear of and contempt for those whom she was poisoning. And always I was aware that she was not acting alone, that from two or three to twenty or thirty other people knew what she was doing, helped her do it, and watched the consequences of the acts with her—Sullivan deathly ill, the Share-A-Home people zombified, Vivek throwing up, Devaraj gasping for air—and did not stop her.

The testimony of Samya, a Brazilian woman who was at one time an intimate of Sheela's and publisher of the *Rajneesh Times*, was particularly graphic.

Samya claimed—in testimony excerpted in the affidavit—she tried to warn Rajneesh about Sheela and was in turn poisoned for her pains. Somehow—this was a bit murky—she remained close enough to Sheela to witness the following events on the day that Devaraj was injected with poison. According to Renfrow, Samya described "entering Sheela's room. . . . Sheela and Shanti Bhadra were in an adjoining bathroom and did not notice Samya's presence. Samya saw Shanti B. acting very excited, literally jumping up and down saying, 'I did it, I did it.' Sheela then teased Shanti B. saying, 'I didn't know you were such a good nurse.' " When Sheela and Shanti Bhadra came out of the bathroom and saw Samya, they changed the subject and "in fact no other conversation took place." Shortly thereafter, on the same day, Samya heard that "Devaraj had been sick and he was flown out of the commune."

The most extraordinary of the ranch offenses was the salmonella poisoning that took place in The Dalles in September 1984. According to secret grand jury testimony that was soon forthcoming from K.D. and others, it was a trial run for election day. The thinking behind this seemed to be that if the ranch residents and Rajneesh Humanities Trust work-study participants and Share-A-Home people voted as a block for the Wasco County commissioners *and* a significant portion of non-sannyasins were disabled on election day—by severe diarrhea, dehydration, fever—then the sannyasins could elect their own candidate or candidates. The mad logic of this plan was exceeded only by that of the hit list. By murdering Turner and Frohnmayer and Zaitz, Sheela and her intimates seem to have believed, in profound disregard for the way law enforcement agencies or newspapers operate, that they would end the investigations these people had begun.

The attacks on sannyasins represented a thoroughgoing attempt at suppressing, if need be permanently, internal dissent and turned out to be far more widespread than even Rajneesh had first suggested. In the weeks following his "revelations" I heard stories from or about Hasya, Mary Catherine, Deva Prem, and Laxmi, as well as Vivek, Devageet, and Devaraj. Unexplained illnesses befell each of them at times when he or she was reluctant to follow Sheela's directions or seemed to her to be a threat.

Often, just prior to becoming ill, the offending sannyasin had had a cup of tea or a meal with Sheela or one that had been delivered at her behest. Deva Prem, the construction coordinator had, I heard, been given Haldol when he announced he was leaving the ranch. Shortly after she told Sheela that it would be impossible, as well as illegal, to fix the Wasco County election, Mary Catherine fell ill for ten days. Laxmi was welcomed back to the ranch in 1985 following surgery for cancer; she felt quite well and then suddenly, after receiving a prepared meal, developed severe abdominal pains. A recurrence of her tumor was suspected, but when she was hospitalized none was found. Hasya developed a terrible headache after a bartender who was close to Sheela served her a drink.

There is something comic as well as criminal about all this poisoning: all these sannyasins suddenly falling ill and suspecting and doing nothing. In the case of Rajneesh's doctor, Devaraj, the attempts reached the proportions of opera buffa.

Sheela regarded Devaraj as a powerful, uncontrollable influence on Rajneesh and, apparently accurately, as an opponent of her regime. When he married Hasya in 1984, he became even more threatening. Devaraj had access to Rajneesh and his trust, Hasya had independent sources of money and a proven talent for raising funds and running a business. From the time Hasya had arrived on the ranch Sheela feared that Rajneesh might choose the film producer to replace her. She bugged Hasya's house and the table at Zorba the Buddha where Hasya and her friends ordinarily sat. In time the bugs Sheela had also planted in Rajneesh's room revealed that he was indeed becoming fed up with her and considering Hasya as her successor. Five years earlier, Sheela had positioned herself to succeed Laxmi. Now she saw Hasya poised to supplant her.

At first Sheela tried to make Devaraj so ill that he would be unable to continue to function as Rajneesh's physician and confidant. During 1984 and 1985, often after eating with Sheela, Devaraj repeatedly and inexplicably developed severe cramps, vomiting, and diarrhea. When he proved as resilient as Rasputin, emerging unfazed from his repeated illnesses, Sheela decided that Devaraj had to be killed. This, she seems to have believed, was the only way to forestall her own ouster and Hasya's takeover.

According to affidavits and testimony later given to a grand jury, Sheela, in order to bring others around to her point of view, produced tapes in which Rajneesh and his doctor discussed their shared fascination with death. Apparently Sheela convinced other sannyasins that Master and disciple were making a suicide pact. Rajneesh had often mentioned that he would die on July 6, Master's Day. July 6, 1985, Sheela maintained, was the one. The only way to save the Master was to sacrifice the disciple before the pact could be fulfilled.

The attack was carried out in Rajneesh Mandir on July 6. Here is the way Devaraj related it to me one afternoon in late September:

"Shanti Bhadra sat next to me." This "surprised" him since ordinarily they didn't get along. "I was sitting with my left buttock out. I felt a discomfort, a pain in it. I realized what was happening. I told Shunyo [another physician], 'I've just been injected with poison.'" Devaraj developed pulmonary edema, coughed up blood; he was treated on an emergency basis at the ranch and then flown to the hospital in Bend, where he remained for two weeks.

"Later Durga [who worked in the ranch medical clinic] found a safety pin in my clothes and said that was what I had felt. Everybody thought I was loony. In the hospital I didn't tell the doctors what I thought had happened. It seemed to me," he grinned as he told me this, "it was my best chance of not being polished off."

By the time I arrive on the ranch on September 22, drawn by Sheela's departure and the crises I know it will bring, Rajneesh is adding unfounded rumors, misinterpretations, and accusations that he probably knows to be untrue to his stack of allegations. I spend time sifting through them. The man whom he says Sheela actually killed on the ranch seems to have been the Share-A-Home person who died of an accidental self-inflicted overdose of a prescription drug, an hour away, in the mountain town of Government Camp. Though Sheela—with Savita's help—may well have diverted money from Poona and siphoned off millions sent to the ranch by individual donors or the European communes, there seems to be no $43 million missing from the ranch itself, as Rajneesh is claiming; there are debts of perhaps $35 million and assets of $75 million.

When interviews with Sheela, now in Germany, appear on television and in *Stern*, Rajneesh devotes his morning discourses to them. He mocks the countercharges she has made and dissects her personality. Sometimes he speaks with anger, more often with condescension, like a sorely tried uncle who has taken in a delinquent niece: Sheela was raped when she was sixteen; she hated men; she is jealous and insecure. And then a refrain: she was "not very much"—pause—"when she met me"—pause—"a waitress in a hotel." Sheela had become "addicted to being famous."

She had responded badly when he broke his silence and drew the spotlight from her, like a junkie suddenly withdrawn from her "drug."

He seems to relish the battle and the debater's points he scores: "She is saying for one more Rolls-Royce that I threatened . . . to commit suicide. One Rolls-Royce brings great joy," he says, raising his eyebrows. "If you have ninety Rolls-Royces, each is less valuable. To say that I am going to kill myself for the ninety-first . . . it doesn't make sense."

"Everything she was doing," he adds, as he has done before and will again, "was against my teachings . . . without my knowledge. . . . I was in silence." She told him "only what she wanted me to know." He is impressive but not believable. I cannot imagine him so ignorant. I wonder too if the uncle wasn't diddling the niece, manipulating her in every other way if not sexually.

From day to day Rajneesh's mood and his focus change. He is clearly in charge, shepherding his flock now in one direction now in another, but never allowing them to rest easy in his guidance. First he spends days evoking their anger at Sheela; next he counsels compassion; and then he is urging independence, responsibility, discipline. He reminds his sannyasins—as if he had never encouraged Sheela to equate the two concepts—that doubt is not negativity, that they must grow up, cease to be his followers, and become his friends: "Whatsoever they did, good or bad, their intention was never bad. They were doing it for you. . . . Sheela has given you a great opportunity for love and forgiveness."

One evening during a press conference he seems uncertain, demagogic: How many people believe my account of what happened with Sheela? he asks. Raise your hands. It is a chilling moment. The tactic is coercive, cruder than anything else I have seen him do. It bespeaks insecurity, meanness. By the end of the evening Rajneesh sounds as if he might well have been the source of and inspiration for the most extreme imaginings of Sheela's paranoia. He warns that if the U.S. government drops a nuclear bomb on Rajneeshpuram—an Italian sannyasin-journalist has asked about a possible CIA plot against the ranch—"they cannot do any harm here. People can also hijack American planes," he adds, to audible audience gasps. In fact, he goes on as if compelled to compound his threat, if worse comes to worst, "no American embassy in any country can function."

In the days since Sheela's departure and Rajneesh's revelations, some sannyasins— perhaps twenty or thirty or even fifty—have already left the ranch. The proximity to so much criminal behavior, the presence of police on the ranch, have terrified them. After the press conference a few more pack their bags. They are sure their Master has lost it. Others regard his words as a device to force them beyond all expectations, all norms. Now his sannyasins can be with him and trust him only, in Kierkegaard's phrase, "by virtue of the absurd." "This man," Isabel tells me, really laughing for the first time since I have known her, "makes Gurdjieff look like Mickey Mouse. There is no reason to stay. If you find a reason, he takes it away the next day."

The next morning at discourse Rajneesh speaks with perfect lucidity. The outburst of the night before is not mentioned, but reassurance of a sort is given: "Nuclear weapons cannot be used, but AIDS spreading like wildfire may destroy humanity."

Afterward, retrieving my shoes, I find myself in the middle of a debate. Sannyasins whom I don't know are coming up to me, asking what I think about Rajneesh's statements on hijacking and attacking embassies. This in itself is a novel experience. Previously everyone was so sure of everything, and debate was impermissible. I say that their Master sounded pretty crazy to me. "Just like Sheela," several sannyasins say. Others argue: "What about the Navy planes flying over?"

Asanga, who twenty years before sifted Rajneesh's motives and found them pure, appears. White-bearded, wrapped in a woolen shawl, he calmly explains: "Bhagwan always speaks to the individual. Last night he was speaking to the paranoia of the journalist in terms she could understand. It wouldn't have made sense to her if he said, 'Existence will provide no matter what happens,' so he put it in terms of retaliation." It is the kind of explanation that only an Indian disciple could give. It is mind-boggling enough to enforce momentary silence on me, while other sannyasins are clamoring for my opinion.

Two days later, as if surprised that some sannyasins were panicked, Rajneesh says that the "hijacking" was a joke.

While I listen, day after day, he pushes on, dismantling the structure that, he claims, Sheela created, urging his disciples to drop the visible signs of their connection to him. "Rajneeshism, the religion," he announces, was "Sheela's creation." He has always been opposed to religion. He wants the name "Rajneeshee" to be dropped. Several days later he announces that all copies of *An Introduction to Rajneeshism*, five thousand of them, will be burned at a mass gathering and, with them, Sheela's robes. Henceforth, he adds, sannyasins will not have to wear orange or red colors or the mala. They can, at least to the eye, be indistinguishable from non-sannyasins — "So we can better take over the world," he remarks slyly a few days later.

A week later he abolishes Gachchhamis, translates "worship" back to "work" and "temple" to "department." He tells his sannyasins to change the name of the city of Rajneesh back to Antelope, to sell their houses to the former residents. Rajneesh Foundation International, he says, emphasizing his own collegial relationship with his sannyasins, should become "Rajneesh Friends International."

Two months before Sheela left, Rajneesh described her as "intelligent and beautiful." Now, introducing the new leadership that he has appointed, he declares them "more graceful and intelligent" than the previous one. Chief among them is Hasya, the coproducer of *The Godfather*. She is taking Sheela's place as Rajneesh's personal secretary and president of RFI. Working with her, as chief financial officer and president of the Rajneesh Investment Corporation, is Dhyan John, the wealthy American physician and businessman. Hasya and John became close in Hollywood, where a common friend, Kaveesha, the Tantra therapist, introduced them. When John purchased Joan Crawford's mansion and turned it into a Rajneesh Meditation Center, Hasya and other sannyasins also lived there. They lavishly entertained performers and other rich Hollywood people and tried to "introduce them to Bhagwan."

When I first met them in fall 1984, Hasya and John were peripheral but highly visible and well-known figures in ranch life. Each had contributed many hundreds of thousands, perhaps millions, of dollars. Both toured the ranch's muddy roads in Rolls-Royces that they bought after Rajneesh had driven them. John, a pleasant but ponderous and self-important man given to philosophizing about the New Age, worked part time at the Rajneeshpuram Chamber of Commerce, showing visitors around the ranch. Hasya, a sophisticated woman who seemed by turns gracious and overbearing, worked at the greenhouse and pizza parlor. Both of them wrote occasionally for the *Rajneesh Times*. When Hasya and John began work on a movie about a seeker who comes to Rajneesh, they were granted access to him. Then Hasya married Devaraj.

Sheela had always been wary of and hostile to others who were close to her Master. Vivek, Devaraj, and Devageet threatened her hegemony with Rajneesh and offered a contrasting style—personal, intimate, more relaxed, a bit goofy. She was his instrument in the world—his hands and voice—but they seemed closer to his heart. She was, I imagine, jealous and also resentful. They had the privilege, the intimacy, and, perhaps to her eyes, all the class that she lacked. She constantly had to scramble to keep her place. They seemed to accept theirs as if it were their due. They must have seemed to her as the British imperialists had to her father and his generation—arrogant interlopers whose influence might reshape every aspect of her life.

Hasya and John compounded her problem. Their independent incomes, their independence from ranch control, their all but impenetrable self-assurance, their capacity to deal with worldly situations, and their increasing proximity to Rajneesh presented an even greater threat to her exclusive authority than her Master's personal caretakers. They could do the job she was doing. She had called them "the Hollywood Gang" and warned her intimates that they were planning a takeover. Now, fulfilling Sheela's worst fears—and Rajneesh's present wishes—Hasya and John are the center of ranch life.

They sit on the sprawling deck of Sheela's former home—renamed Sanai Grove, after a Sufi mystic—and play out a scene that could easily have been set in Hollywood. At one table Hasya, in a floppy red straw hat and lounging clothes, sips at a cup of coffee and listens to Kendra, a pretty young blond aide, read her schedule from a clipboard; at another table John, in dark sunglasses, is on the telephone to a sannyasin investor who wants to bankroll high-tech industry on the ranch. A few feet away reporters and TV crews wait for interviews. A hundred yards from Sanai Grove, in City Hall, a task force of seventy local, state, and federal law enforcement officers is investigating Rajneesh's charges, questioning sannyasins, and sifting through the evidence that has been turned over.

The day that Sheela left, I am told, sannyasins sang and danced in the streets of Rajneeshpuram, like Munchkins celebrating the death of the wicked witch. When Rajneesh began to disclose Sheela's "crimes" many became depressed and angry—at Sheela for deceiving and using them, at Rajneesh for not protecting them, and most of all at themselves for allowing it.

"Every day since he began talking last October," one long-time sannyasin recalls, "Bhagwan was telling us how dangerous and limiting organized religion was, how important it was to doubt, to rely on ourselves, to trust no authority. And all the time that I was saying 'Yes, yes' to him I was also saying, 'Yes, yes' to Sheela and 'moms' and 'unity.' " German sannyasins, recalling the behavior they have condemned in parents who were Nazis or their sympathizers, seem most ashamed.

Almost everyone I know tells me a story about the time or times they decided to go along or shut up rather than speak out and risk expulsion. People apologize for lying to me—when I challenged them—about their feelings for Sheela, the atmosphere on the ranch, the Share-A-Home program, the treatment of the Antelopians: "We were told that it was necessary to protect Bhagwan and the commune."

During the first weeks after Rajneesh's revelations, the mood on the ranch oscillates wildly. Some who no longer trust Rajneesh—or anyone else—to guide them, leave the ranch. Others stay away from work for hours and days at a time. The vast majority, however, seem grateful, and energized. Sheela and Vidya and Savita built the foundation for the commune. Now they have the opportunity to really make it work.

Mary Catherine points with pride to articles in the first post-Sheela issue of the *Rajneesh Times* that express doubt and dissatisfaction. Mangala, an old friend from Suryodaya, who has been with Rajneesh for thirteen years and has her twin boys on the ranch with her, runs up to tell me about a parents' meeting. "Now children will be allowed to live with us." When I say, "It's about time," she shakes her head. "We've fucked up, we've been stupid, but don't forget we're here to learn. We've experienced fascism and we know we don't want it." A newly invigorated Citizens' Involvement Group is demanding information from and access to the Rajneeshpuram City Council.

At Rajneesh's morning discourse a band plays in the back of Mandir. Four thousand people are there, standing or sitting, swaying or still. The music starts slowly and picks up tempo as the time for Rajneesh's arrival approaches. This particular morning, I sit next to Major Robert Moine, district commander of the state police in Bend and the liaison between the law enforcement agencies and the sannyasins. Major Moine's gun is on his hip but his hat is on his lap as if he were in church. "He's a smart man," Major Moine says, gesturing to the wing chair far away on the stage, which Rajneesh will soon occupy. "His teachings lifted guilt. There's no loneliness here. Did you ever," he goes on, "read a book called *Jesus: The Man Nobody Knows?* It reminds me," he says, to my considerable surprise, "of him."

The music is faster and louder now, and there are singers at the microphones. They begin, in harmony—two are black Share-A-Home people—"Dancing in your light again, Bhagwan." Almost everybody is joining in. People are moving their heads and shoulders from side to side, clapping hands. Major Moine is tapping a large, shiny black shoe in time to the music. It seems as if the anger and doubt and self-doubt of the day before are dissolving in celebration. "Dancing in your light again, Bhagwan."

For many sannyasins, each of Rajneesh's pronouncements, each change in ranch direction, each sign of affiliation abandoned, seems an opportunity to drop past attachments—to Rajneesh as all-knowing authority, to a ranch structure they had unquestioningly accepted. The contradictions in Rajneesh's daily discourses, the unpredictability of it all, and, most of all, the unseen but felt power of his guiding presence remind them of why they were drawn to him in the first place.

One afternoon on the deck of Sanai Grove, John recalls to me a fable in which paradox and contradiction are the two pillars of the gates to enlightenment. "If chaos is producing change," Devageet, Bhagwan's dentist, gleefully chimes in, "he will produce more chaos." "I'd heard," says Srajan, the carpenter who'd once been a Zen monk, "about the Master pulling all props from under his disciples. Now I know what it means."

I understand what they are saying, feel the exhilaration of the precarious path along which Rajneesh is leading them. But in forgetting so quickly where they have come from, it seems to me, they may soon be lost again. I'm not at all sure that once the initial rebellion has passed, they won't follow the new leadership as blindly as the old. Even more important, as I point out to one sannyasin after another, there has been no real criticism of Rajneesh in the newspaper or in the morning discourse, no challenge to his bland assertions that he did not know, no serious questioning of the soundness and sanity that are supposed to be the foundation of his crazy wisdom.

Rajneesh is speaking as if Sheela alone created and maintained the "concentration camp" in Rajneeshpuram. But that is — sannyasin faith aside — impossible. The Master was "in silence," but he spoke with Sheela daily, advised her in detail. He publicly praised Sheela's actions. And many of her decisions clearly came from him. He is the one who told her to be more "assertive." He fired Bob Davis, the lobbyist who might have helped the ranch to accommodate its neighbors and their objections. He is the one who announced the formation of Rajneeshism, who took credit for dismantling the local centers around the world and centralizing them in communes. He is the one who condemned Laxmi as "cunning and deceptive." Surely he knew Somendra and Shyam, Prageet and Chetna, were expelled. Just two months before she left, he said Sheela was beautiful and intelligent.

He also had contact with other sannyasins who could report what was happening on the ranch. He saw Devaraj and Devageet and Vivek, all of whom moved freely about the ranch, all of whom sannyasins no doubt importuned to "tell Bhagwan" about the lying and spying. Nor was he ignorant of the reactions that Sheela was provoking, of the way the world outside perceived life in Rajneeshpuram. I know from people who worked in Edison, "the electronics temple," that TV news summaries were prepared for him.

As I listen to Rajneesh heap blame on Sheela, as I watch sannyasins accommodate themselves to his self-serving revelations, I feel anger and disappointment and confusion: I have never been a sannyasin and have for years been impatient with their unquestioned acquiescence to communal authority and their arrogance toward the world. But I have shared many experiences and hopes and perspectives with them. Though I have been and still am an observer in Rajneeshpuram, I have some kind of "connection to Bhagwan" and an investment in his new commune.

Earlier in my life psychoanalysis and my role as a psychiatrist served as a vehicle for my desire to help and understand, to be a doctor and an intellectual, to work on myself and with others. The therapeutic community, with its openness to self-exploration, conflict, and change, helped shape my understanding of what an ideal community and a more humane world might be like. In time, my involvement with political activism, participatory democracy, and therapeutic communities showed me the limitations of both politics and psychotherapy. Like many of the people who became sannyasins, I came to believe that resolving our personal and collective dilemmas would require us to bring to political action and psychological understanding some more encompassing, more generous wisdom, one that we were accustomed to call spiritual or religious.

Through his meditations and his writings and the force of his presence, Rajneesh was a catalyst in this process, a teacher if not a Master for me. I wanted Rajneesh and the ranch to be an example as well, the next large step beyond the therapeutic community, a commune that encouraged both introspection and cooperation. And I have been disappointed. If this remarkably intuitive and intelligent man could not help people change; if he could appoint, support, encourage, and guide someone as destructive as Sheela; if these talented, smart, energetic, and cheerful sannyasins with their commitment to loving openness and self-examination, cooperation and celebration, could not make it; if in fact he and they have created the ugly disaster they seemed to have—then it does not bode well for me or for others who might want to create and be part of loving and productive communities.

On the ranch this time I feel like the Ancient Mariner haranguing wedding guests as I talk to sannyasins about their Master and his and their responsibility. Though most sannyasins listen patiently to my concerns, they are, as the days pass, less and less willing to talk with me about them. If I would like, they say, with an unaccustomed spirit of humility, to help with their present work—on the new city council or at the health center or newspaper—they would appreciate it. But they are not, finally, interested in why Rajneesh did or did not do something, or in what, as the lawyers used to say in the Watergate hearings, he knew and when he knew it.

That time has passed. Now they have the opportunity, as Rajneesh and Tantra have taught them, to put the present situation—Sheela's departure, Rajneesh's accusations, their own growing sense of themselves as survivors—to good use, to use it as a device. One sunny morning I sit with Mona, now Rafi, outside the bus near Mandir from which she serves coffee and pastry. She tries to explain it to me: "He's got everybody in Oregon waiting to hear what he's got to say," she happily announces. "He's on 'Good Morning America' and 'Nightline.' So what if he's talking about Sheela and her crimes. People will hear him and get curious. Maybe they'll buy a book. . . .

"Sure," she goes on, "there was a lot wrong with us when Sheela was here, and there is still plenty wrong with us. But it's better. We're just babies. Look at what we've done in just four years. When we first got here we had too many people for the buildings. We had to sit outside even in winter; sometimes our soup froze before we could sit down. Now look at all this: five thousand people dancing with Bhagwan at morning discourse, houses for everybody, the hotel, the food we produce for ourselves, Devateerth Mall. It's taken him thirty years to get us together, a core group to make his vision come true—no boundaries, no races, no religions. He's here with us, someone who is trying to unify the earth."

11

"I'M A RISKY PERSON"

I finally speak with Bhagwan Shree Rajneesh at the end of September 1985, twelve years after I first heard about him. In Poona he talked only to sannyasins; then he was in silence. But during the past few weeks he has begun to give nightly press interviews. Each evening he descends from a stretch Rolls-Royce at Sanai Grove and walks between a double line of swaying, clapping men, women, and children. Musicians follow, in bright silk shirts with sashes around their waists, playing Eastern European melodies. Rajneesh walks slowly, stopping to clap and smile and move—"the Bhagwan shake," some sannyasins call it—first with one disciple, then another. When I watched him one evening I saw a gypsy king with his subjects, a Zaddik passing among his Hasidim. Now I wait for him in a room chilled for his comfort to fifty degrees.

He enters ahead of the musicians and takes his place in the special chair that Devageet has lugged in. I sit in a chair across from him. There are bowls of fruit and glasses of water on tables next to each of us. Floodlights warm the space we are in. Three video cameras and elaborate sound equipment record every gesture and word. Thirty sannyasins are on the floor behind me, cross-legged, motionless, and silent, except when they laugh. Like me, they are dressed in long underwear and scarves, slacks and sweaters and parkas, layers of cotton and nylon and down—but not wool, to which Rajneesh is allergic.

Up close Rajneesh looks like a gnome, a tiny man appearing much older than his years, with a long, white beard and dark, liquid eyes. He is wrapped in a floor-length slate-blue gown and a matching knit hat, enclosed by the high wings of his chair. He wears a watch that sparkles with stones that look like diamonds. He seems incredibly still, like a pond very early in the morning before the wind has come up, and quite relaxed. His voice is soft at first, as dry as fallen leaves: "Glad to see you."

I tell him I have waited a long time to see him.

"And I also have waited a long time," he says. "It is never"—the s's and r's stretch out—"one-sided."

I can feel a pull then, in the respectful inclination of his head, in the sibilance of his slowly spoken, gracious words, in the graceful opening of his left hand toward me, and in the unblinking soft eyes that drew Laxmi and Teertha, Chetna and Sheela, and so many others. He seems to be speaking only to me, inviting me to say exactly what is on my mind.

I tell Rajneesh that I first heard about him from Shyam Singha years ago, that I have done his meditations and read his books and spent time at his ashram in Poona and been on the ranch many times. I have been touched by him, I say, but now I am here as a doubter, a journalist.

"Come as a friend," he says. "You can take care of the journalism . . . but come as a friend. You can explore more easily as a human being than as a journalist."

And so, amid the floodlights and the palpable, rapt attention of his disciples and my own suspicions and wariness, I speak to him as a friend might—as, I think, some friend should have—a puzzled, disappointed, critical friend who wonders how someone who seems to know so much and to know people so well, who has inspired and apparently given so much love to so many, has permitted, if not created, so many things that are ugly and dangerous.

I begin by asking about the pressure on sannyasins in Poona—to engage in violence in the therapy groups, to be sterilized—pressure that seemed then, as it still seems, to have been the seed of the coercion that thrived on the ranch. Why had he allowed, even encouraged, it?

He ignores my question, or rather isolates one element of it—"the need for birth control." He speaks quietly but distinctly, each word as carefully chosen and presented as the stones on his watch. "I was in favor of it and still I'm in favor of it. The world is already overpopulated and only an *in*human being who has no respect for children can give birth to a child." Slowly he paints a picture for me—of a world "already in a mess," in danger of a third world war; of thousands of infants dying in Ethiopia; of Indian children whose bodies survive while their brains, more sensitive to malnutrition, gradually die. Children who will never appreciate music, beauty, literature, and art—"Mozart and Picasso and Bertrand Russell"—children who will never even read or think clearly.

For a few moments the questions I have planned to ask disappear. I feel, as surely as if they have reached out to touch me, that these starving children are my own. Tears creep down my cheeks. Why am I so worried about a relatively few young women who now regret that they decided to be sterilized? There are so many children in the world already, children who need them, who need me. "If you want children, adopt," he says. "Why be so fixated that it has to be your semen? . . . And can you recognize your semen if the samples are placed before you?" The laughter rises behind and around me, in me. "I am still," he concludes, "for absolute birth control, at least for twenty years. Then there will be no need for communism, we can create a supercapitalist world, and yet classless. We can have abundance of everything."

Yes, Rajneesh, I think, there is truth in what you say. You have put my question in a larger context. I see the sense, even the humanity, in what had only seemed like tyranny. But that doesn't excuse or explain what happened in Poona or the coercion and criminality on the ranch. It doesn't really answer my question.

We talk for a while about his concern for the destructiveness of governments and of nationalism, and then we turn to his plans for the ranch. He wants, he says, to have a "World Academy of Sciences," a place where scientists from all nations can pursue their work free of the governmental influence that has forced them to work for war. "On the ranch we will give them music, dance, and song, then they cannot create destructive things. . . . Meditation"—the 112 kinds that Lord Shiva described in the *Vigyana Bhairava Tantra*—will be available. "Out of that calm, serenity, destruction is impossible. And they can see my people. They are living so joyfully . . . it is infectious. . . . We can make them dance, and all the scientists need to dance, to play music, to sing. Then they cannot make destructive things. And if they can meditate also, we will be developing a totally new kind of scientific investigation."

I feel, though I asked the question, that he is somehow leading me—like a parent recounting a fairy story to a child, or George to Lenny in *Of Mice and Men*, telling him once again about the farm on which they will someday live. And then for a moment I wonder if he has lost contact with reality. "Yes," I say, not wanting to be rude but feeling impatient, "it sounds beautiful, but it also sounds"—in the context of all the opposition and mistrust he and his disciples have aroused, all the crimes they have committed—"like a pipe dream."

"It is a dream and it can become a reality. Better to choose a dream," he replies quietly, "and give it a try . . . than destruction." I cannot argue with this, but an uneasiness remains in me. Does he really believe that scientists will want to come to a place so tarnished by scandal?

He goes on to discuss meditation and the difference between his approach and that of other leaders of new religions who, I suggest, also want to bring meditation and science together. What Maharishi Mahesh Yogi offers is "not meditation" but "autohypnosis that leads you to sleep." Reverend Moon is "only a Christian." He offers only "prayer, petitions to God, not meditation." By contrast, "My method leads you into more awareness. You have only to witness all actions of your body, all actions of your mind—thoughts, dreams—all actions of your heart—moods, happiness, sadness. And when you become capable of watching these three, then the fourth happens of its own accord. . . . The more you become aware, thoughts and feelings become lesser."

Listening, I feel my own mind slowing down. Thoughts are like crystals now, defined, isolated. "When it happens totally that on all the three steps you are simply alert—no mind, no thought, no action—a quantum jump happens. Suddenly you find yourself at the center of the cyclone. You are in a state in which you have never been which gives you immense insight into everything, which gives you twenty-four hours of immense blissfulness. Whatever happens outside, you remain the same." I feel it for a moment, in the silence after his words, appreciate it as a gift. But I am not quite ready for it. My mind still has questions.

I want to know what has happened on the ranch and why. Why did he, knowing Sheela's character and her limitations—her insensitivity and ruthlessness and meanness—appoint her as his personal secretary and trust his commune to her and encourage her?

"It is not a question of thinking pros and cons," he says, "it is my insight. . . . I could not give the commune in the hands of innocent people. They would have destroyed it. . . . Whatever happened, although it was not good—but looking at the world, only bad people could have managed and good people could not. . . . She served her purpose," he concludes, "perfectly well."

"You used those people, used Sheela," I say.

"I did not abuse them," he counters.

No, it wasn't abuse. Sheela was not forced to do anything, certainly not to violate her own code of behavior. Already in Poona she may have been responsible for the warehouse fires and the landlord's frameup. Still, his admission is chilling. Knowing her well, he allowed and encouraged her to do whatever seemed necessary to establish the commune he wanted. He could probably have predicted that her zeal would at some time become the fanaticism, grandiosity, and paranoia that would eventually insure her exile from the commune she had done so much to create. But it doesn't seem to matter to him. He gave her the opportunity, probably goaded her, perhaps even ordered her, to act out the shadow side of her character, to take it almost to its limit. But it is, he maintains, her responsibility, not his.

A few moments later Rajneesh is justifying Sheela's behavior. He and his sannyasins were a minority. Sheela's actions against the people of Antelope, her fights with the state government, "everything illegal she did in Oregon . . . she did exactly as they were doing. When it became clear that they are going to hinder everything, Sheela had to take the step and take over. I did not stop her. I let her do till I saw the commune is established. Oregonians have understood one thing, that we are here to stay."

I am objecting, suggesting that Rajneesh and Sheela might have been more compassionate, more intelligent. It wasn't necessary, I say. The sannyasins were a minority in the state, but they were a powerful majority in and around Antelope. You could have compromised and been more patient. Other groups, like The Farm in Tennessee, the Hare Krishnas in West Virginia, seemed to have learned to respect and to compromise with hostile neighbors. They provided services—an ambulance in Tennessee, food for the poor, jobs for the unemployed in West Virginia—and gradually the animosity and opposition abated. The sannyasins didn't need to control and intimidate.

"We have not refused any permit to anybody," he responds.

"You were infringing on their actions," I say, trying to get through to him, "violating their customs."

"How," he says, shifting to the offensive, "did you manage to take the country from Red Indians?"

Though I don't see the relevance I find myself playing his game: "Not my idea." Laughter erupts behind me.

"Whose idea?"

"Basically," I begin, knowing that I am setting him up and knowing that this whole contretemps is a distraction, "the idea of a bunch of arrogant Christians who thought they had the right to the whole country."

"So these people must have been your forefathers."

"Not mine. I'm a Jew from Russia." The whole place is roaring now. I have won a skirmish, but I sense that I am losing the battle to unearth his motives. We are for the moment partners, performers doing a shtick. He has seduced me.

"That is good. That is why you can understand a little humor. To be a Jew," he giggles now, "is really great. They should think," he goes on, now returning to the subject at hand, "that they have taken this whole country from other people. And we have" — all innocence now — "purchased the properties from them. They should not have sold. We are not forcing ourselves on them."

He proceeds to remind me that he has asked his sannyasins to change the name of the city back to Antelope, that he is willing to sell the properties back or to buy the remainder of their properties. "No," he is impatient now. "Persecution came from the other side only."

He goes into great, almost lawyerly, detail about the history of the conflict, the need for improvements in the town, giving the lie once and for all to his claims of ignorance. The sannyasins bought the houses legally. They had the right to permits that were denied them. At present a hundred sannyasins paid far more taxes than the twelve Antelope families who remained. And finally, as if speculation about who did what to whom were no longer relevant, "I'm not concerned with them. They should purchase the property from us or sell it. I'm not a bit interested in those people."

I find myself disappointed in and angry at his arrogance, thinking back, not amused but uneasy now, to a quote from *Glimpses of a Golden Childhood*: "I've never asked anybody whether I am right or wrong," Rajneesh said. "Wrong or right if I want to do it, I will do it and I will make it right. If it is wrong I will make it right. But I've never allowed anyone to interfere with me."

Why, I go on, pushing aside the fiction that he hadn't, at least in its broad outlines, known all of Sheela's behavior, did you keep Sheela in power when you knew she was creating a "concentration camp"? Why did you wait almost a year after she first poisoned your doctor, Devaraj, and two months after the second, more serious, attempt, to confront her?

"It was needed," he says. "She was fighting so many cases I didn't want to end in the middle. I wanted things to come to a conclusion from where a new group could start, and this was the time many cases were concluded."

"You play a very risky game," I say, provisionally crediting his account, glimpsing him moving the living pieces — Laxmi, Sheela, Devaraj, Hasya — around the board of ranch life.

"Certainly," he says, with pleasure. "I'm a risky person and it is a game and I know the right timings . . . I'm just" — hands opening out now, disclaiming responsibility again — "a referee."

Referee, I think, and rule maker, director and star, Machiavelli and Mephistopheles. I remember the stories of young Raja, leading his friends on lightless walks on the cliffs high above the river Shakkar; daring them to jump into the whirlpool; pushing his new disciples harder and faster through the stages of Dynamic; rearranging their psyches and assigning them jobs and lovers with the same impunity.

Why didn't you ask others besides Sheela to report to you? Why not balance her character and her view of things with someone less truculent and devious, more subtle and more informed? That, I think, is the way I would have done it.

"I was in silence and did not want to be disturbed."

"Look," I say, "on one hand you are trying to create an experiment here on the ranch, a movement in the world, but on the other hand, you don't want to be bothered."

"My silence," he announces with finality, "was more important than the whole experiment." This—like it or not—is who he is, not "nice," not "your uncle," not consistent, certainly not saintly and sweet. If his sannyasins want to walk "the razor's edge" with him—to be themselves even as he insists on being himself—they are welcome. If not, it isn't his problem or concern.

Finally, I ask Rajneesh about Shyam, who helped open his first center in the West, who twelve years before first spoke to me of him. Why had he and many other strong people—Shiva and Somendra, Pramod and Nandan—been forced, by Rajneesh or his organization, to drop sannyas or leave the ranch?

"It was my doing," he begins. "I kicked Shyam out. And I don't want him here ever." And then, ignoring any others who may have left, he details his grievances against Shyam, sounding angry, exasperated, and petulant: Shyam insisted on "wearing perfume" when he visited and made his allergies worse; Shyam wanted to treat Rajneesh with acupuncture and Rajneesh didn't want it. Shyam was "exploiting sannyasins for his own work" as well as Rajneesh's and did not always wear orange clothes and the mala.

The denunciation of a man who was once his friend, who is my friend, builds to a crescendo. Shyam is forbidden "ever" to come to the ranch. I feel my jaw drop. Such pettiness and vindictiveness, or maybe it's a version of competitiveness, or jealousy. I remember that there are no men in positions of real power in Rajneesh's organization. He is putting Shyam down because he is too independent, because he commands too much allegiance from too many sannyasins. What kind of Master is this? And then, just as my outrage and disappointment are peaking, he pauses. "But," he concludes, as if he has exhausted his anger and now is shed of it, "I love him. You tell him he is always welcome—if he behaves. OK?"

The interview is over. I realize that like any great performer he knows when to end. Rajneesh rises and namastes. I stand, still a bit bewildered by his tirade and its abrupt reversal. I namaste to the tiny man who stands in front of me. An image from *The Wizard of Oz* comes to me: the little old man who sold nostrums in Kansas is emerging from behind the control panel that gave him the mighty voice of the Wizard. The image fades, Rajneesh takes my hands in his.

After a moment, I remove my hands and clasp his. Feeling his soft, dry hands in mine, the eyes of his sannyasins on us both, I sense power—I do not know if it is borrowed or shared, his or mine—growing in me. The music begins, immediately in full career. I find myself next to Rajneesh, slowly moving to it, with him. Then, while he moves his hands as if to shake water from them, I am dancing.

It is no dance I know or ever remember having done, a wild, unwilled movement. I close my eyes against the crowd of clapping sannyasins, against my own sudden feeling of foolishness. I have come to question, not to dance. But I am filled by the music—Russian music, gypsy music, the sounds of the Jewish shtetl of my grandparents' childhood—and do not want to resist the dance. I move faster and faster, jumping now and squatting and kicking like a Cossack, on and on. Rajneesh and the musicians recede out the door, but the clapping and my dance continue, faster and faster.

Some time—I don't know how long—later I fall down, exhausted, and I begin to laugh: at this mad contradictory man, now loving and compassionate, clear-sighted and straightforward, now self-absorbed, angry, petty, jealous, deceitful, willful, contemptuous. I laugh at myself, and the equally absurd contradictions in me—the doubter and dancer, Rajneesh's would-be analyst and fascinated student, reporter and celebrant. I wonder at the ugliness he and his sannyasins have produced and his ability, at least for moments, to get me to suspend my judgment of it; at the strange catalytic power of his presence; and at the dance that he and I, interviewer and interviewee, are doing, which does not begin or end, I know, with this evening's music.

In the weeks after I left Rajneeshpuram the sannyasins divided their attention between restructuring the ranch and the ongoing legal dramas. Search warrants, issued on the basis of Lieutenant Renfrow's affidavit, had unearthed several thousand tapes, presumably made by Sheela. Rajneesh and approximately one hundred sannyasins received subpoenas to appear before federal and state grand juries. K.D., looking gaunt and haggard, returned to the ranch for a few days amid rumors that he and several other sannyasins had received immunity in return for testimony on the poisonings and murder plots. On October 24, 1985, the state grand jury handed down indictments for the attempted murder of Devaraj. On October 28, Sheela, Puja, and Shanti Bhadra were arrested in Germany, where they were held for extradition. Meanwhile, the grand jury that had been investigating possible immigration law violations was rumored to be ready to indict Rajneesh and other sannyasins.

In the midst of all this, on Sunday, October 27, at approximately 4:00 P.M., Rajneesh and six sannyasins, including Devaraj and Vivek, left Rajneeshpuram in two Learjets, with more than $400,000 in jewelry and $58,000 in cash aboard, bound for Charlotte, North Carolina. At the Charlotte airport two more planes, chartered by Kaveesha's sister Hanya, were ready to fly them to Bermuda. In Charlotte, Rajneesh and his companions were taken into custody by U.S. marshals. Rajneesh was charged with unlawful flight to avoid prosecution and his disciples with aiding and abetting his flight and harboring a fugitive.

In court, the U.S. attorney from Portland, Charles Turner, maintained that Rajneesh had found out that he was to be arrested on a sealed thirty-five count indictment that was handed down on October 24. To forestall the possibility that Sheela and the others, forewarned, might try to escape from Germany, Rajneesh's arrest in Oregon was to take place on the same day as theirs. Later, Turner told me he was sure there was a leak in the Justice Department in Washington to someone at CBS who then called the ranch.

Rajneesh's immigration lawyer, Peter Schey, said that he only heard rumors of the indictments, as he had four times previously. On this occasion, as on the others, he had spoken with Turner—at 2:00 P.M. on Sunday—and had been assured that when an arrest warrant was issued, they would negotiate the time and place and conditions of Rajneesh's surrender. Turner agreed that he spoke with Schey but denied that he acknowledged the existence of the grand jury or that he would agree to any particular mode of surrender: "I said, 'We'll talk about it.' "

Swami Prem Niren, Rajneesh's personal counsel, claimed to have advised Hasya, after Schey's conversation with the U.S. attorney, that Rajneesh was not about to be arrested. Hasya claimed, according to Schey, that without consulting either Niren or Schey, she confirmed Rajneesh's plans to fly to Charlotte, or perhaps Bermuda, for a "vacation" from the tensions of the ranch and the rumors of arrest and physical harm that continually circulated there. And in the Charlotte jail, Rajneesh, interviewed two days later by Ted Koppel on "Nightline," claimed not to know where he had been going. His "friends," he said, thought he "needed rest." Nor was he aware that he was going to Bermuda: "I don't know where my friends were taking me."

Everything about the episode seemed implausible but familiar, another instance of unnecessary and self-defeating sannyasin evasion and government overreaction, of the confusion and contradictions that seemed to embellish every move Rajneesh made. Watching him on television, Surendra Kelwala, the Indian psychiatrist, was "reminded of the village boy caught by the English schoolmaster. He denies everything, 'No, no, I knew nothing about nothing.' "

Though the charges against Rajneesh seemed grave—convictions on the thirty-five felony counts on which he was indicted could have put him in jail for 175 years—they were, on close examination, flimsy. Thirty-three counts alleged in vague and general terms, that Rajneesh participated in a conspiracy along with Sheela, Vidya, Arup, Karuna, and three other sannyasins to "aid, abet, counsel, command, induce and cause" twelve sannyasin couples to enter into "sham marriages." The thirty-fourth count alleged that in his October 21, 1981, application for an extension of his temporary visa, Rajneesh "falsified, covered up and concealed" the fact of his "intention" to remain permanently in the United States. The thirty-fifth count alleged that on October 14, 1982, in an interview with the INS in Portland, he "knowingly and willfully" made "false, fictitious and fraudulent statements" by declaring "that he had never discussed immigration to the United States with anyone prior to coming to the United States."

As I read through the indictments and consulted with neutral immigration lawyers and former INS officials, it seemed that the INS was reaching pretty far to arrest Rajneesh. He might well have known about the sham marriages, but I didn't see how, apart from taped evidence of a conversation with Sheela, this, or his aiding and abetting them, could be proved. The people I spoke with were even more dubious about the other two counts. None of them recalled anyone who had previously been indicted for, let alone convicted of, concealing an intention to remain permanently at the time he applied for a nonimmigrant visa, or for discussing immigration prior to coming to America.

The ranch's behavior seemed equally exaggerated, and once again counterproductive. If Hasya and the others knew the approximate contents of the indictments and that an arrest was impending, why encourage Rajneesh to leave? If he was indicted, Rajneesh, who had hitherto shown no inclination to flee, would have been out on bail in hours. If he was tried and convicted, which did not seem likely, the conviction could have been appealed for years. If the conviction was ultimately upheld, he would probably only have had to do what he had just tried to do—leave the country.

If, as Hasya maintained, she didn't know that his arrest was imminent, why send Rajneesh outside the country to Bermuda for a "vacation"? His life on the ranch was quite calm, and he was certainly better protected there than anywhere else in the world. If he had left the United States he probably would not have been allowed back.

Rajneesh's claim—"I don't know where my friends were taking me"—was unseemly but comprehensible as a legal necessity. But the reason for his departure remained obscure. In the past when I had not understood his words or actions, I had wanted and tried to give him the benefit of the doubt. Now I sensed, much to my discomfort, that the official mystification concealed not a mystery but a crime, not some rich paradox or surprising contradiction, but ugliness and lies.

While his lawyers maneuvered to secure Rajneesh's release and the government warned that he was "a danger to society," Rajneesh remained in prison, first in North Carolina, and then, following his extradition, in facilities in Oklahoma City and Portland. The national media showered attention on him. Rajneesh in green prison-issue shirt and blue jeans, seemed frail, bewildered, and bombastic at first, then more relaxed.

In the "Nightline" interview on October 29, he announced he was "not going to leave this country. I am going to fight for American Constitution against American politicians. They are prostituting the democracy and Constitution both." "It has been a good experience," he confided on Cable News Network two days later. "Thousands of people are in jail in the world, and to be a prisoner for a few days is a good experience. "Be happy," he told Vivek to tell his disciples when she was released on bond.

During Rajneesh's twelve days in jail sannyasins on the ranch and around the world closed ranks. Doubts raised by Sheela's alleged crimes, her departure, and accusations, and by Rajneesh's response to them and his flight were overwhelmed by concern about his health and anger at the treatment he was receiving. Sannyasins were horrified by the televised images of their Master, a frail "man of peace," in shackles and handcuffs; by reports that he had been denied his orthopedically designed chair, that he was confined in a stuffy, smoke-filled cell with violent felons. "I do feel betrayed," Subhuti wrote in the *Rajneesh Times*, "but not by Bhagwan. I feel betrayed by America."

Sannyasins placed calls asking one another and anyone they knew—three people, presumably acting separately, called me—to apply political pressure for his release, to call the jail, to raise money for his bond. When the government, apparently trying to harass and intimidate Rajneesh, kept him incommunicado for three days, they became frantic. Even sannyasins who had left the ranch in disgust, like Nandan—now Anna Forbes again—and those who, like Shyam, had been excommunicated, worried that under the harsh conditions of life in jail, Rajneesh's body might suffer irremediable damage. Subhuti and others, on and off the ranch, compared his imprisonment to Jesus' and Socrates' arrests, and feared that he might be similarly martyred.

On November 8, twelve days after his arrest, U.S. District Court judge Edward Leavy released Rajneesh on $500,000 bail. Six days later, he pleaded guilty to intending to remain in the United States when he applied for his visa and conspiring to have followers illegally stay in the country. According to a peculiar legal precedent created in the Alford case, Rajneesh, who had to admit that the evidence presented was sufficient to convict him, was allowed to maintain his innocence. Under the terms of the agreement he made with the U.S. attorney, he received a ten-year suspended prison sentence and paid a fine of $400,000, including $160,000 in court costs. He agreed to leave the country within five days and not to return for five years without written permission from the U.S. Attorney General. In addition the sannyasins agreed to drop their suits against Meese, Shultz, and the INS.

According to Sunshine, who was now in charge of the ranch press office, Rajneesh was exhausted and in pain from the days he had spent in jail. His back was hurting badly and he had lost eight pounds. He was unwilling to spend his days concerned with or testifying in this or other court cases. His attorneys had estimated that the trial on the immigration charges alone would have required him to be in court every day for six to eight weeks and they expected that the government would try to make him a defendant in as many of the upcoming court cases—on wiretappings, poisonings, and so on—as it possibly could. His body, Sunshine said, couldn't take the time in court. He and his disciples also feared he might be assassinated on his way to or from the courtroom. Besides, he told his sannyasins, he was disillusioned with an American democracy that permitted its government to arrest and detain an innocent person. "I never want to return again," he announced at his hearing.

While sannyasins sang and danced at the Rajneeshpuram airport, Rajneesh—with Hasya, Vivek, Devaraj, and a dozen others who cooked and cleaned and cared for him—left the ranch. The plane circled over the snow-dusted hills and then headed into the sunset, for Portland. Two days later he arrived in New Delhi. Rajneesh said he was on his way to the far north near Manali, in the Himalayas, where for almost half the year he would be inaccessible amidst the ice and snow. I heard that Laxmi, whom he once dismissed as his secretary because "in ten years she has never found a place for the new commune," had located a site for him. He was going to be in silence again.

The sannyasins on the ranch and around the country were relieved for him and as proud of him as a medieval maid of her champion. He would have stayed and fought, they said, but the government was trying to get to him through his body and his body couldn't take it. "A man of freedom," added Sunshine, who had spoken with Rajneesh just before he left, "always takes care of himself first. Choose freedom first. That's the most important lesson he taught us, and it's time to practice what we've been taught."

They were also terribly sad. "I feel," said Sunshine, "like my heart is turned upside down." Rajneesh had asked his disciples not to follow, at least not for now. Many doubted they would ever see him again: "He seems so totally inaccessible," one unhappy sannyasin in Washington told me. "I know I'll recover, but right now I feel like the center of my life is gone."

Others were more optimistic. Rafi believed that "maybe, like Jesus, he had to disappear before his message would catch hold." Besides, tens of thousands of sannyasins would be freely "running around," as Sunshine said to me, "without the colors and mala," giving workshops and teachings, doing therapy and serving clients, working in businesses, sharing his vision each day with all whom they touched.

On the ranch, the sannyasins had been asked to wait a few weeks or a few months to see how things went before making plans to leave. But everyone was in a state of high excitement, talking about the future. "It's incredibly juicy," Mangala, who worked as a cleaner on the ranch, told me. "The restaurants are packed with people dreaming up new ideas, exciting places to go, and ways to make money." She was planning to resume work as a massage therapist at Suryodaya or in London, perhaps help open a healing center. "Six months ago I would have said we'd all freak out when Bhagwan left," another sannyasin, who had just decided to go into business in India, told me. "Now this seems fine. This is what sannyas is about anyway — not being attached, always changing."

Without Rajneesh there as the attraction and guiding force, the center and source for the Buddhafield, the sannyasin city of 50,000 or 100,000 would certainly not happen — at least not now, not in Oregon. Still, a week after his departure, a thousand people said they wanted to stay in Rajneeshpuram. They loved the ranch, "the oasis in the desert" they had created with their love and work and money. There were, sannyasins told me, so many people who cared so much for one another, who had learned so much from Bhagwan and each other. The large European communes had survived, economically and interpersonally, without Rajneesh's presence. Perhaps they too could put some part of his vision into practice. John announced that now they could exploit the ranch's natural resources — coal and oil, gold and silver. Even with most of the sannyasins leaving or planning to leave, the ranch was still, they reminded me, the largest and most successful alternative community in America.

But a few days later, less than two weeks after Rajneesh left, Niren, the lawyer, who was the new mayor of Rajneeshpuram, announced at an evening community meeting that Rancho Rajneesh would be closed and sold. It had become clear to the new leadership that the ranch was no longer economically viable. Without Rajneesh there to draw sannyasins to the commune, the university, the RHT program, and the festivals, there would not be — with or without mining — sufficient income to keep the huge operation going. Besides, they believed that federal and state prosecution would not end until the commune had been destroyed.

Attorney General Frohnmayer had recently threatened to invoke racketeering and organized crime laws, which would make the ranch corporations liable for the actions of their officers — Sheela, Vidya, Puja, and the others — and allow their assets to be confiscated. Most important, earlier that day K.D., the former mayor of Rajneeshpuram, had pleaded guilty to federal immigration and state wiretapping charges. He had turned state's evidence on immigration and wiretapping cases and on the violent incidents in which he and Sheela and many others were involved. He had also given a detailed and thoroughly damning deposition that investigators believed would clinch the church-state case: "As mayor," it began, "I reported directly to Ma Anand Sheela, president of the Rajneesh Foundation International. Sheela in turn reported to and consulted with Bhagwan Shree Rajneesh regarding many of the day-to-day operations of Rancho Rajneesh, including the operation of the city government." If the church-state case were lost, as now seemed certain, and Rajneeshpuram were no longer a city, then the ranch would cease to be a viable project.

The ranch, Niren announced, would be phased out as quickly as possible. The approximately one hundred Share-A-Home people who remained would receive money to travel back to their cities of origin. Sannyasins who had no cash would also be provided with transportation, but they would not be paid back any money they might have donated. Those who had put money into the Rajneesh Debit Card System, the ranch credit system, would be able to obtain goods but not cash in exchange for their deposits. Plans were being made to move the university and its therapists to Europe, perhaps to southern Spain or Italy. As the ranch's assets were liquidated, John announced — already negotiations were under way to sell the Rolls-Royces — local creditors would be paid. Sannyasins from whom the ranch had borrowed money — more than $30 million — would also be reimbursed. No one could or would say how much money Rajneesh had taken with him or how much Sheela had in Swiss banks.

The local people were delighted. They had greeted Rajneesh's promise to give back Antelope, the change in ranch leadership, and even "the Bhagwan's" departure with skepticism. Don Smith, who had once served on the Antelope City Council and had run unsuccessfully for mayor against Karuna, told me he was "reminded of a restaurant which puts a sign on its window, 'Under New Management.' You have to wait and see if the food and service improve." But now it was over or almost over, and the Oregonians were relieved if not yet totally satisfied.

Jon Bowerman's father, Bill, who had helped finance some of the Antelopians' battles, reminded me on the phone that not all of the court cases had been settled: Rosemary McGreer, a local rancher whom Sheela publicly defamed, had not yet received the $75,000 the court gave her when Rajneesh refused to testify in her suit; the defamation award to Marcia Wichelman — $625,000 — was on appeal; and the local people still wanted the sannyasins to repay the debts that Antelope incurred for the Peace Force and improvements in the water supply.

Jon Bowerman was sorry for "the ordinary working-class" sannyasin who he felt had been duped and victimized ("There are going to be some big holes on those people's résumés) but not for Rajneesh or the leadership. He was proud that in spite of the fact that he and his friends and neighbors "grew up with the Western six-gun mentality . . . there was never any violence." People whom he cared about had left and many local people had put an enormous amount of time and money into their struggle, but finally things had worked out for them: "Despite the fact that it is amazingly slow," Bowerman concluded, "the American legal system and our Constitution do work."

If the local people were pleased with the American government, the sannyasins seemed as disillusioned with it as their Master was. Rajneesh had said that America was the world's hope, that here, in a democratic climate and amidst material wealth, "consciousness" might grow and change on a large scale. But the sannyasins told me, with almost as much regret for the country as sadness for their Master and themselves, America "missed." America "wasn't getting it." Rajneesh's name and face were now known, but to most people he was just a con artist — the "sex guru" or "the Rolls-Royce guru" — and a criminal.

Rajneesh, they said, seemed to have touched the Charlotte sheriff, who said he was a "humble man," and the jail nurse who cared for him, as well as some who saw him on television, smiling peacefully in shackles. But there was no massive outcry to match the sannyasins' horror at the treatment he received. There was no sign that the mass of Americans understood who or what his sannyasins believed Rajneesh to be—a revolutionary and world-changing spiritual teacher, a man like Jesus or Krishna or Buddha. Instead, the country's law enforcement agencies had hounded him from the country.

12

THE JOURNEY
CONTINUES

Most sannyasins remained on the ranch after Rajneesh left, and many stayed even after the decision to close the commune. Mary Catherine continued at the newspaper, but others, in the wake of Sheela's departure, had new jobs. Bodhicitta was in the medical center now instead of the recycling center; Mangala was cooking for the children, not cleaning; Rafi, once a "deli mom," was helping to sell off assets and deal with the tangled heap of litigation.

Other sannyasins were preparing to leave. They made calls to family and friends, sent away for licenses and diplomas, and checked out living situations and business opportunities, sometimes in half a dozen cities and on two or three continents.

At first those who had put cash—hundreds or thousands of dollars—in the Rajneesh Debit Card System, a kind of non-interest-bearing bank account that sannyasins could spend in ranch businesses, were able to withdraw their money. After the accounts were closed, they were briefly able to take ranch goods in lieu of cash—a four-wheel-drive vehicle, a van, a car, a couple of bicycles, mechanic's or electrician's tools, a computer—something to help them get started outside. Then, under threat of bankruptcy proceedings, the money was frozen.

In November and December 1985, the number of ranch residents decreased precipitously from several thousand to several hundred. They were taking apart what they had bought and built, leaving more and more of the ranch unoccupied, unused. The legal entities they created, their communal and corporate structures, were shrinking, dissolving, or disappearing. The commune grew smaller each day; RFI moved its copies of Rajneesh's books and tapes to Boulder, Colorado, assigned its copyrights to the Rajneesh Foundation Europe. Instead of accumulating assets, the Rajneesh Investment Corporation (RIC) was liquidating them. Even the land, now inadequately tended and protected, began to return to the state it was in before the sannyasins came to the Big Muddy.

Farm and construction equipment, furniture and bedding, video equipment and computers, the buses of Rajneesh Buddhafield Transport, planes and portable toilets, tents on the ranch and houses in Antelope—all were for sale. The *Rajneesh Times* stopped printing and the stores in the mall closed down. Some farm operations were disbanded and ranch bus service was halted. On November 29 and 30 Bob Roethlisberger, a flamboyant Dallas car dealer, bought eighty-five of the Rolls-Royces for about $6 million; the sannyasins who donated them were reimbursed.

Other debts were being paid. At the insistence of a former German sannyasin, Eva Maria Mann, who claimed that Dipo, Sheela's third husband, had improperly transferred $800,000 of her money to the commune, a judge appointed bankruptcy trustees. Mann was repaid. The judge ordered the commune to cut its population still further and granted it $50,000 to cover travel expenses for sannyasins who would have to leave.

During the hard winter months, the bankruptcy trustees were removed, but the ranch continued to contract. The town houses and trailers and A-frames were closed and sold. Beds, desks, linens, and typewriters were piled up in aisles in Mandir. Where thousands of sannyasins once sat silent in their Master's presence, prospective buyers from Portland and The Dalles now roamed. All business took place in the mall. The 160 sannyasins who remained ate in the Zorba the Buddha restaurant and stayed in the hotel and at Sanai Grove, where "Sheela and her gang" once lived. Life had slowed down. The work of cataloguing and selling and caretaking began at nine and, after a leisurely lunch, continued only till seven. There was time to meditate again. And there were long evenings in the restaurant or in front of the cable televisions in the hotel, where now movies as well as videos of "Bhagwan discourses" were shown.

In February the work force was cut to one hundred. No longer volunteers, each was paid $1,250 a month by RIC. By June 1986 there were only twenty sannyasins left, volunteers again. Moses, the health planner who was not sure whether he wanted to "blend in" in Poona, had taken over the job that Savita and John once held. As head of RIC, he was in charge of selling off the property. There was, he told me, "no reason to pay the people closing the ranch who want to stay." He and they were "doing this in the same spirit in which we have always worked in sannyasin organizations."

The spillway on the huge Gurdjieff Dam needed repairs, and small dams and footbridges on the Big Muddy had been washed away in the winter floods. But the sannyasins were doing their best to keep the buildings in shape and the land alive—a thousand acres of orchard grass had been planted. Kingfishers and red-tailed hawks were still visible, and deer grazed in the hills.

In May 1986 Multnomah County paid $1.6 million for the Hotel Rajneesh in Portland. In the future it would be used as a "restitution center" for felons. No buyer had yet been found for the ranch. The assessed value was $65 million, but the asking price was $40 million—it would go down to $28.5 million in July—for the property and all of the improvements that had been made on it. Moses told me that the state had considered it for a prison and that private groups had evaluated it as a site for social programs and a resort. If the ranch could be sold for $28.5 million, Moses assured me, all of its creditors, including the sannyasins whose money was tied up in the Rajneesh debit cards, would be repaid.

When I called in December 1986, the ranch was still on the market. A dozen people were living there quietly. There was no switchboard, no operator answering the phone with the bright salutation, "Rancho Rajneesh."

Moses was in Portland, where he would be more accessible to prospective buyers. Over the last year, he told me, as he had supervised the sale of goods and negotiated with state agencies, he had felt the "loss" of his Master's presence, of his friends, and of a "community where we were doing miracles, reclaiming the land, living a rich, satisfying life, spiritually, emotionally, economically." And yet the loss of the ranch and his Master's departure now seemed less an ending than a reminder. He realized that his "existential reality," his search, was in a way no different from what it had been eight or nine years earlier, when he first went to Poona: "Bhagwan's job is working with individuals on their inner growth. That is the path to making an impact on the course of human evolution. That is the reason I'm interested in having something to do with him."

Rajneesh had left the country, but the accusations he raised and the federal and state investigations that pursued his leads produced dozens of indictments. While the ranch was closing down, criminal cases and a host of civil suits were settled.

The most dramatic ones were against Sheela, Puja, and Shanti B. After complicated negotiations these three were finally extradited from Germany in February 1986. The news photos showing them coming off the plane and entering the courthouse in Portland were telling: in their prison-issue clothes, the women looked as small and plain as wrens. I remembered them in sannyasin red—silk and satin and velour—as bright, as noisy, as arrogant as cardinals.

In July, when the plea bargaining arrangement was finally worked out, they admitted to all the mad crimes of which Rajneesh had accused them. Sheela pleaded guilty to federal charges of conspiracy with respect to immigration fraud, wiretapping, and "tampering with consumer products" (a euphemism for the salmonella poisoning in The Dalles). On the same day she also pleaded guilty to the attempted murder of Devaraj, to first- and second-degree assaults on Wasco County commissioners Hulse and Matthews, and to arson at the office of Wasco County planner Dan Durow. She received two twenty-year and two ten-year sentences, to run concurrently and would probably actually serve about four and a half years' time. Sheela was also to pay a $400,000 fine and $69,000 in restitution for the fire. She wore a sly, secret smile as she listened to the judge sentence her.

I learned when I called up Steven Houze, Sheela's attorney, that none of these settlements exempted her from civil suits. That was one reason, he explained, why she wouldn't give me or anyone else an interview. The other was that she planned to write a book. He wouldn't say whether she had hidden tapes of her conversations with Rajneesh in Europe before she was arrested, though I had heard that she had. "All I'll say," he told me, "is that she has an incredible story to tell." I didn't ask—because I knew he wouldn't tell me—how much money she and Savita and the others had salted away in Switzerland. But the figures I was hearing started at $10 million to $12 million.

At her sentencing, Puja called herself by her original name, Diane Onang. Others in Oregon, impressed by the persistent rumors that she was planning to engineer an AIDS epidemic, referred to her as "Nurse Mengele." She received fifteen years on the wiretapping, salmonella, and attempted murder and assault charges and would probably serve three years. Shanti B., now Catherine Elsea, got a ten-year sentence—she'd be out in a year—for her part in the attempted murder. All began to serve their time in Pleasanton, a medium-security coed federal prison in California.

Most of the rest of the several dozen indicted sannyasins, including Arup, Karuna, and Padma, pleaded guilty to wiretapping and/or immigration charges. As is customary in cases where the defendants have no previous records, almost all of them were put on probation, usually for five years. Some, like Vidya and Savita, had left the country to avoid appearing in court. The government was not pursuing them but would arrest them if they returned. Vivek and Devaraj, who were charged with aiding and abetting Rajneesh's flight to Charlotte, failed to appear for a hearing and forfeited their $75,000 bond.

A few weeks after Sheela, Puja, and Shanti B. pleaded guilty, the various Rajneesh corporations reached a complex agreement with the state for the compensation of victims of the salmonella poisonings. The corporations agreed to provide a "relief fund," which might eventually total as much as $5 million, to the state of Oregon. The state was to retain about a quarter of this money for investigative and attorney costs. The rest would be disbursed to four of the restaurants where the poisoning occurred, and to the victims of the poisoning, some of whom were, according to a report in the *Oregonian*, still suffering from intestinal problems and food sensitivities. By December 1986 some five hundred people had applied for "real damages" and money to compensate them for their "pain and suffering." The bulk of the fund was to come from the eventual sale of the ranch by the Rajneesh Investment Corporation.

As part of this agreement, the sannyasins withdrew their appeal, to the Ninth Circuit Court of Appeals, of a December 1985 ruling that the incorporation of Rajneeshpuram was in violation of the separation of church and state. And Attorney General Frohnmayer, in turn, dropped the racketeering suit, which was asking $6.5 million in penalties and forfeiture of the ranch.

Most of the other civil suits, the ones that Bill Bowerman had been concerned about, were settled. Bob Harvey, the former ranch foreman, was awarded $175,000 by the court and paid. Though they did not admit liability, the Rajneesh organizations made a May 1986 settlement with Marcia Wichelman, whom Sheela had savaged at the school board meeting. The Rosemary McGreer decision—she claimed that Sheela defamed her on a TV show and was awarded $75,000—was still on appeal.

"This," said Attorney General Frohnmayer after the relief fund was set up, "is the conclusion of one of the most startling and dismaying episodes in Oregon history." The resolution of the church-state case, was, he added, "a vindication" of his theory that Rajneeshpuram was a "theocracy in flagrant violation of the U.S. Constitution."

Several months after Sheela and Puja and Shanti B. began to serve their jail terms, after the financial settlements were made and most of the civil suits resolved, I talked with Charles Turner, the U.S. attorney, and Dave Frohnmayer, the Oregon attorney general. Both men were courteous, thoughtful, and generous with their time, qualities that among politicians, at least those in Washington, D.C., are in short supply. Both wanted me to understand very clearly what the situation was like in Oregon and what the facts of the various cases were, why they proceeded as they did, and, perhaps most interesting, how they felt about Rajneesh.

Frohnmayer, a precise man whose speech was part folksy Oregonian, part Harvard/Oxford/Berkeley, explained, "Oregon is like one big small town." Long-term residents often had relatives and friends in the north and south and on both sides of the Cascades. Events that happened to a cousin or high school classmate in the east reverberated across the state. In any large investigation, Frohnmayer, like the Oregonians who had elected him, might well find that someone close to him was personally affected by the alleged crime.

Frohnmayer grew up in southern Oregon but he heard about the sannyasins' "bad neighbor policy" from friends and family in the east within the first few months of their arrival. His assistant, Marla Ray, came from Gateway, near the Warm Springs Indian Reservation, about twenty miles from Antelope. She told him that the local reaction was mixed. The merchants liked the sannyasins because they paid their bills on time, but most other people felt mistrustful. From Bill Bowerman, who was "a lifelong friend of my father," Frohnmayer heard about "the dark, confrontational side" the sannyasins were showing in Antelope. Shortly after Frohnmayer began to prepare his opinion on the church-state issue for the legislature in 1983, John Silvertooth Stewart brought around the coordinators' minutes he had found.

Charles Turner, the U.S. attorney, was from Chicago, but he had been in Oregon long enough to have a grapevine of his own. He was, as well, subject to pressures from elected representatives. Almost from the time the sannyasins arrived on the Muddy, the state's politicians were being lobbied by Oregonians who were furious at "the Rajneesh's" incursion, at the monumental arrogance of "the Bhagwan." "Can't you get something on them?" queried U.S. Senator Mark Hatfield, who had supported Turner's appointment. To which, the U.S. attorney told me, he replied, "We're trying."

Turner wanted to make sure I understood 1) that he did not give Peter Schey, Rajneesh's immigration lawyer, a specific commitment about Rajneesh's surrender, and 2) that despite the technicality that allowed Rajneesh to maintain his innocence, the Alford plea was in fact a guilty plea. It was very important to him that Rajneesh had made a "public confession." He sent me the transcript of the sentencing so I could see it in print. Frohnmayer wanted me to know that he did his best to hear the sannyasins' side of things and was willing to compromise. He too sent me material to support this contention, letters to and from the Rajneeshpuram city attorney, Ma Prem Sangeet, a former student of his at the University of Oregon Law School.

Both men knew that they had to build the cases against Rajneesh and his sannyasins slowly and methodically, avoiding prejudice and its appearance. Turner's focus was to be on the immigration cases, but it often seemed to him as if the aggrieved agency, the INS, was more the problem than the solution. Frohnmayer had a clearer field. A constitutional lawyer himself, he enlisted two preeminent constitutional scholars — Lawrence Tribe of Harvard and Jesse Choper, dean of Berkeley's law school — to help him build the church-state case. "We did it by the book," Frohnmayer told me, but, he also said, he "took a lot of crap for not demagoguing the issue."

Each of them, separately, reminded me that the sannyasins had committed the most significant crimes of their kind in the history of the United States: the largest single incident of fraudulent marriages; the most massive scheme of wiretapping and bugging; and the largest domestic mass poisoning. "No man," Turner told me, "has ever touched so many Oregonians as this one. Not Mark Hatfield, not Governor Tom McCall, not Wayne Morse, not Bill Walton."

As I talked to them—Turner on the phone and in person, and Frohnmayer on the phone—it became apparent that these cases got to them.It was not simply that old friends or neighbors were harmed by the sannyasins' actions. Nor, I suspected, was it even that Rajneesh's very existence in Oregon was an ongoing affront to everything that they were charged with upholding and protecting: the democratic process; the separation of church and state; individual privacy and collective safety. To Turner and Frohnmayer, Rajneesh was not merely personally threatening or morally offensive or legally outrageous; he was also ontologically and theologically abhorrent.

There was not enough evidence to bring charges against Rajneesh in the wiretapping, the salmonella poisoning, or the assault cases, but both Turner and Frohnmayer seemed to hold him responsible for all of them. Based on the affidavits they took and the tapes they heard, they seemed sure that little took place on the ranch without his knowledge and that, in Frohnmayer's words, his "philosophy" was not "disapproving of poisoning." When push came to shove, these officials of the court expressed themselves in a way that was, if more sophisticated, not unlike the language used by the woman in the Christian bookstore in Madras or the preachers who had organized demonstrations against "the Bhagwan" and his sannyasins.

Frohnmayer, who had written his Harvard honors thesis on Nietzsche and Lenin, saw in Rajneesh the same "individual self-aggrandizement," the same "relativity of truth," the same "disengagement from ethics," that he had discovered in Nietzsche's concept of the Superman. "I wanted to say to Bhagwan," he told me, " 'I've read your book.' " Rarely, he told me, had he seen people who were "genuinely evil," but from what he could tell, Rajneesh and Sheela fit in that category.

Turner, who called himself a born-again Christian, was, if anything, even more emphatic. When he finally saw Rajneesh in court he discovered that he "didn't like to look at the guy. He was small and unprepossessing, but he did have a certain magnetism about him. His eyes were luminous, almost with a satanic glow to them. There was a feeling of evil around that person. A number of investigators," he added, "told me that they had that feeling." When we spoke again, a few days after this conversation, he came back to this point: "I never found a single, solitary redeeming feature in this man. Even in a robber or a dope peddler I could find something."

Some sannyasins left the ranch alone. Most traveled in couples or small groups, in vans and buses and cars. Freed of the ranch's centripetal pull, they kept moving, wherever pent-up energy took them—toward friends, family, or enclaves of the hip subculture where there were other sannyasins already living.

Sannyasins with professional backgrounds and skills began to write up their résumés, to debate how they should fill in the holes that Jon Bowerman had known would be there. "Shall I say," one MIT-and-Harvard-trained architect mused, "that

I've been doing construction work and gardening for eight years, and that my most recent job was as a tour guide in Rajneeshpuram?"

Some of those with the most impressive credentials and self-confidence simply presented the facts. Bodhigarba, an eccentric German electronics and computer expert who settled in Boulder, told his prospective employers "everything. I said, 'I worked in electronics at Rajneeshpuram. I worked with top management there. If you want to ask about my work call Sheela, she's in prison. That period of my life is finished.'" He showed what he could do and got the job, a high-paying, responsible one.

Others moved back into their professions gradually. Doctors who had for years worked as carpenters, cooks, and laborers began with part-time work in emergency rooms or covering for other sannyasin physicians who had never come to live on the ranch. Architects worked as draftsmen and reporters as proofreaders and copy editors. Nurses who had been in charge of whole medical wards before they came to the ranch worked private duty or part time in clinics.

Sannyasins who were carpenters and electricians, mechanics, beauticians, secretaries, waiters, waitresses, and bartenders did well. If they were good at their job — and almost everyone who had been a commune member was very good at the job he or she did — it didn't matter if they had spent the last five or ten years in India or on the ranch.

Those who didn't have money or family or profession, who had not brought skills to the ranch or obtained them there, had more trouble. But they could at least do what they had done in Oregon — clean houses or work in restaurants or drive a cab. And there always seemed to be some other sannyasin somewhere who could give them a place to stay and an opportunity to get started.

Still, for everyone, from the most highly skilled and credentialed to the least, living and working back in the world was a shock. On the ranch, everything had been arranged. One awoke and ate and went to work; one went to drive-by or discourse; at night one might go to the restaurant or disco, to Mandir to hear music or watch a video. The structure of life, the economics of living, the goals of work, were planned elsewhere. The choices were only instrumental ones — whether to buy machine parts or Rolls-Royces from this merchant or that, how to bring the paper out or to repair a tractor.

They quickly discovered — as they had certainly suspected — that it was one thing to work as a cleaner or landscaper or security guard or even as a physician or nurse on the ranch, and quite another to do the same job by oneself or within another institution or organization. On the ranch one was contributing to one's own community, helping people whom one loved, making their life a bit easier, their world a bit more lovely. Outside, one was often alone, at least during working hours, working for or with people with whom one was not emotionally, let alone spiritually, connected. Work was not worship but alienated labor.

After a few months on their own, many former commune members tended to gravitate toward communities where there were high concentrations of sannyasins, toward the Rajneesh meditation centers that were being revived or reestablished. In San Francisco, Marin County, and Santa Cruz; in Los Angeles and Laguna Beach; in Seattle and Santa Fe and Boston, sannyasins set up small businesses, many designed to serve other sannyasins primarily or in part: a law firm to deal with immigration problems; holistic health centers where massage therapists and nurses worked; small enterprises joining housepainters and contractors, cleaners and landscapers. Some of the ranch's spiritual therapists traveled from city to city, drawing sannyasins and their friends to weekend or week-long workshops. Others, like ministers among their flocks, settled in the growing sannyasin communities.

A few ranch enterprises dissolved and reformed elsewhere. Rajneesh Publications stopped operating on the ranch and resumed in Boulder. Two ranch massage therapists set up training programs near Florence, Italy. Teertha and some of the other former group leaders and therapists created an Institute for Meditation and Growth—omitting Rajneesh's name—at Villa Volpe, on Italy's Lago Maggiore. The *Rajneesh Times* closed down in Rajneeshpuram. But within several months Bodhi—with Hina and Maitreya, a businesswoman and a graphic artist—began publishing a new paper, *Rajneesh: The Newspaper,* in Boulder.

Everywhere they went, sannyasins found themselves questioned, if not interrogated, by family and friends and—if they wore the colors and the mala—by employers and people on the street as well. "Why did you go with that guy? What about those Rolls-Royces? How could that woman Sheela have done all those things? Didn't you know what was going on?" Some still enjoyed these confrontations as a device. But most sannyasins, including the ones who settled in again at Devadeep, wore red and the mala less often or only among other disciples. Before they were blending into the commune. Now they were trying to blend into the world.

In fact, many of them were quite uncertain about what their "connection to Bhagwan" still was. From day to day, they put on and took off the mala and the red clothes to reflect their changing feeling of involvement with a Master whose power and integrity they sometimes doubted. On their own, away from the continual mutual reinforcement of the commune and its world view, exposed to criticism, sympathy, and ridicule, some people were deeply troubled. They pored over the evidence of Sheela's guilt, Rajneesh's knowledge, and their own complicity and wondered if they had been fools or worse.

Many were very unhappy that they had lost their community, that the dream that had sustained them for years had disappeared. They were anxious about the inhospitable world into which they were moving. Others felt challenged by the events on the ranch, the revelations of criminal activity, Rajneesh's departure, and their own loss of support. They were on their own but still connected to their Master. Their loss of his continual guidance was, they believed, their Master's hardest, most important lesson.

Rajneesh was on the road but not, apparently, uncertain. Arriving in Delhi in November 1985, he held a press conference in which he publicly condemned the Americans whom he had previously regarded as "the great hope of humanity." They were, he said, without obvious irony, "subhuman." India, which he had not so many years before excoriated, was now—one can almost hear the sitar playing—"my motherland, though poor." In America, he went on, "I was simply a witness to all this idiotic, fascist strategy." Though it was not clear how he arrived at his conclusion, he declared that "I have come a winner. . . . This proves that a single man of innocence is more powerful than any nuclear power."

He moved into an elegant resort in the town of Manali, high up in the Kulu Valley in the state of Himachal Pradesh. He told a reporter from Delhi's *Hindustan Times* he would remain in India only if he felt welcome: "He made it clear," the reporter wrote, "that he would remain in Manali if he felt comfortable, otherwise the whole world was in front of him."

Within weeks the Indian government was making him feel less comfortable. It denied visa extensions for Devaraj, Hasya, Vivek, and the other disciples who were taking care of him. By the end of December the government had told its embassies to refuse visas to his disciples. "The country," Rajneesh responded, "is much more materialistic than I had expected. The bureaucracy is endless. Besides, the country is under heavy political pressure from America."

Rajneesh retold the events of recent years to an Indian audience that had only heard secondhand accounts and rumors. He painted himself as the pained observer and survivor of Sheela's machinations, concluding that "we had to pass through that phase, and we have passed through it without any damage because unless I am damaged, nothing is damaged." He did not mention the people in Antelope who had to leave their homes, the adults and children who still suffered from intestinal damage after the salmonella infection, the Share-A-Home program, the sannyasins who had lost their money and their homes, or those who felt hurt and angry and betrayed.

Rajneesh, apparently indefatigable, began to talk about a "final attempt" to start a commune on an island in the South Pacific, perhaps near the Fiji Islands. "For the first time we could manage anarchism and communism both together. Where no nationality is recognized, no religion is recognized, no political boundaries." He imagined gardens floating on water, underwater houses, an island paradise—"a model for the universe"—to which sannyasins who now must live in and cope with the world could periodically retreat.

Previous discourses with their talk about the "new commune," where work would be meditation and sannyasins would build a city of a hundred thousand, were no longer relevant. "I don't," Rajneesh told a questioner, "want a very organized commune. For the simple reason that whenever you become very organized you start losing something for which in the first place you had started to organize. . . . Sooner or later," he went on, "that kind of commune was going to break down. There was no time to meditate, no time to dance, no time to sing your songs or play your flute.

"Once again it is good there are small centers where people come to meditate, to read. . . . And these people have to work in the world, that's why I have given them the freedom to wear all colors. . . . And if you are working for a year you can certainly save for a month, two months, three months, to be with me." In the new place—sometimes he called it a commune, sometimes a school—"there will not be therapy groups. There will be meditation groups, music groups, sculpture groups, poetry groups. You can sit by my side and ask questions. Rather than having an institution, you become a moving institution, you can be my wandering messengers."

Rajneesh was speaking to men and women who had believed in him, given money to him, worked tirelessly to create the utopian community he promised them, and had then lost it. His praise for wandering messengers and his offer of a retreat from the world into which they had been summarily expelled were meant to be reassuring reminders that all necessities could be regarded as virtues. But now there was an aura of opportunism as well as Tantra about his words. As I read Rajneesh now, lines from *Glimpses of a Golden Childhood* came to me: "I have learned the art of moving ahead of things so it looks like I am making them happen." I thought I could hear the Master breathing hard.

On January 3, 1986, Rajneesh left India for Kathmandu, where hundreds of Nepalese sannyasins welcomed him, and Hasya, Vivek, and Devaraj were able to rejoin him. In Nepal he elaborated on his concept of "a new community where two hundred people are there at a time," people who could "just sit by my side and have a more close, more intimate contact." For the time being, though, the Master, apparently feeling restless and confined in the East, would be visiting his sannyasins, making a "World Tour."

The first stop on the World Tour, on February 16, was the Greek island of Crete. Rajneesh was admitted there after friends and disciples made contact with Prime Minister Andreas Papandreou. The actual arrangements were made by Papandreou's son George, the deputy minister of education and cults (religion). A sociologist who was educated at Amherst and the London School of Economics, Papandreou, Jr., as the Greeks called him, believed that Rajneesh's presence would boost the island's flagging tourist industry. Because of terrorist activities at European airports, the overall number of visitors to Greece was down by 60 or 70 percent and the number of wealthy Americans by even more.

It seemed a natural. Papandreou's socialist government depended on Cretan votes to stay in power, and Crete depended on tourism for its economic well-being. And admitting the controversial Rajneesh demonstrated the government's liberalism to its critics on the left. Besides, Papandreou was only issuing Rajneesh a "temporary residence permit," not a visa. It was good for only thirty days and timed to end before the beginning of the tourist season.

The seventeenth-century Venetian villa the sannyasins rented completed the picture. It was in the port town of Ayios Nikolaos and was owned by Nikos Koundouros, a film director who was himself something of a cult figure to Greek moviegoers. Koundouros' most recent film, *Brothel*, had been a Felliniesque melodrama about the 1897 Cretan rebellion, set in the bordello of Madame Hortense. Koundouros' house had previously been used by the Beatles and Joan Baez.

Within a few days Rajneesh was giving talks twice daily on the terrace in front of Koundouros' villa. From his orthopedically designed chair, which Devageet had placed under a gnarled carob tree, Rajneesh could see the boats in the harbor at Ayios Nikolaos and the turquoise waters of the Aegean. His opening themes were, appropriately, Greek. "Socrates was asking only one thing, that nothing should be believed, everything should be experienced, experimented. . . . I have loved Socrates more than anyone else for his humbleness, for his scientific inquiry, for not creating a religion, not creating a theology, not creating a following, not becoming a prophet. . . . What Socrates was doing twenty-five centuries before," he announced, "I am doing now."

On the phone Bhagwati, who was in charge of public relations, told me everything was "very beautiful, very peaceful." Certainly she would be able to arrange "interviews with Bhagwan" for me.

By the time I arrive on Crete, on March 3, two weeks after Rajneesh, there is turmoil in the island's churches. Orthodox priests, acting on instructions from the local bishop, Metropolitan Dimitrios of Petra, have threatened to stone Rajneesh's disciples for taking part in "sex orgies." In their churches, they are collecting signatures—three thousand so far—on a petition to have him expelled. It turns out that the Cretan Orthodox church was not consulted by the Papandreou government before Rajneesh was admitted, and any approval given by the Greek Orthodox church means nothing on the island. The Cretan church is "autocephalus," an autonomous branch of Eastern Orthodoxy that reports directly to the patriarchate in Istanbul.

Already Rajneesh, who didn't pick this fight, is relishing the head-to-head confrontation with local religious authority: "If people had followed Socrates and Aristotle, Greece would be the cream of the world," he confides, "but you have followed those idiots, the Byzantines, and you are still in the grip of idiots."

The war of words quickly escalates. Rajneesh, sounding a familiar Tantric theme, and knowing it will enrage the bishop, urges his listeners to "go through the sexual experience to such an extent that you are completely satisfied with it. Only then will you be able to become meditative like Buddha."

Dimitrios issues an encyclical telling church members to "beware of this modern god with his Rolls-Royces and vast wealth. . . . He is," Dimitrios adds, "a menace to public safety." The bishops on Crete join together to suggest that Rajneesh's presence on the island violates a clause of the Greek constitution that forbids proselytization.

Rajneesh responds in kind. "Jesus Christ was crazy," he says. "There was no need to crucify him. But Socrates' devotion to truth was total."

The newspapers are full of the war of words between the guru and the church, but Ayios Nikolaos feels peaceful and inviting. I am here because I have a commission from *Penthouse* to interview Rajneesh. The magazine wants information on the sex guru and his much publicized battle with Sheela. I am trying to figure out how I feel about Rajneesh, to piece together my experience of him—his friendliness and intelligence, the catalytic power of his presence on me, my affection for him—with what he and Sheela did in Oregon, his cowardly flight from the United States, and his petulance. Maybe, I think, if I spend more time with him, get to know him better, my picture of him will become clearer. Besides, I am still drawn to him, still eager to be in his presence.

I have a room in the Ormos Hotel, a couple of hundred yards from the gate of Koundouros' villa. The sky is clear and the days are warm. *Penthouse* will pay my expenses even if ultimately it decides not to take the interviews. I feel like I'm on a paid vacation. And then too there are people here I want to interview for this book, which I have now decided to write. Do they, I wonder, still believe, even after Rajneesh has abandoned his commune and retreated from the United States, that he is infallible and courageous?

The scene at Ayios Nikolaos is as playful and colorful as the boats in the harbor. There are flowers in the fields and on the hills overlooking the hotels—geraniums, hibiscuses, bougainvilleas, poppies, almond trees in bloom. Sannyasins fill up the Ormos bar and lobby and porch, the terrace of the restaurant across the street, and the huge semicircular café in the center of town. Most are dressed in orange and red, although some are wearing their malas over green, turquoise, and bright yellow. They are young and tan and healthy-looking, mostly Europeans. A number have not seen their Master since Poona or only at one of the World Festivals. Their voices, all the languages of the continent, rise from the packed tables, blend together. There are students on vacation and sannyasins who have invested the last dollars they brought from the ranch for the ticket.

Arup and Mary Catherine and Asanga and Devageet are here; John, Kendra, Kaveesha and her nephew David, and Devaraj are staying with Rajneesh in Koundouros' villa. Most of the rest are in the Ormos. Already sannyasins are filling up nearby hotels, renting rooms and apartments by the week. There are 250 disciples in Ayios Nikolaos on the first day I arrive. Three days later there are 700. More are arriving on every plane into Heraklion.

If the church is repelled by Rajneesh and his sannyasins, the local hotelkeepers and restaurateurs are not. These attractive young people have as much money to spend as the tourists who ordinarily come to the resort town and are, on the whole, more cheerful and better behaved. They don't get drunk or get in fights. They tip well and treat the clerks in the hotels and the waiters in the restaurants in a good-natured, comradely way.

The whole scene feels a bit like a camp reunion or a spiritual Fort Lauderdale. There is no security, no sniffing of hair, no armed guards or, for that matter, guards of any kind. We line up half an hour before discourses, morning and evening. The gate to Koundouros' villa opens and we file up the hill to the stone terrace. Musicians play and, after some time, Rajneesh, holding Vivek's hand, descends the stone steps of the villa, sits in his chair underneath the carob tree, and begins.

There is only one prohibition in force. Cretans, with the exception of journalists, are not allowed into the discourses. This, I understand, is to forestall accusations of proselytization, which is illegal. In Greece, all citizens are born into the Orthodox church. Jehovah's Witnesses and Protestants who have tried to win converts have been jailed, beaten, and expelled.

On my first day I spend time with white-bearded Asanga. Since leaving the ranch, he has lived in Switzerland, a jet-age saddhu, with sannyasins. After a few days in Crete he will return to see his family in India. I want to know whether he thinks his Master is responsible for what Sheela did to Oregonians and other sannyasins and how the whole experience has affected him and his commitment.

"Bhagwan," he explains, "loves and gives total freedom to individuals. He never interferes. A person cannot grow unless given total freedom. At that stage the real inside comes out. Bhagwan makes everyone's insides come out. He uses you optimally. If a person isn't aware, Bhagwan will, or the people around him will, make that person aware. And if not . . ." he shrugs. "So for Sheela nothing is yet lost. If she becomes aware and accepts everything that happened, then she will have a greater spiritual growth. If Bhagwan stopped her, then she wouldn't be able to realize. If she has this offensiveness it has to be finished." When I ask about the ranch, he says that he is sad to see the passing of that time. But "sadness comes and goes. It too can be an opportunity. Others," he reminds me serenely, "may see the destruction of Rajneeshpuram simply as destruction. We see it as the creation of something new."

That night at discourse, Rajneesh is in good form. He has been asked a question about Krishnamurti, who died a week ago. He knows that Krishnamurti often criticized him, and I'm sure he is aware of what Krishnamurti said to Deeksha about his "criminal" behavior, but he treats it all as a "joke": "The color red was to him as to a bull. He criticized me, I criticized him. We did not mean it. I love the man and a joke with him once in a while is not contradictory. Only on one point does he not agree with me. He is too serious. and religion needs a certain quality of humor to make it more human." He goes on a long, funny detour as the light fades from the Aegean and a breeze springs up, and then he comes back to the matter at hand, turning Krishnamurti's criticism to his advantage. "Krishnamurti has prepared the ground for me. My work will take people deeper than the intellectual, to the heart, and deeper than the heart, to their being. Our work," he concludes, "is one."

The next day I prepare my questions for the interviews. I figure the first day for politics, the second for sex. Bhagwati asks me to write them down. They will be presented to Rajneesh and he will decide which one or ones he wants to answer. Bhagwati warns me that this interview won't be a dialogue as in Oregon; also, she says, he doesn't want to talk about Sheela. The last time someone asked a question about her he said, "Who is Sheela?" and then, "Next question."

I can understand his not wanting to dwell on the past, but I also know that my doubts are strong, that nowhere has he dealt honestly and fully with the issues that still trouble me and many others. More speeches won't clarify anything. I preface the questions I write down with a request to have a dialogue.

"When you appeared on American TV on 'Nightline,' from the jail in Charlotte, North Carolina, you told the interviewer, Ted Koppel, you didn't know where your friends were taking you on your plane. This is extremely hard to believe. Then you said you were going to fight for the American Constitution and you plea-bargained to leave the country. What was going on?"

"Why do you permit violent and destructive activities and at what point do you stop them?"

"What have you learned from your experiences in Oregon, your experiences in jail? Have they changed you?" There are five more in this vein.

The next morning Rajneesh is in a cheerful mood. He has been looking around, I'm sure, feeling the lively, expectant presence of all these European young people who have been coming to Crete, to eat and drink and dance in the discos and sit twice a day at his feet. There is no question that he feels himself the new Socrates, that he now welcomes the bishop's charge that he is "corrupting the youth."

He is reminding his listeners about the "gap between generations." It is time for a "quantum leap. . . . The past is irrelevant, a hindrance too. The old man was a part of society, the new man an individual being, not a cog in the wheel. The new man will live spontaneously without rules or regulations or anyone telling him how to live. . . . Existence wants a new man, new ways of thinking. There is no Messiah. The new man is the Messiah. I have chosen the right time and the right place. . . . I am the right man at the right time. . . . I'm talking to people who are already dropping the past. The archbishop," he goes on, throwing out yet more bait, "is saying I should be deported because I am corrupting the youth. If a religion of two thousand years can be destroyed by this man on a tourist visa" — his voice lowers, he pauses and shrugs — "for four weeks. . . ."

Rajneesh is clearly enjoying himself on Crete. So am I. Mary Catherine has just arrived. She's covering the World Tour for *Rajneesh: The Newspaper*, which Bodhi is editing in Boulder. We have breakfast and check out the bulletin board in the hotel lobby. Several of the notices are from sannyasins who drive cabs between Ayios Nikolaos and Heraklion, where the planes arrive and depart, and to Knossos, where the Minoan ruins are. Tarot readings and horoscopes, past-life regressions and half a dozen different kinds of massage are advertised. One sannyasin is selling "Pictures of Bhagwan on the Ranch," and another offers to mend clothes. Shares are available in apartments that sannyasins have rented. Tickets back to London and Rome are on sale at cut rates. Devageet has brought his dentist's tools and is cleaning teeth for $10 U.S. As in Poona, the underground economy is thriving.

Bhagwati calls me over, suddenly solemn. "Jim, I have bad news. You can't do the interview tonight. I have a note from Bhagwan. He says" — she takes out a type-written message — " 'The questions are all rubbish. They are yellow journalism. I don't want to be interrupted. You're welcome to ask other questions.' "

My sense of well-being evaporates. I feel momentarily hurt, and rejected. This sur-prises me. And then the anger is rising. What's all this bullshit about spontaneity and "the new man"? These questions aren't "yellow journalism." They're simply serious attempts to find out what is going on, to get some answers to questions he continues to avoid. He's arrogant and petty, cowardly and defensive. He's no Socrates taking on all comers, just a self-protective man, a child who wants to play only according to his rules. He won't allow me or anyone else to get too close, to engage him too intimately, push him too hard.

The next afternoon Kaveesha and David come up to me. "I'd like to help you ask Bhagwan some really juicy questions about sex," Kaveesha offers. "Having an interview in *Penthouse* is a wonderful opportunity to get his teachings across to people." Why not? I still have work to do.

We finish going over the questions. I feel good. My work is all but over. I will ask about the connection between political repression and sexual repression; the relationship between meditation and sexuality; Rajneesh's views on pornography and censorship; the causes of and cures for premature ejaculation and impotence. *Penthouse* will be satisfied. If things go well, I'll get another interview and try once again to pose the more pointed and political questions. Now Kaveesha and I are on the terrace drinking wine, watching the boats in the harbor, talking about what has hap-pened since Rajneesh left Oregon. Kaveesha has no regrets. "Bhagwan will reach more people on this World Tour than he ever could have in Oregon."

Suddenly, sannyasins are running toward us, shouting, "The police have come. They're arresting Bhagwan, come quickly. Bring your camera." At the gate to Koun-douros' villa there are eight or ten police cars, most unmarked. There are stiff young cops in uniform and older men in black suits and white shirts who look like inspectors or government functionaries. And there are cops in designer jeans and windbreak-ers — Cretan Vice.

My first thought is that it's simply a drug bust or harassment. The sannyasins pour out of the hotel and line the road. Cretan youths on motor scooters arrive. The uniformed cops keep us from going through the gate but seem to know nothing. I feel their fear and the possibility of violence in them. The men in the suits and windbreakers confer among themselves, refuse to answer my questions.

All around me sannyasins are debating whether or not to sit down in front of the gate to keep the police from leaving with their Master. It reminds me of the sixties—the civil rights movement in the South, antiwar demonstrations in Cambridge and San Francisco and Washington. But the sannyasins are inexperienced, frantic, almost hysterical. It seems more like they are trying to prevent a child from being kidnapped than a leader from being arrested.

Twenty minutes later a police car barrels through the gate. In the back seat is Rajneesh, with Devaraj. As the car passes I can see the back of his head and his hat.

Within five minutes I'm in my car with Mary Catherine and a Greek sannyasin whom we've brought along to interpret. We careen around Ayios Nikolaos, up and down the hills, past fruit sellers, around circles, the wrong way on one-way streets, shouting to get directions, looking for the road to Heraklion. All the while I'm alternating between paying attention to my driving and thinking about my story. Now it's not just a question of my interest or good journalism but of economics. If I don't get any interview at all, I wonder if *Penthouse* will even pay my expenses. We tear along the road to Heraklion, passing men in donkey carts and new Mercedes cabs, fields and mountains and orchards I would ordinarily want to stop to walk in.

I start to laugh at the whole chaotic situation. The trip was to be so relaxed; the interviews were arranged ahead of time; the place is beautiful. It had been more pleasant than ever to be around Rajneesh and his sannyasins. And now everything is turned upside down.

At the airport there is confusion. The woman at the information counter tells us that "the Bhagwan will be sent to Athens." The airport officials say, "No, he is going to Rhodes." We buy tickets for both places and head for the Harbor Police Station, where he is being held.

Already there are sannyasins outside the police station, and longshoremen from the nearby piers. Shyam's old friend Veena is there, keeping things orderly. Mary Catherine and I push through the crowd and show our passports and credentials to the policeman at the door, who hands them inside. A few minutes later, to my great surprise, he lets us in. A plainclothesman leads us back to the room where Rajneesh is being held.

The room is ten by fourteen feet and already there are fifteen people jammed into it. Rajneesh is sitting in a chair, flanked on one side by Devaraj and on the other by Anando, a lawyer who is acting as his "secretary." Reporters are waving their hands and shouting questions in Greek. Mukta, his benefactress in Bombay, his gardener in Poona, is sitting at Rajneesh's feet, translating. The room is ringed by policemen who are fidgeting with cigarettes they are not allowed to light in the allergic guru's presence. One is puzzling over an autograph he has solicited from Rajneesh. Outside, the noise of the crowd is louder. More people are coming. There are shouts, laughter, and the first strains of guitar music. Flashbulbs are going off at the window.

Rajneesh is sitting quietly, inclined toward Mukta. He's wearing a floor-length gray and white silk gown, a diamond-studded watch, and a white hat in which two rings of stones are sparkling. On the table next to him there is a bowl of fruit. I push forward, amazed that I am here, surprised at my temerity, but determined to get my interview. Feeling very much the journalist, I take pictures, color first, then quickly change the film to black and white. I sit down in front of Rajneesh—only the floor is available—and put my tape recorder on the table next to him. I catch Rajneesh's eye, we nod to each other like a conductor and his concertmaster. The Greek reporters ask one or two more questions and then, as if my wish had made it happen, disappear from the room. We begin the dialogue that two days before he had refused to have with me. Though he is clearly tired, Rajneesh is gracious and calm in the middle of the frenzied activity inside and outside the police station. We talk as if we were in his living room.

Rajneesh has already told the Greek reporters that twenty police broke down the door at Koundouros' villa, that they threatened to "dynamite" the house if he didn't come with them right away. He has made it clear that he has done nothing wrong, that he was only talking to "my people." I explain my situation and quickly move into the list of questions that I know *Penthouse* will want answered. He is "perfectly happy" to oblige and we are off and running: of course there is a connection between political and sexual repression; people who are sexually repressed will have no energy for political change. It suits the churches and—there is a twinkle in his eye—it suits writers like me as well. Magazines such as *Penthouse* and *Playboy* would not exist if there weren't sexual repression.

I steer him through the questions firmly but I think rather gracefully. It is as if we are playing roles—I the reporter and he the interviewee—or, once again, dancing. We talk about Socrates and the threat that thought and introspection will always pose to dictators. I wonder if he appreciates the irony. The people outside are clapping their hands and singing louder and louder. There are guitars and drums and flutes. The words fill the holding room.

"Ecstasy, when I see your face.

"Ecstasy, when I feel your grace.

"Ecstasy, when I look in your eyes."

Rajneesh gets up, goes to the window, and waves to the crowd. "You will see me," he says, "in many jails." He sits down again and turns to Anando. "We will have to start a list of all the countries," he says, meaning all the countries that have thrown him out or won't let him in.

The interview, by turns sensitive and outrageous, continues for the next hour. Rajneesh explains why he holds the Vatican responsible for the world's sexual ills, up to and including AIDS, and gives advice to those who cannot relax in sex. I know it's perfect for *Penthouse*. By the end of the interview, my feelings about Rajneesh are no clearer, but once again I sense there has been a certain fit, a certain grace to our meeting. After I leave the room Rajneesh and his sannyasins turn out the lights and sit quietly for forty minutes.

Later that night Rajneesh arrives at the Athens airport, flanked by Devaraj and Anando. The chief of police of Attica is there with twenty armed men in uniform. He has a warrant signed by Athanasias Tsouras, the alternate minister of public order.

Rajneesh is to be expelled for "reasons of public interest," a proviso most commonly used for Palestinian terrorists. Before heading for the private plane that will take him out of Greece, Rajneesh holds a brief press conference. Forty reporters are shouting in half a dozen languages. The floodlights and flashbulbs are blinding. "I was thinking," he says, "that after poisoning Socrates you must have learned something, but it seems that you are still as barbarious [sic] as you have been two thousand years before."

The police chief signals, and the men in uniform crowd Rajneesh toward the other end of the airport, where a private plane is waiting to take him to Madrid.

After he leaves, Metropolitan Dimitrios orders the churches in Ayios Nikolaos to ring their bells. "His expulsion," proclaims the bishop, "is a victory for the people of God and the local church." Apparently the Cretan church put heavy pressure on Papandreou. The Greek government, which had hoped to win votes by bringing tourism to Crete, was in danger of losing them by offending the church. It was time for Rajneesh to go.

———————————————■□———————————————
□■

After he left Greece, Rajneesh was refused entry into Spain, Switzerland, Sweden, and Great Britain; already Germany and Italy had indicated their unwillingness to have him. He landed in Ireland, stayed quietly in a posh hotel in Limerick—what could he possibly say in Ireland without getting in trouble?—and headed south and west to Antigua, where once again he was turned away. He finally came to rest in Uruguay. He stayed there on a three-month visa at the seaside resort of Punta del Este—I noted that bills for hotels, airfare, and so on were mounting—accompanied by Vivek, Hasya, Devaraj, Kaveesha, David, John, and cooks and cleaners, the caretaker sannyasins. There were rumors that Rajneesh would be allowed to stay for a year and set up a commune.

Rajneesh gave a few low-key interviews in Uruguay. He seemed less focused now on building a movement, more on the individuals who made it up. He reassured his disciples that physical closeness to him, now impossible, was not necessary. "Even without it, your heart can beat in the same rhythm, your being can be silent to the same depth . . . and then there is no distance, then you are not lonely, you are alone. . . . All the politicians who have been desperately creating walls between me and my people can be foiled. I find a deeper way, an invisible way, that is a connection between the Master and disciples. . . . I am with you wherever you are. Just remain open, vulnerable, receptive."

More and more sannyasins were questioning that connection. They felt abused by the organization Rajneesh had created, exhausted by the contortions through which its policies had put their lives. What they had accepted as devices sanctioned by their Master turned out to be derelictions he now disavowed. They had been "open, vulnerable, receptive," and they felt their trust had been betrayed. Most sensitive to this, perhaps, were the therapists who had followed him.

In September 1985, after Sheela left the ranch, Poonam got a note from Rajneesh. "He said to me, 'I know Sheela wanted to destroy Medina and you.' He asked me if I wanted to get a new commune together." She had been content as a therapist on her own. Now for a while she was elated. Her Master had called on her again. Her mistreatment had been a mistake. But, she discovered, "My heart wasn't in it. . . . People weren't so interested in getting together; communes were closing down." She didn't do it. Instead, she told me, she was opening a therapy center outside London, called Quaesitor II, after the center she had left fifteen years before to join her husband, Teertha, and his new Master in India. Many of the Poona group leaders, including Amitabh and Teertha, now Paul Lowe again, were doing workshops there.

"I'm doing therapy and I've taken a house in the country. I love it. And I'm not at all sure of my relationship with Bhagwan. I need to see him, to talk to him." She didn't know how much he knew or why he allowed what happened—to her, to Medina, to the ranch—to happen. She wore a black sweater and no mala, but her house was filled with sannyasins and pictures of her Master looked at us from the walls and tables in her sitting room.

Poonam was not the only therapist who loved Bhagwan and had doubts. While Rajneesh and his entourage were traveling and living well, they were having to contend with the ordinary realities of living and making a living in the world. As they did so they were forced to confront the feelings of anger and betrayal—in their sannyasin clients and in themselves—that many had denied. They had been Bhagwan's vehicles. Now they were resisting his guiding hand. I heard that Amitabh said that "Bhagwan has lost it," that now he would like to "meet him man to man." Lowe, angered by the financial plight in which Rajneesh left the ranch dwellers, was reported to say that he had "not been a disciple since Poona, but at the same state of consciousness as Bhagwan [i.e., enlightened]." I heard that Lowe refused to allow Rajneesh to stay with him in Italy or to donate the money that he and the others were making. They reportedly believed that Rajneesh's presence would damage their standing with the Italian government and with potential non-sannyasin clients; and there was no extra money to give.

Though he was silent about the Uruguayan government, Rajneesh was quite vocal about the therapists. "Therapy," he announced in a communiqué that Hasya published in *Rajneesh: The Newspaper*, "basically has nothing to do with spirituality. I was just using it to clean the rubbish the mind has gathered down the ages. The people that pass through therapy go deeper into meditation than the therapists. The therapists were going deeper into their egos. . . . They started feeling that they had become some kind of gurus, masters." He singled out Lowe in particular. "Teertha has taken it for granted, without anybody saying it to him, that he is going to be my successor." He accused them all of "having been failures in the West" before they came to him.

Though this kind of public attack, mixing truths—about the limitations of therapy and the pitfalls of its practice—with half-truths and lies, was no different from many others he had launched, it no longer had the same force. Some sannyasin therapists listened receptively, nodded their heads, and wrote letters—also published in *Rajneesh: The Newspaper*—in support of "Bhagwan's hit." The danger of believing that one "has it together" was ever present; they realized, as any sensitive therapist must, that some of their patients were able to deal with themselves and their world—at least on occasion—more intelligently or lovingly or spontaneously than they. Prasad, the German who ran the Centering group in Poona, quoted Rajneesh in his own favor: "A disciple is willing to learn, a follower is closed." And Maitri, an American therapist, saw his words as just another of her Master's lessons: the praise, the status of the therapist, "everything which can be given can also be taken."

But other therapists were more skeptical. They were beginning to apply to their Master the therapeutic tools that they used on themselves and their clients. "He's pissed off," said Rajen, a British psychologist, "because the therapists are doing their own thing." "He miscalculated," Radha, who had been Rajneesh's medium as well as a therapist in Poona, told me. "He's just not in touch with reality."

Perhaps the strongest response came from Poonam. "I have felt so hurt, so used and so uncared for," she wrote in a letter published in the newspaper. "And you know and I know how many lies were in that statement [of yours]. You also know that far from coming to you because we were failures in the West, and 'losing our clients,' many of us came at the very peak of our careers. I have so very much to thank you for, but your statement felt to me like the words of an old lover who wants to stay in control. . . . For better or worse, right now, I have to be on my own."

When Hasya issued another letter, two weeks later, claiming that the first was only to provoke a "catharsis" in the therapists, reminding them of the "inner sannyas" of their connection to him, and assuring them that "Bhagwan loves you more than he has ever loved you," some were unimpressed. It might be—and to those who remained unquestioningly loyal, it was—a Master's device, but it felt on balance like a manipulation, an attempt to appease and seduce, to use cunning when force would not work. Before, Rajneesh's hits, like the blows of the Zen Master's stick, were gratefully accepted as teachings. Now they seemed like acts of aggression designed to beat disciples into a surrender they no longer freely embraced.

In the middle of June 1986, the Uruguayan government declined to extend Rajneesh's visa and he was compelled to leave. Rajneesh claimed, according to Hasya, that the president of Uruguay himself embraced the guru while bidding him a tearful farewell. Hasya noted in a message to sannyasins in *Rajneesh* that the Uruguayan president had been in Washington just prior to Rajneesh's departure and that an agreement providing millions in U.S. aid to Uruguay was signed. These were facts, but there was no evidence to link American aid to the Uruguayan government's denial of Rajneesh's visa.

Leaving Uruguay, Rajneesh stopped in Brazil before going to Jamaica, where, after a three-day wait, he was denied a visa. He went from there to Europe, where he stayed incognito until the end of July. At that point Hasya announced that "Bhagwan's World Tour" was "a great success" and was at an end. He was returning to Bombay, where he would speak not about politics or to the world—"I drop all hope for this humanity and all hope for the planet"—but only to individuals who wanted to "grow into meditation, into peace, into silence."

While Rajneesh traveled and talked, arousing the enmity of prelates and politicians, now spinning out new plans, now sparring, now retreating, his disciples continued settling into their new lives. With this settling came new perspectives on their feelings about their Master.

The connection of Yashen, the mathematician, with Rajneesh was uncomplicated by the expectations or disappointments of intimate personal contact with his Master or by a long-term investment in communal living, either in Poona or on the ranch. This connection continued to give him a feeling of peace and joy, a freedom from expectations. We talked about it on the plane from Athens back to London in March 1986.

"I'm in love with Bhagwan," he said. "It's so easy. I went to be with him in Crete because he's fun to be with. You don't get anything out of it and yet you get everything."

"What is that everything?" I asked.

"I no longer bother about someone else's opinion much. I read things I need to know technically [he's now an accountant]. But I'm no longer very interested in what someone else feels about the way I am. It's irrelevant. I might talk about it in a conversation and then it's exciting, but I don't need books telling me someone else's idea, someone who didn't live what they wrote, trying to communicate what they never experienced."

There were many others who continued, in spite of everything, to be totally in love with Rajneesh. They were as comfortable with his changes of mood and plans, his obvious lies and questionable decisions, as ducks floating down a winding river. No matter the fate of any particular project or announcement, their lives seemed richer, easier, more relaxed. In London I talked with Bhagwati, who was a high-powered and highly paid computer programmer before she was a Twinkie on the ranch and a spokeswoman in Crete. "It always turns out better," she told me two weeks after Rajneesh had left Crete. "I loved Poona and I hated leaving. And then I went to Rajneeshpuram and that was beautiful and I hated leaving. And then I went to Crete and that was even more beautiful. Now my bags are packed. I always live well. Money comes. No sannyasins will let you down."

Gopa, after leaving the ranch, lived with her parents in New England. She knew she was seeing them more dispassionately, more compassionately, than she ever had; but sometimes she would watch with dismay as the family patterns of a dozen or two dozen years earlier re-formed, as the same feelings of frustration tightened her muscles. Later she moved to Washington, D.C., not far from me, where she worked as a research assistant for a political writer and took drawing lessons.

For some time Gopa wasn't terribly eager to see other sannyasins. At thirty-two she wanted to have some sense of what it was like to be in a world she had left eleven years before. Living in Washington, she discovered how much she missed the community she'd had in Poona and on the ranch—the family feeling. In Poona and on the ranch she felt "intensely alone," but there was a "kind of cooperation and friendship. . . . We all wanted to see the commune work. We'd wake up with three hours' sleep and nobody felt forced or resentful. We wanted to work because we believed in what we were doing and we felt we had to keep it going, and this carried us through." When it became clear after Rajneesh left that the ranch would be abandoned, "there was a feeling of someone dying, of utter loss. I remember one day when I woke up and walked up the hill and lay down and cried myself silly and then everything went still."

Though she did it well, her job in Washington didn't interest her. Once she had saved some money she took off again for Canada, then England and Italy, where she stayed with sannyasins. She telephoned from Milan, happy. "I've realized," she said, "that the only thing important to me is meditation, becoming more aware, more alert, more quiet, more peaceful." In October 1986 she was on her way to India, not to stay, but "just to see Bhagwan."

At about the time that Gopa was on her way to India, I talked again with Mary Catherine and Bodhi. They were in Boulder, a kind of pilgrimage site in the mountains where Tibetan Buddhists, Zen Buddhists, Sufis, and a dozen other religious groups have all formed communities. They were jointly editing *Rajneesh: The Newspaper,* bringing their Master's words and news about him to his disciples and "friends" in America. They lived in Boulder among two hundred other sannyasins, in one of the dozen group houses that had been formed there. They worked with sannyasins, and many of their friends were sannyasins. The ranch was gone and Rajneesh was in India, but the connection with him was as strong as it had ever been.

Years before, in Poona, Bodhi had realized that "Bhagwan was the man that Wilhelm Reich had theorized about" and that it might be possible for him to become like his Master. Rajneesh helped Bodhi to see "my jealousy, my fears, and my anger, my hunger for power, and to go through them. Without him I would not even have started. The best therapist in the world would not have convinced me to do it." In Poona and on the ranch he learned "to become aware of the chatter of my mind, the tone of my body talking, to tell what emotions are going on, to breathe deeply and to let them go."

After Sheela left, Rajneesh had advised his sannyasins to "never again let anyone have power over you or have power over anyone." Bodhi realized that he had "allowed that to happen," in the last year with Sheela. She was "consciously trying to protect us but she was unconsciously trying to provoke a reaction from the outside." From his point of view, "Bhagwan kept himself out." Like Asanga and many other sannyasins, Bodhi believed that Rajneesh set things up, or at least allowed them to happen "so we would follow our desires, so we would fuck up and learn a lesson."

Once, during a long night of eating and drinking, I marshaled for Bodhi my facts and my suspicions: the absurdity of Rajneesh not knowing what was happening, the evidence that he did know the things that were done, the stories I had heard from Shiva and Nandan, from Deeksha, Radha, and the Oregon attorney general, even Rajneesh's own words to me. I saw what I believed to be doubt come into Bodhi's face — and then disappear, like a headlight's beam on a roadside sign. "Even if it's true, I love the man no matter what he does. I will do everything in my power to keep him free and healthy. Without him, without his living example, I would have wound up with only an ideology about growth. I would have despaired about making the world a better place.

"He is the only man in the world," Bodhi went on, "speaking truth in detail and pointing to solutions that may save mankind. Others are pointing to a political revolution, a shoring up of what's falling apart. He's created a psychological revolution, a change in individuals."

Now with the newspaper Bodhi felt for the first time that he was doing the work he was always meant to do. He was trying to reach out beyond the sannyasin community; to report on and make contact with others who were concerned with the environment and with prison reform, spiritual development and the abolition of national boundaries. He was working for "everything and anything that brings more responsibility to individuals and increasing awareness, love, and connectedness between them and nature." And in this work, he said, Rajneesh was guiding, inspiring him. "I feel," he concluded, "as connected to Bhagwan as my hands are to my arms."

During the year after she left the ranch, while she traveled, Mary Catherine felt her "rootlessness and restlessness" drop away. Eventually, inevitably it now seemed, she too came to Boulder, to work on the newspaper, to live in a community with other sannyasins.

After I left the police station in Crete, Mary Catherine stayed on. The lights were turned off and for forty minutes she sat silently with her Master, fulfilling "a dream that I'd had for four years." And "some little empty place got filled up and it still flows over, some kind of light gets lit again." She knew that it might not make sense or seem important to most people, but now for the first time it seemed possible for her to meditate — to "just sit with something, just acknowledge it," and then to watch as "something shifts. It is not done with the mind. It is possible only for moments. But in that shifting there is some kind of transformation of consciousness, a certain grace, a gracefulness that happens. It is some kind of quality that Bhagwan has, a tranquillity that stays with him, even in the courtroom or in pain." It was that stillness, that centeredness, that watchfulness, in which she felt that her Master lived permanently and for which she had come to him ten years before, that was preeminently important to her.

For Mary Catherine the process of meditation, and of creating a meditative community, was beginning, perhaps for the first time. "At the newspaper we're learning more about ourselves and each other. It's turbulent, but there's more honesty about it and a more open affection than in most places. Also, people are reemerging in small groups. We're watching videos of Bhagwan together, putting our toes back in the water, to see what meditativeness is." They were doing Dynamic again, eating and drinking and dancing. Recently Kaveesha, on a tour of sannyasin communities, had come through Boulder. She brought with her a new "quiet meditation" that Rajneesh had given her. And now the sannyasins were meeting regularly to sit in meditation together.

Mary Catherine was not inclined to look at what happened on the ranch, not sure she saw the point, when I pressed it, of trying to figure out "what Bhagwan knew or when he learned it. Let's say he knew all along what was happening and he chose not to intervene. Then at the end he says, 'Look at the mess you've made.' It's a reflection of our minds and our behavior. And there's no question in my mind that he says different things at different times."

For her, all her Master's actions, all his apparent lies, were "arrows" pointing to something that dwarfs or should dwarf analysis and judgment and blame: "He's trying to bring people through all this nonsense, out of our madness and into meditation. A friend of mine described the ranch as a huge immunization program. We are exposed to certain viruses — authoritarianism, fascism — and now we've developed antibodies. We've dropped politics and we're off into meditation pure and simple. We're in a new phase," she said, a perfect echo, a reflection, it seemed to me, of Rajneesh himself. From this point of view the ranch was "a four-year gift. If it's gone now, why be bitter?" When I mentioned the people in Oregon who were bitter, who still had diarrhea and food sensitivities from their poisoning, she was not moved. "It's possible to recover from salmonella," she went on, "but I don't think that people in The Dalles can ever recover from the community-wide hate."

Mahadeva reminded me of a sleeper awakening in an unfamiliar room in a strange city. He was eager for any information about himself, Rajneesh, and other sannyasins that would help him get his bearings, sort things out.

In November 1986, months after he stopped wearing the mala and the red clothes, he was at a Knicks game at Madison Square Garden. "I saw some guy wearing a mala and I called out to him, 'Hey, Swami.' He seemed defensive, so I said, 'It's OK, I'm a sannyasin too.'"

"Why did you say it?" I asked.

"I'm not sure if I responded out of an old habit or whether I just meant I was still open-minded, still a seeker. I suppose too that if I was once a disciple of Bhagwan, I'll always have some kind of connection to the guy. Whatever my connection is, I call it sannyas."

Mahadeva had begun to feel that he deceived himself. "Ten years ago I was wanting something more from reality, and he promised it. I've been depressed most of my life. I think all of us were depressed. I saw him as a way out of depression, a way to be fully alive. Something was missing. In the early days I tried to fill it up with drugs and athletics and sex. When Bhagwan spoke of enlightenment I decided that's what I was going for. Through this explosion into enlightenment would come some kind of overwhelming bliss and joy.

"My need for him to be there for me, to receive this thing from him, was so great that I didn't apply the usual perceptions and insights about human beings to him. I was a rebel sannyasin here in New York; I didn't like the organization telling me what to do when I knew how to do it better. I dropped sannyas, and then I took it again. I think I saw the organization clearly, some of the stuff going on on the ranch, but no matter how Bhagwan acted he was OK."

Now Mahadeva was stepping back, bringing the kind of perception that he applied to himself and his clients to a man whom he once regarded as beyond question or criticism or analysis. "I think," Mahadeva began, "Bhagwan went into a depression after he left India. It may have been a little like what happened to him before he became enlightened. He said he would never leave India, and I think he was wounded by the Indian government, so he went into silence and he got withdrawn. He dealt with his depression in symptomatic ways, like drugs and nitrous oxide and the Rolls-Royces and the jewelry. These were ways to turn himself on, thrills, titillations. And pushing Sheela to become more provocative with the press. It was like living on the edge to know he was alive.

"Bhagwan," he went on, sharing with me the analysis he had made, "started to come out of his depression when he started to speak again. He was no longer just taking. He started to give. But he miscalculated. His contact with reality must have deteriorated. Obviously it did if he ends up getting himself arrested and spending time in jail.

"For ten years I took a detour into his reality. That reality had a promise: the closer you got to Bhagwan, the closer you got to enlightenment. It was like a carrot held in front of our noses. But I don't see him as caring. He had contempt for people. He pushed Sheela too hard. He created a commune and then he tore it apart. He said he would fight the charges in Oregon and then he ran. We all came to him as utter supplicants. He took from everybody.

"Sometimes I wonder where I'd be if I hadn't taken this trip for ten years. Was I running away from something? Was I fooling myself? Now it's all gone. The diehards, they're still holding on to something. They don't want to deal with reality. I still feel like I'm going through the same thing I came to Bhagwan for. I'm seeing a therapist. I'm trying to live my life to the fullest. I haven't given up the quest.

"I like to say the trip was wonderful. There's this tremendous intelligence that I was privy to," he went on, "through his books and his writings. I still pick up the books and get something from them. I got a lot out of being a sannyasin. I became more intelligent, more aware. He helped me to see things from the positive and to be more relaxed and trusting and at ease. I needed it.

"A friend of mine just came back from Bombay and said, 'He's very beautiful. He's helping people to become less dependent.' I'm curious about him and I care about him. But I can't see myself going to Bombay and asking for advice. What would I ask? 'I followed you for ten years and you've been a tremendous disappointment. Have I been an asshole?' What's he going to tell me? He's going to justify his position as a leader. I guess I don't trust him. He doesn't warrant my trust."

Every time I talked with Anna Forbes she seemed less angry, more self-critical, and more distant from the sannyasin experience that had been the center of her life for seven years. She no longer used the name Nandan and now, with a bit of effort, called her former Master "Rajneesh," not "Bhagwan." She still believed that Rajneesh "had a satori and a number of mystical experiences," that he had the power to cause people around him to have psychic experiences. But, she said, he failed the spiritual test that Jesus passed: "He went for power." The Master became a "master scammer." And she saw, though she didn't make the connection between her desires and those she imputed to her former Master, that she too wanted power: "I tried to be a nobody and I always wound up working with the boss types. . . .

"The last time we talked I had a lot of investment in making you see 'the truth,' but now I don't have to hate Rajneesh anymore and neither do you. There was a period," she went on, "when I felt so angry about my sterilization. I really would have murdered him if he came in my house." She was still angry about the sterilization, but she now saw it as a choice she had made. "I bought it lock, stock, and barrel: if you're a good sannyasin, you do it." And now, looking back on her experience, there were many things for which she was grateful. "He gave me permission to be angry, to be total in my work, to experiment and get involved deeply with meditation. He was a catalyst, he drew incredible people to a beautiful environment. We always attributed the experiences to him directly, but it was us. He said it. There was a Buddhafield, but it had nothing to do with him. I'm grateful for these experiences, even for seeing the darker side of things. I've grown up. I'm less gullible."

Anna Forbes was still "very much a seeker." She did Vipassana and went to Benedictine and Zen retreats. And once a week she got together with friends, many of whom were also ex-sannyasins, to sit in quiet meditation.

By late fall 1986 Hasya, Rajneesh's new personal secretary, was in Europe, based in Cologne, where there were a commune—now reduced in size from 300 to 150 sannyasins—a disco, a restaurant, and other sannyasin businesses. Arup was with her and so were others concerned with administration. For several months I had been reading Hasya's communications in *Rajneesh: The Newspaper.* They were a strange compound of loving enthusiasm for her Master, news of the structure that he was giving his movement, and sweeping but undocumented accusations against a variety of governments.

A May 12 letter from Uruguay began, "Shortly before leaving for India [from Oregon], Bhagwan started talking to me about his vision about a new university, which is spread across the whole world, Rajneesh International University of Mysticism, of which he said, 'Our work is to help people become mystics and meditators.' " The new university would have many "Institutes" scattered throughout Europe, the Americas, Australia, and the Far East. Before, when sannyasins had wanted to be with him, Rajneesh wanted centralization, larger and larger communities and Buddhafields, a sannyasin city of 100,000. After the ranch collapsed, while his disciples still hoped for a new, less vulnerable, more isolated community, he dreamed of an island paradise. Now, with characteristic astuteness, he was giving his blessing to—or stealing the march on—the diaspora that was already under way.

When Rajneesh, rejected by a dozen countries, ended his World Tour and returned to India, Hasya hailed her Master as a kind of guru to the globe, revealing the truth about themselves to nations that had been unable or unwilling to see it: "We have caused countries which considered themselves free and independent to see their helplessness in the face of economic pressure brought to bear by the biggest superpower. Isn't it exciting that this superpower is afraid of 'just one, ordinary man,' our beloved Bhagwan."

When I spoke with Hasya by phone in November, she assured me that "the intelligentsia of Europe is seeing that what the press put out about Bhagwan is not true." They were reading *The Rajneesh Bible* (the talks he gave in Oregon) and *The Last Testament* (a collection of Rajneesh's interviews with journalists). And they were asking for sannyas. She told me that there were in the last week forty-five applicants in Munich alone. "Old-timers," she added, "are becoming strengthened. Some are dropping out and new ones are coming forth."

It felt like Hasya's metamorphosis from private person to personal secretary was well under way. When I asked what she had learned—meaning what she had learned about herself—she answered in global terms: "I have had the opportunity to travel with him, to see the free world and how it works and how little freedom there is for individuals anywhere. I'm seeing what happens in the United States, how the U.S. Constitution is being prostituted, how the Moral Majority is setting up the country to go back into . . . the Dark Ages. . . . If he could have survived in America he would have been the only balance against fundamentalist religion." Her words made me uncomfortable, not because I disagreed with her analysis of the Moral Majority—I didn't—but because of the unearned sense of superiority I heard in them, the certainty of Rajneesh's and her own importance. She sounded imperious and oracular, as if she were Aaron to Rajneesh's Moses.

I asked Hasya for evidence of the "personal vendetta against Bhagwan" which she had said Attorney General Meese was waging. I told her I wanted to follow up any leads she might have on Justice Department influence on foreign governments.

She said she couldn't give me the information, at least not yet. She felt it would "endanger too many lives."

She went on: "In India he told us that he would take us into the collective unconscious. I thought he would take us to some secluded place where we would dredge up all the demons you read about in the scriptures. In fact, he did take us into the collective unconscious, on the ranch and since then. He showed us our projections. He encouraged all of us to bring out what we couldn't see otherwise. . . . It was an experiment." The mistakes of the past would not be repeated.

When I suggested, as I had in other conversations with her, that Sheela's illegal deeds started long before the Oregonians opposed the sannyasins, that Rajneesh knew about a great many if not all of the things that happened in Poona and Oregon, Hasya asked me to prove it. I began to display the evidence—so-and-so told me he was involved in the warehouse burning in Poona. . . . She quickly moved on, quoting people who had testified to things that she knew or believed to be untrue. "People were lying. They were hurt and they wanted to get even. When people get angry they become destructive, and the mind creates all sorts of illusions."

Meanwhile, Rajneesh was back in Bombay, where he first initiated disciples seventeen years earlier. He was staying at a sannyasin's house in Juhu Beach, a neighborhood of hotels, expensive private homes, and small multifamily dwellings where the poor live. At night he gave talks to 150 people in the house's living room. From visiting there in earlier years, I remembered that on the long beach, among the bathers, were donkeys and camels and tiny traveling shows with contortionists, pipers and drummers, acrobats, jugglers, trained monkeys, and snake charmers. The Hare Krishnas had their hotel and temple nearby.

Rajneesh was entering yet another "new phase of his work." He was calling his first series of lectures "The Rajneesh Upanishads." "Upanishads," he began, "means sitting at the feet of the Master." Laxmi was at the evening lectures and so were Darshan, who once sat at the gate in Poona, and Taru, who danced in India and on the ranch; so were Vivek and Devaraj, who had managed to evade Indian immigration officials. For a few weeks Bodhicitta and Carolyn were there, on leave from the health clinic—the Rajneesh International Medical Clinic—they now ran in Nepal.

The Westerners were not wearing malas or red. If they had been when they arrived in the country, they would probably have been denied entry by the Indian immigration service. Visiting Rajneesh was not considered a proper activity for tourists. Even within the country, sannyasins were still being discreet. In September I heard there were several hundred of them in Bombay. Those who did not have tickets for the evening watched the discourse on video. Every day there were meditations.

Rajneesh was speaking as confidently, sometimes as grandiosely, as ever: "The Attorney General of America told the press that he does not want to hear my name, see my face on any newspaper, any news magazine, does not want to know whether I am still alive or dead." He was presently deemphasizing the role of the Master and, no doubt responding to sannyasins' disillusionment, emphasizing the "responsibility" of the disciple: "No expectations should be projected on the Master, otherwise there is going to be frustration. It is your expectation which has turned into frustration."

When asked about Hugh Milne's recently published book, *Bhagwan: The God That Failed*, he ignored its many accusations and criticisms, and instead, with characteristic trenchancy, exposed its deepest flaw: "He is disillusioned with his own image, not with me. If you make me a god you are stupid. And then when you don't find the god you are disillusioned. And now I am responsible for that. Do you think so? I am an ordinary human being with all the frailties, all the weaknesses of human beings." A few days later he returned to the subject for a few more swipes at his ex-bodyguard: "It took ten years for this idiot to find out he was with the wrong Master." It was hard even if one was very critical of him not to laugh with Rajneesh.

He spoke again of old themes, often with simplicity and elegance. "The Master does not give you knowledge, he shares his being. And the disciple is not in search of knowledge, he is in search of being. He *is*, but he does not know who he is. He wants to be revealed to himself, he wants to stand naked before himself. . . .

"The Master can only do a simple thing, and that is create trust. Everything else happens. The moment the Master is capable of creating trust, the disciple drops his defenses, drops his clothes, drops his knowledge and becomes just a child again—innocent, alive, a new beginning. . . . I do not ordinarily make prophecies but about this I am absolutely prophetic: the coming one hundred years are going to be more and more irrational and more and more mystical. The second thing: after a hundred years the people will be perfectly able to understand why I was misunderstood—because I am the beginning of the mystical, the irrational . . . I am a discontinuity with the past."

At the end of September an Indian disciple, Govind Siddarth, declared that he had had a vision: the Buddha's "third [astral] body . . . touches the feet of Bhagwan and merges with his body. . . ." Buddha announced that Rajneesh was now "Bhagwan Rajneesh the Buddha Lord Maitreya, a buddha, a true friend to all," thus fulfilling a prophecy that Buddha had made twenty-five hundred years before.

Rajneesh acknowledged the "absolute reality" of his disciple's vision, then declared his independence if not his preeminence: "I am nobody's vehicle . . . my message is parallel."

It was hard to know what to make of these extraordinary claims. They were so outrageous, so at variance with Rajneesh's previous attempts at demystification, so redolent of the kind of esotericism that he had often mocked, but so convenient for juicing up the expectations of doubting disciples. He seemed to be deliberately exciting the imagination of reincarnation-loving Indians, preempting and one-upping the latest Western religious fad—the "channeling" of the words of disembodied Masters by people in trance states. Perhaps this was his latest con (Govind Siddarth was, incidentally, a wealthy man), perhaps it was simply another drama that he was enjoying, another device for his disciples.

None of this—nor discussions about reincarnation or why the therapists left him or why he "hit" them—mattered much to Gopa when she visited him in November. "It was beautiful to see him," she told me. "It made me feel much more settled. There's no organization . . . just someone who issues tickets. I sat and listened to him and during the day I walked on the beach and meditated. I hated India at first but I did Nadabrahma [the humming meditation] and in the part where you move your hands toward you and take everything in, I took it all in—the pigs in the street, the beggars, the dead horse on the beach—and it lost all its charge, and then I started taking in the nice things.

"I sent him a letter, it wasn't a question but he answered it. I said, 'In the last year I was in the world for the first time in eleven years. No matter what I did I didn't seem to care. . . . I don't know what your work is'—he had once told me I would do his work—'but I feel like it's the only thing that means anything.'

"He said, 'I'm not going to tell you what my work is. You are doing it. It's all happening so naturally. If I tell you, you'll interfere. You have all my blessings.' " I could see the extraordinary intelligence of his reply and feel the love that she felt in it as she told it to me: Do what you are doing. Whatever it is, is my work.

That same week I spoke to Shyam, who first introduced me to Rajneesh. He was getting ready to go back to India for a nephew's wedding. He might see Rajneesh in Bombay or perhaps, on the way back, at the ashram in Poona, to which Rajneesh was once again moving. "Someone just came from Bombay and told me," Shyam said, "that his back is so bad he sometimes has trouble walking around." If Rajneesh wished, he would treat him. But he would not go to listen to discourse or pay homage. He wanted to be the kind of friend Rajneesh had said he was looking for. He would not say that he was a sannyasin or that he wasn't. When I pushed him about it, asked him why he still wore the mala when he felt Rajneesh had made so many mistakes and been responsible for so many crimes, had become so enamored of power and so petty toward him, he shrugged.

"It's not that he's my Master and it's not that he's given me anything. It's just that in his presence something happened to me which changed me forever. And so for that I wear his picture."

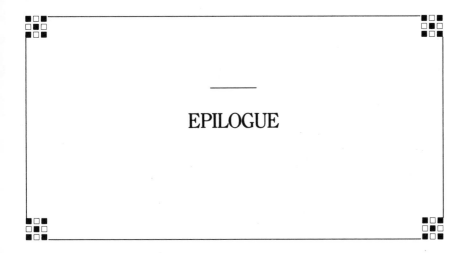

EPILOGUE

On Crete in March 1986, Rajneesh told his young listeners that he shared their perception of the generation gap, that he understood their need to drop the past and its rigid, worn-out ways of making love and money, of being worshipful and political. "I am," he declared, "the right man at the right time," the one who knew how to live spontaneously and ecstatically, in tune with nature and his own nature, the one who could help them do likewise.

The right man at the right time. The phrase is an apt one to describe the remarkable fit between his life — including those qualities he cultivated or created — and the lives and aspirations of his disciples. Out of the raw material of his childhood, the stuff of his experience, the circumstances of his time and place, the wisdom of the books he read, and the fecundity of his imagination, Rajneesh created a myth. And then — how much according to nature's dictates and how much according to art's is hard to tell — he lived it out.

His life and his myth are rich with complementarities and paradoxes. He is by turns peaceful and rebellious; a brilliant man who derides the mind and appeals to the heart; a solitary man who issues an invitation to community; a trenchant critic of the manipulative political mind who is himself a master manipulator; a "man of the truth" who often lies and a "man of freedom" who coerces his disciples and entraps himself; supremely sane and mad. He is dedicated to the celebration of every aspect of life, and yet he flirts with death and invites martyrdom.

According to his and his family's account, Rajneesh's life was from its first moments poised between predictions of unimaginable greatness and total destruction. He "lost" his mother and father but gained preternaturally good grandparents: a grandmother who gave him a wiser and purer love than any mother's, a grandfather who was supernally generous and understanding. From this turn of events he derived a sense that every loss would or could presage greater gain. Rajneesh brought his sense of blessed self-assurance into the childhood and adolescence he spent with his parents. The more chances he took with them and in the world of the village and its institutions, the freer from restrictions he became. As an adolescent he was always the leader, alone but not lonely, the master of games, the rebel, the precocious scientist putting his subjects—family, friends, village authorities—through risky, sometimes sadistic experiments.

In his late teens Rajneesh left home for college, and the universal aspect of his early years took on a particular social cast and historical dimension. The small-town boy, victor in the Oedipal struggles with parental and adult authority but inhibited by the limitations of caste and background, exaggerated, played out, his rebellion on the stage of the city university. He was, in the early 1950s, not merely the rebellious adolescent but the particular rebel of his time—the cool Bohemian, the beatnik: "I lay in bed for days at a time staring at the ceiling. I put my bed near the door so I wouldn't have to move too far to go out of the room."

Rajneesh's "enlightenment" in 1953 was the repetition of an age-old drama of the hero's death and rebirth, an example of the Tantric approach—pursuing a way to its limits—that he would later espouse. It was also an affirmation of the similar rebellion in which his future disciples were or would be engaged. Rajneesh took his rebellious individualism to its extreme and it exploded, revealing to him in his enlightenment experience in the garden the underlying unity that bound him to his own nature and to the larger nature that worked on and through him. And once again there was a paradox, even a miracle. This merging of "the drop . . . into the ocean" confirmed his individuality.

In the 1960s Rajneesh's mood, like the times, changed. While a graduate student and lecturer at Jabalpur, he stormed across India lecturing, provoking, like some itinerant anarchist organizer. These talks revealed Rajneesh's affinity with the contemporary Western rebels who would soon be drawn to him. Like the yippies who scattered dollar bills on the floor of the New York Stock Exchange, Rajneesh was being deliberately, publicly outrageous. Like Ken Kesey spiking fruit punch with LSD, he was trying to disrupt conventional patterns of thought and behavior. "With or without reason," Rajneesh would say a few years later, "I was creating controversies, creating criticisms."

In the early 1970s, just as the antiwar movement and the student rebellions in the West were exhausting themselves, Rajneesh was fresh. He wanted to reach more people, to create a community, to start his own movement. The Westerners who were drawn to him were discovering the limits and limitations of leftist politics, the sexual revolution, psychotherapy, feminism, and psychedelic drugs. They felt the need to take a journey into themselves that would definitively alter the fearful or selfish, limited or anxiety-producing ways they had been relating to their friends and families, their political goals and sexual experiences. He seemed to have taken the journey and was willing to be their guide.

Rajneesh's message was in many ways similar to that of other mystics. He was using techniques to promote introspection and awareness, trying to strip away familial, social, and environmental conditioning, to allow people to become present to each moment as it passed. And he spoke with the same assured authority as the mystics of the past and their heirs. But he presented his message in a way that was more accessible and modern, more immediately relevant to the way that searching Westerners actually lived and felt and thought.

The multinational, multiracial community that Rajneesh created in Poona was at once the response to the isolation and needs of those who came as disciples and the fulfillment of the utopian dreams and universalist hopes that pervaded the culture of the 1960s. It united, or seemed to unite, all the best features of capitalist creature comforts with the selfless sharing, the limitless sexual experimentation, and the creative playfulness of the ideal—or idealized—anarchist commune.

In Poona communards lived with a feeling of infinite possibility in a paradisiacal time out of time. Distinctions of age and class, nationality, race, and religion blurred. Adults comforted by the maternal reassurance of the community, sustained by the paternal strength and authority of their Master, were as free as children to play and to play out and explore every side of themselves, every fantasy and fear. Adolescents were granted full adult status in the community. Past and future were abolished. The only time was a now that, in the flow of the Buddhafield that Rajneesh seemed to generate, changed and renewed itself every moment. Even death was a moment in the flow, an occasion for celebration. The ashram was thus an individual and collective altered state of consciousness, as well as a physical place.

While creating this kind of community Rajneesh used a variety of devices to enhance the psychological and psychohistorical fit between him and his disciples. The meditation techniques and therapy groups were ways of helping people to shed their social conditioning. The discourses provided specific guidance and a new and coherent world view. The orange and red clothes, the mala with his picture, the new name and the new identity—all these bound the sannyasins to each other and to him, in the new community, the new order.

In discourses and darshans Rajneesh also used hypnotic techniques to bypass his disciples' conscious defenses, to win their assent to his words, and to enhance their transference to him. He created confusion and elaborated paradoxes and contradictions, which baffled their rational minds and the habitual ways they looked at themselves and the world. He used his voice, varying the volume and pace of speech, punctuating, modifying his words with his hands and eyes, even with his stillness. As his disciples listened and watched, their minds slowed. They followed the winding, discursive thread of his stories the way the eye follows the motions of a tiny falling feather. In trance they were more receptive and suggestible.

In Poona and later in Rajneeshpuram, Rajneesh used other devices as well to heighten his effectiveness and his listeners' receptivity: barriers to entry (sniffers and guards); identification bracelets; elaborately staged entrances and exits; repetitive music; sentimental songs; a bare setting; the raised place of his chair and the increasing remoteness of his person; absolute silence. One came to Rajneesh as if in procession to a temple deity. And, like all great performers, Rajneesh played the crowd, multiplying the power of his words and his presence by the attention his audience paid to him; augmenting, as any charismatic leader must, the power of those who were attributing power to him, as if in a continual and continually recharged circuit.

The psychological fit, the hypnotic and ceremonial devices, were enhanced, animated by subtle connections between Rajneesh and his disciples that could not be reduced to or explained in the context of psychological or sociological formulations. Something had happened to Rajneesh that made him unlike other men. He had undergone some change—enlightenment, the rising of kundalini—and his being had been altered in palpable ways. The change in him in turn affected his sannyasins and created a persistent and catalyzing resonance between them.

In choosing America for the new commune, Rajnesh was of course responding to the exigencies of life in India. Whether or not he deliberately provoked the Indian government's antipathy toward him—and there is certainly evidence to suggest that he did—it was clear that he could no longer stay there. At the same time there was once again a remarkable resonance in his choice of America for his new commune.

Since the earliest European explorations, America has been the Promised Land, a landscape on which the dreams and visions of explorers and pioneers might be played out. Like the Puritans who first settled the North American continent, Rajneesh and his sannyasins were embarked on a sacred "errand into the wilderness." And like those first immigrants, they believed themselves different, superior, chosen—if not "the elect," then Superman. Landing in America, Rajneesh picked up on this theme: "I am," he reportedly said, "the Messiah America is waiting for."

The possibility of cross-fertilization between the energy of democratic America, and the contemplativeness of the East had long fascinated influential American writers, from Emerson and Thoreau to Jack Kerouac and Allan Ginsberg. By the 1970s this possibility seemed almost a necessity to Eastern religious leaders as well as to Americans who adhered to Eastern traditions or those who joined the new religious and consciousness-expanding groups that were influenced by them. Tibetan Buddhists, Zen practitioners, Hare Krishnas, Moonies, esties, and many others, as well as Rajneesh's sannyasins, all shared a common conviction that a fruitful, if not world-saving, marriage of East and West, of meditation and materialism, would happen first in experimental, affluent, democratic America.

For sannyasins, Rajneesh's new western commune would be the form into which they could pour all the energy and money and hope that they had generated in Poona, all the resources and talents they had accumulated in the West. On Rancho Rajneesh, with the guidance of the visionary prophet Bhagwan, they would build heaven on earth.

In Oregon Rajneesh infused his utopian project with an apocalyptic urgency: the new and potentially world-saving man had to be created; an organized religion—Rajneeshism—was necessary to preserve and propagate the Master's teachings. All this had to happen now so he could personally guide his disciples before he died, so they would be able to survive the nuclear holocaust or the AIDS plague that would surely come. The sannyasins and, most particularly, their midwife and Master, Bhagwan, had to be protected so they could accomplish their aims.

Soon the boundaries of the ranch became the dividing line between righteousness and error. Inside was life, a loving community of new men and women, a vanguard, a chosen people. Outside lay a dying world in which dangerous reactionaries roamed. Like the fascists and fundamentalists whom Rajneesh and his sannyasins had mocked and condemned, the ranch dwellers created dogma and rules, ordeals and elites, which would insure obedience and protect them from contamination. Rajneesh and Sheela became increasingly dictatorial, the mass of sannyasins more and more slavish.

Sheela's defection, and Rajneesh's report of her "crimes"; his flight, prosecution, imprisonment, and expulsion—these at last awakened sannyasins to the truth they had refused to see. They had indeed collaborated in creating their own "concentration camp." But whose idea had it been? Rajneesh had accused Sheela, but how could he not have known? Many sannyasins became disaffected, disillusioned. The man they believed to be—who claimed to be—perfect was not. Others resolved the cognitive dissonance between their trust in their Master and the facts that suggested his complicity in a multitude of ugly crimes by denying the latter, rationalizing his behavior, and redoubling their enthusiasm for him. He was no longer the challenger unheeded but the savior denied, martyr as well as Master.

In India the next act is now being played out. Repudiated in this time and place, Rajneesh now claims he has been confirmed across two and a half millennia by the ancient Master, Buddha. He is encouraging disciples who have been frustrated in their effort to create an earthly paradise and who have been appalled by their participation in an authoritarian community to take responsibility for themselves, to find the truth in quiet meditation and a silent connection with their Master. The hope of the commune is dormant, the promised land no longer visible or relevant, the kingdom of heaven once again only within. And yet sannyasins can, like early underground Christians, participate in the drama of truth martyred and ongoing personal martyrdom.

Just as Rajneesh's character shaped his relationship with his disciples and his movement, so his unacknowledged imbalances and unobserved blind spots warped and deformed them. What only seemed to be accepted, integrated, and transformed, what was in fact consciously suppressed or unconsciously repressed, would emerge later in a distorted shape. As Rajneesh's personal power and charisma increased, as his movement grew, so too did these imbalances and distortions and their potential destructiveness.

This will happen with any powerful leader, but it is particularly true of charismatic spiritual leaders, who teach through nonrational devices and ask their disciples to enter a relationship predicated on surrender and trust. The Master asserts his own perfection, and disciples—who in any case are inclined to project their idealizations onto him—agree to it as an article of faith. In this context, even foibles and flaws that are noted are almost instantaneously redefined—as lessons for the disciples, as mysteries that defy analysis and invite still greater surrender and trust.

In Rajneesh's case, some of the qualities that were most central to both his development and his appeal to others—the greatest assets of the brash student and the wandering acharya—grew, fed by his increasing power and fortified by his need to maintain it. Unacknowledged and unchallenged, they became the greatest liabilities of a man who purported to be Master of a world-saving movement.

Rajneesh's belief in himself and his capacity for aloneness—which he dated from his grandfather's death—gave him the confidence to pursue his own path, to experiment on and with his mind and body, and to inspire others with a similar confidence. But this belief was built on a shaky foundation. The child Rajneesh had survived early interpersonal losses and life-threatening physical illnesses, but the adult showed the long-term effects—a preoccupation with accumulating unnecessary goods, a vulnerability to chronic debilitating illnesses. His confidence, alloyed with and flawed by an insecurity he could not admit, slowly hardened into self-protective arrogance. He allowed no one to turn him aside from a purpose he refused to question. He defended against criticism by claiming an authority based on omniscience and omnipotence: "Nothing happens in this ashram without my knowing it," he said in Poona.

Rajneesh's willingness to live at the edge of his capacities, to risk danger and death, augmented his sense of power and his appreciation of life, but it also gave rise to a forced and false sense of invulnerability and led him to indulge in titillating and self-destructive risk-taking. His youthful rebelliousness permitted him to see and speak out against hypocrisy and cant, but he never came to appreciate or admit the aggression with which it was mixed. Untempered by self-criticism and indiscriminately acclaimed by his disciples, Rajneesh's iconoclasm ultimately became a mindless and counterproductive reflex.

Rajneesh's love of experimentation gave form to his leadership and made it congenial for him to work on large numbers of people. But in his self-imposed isolation from his disciples and the larger world in which he and they lived, it degenerated into the indifferent coldness of the experimenter. His ambition carried him from a small town to and through the university and out onto a national, and eventually an international, stage; it enabled him to conceive of himself as a powerful catalyst, a midwife to the new man. But, unchecked, inflated by the adoration and idealization he sought and received from his sannyasins, it led him to claims he would have scoffed at in another, that he was the Messiah, the source of "the first and only religion."

Potential sannyasins had been drawn to Rajneesh by the hope of liberation from the condemning, life-denying voice of external or internalized authority; from inhibitions and fears; from the ego, the false idea of separateness that divided them from their own naturalness and the natural world around them. They saw Rajneesh as an Enlightened Master who could, by example and instruction, lead them to it.

In the meditation groups and daily life of Rajneesh's mystery school, sannyasins relived traumas and shed their psychological defenses. They fulfilled suppressed desires, became sensitive to their own thoughts and feelings, more open, vulnerable, and loving toward one another, and exquisitely receptive to their Master.

In time, intoxicated by their devotion to Rajneesh and blinded by the attractiveness of his vision, they claimed their Master's individual limitations as their collective policy. Thus they could shield themselves, their movement, and their Master from their own doubts and others' criticisms. Little by little, they replaced the false idea of separateness with a false idea of togetherness, the individual ego with a self-perpetuating, self-confirming group ego. Rajneesh's withdrawal and isolation became the model for their community's; his sense of superiority, his ambition, and his grandiosity became theirs. They rejected the dogma of their past as their Master had encouraged them to, but they enshrined Rajneesh and his opinions as a far more powerful, unquestioned, and unquestionable authority.

Rajneesh's way, unchallenged, became magnified, institutionalized, even caricatured, in the dictates of his coordinators, the tactics of group leaders, and the policy of the ashram. Rajneesh's experimentation with intense and collective pressure in therapy groups made them seem like plausible tactics for change in every situation. His belief in birth control became a coercive party line within the ashram. His rebellion against, if not contempt for, the sensibilities and laws of Indians outside the ashram encouraged a similar rebellion and contempt in his disciples. His unshakable belief in the overriding importance of his teachings and his way allowed him to encourage his disciples to do anything—give up their children, engage in prostitution, sell drugs—to stay with him. In time his disciples would convince themselves that no sacrifice, including the abdication of their intelligence and judgment, was too great. Increasingly, the end—being "with Bhagwan," surrendering to him, "blending into the commune"— overshadowed both the means taken to achieve it and the reasons why people had first come to him.

Leaving India probably exacerbated the situation. Like many people who incessantly challenge those in authority, Rajneesh seems secretly to have hoped to be loved, if not for his provocations, at least in spite of them. That is what he said happened in his family and his village. When India, which he considered spiritually superior, rejected him, he may well have felt not only wounded as Mahadeva suggested to me, but aggrieved. Deeksha told me that during his drugged ramblings, he talked about returning in triumph to the country of his birth.

In the United States, a country of which he was almost totally ignorant, Rajneesh was loosed from whatever restraints his native country and culture might have imposed on him. His fantasies were unbounded.

Still, in the United States it might have been possible for Rajneesh and his sannyasins to have made a fresh start. Their money allowed them to buy a large piece of property suitable for a protected, self-sufficient commune that would neither be intruded on nor offend its neighbors. But Sheela and Jay, acting with the haste and arrogance that had come to characterize the organization, hadn't checked things out. Even a brief inquiry would have informed them that Oregon had very strict land use laws and a tough, if not hostile, attitude to newcomers. Inevitably, these would threaten and provoke the sannyasins and lead to confrontations.

Once Rajneesh was on the ranch, his impatience, his absolute authority, and his isolation from the ordinary realities of day-to-day life and from intercourse with other people produced more problems. He—and Sheela, his pupil—began by dehumanizing the Oregonians, who questioned their motives and behavior. They treated them as abstractions, objects to be manipulated, obstacles to be avoided or removed. They concluded by behaving in the same cavalier, instrumental way toward the sannyasins themselves. Increasingly Rajneesh seemed to control rather than guide and inform the lives of his disciples. He used coercion and guilt, shame and deceit—tactics that he had mocked in the leaders of traditional religions and apocalyptic cults—to bind sannyasins to him. The more he defended against threats to his authority and security, the more isolated and grandiose he became. The more convinced he was of his special mission, the more he felt justified in doing anything necessary to further it. The more illegal his actions, the more secrecy and self-protectiveness were necessary, and so on in an accelerating, amplifying loop.

Rajneesh's physical ailments heightened his sense of vulnerability, restricted his actions, and limited his pleasure. If indeed his sexual potency was diminished by diabetes, this added embarrassment and feelings of inadequacy to his problems. The drugs on which Rajneesh seemed to become increasingly dependent exacerbated the situation. They may have created a euphoria that protected him from physical pain and discomfort, and from the feelings of insecurity and inadequacy that may have threatened him, but they clouded his judgment, removed him still further from his disciples, and heightened his grandiosity.

Even if Sheela's style was far cruder, she resembled her Master in many ways. Her feelings of insecurity, her preoccupation with money and material goods, the language and form, if not the details, of her attacks on Oregonians and her strategy for dealing with sannyasins, even the proliferation of physical illnesses and the drugs she took to cope with her situation were reminiscent of her Master. At once obedient and manipulative, she amplified Rajneesh's arrogant offensives when his mission, her authority, or their commune was challenged from within or outside. After she left, Rajneesh himself declared that Sheela was "a perfect parrot."

Those sannyasins who did not leave the ranch and Rajneesh participated or acquiesced in its crimes and excesses. They governed with Sheela, as her lieutenants, or served as privates, carrying out orders. They refused to give up their idealized image of their Master, their sense of participation in his mission, the reassurance of contact with him, and the serenity that blending into the group afforded them. Blinding themselves to the contradictions between Rajneesh's liberating words and Sheela's administration and their own deeds, they became as faithful and dogmatic as any religious zealots. Long before Rajneesh left the United States, he had become the "Big Daddy" whom he mocked in his discourses, and his sannyasins, once rebels and adventurers, the frightened conformists who "cannot trust in themselves."

For months before Sheela left and months after Rajneesh's expulsion I tried to sort out what Rajneesh knew and when, which of Sheela's activities he had ordered and supervised, and which she had concealed from him. It seemed terribly important to me, as it did to many sannyasins. I knew he couldn't be as ignorant and preoccupied as he would claim—obtuse Lear giving his kingdom to cruel ingrates, Prospero "neglecting worldly ends" while his brother usurped his crown—and I hoped, because I had learned so much from him, that he wasn't as responsible as I feared.

The more I found out, the more I felt myself fighting a losing battle to give Rajneesh the benefit of the doubt. He was certainly responsible for the ranch's arrogant attitude, the consolidation and sclerosis of power, the paranoia. He had decreed the religion of Rajneeshism and the centralization of the communes. He knew about the Share-A-Home program, the wild attacks on the Oregonians, and the authoritarian structure of the ranch. He not only knew there was no separation of church and state in Rajneeshpuram but approved officials and directed civil functions in the city.

In my interview with him at Rajneeshpuram, I discovered that many of his professions of innocence were untrue. He told me he knew Sheela was doing wiretapping but claimed that he believed it was only in self-defense: "She did exactly as they were doing." He knew about and approved of the immigration fraud. He later said he knew Sheela was "turning a meditation camp into a concentration camp," harassing and expelling loyal disciples, suppressing doubt and dissent, but hadn't stopped her. It wasn't "time" he said and justified his inaction with excuses that seemed lame: there were "so many [legal] cases," he told me and, later, in India, Sheela would have "made sannyasins miserable" if he had tried to stop her.

It was painful for me to realize that this brilliant man, who had seemed such a graceful, generous, untroubled observer, had behaved in a way that was so contemptuous and controlling, so cruel and wasteful. He had seemed so sensitive and alert and now it appeared that, drunk with his own power and pride—and several different drugs—he had fallen into a kind of stupor. I wondered what had happened to Rajneesh's enlightenment, if in fact, he had ever been enlightened. Puzzling it out for myself, reading about other Masters, I realized that enlightenment was itself a moment-to-moment experience, as subject to the same laws of change as any other state. A willingness to accept one's limitations and continual alertness were ongoing requirements.

I began to wonder also whether Rajneesh was capable of even greater sadism than I had suspected. Had he known about or even ordered some of the violent crimes that he and everyone else were attributing to "Sheela and her gang"? What Deeksha and other sannyasins, who insisted on anonymity, had told me suggested but didn't prove it.

The law enforcement authorities who had listened for hundreds of hours to tapes that Sheela had made, and pored over affidavits that were never made public, hinted—insistently, angrily—that Rajneesh was guilty of far more than he had ever admitted to. There was a plan, Major Moine of the state police told me, for sannyasin women and children to form a human wall around Rajneesh should the authorities come to arrest him. In Poona this had been protection; in Oregon, Moine assured me, it was a prelude to aggression. While the police tried to cope with this defense, sannyasin guards would shoot them. "Don't you think he knew about it?" he asked rhetorically. Rajneesh's "philosophy," Attorney General Frohnmayer told me in one of those asides that escape the impropriety of disclosure even as they accomplish the fact, was not "disapproving of poisoning."

Sannyasins who had been close to Sheela told me of tapes that she played when they questioned whether her orders were coming from their Master. And Sheela, though publicly silent, had spoken from her jail cell in California. She had told several people who were still close to her that "Bhagwan knew everything."

None of this proved to me that Rajneesh ordered Sheela to poison the Wasco County commissioners or the people of The Dalles, to culture the AIDS virus or to draw up a hit list of the ranch's political opponents. But I was sure he had created the climate in which such acts could take place and thought he might even have ordered them. I couldn't imagine that he would have wanted Hasya and Vivek and Laxmi disabled or Devaraj killed—these seemed certainly to be actions Sheela undertook to preserve her power—but I was no longer positive about even this.

As I felt my way gradually, uncomfortably, but inevitably into the territory of Rajneesh's complicity, I was still puzzled by two pieces of his behavior: his revelations about "Sheela's crimes" and his attempted flight from the United States. Neither one made sense, and both proved disastrous for him.

Until Rajneesh spoke publicly, the only charges pending against him or anyone else on the ranch were related to immigration fraud. If he hadn't exposed Sheela's wrongdoings, the authorities would probably never have found informants to testify, let alone obtained convictions on wiretapping, poisoning, and arson. And if Rajneesh hadn't tried to flee the country, both he and his commune would in all likelihood still have been in Oregon.

Many sannyasins and some law enforcement people attributed Rajneesh's public attacks on Sheela to a sense of betrayal: his were angry words spoken impulsively. Major Moine compared it to a divorce, "where all of a sudden you talk in public about things that you always kept private." Several of the prosecutors suggested that Rajneesh tried to leave the country because he was "terrified of jail": that had been their impression when they saw him in North Carolina. Some sannyasins agreed, but they believed their Master's fears of jail were realistic, a sign not of cowardice but of his compassion for sannyasins who still needed him. There was, they told me confidently, a plot against Rajneesh's life; later some of them, including Hasya, would tell me that the U.S. government had put a half-million-dollar contract out on him. Other people viewed both Rajneesh's public denunciations and his departure as the end products of bad planning or advice: the lawyers were either ignored or not consulted.

None of these explanations really made sense to me. Rajneesh's first revelations followed Sheela's departure by two days. He may have been angry, but he certainly wasn't hysterical or out of control. He had had plenty of time to organize his thoughts, to discuss his course of action with his lawyers. In other situations—regarding immigration and church-state matters, for example—he had obviously had legal advice. Nor did fear of jail, realistic or unrealistic, seem an adequate motive for flight. There was in fact no danger of jail. In an immigration case like this one, Rajneesh would have surrendered, been arraigned, and been released on bond almost certainly within a matter of hours. He might well have never been convicted, and even if he had been and the conviction were upheld years later on appeal, the worst that would have happened would have been deportation, not jail.

Others with whom I spoke offered psychological or spiritual explanations for Rajneesh's behavior. Some disaffected sannyasins believed that Rajneesh was depressed and self-destructive: in speaking out against Sheela and leaving the country, he was attempting to destroy what had been created in his name. He had done this, they theorized, because he hated himself for pretending to be enlightened when he no longer was.

Sannyasin loyalists continued to see Rajneesh's actions as preternaturally wise: he had exposed Sheela and left Oregon in order to give the coup de grace to a commune that had already been destroyed by individual and collective authoritarianism. This was his way of showing his disciples how destructive their sheeplike behavior had been. In this scenario Rajneesh's arrest and imprisonment were devices designed to reveal to the world the religious bigotry that still existed in "the land of the free," the cruelty and inequity of the American legal system.

For months I kept trying to sort all this out, convinced that if I understood these apparently inexplicable behaviors I would have a key to Rajneesh's character. One day, almost a year after he flew out of Portland toward India, another explanation, simpler but far more distressing than any I had heard, occurred to me. And, as is so often the case when I have tried to understand a person's motives, the clues were available in his words, and in my reactions to them.

I remembered that during one morning discourse shortly after Sheela left the ranch, Rajneesh had interrupted a diatribe against her to say that he feared that Sheela would receive immunity from prosecution and accuse "innocent sannyasins." He was trying, he implied, to protect his sannyasins by exposing the crimes that had been committed as Sheela's doing; that way she would not be able to put the responsibility on others. I remembered that at the time I had sensed a false note in this solicitude. Rajneesh was not a stupid or ill-informed man. Even if he hadn't known American law well — and in view of the quality and number of lawyers around him, this was unlikely — he was intelligent enough to understand that no prosecutor would grant the principal offender criminal immunity so that she could testify against those to whom she had given orders, or against innocent people.

The only "innocent" one, I now realized, who would have been threatened by a grant of immunity, the only one whom the authorities wanted more than Sheela herself, was . . . Rajneesh. If he believed that Sheela, desperate to stay out of jail, furious at her replacement by Hasya, and in possession of tapes of their daily conversations, was going to make a deal by exposing him, then — and only then — did it make sense to reveal "Sheela's crimes." Once their extent had been made public, the authorities would not be able to promise her immunity from prosecution for them.

A similar explanation would also account for Rajneesh's precipitous flight from the country on the day before his arrest for immigration fraud. I knew that the ranch had heard, via a source at CBS, that Sheela's arrest in Germany was timed to coincide with Rajneesh's in Oregon. He may have feared once again that she would, under arrest, try to make a deal for herself. And he would have known that she had evidence that would implicate him in crimes far more serious than immigration fraud. If she had tapes that recorded him ordering, or even hearing about, the poisonings or the arson or the hit list, then he did indeed have reason to fear that he would not only be arrested, but jailed without bond.

Not long ago I spoke with Gopa again. I told her some of the things that Nandan and Shiva, now Anna Forbes and Hugh Milne, had said to me, and some of what I had heard from the law enforcement people. I said that it now seemed to me that Rajneesh was guilty of some or all of the crimes of which he accused Sheela. How, I tentatively asked, did she feel about her Master's possible involvement? Did it affect her respect for him? Did she feel betrayed or deceived?

Gopa was quiet for a while. Then she said, as I believed she would, that she didn't know what Rajneesh had done but it really didn't make much difference to her. It was beside the point of her experience of him, her love for him. A week later she sent a note with the photographs I had asked for: "In the end," she wrote, in explanation of her devotion, "I don't think anyone who isn't a disciple, willing to jump into total emptiness, will ever understand the whole story. If it could be understood intellectually it would not be what it is."

Reading Gopa's words I could see how easily such an attitude could serve and perpetuate mystification within the circle of disciples and obliterate criticism from without. But I knew also that they described how Gopa felt and that she was expressing the kind of observations that mystics have always made about religious experience: that it is nonrational, purely subjective, unsupportable, risky, experiential, and ultimately incommunicable. "You cannot taste the honey," Indians are fond of saying, "by licking the jar."

Writing this now, I remember some of my own experiences: the power I felt doing Dynamic day after day in my barn; the moments of light and silence in Enlightenment Intensive in Poona; standing on the side of a road in Oregon, watching a man drive by in a Rolls-Royce, feeling his presence enter me and turn my moods like a wheel; crying and dancing with Rajneesh in my interview; playing a game with him in the police station in Crete; writing about him now. Like Shyam, I realize it is not that he was responsible for what happened to me, or that such powerful things have happened only with him—but only that they did happen with him.

This does not mean that Rajneesh has not manipulated people—including, as best he could, me—used them contemptuously, and perhaps even poisoned them. Rajneesh was fond of telling worshipful sannyasins that the God to whom they were praying was "not a nice man, not your uncle." The same might be said of people who have learned how to use psychological and psychic power and particularly of Rajneesh himself. Kundalini energy does not rise only in those who are quite prepared. Extraordinary powers—to stimulate sexuality or produce wealth or manifest love or understand and manipulate the psyche of others—do not come only to the virtuous.

Even enlightenment doesn't mean perfection. It is an authenticity characterized by contradictions: truth-telling and deception; great wisdom and fallibility; areas of blindness as well as great vision; darkness as well as light. Two hundred years ago Rebbe Nachman, who was said to be a Tzaddik, an enlightened Hasidic Master, pointed out, "There are two erroneous concepts going around the world: the first that a Just Man cannot make a mistake, and the second that he cannot remain great even if he has made a mistake." "The emphasis," the contemporary Zen Master Suzuki Roshi has written, "is not so much on the Master being a perfect person as being a perfect mirror."

And, enlightened or not, Rajneesh—and his disciples—have been mirrors and teachers for me. His teachings are, if not original, wise, well put, and easily understood. His commentaries have helped me to explore rich traditions and useful techniques. His meditations are accessible and elegant and have been useful in my life and my work. Rajneesh's ways of peeling the onion of our conditioning have contributed materially to my own and my patients' well-being. He has inspired me to take chances with, to celebrate, my life and my work in ways I might not otherwise have done. His and his disciples' projects—bringing together the ancient wisdom of the East and the material well-being and enterprise of the West; trying to create the new joyous, meditative man, Zorba the Buddha; forming a meditative community that is harmonious and in harmony with nature—are, cannot help but be, my own.

And yet Rajneesh, falling asleep—choosing to fall asleep—failed to live what he knew and taught. He ignored what he did not care to deal with in himself, tried to silence or obliterate people or situations or points of view that threatened or contradicted him. From the time he broke his "silence" in October 1984, he said again and again, 'I am just an ordinary man . . . ordinariness is blessed. . . . Gods are projections. Change is endless." But every day he continued to act more special, more controlling and godlike, more removed from the flux of life and from his own and others' ordinary humanity.

In the end, Rajneesh became the kind of man, the kind of religious leader, he had always derided. If indeed his ego had once dissolved and melted like a drop into the ocean, it seemed over the years to have renewed and enlarged, and in his isolation it grew gross with his attachment to power and luxury and position. He became more power-hungry and more deceitful than any of the politicians he attacked, more papal than "the Polack," more sanctimonious than saints he derided. On his ranch, surrounded by armed guards, dressed up and doped up, imperious and imperial, he resembled Jim Jones far more than Buddha or Krishna or Jesus. He was unwilling to learn or change, or to admit that there was anything to be learned or to change.

Ultimately, perhaps Krishnamurti, whom Rajneesh considered his great rival, is more right than Rajneesh: we don't need Masters; they will inevitably become intoxicated with their power and encourage those whom they promised to liberate to become slaves. But Rajneesh, the Tantric Master, is also right: we cannot see what we do not need until we have explored it, taken it to its limits, exhausted its possibilities, and found that it will not, cannot satisfy.

It would have been wonderful if Rajneesh was who he said he was, if, like the Master described by Buddha, he had been content to be a boat, a vehicle for his disciples' use, if he had been able continually to renew the experience of enlightenment that he seemed to have had. But it appeared that Rajneesh had to—probably still has to—learn the Tantric lesson he has been teaching.

Nevertheless, during the last twenty years, the wisdom and generosity of the ideal Rajneesh offered have helped his sannyasins and me and many more people to see the generous, spontaneous, celebratory aspects of ourselves. His vision of a loving, cooperative community dedicated to the creation of new men and women living in harmony with their own nature and the natural world have provoked and inspired us. Similarly, his self-absorption, and self-deception, his destructive, controlling actions and his sannyasins' collaboration in them, can help show us our own willingness to be self-absorbed and destructive, to be controlled individually and in groups, and to deceive ourselves. The contradictions in Rajneesh and in his sannyasins remind us that the ideals to which we aspire and the flaws which we fear are both already present in us.

For me, it is not finally a question of agreeing or disagreeing with Rajneesh, of praising or condemning him or his sannyasins. It is, rather, a matter of learning from him and them, of appreciating his remarkable talents and gifts and recognizing his perverse uses of them, of seeing myself in him and his sannyasins, of using his extraordinary story and strange, as yet unfinished journey as a mirror for my own.

INDEX